BOUND IN FLAME

BOUND IN
FLAME

THE HAWAIIAN LADIES' RIDING SOCIETY

KATHERINE
KAYNE

Passionflower
p r e s s

Kona • Seattle

Published by Passionflower Press, Seattle and Kona
www.katherinekayne.com

Edited and designed by Girl Friday Productions
Cover design: Paul Barrett
Project management: Sara Addicott
Hawaiian language consultant: Malani DeAguiar

Image credits: Cover © Shutterstock/Rosapompelmo

ISBN (paperback): 978-1-7336077-0-4
ISBN (ebook): 978-1-7336077-1-1

Library of Congress Control Number: 2019901196

First edition

Traditional Hawaiian proverbs are quoted from ʻŌlelo Noʻeau, first published in 1983 by the Bishop Museum.

"Every now and then, a flower wreathed Hawaiian woman, in her full radiant garment, sprang on one of these animals astride, and dashed along the road at full gallop, sitting on her horse as square and easy as a hussar."
—Isabella Bird, 1872

To the fierce and fearless women of Hawaii who keep the tradition of pā'ū *riding alive. Gallop on, ladies!*

AUTHOR'S NOTE

Hawaii is a rare place, one where the very heart of the earth comes near; if you go there, you will feel its heat. *Bound in Flame* was never intended to be an accurate portrayal of history, but rather a reimagining, a consideration of what might have been. Here, in the world of the Hawaiian Ladies' Riding Society, the reality of the unlawful American takeover of the islands remains, but so also does the magic. *Bound in Flame* seeks to capture that magic, if only in a small way. Is this a romance? Is this a fantasy? Or merely the ramblings of an old woman who has spent too long in the sun? I leave that for you to decide.

PROLOGUE

Maka Mua

THE BEGINNING

Lang's Livery, Oahu, the 15th of August, 1906

The parlor windows lay shuttered against the day's heat. Tiny bars of sunlight dappled the hulking Victorian furniture, coughed up years ago by some Irish ancestor's sailing ship to honor his royal Hawaiian bride. Letty used to think there might be spirits lurking in those shadows. Not so now. Now, something worse was in store.

Leticia Lili'uokalani Lang stood stiff, still, waiting. Her bare brown toes clenched the thick Persian rug for comfort, although comfort was not to be had. Her grandfather, her beloved *tūtū kāne*, might issue the verdict. That there would be a verdict? Of this she had no doubt. This time she'd really done it, her little escapade a disgrace to her entire *'ohana*. All she had wanted was to garner her new stepmother's attention. Not this. No. Never this.

Letty might blame the flames if she dared. The flames were her constant companions. Unseen, of course, but constant. Sometimes just a tickle in the small of her back. Sometimes a raging inferno up her spine. Always urging her to move, to act, to do *something*. Unfortunately, that something was often not the very best of ideas.

Like riding her horse through her stepmother's first garden party, sending a dozen of Honolulu's society matrons running. Not the best of a string of her latest ideas—none of which might ever have seen the light of day had it not been for the flames.

No one knew about the flames, of course. How could Letty ever explain? And wouldn't they simply think her crazy?

This time she'd surely be sent away. To that school. The one the Princess touted. Might she ever come home?

Praise the *'āina*, she hoped they had horses in California.

PART ONE

Aia ke ola i ka ihu o ka lio

LIFE IS WHERE THE HORSE'S NOSE POINTS

CHAPTER ONE

Lu'u Iho

DIVE HEADFIRST

Moran Sugar Plantation, Hawaii Island, the 9th of June, 1909

"Mr. Tim! Mr. Tim!"

Timothy catapulted up from the row of sugarcane, slapping his machete into its holster. His knee grumbled; he ignored it, just as he always did.

Joshua came running down the cane road with Champagne trotting behind. Tiny clouds of red soil puffed up under the big gelding's hooves.

"Mr. Tim! Boat is early! You best go!"

Timothy nodded his thanks, mounted Champagne, and saluted his crew. Two weeks earlier he'd received a message from Grandmama to expect an exceptional birthday gift . . . alive . . . named Diablo . . . on today's interisland steamship. He could only pray it was not an elephant or a crocodile, given Grandmama's proclivity for the grand gesture.

Settling into the saddle, Timothy fingered well-worn reins as he eased Champagne into a rocking canter down the harbor road.

Scarcely two years had passed since he—and the pigs destined for a princess—arrived at this selfsame harbor. Today he simply hoped to get his grandmother's "gift" safely delivered up to the ranch, then head back to the plantation. Please, please let this not be another pig. Or some damned fancy rooster. He loved his grandmother, but the dowager countess's attachment to livestock as gifts strained credulity. He'd be happy with a nice book.

Besides, Timothy had a bumper crop of cane on his hands and a chance to buy his own sugar mill with his crop share. Animal nanny was not on the daily agenda.

As he crested the ridge above Kawaihae, his bubble of self-absorption burst. The steamer already rocked at anchor. Boats plied the harbor, unloading passengers and goods. Damnation, he was late.

The steamship *Pele* rolled in the coastal surf. Letty's booted foot slid a bit on the deck until she righted herself. She preferred bare feet, but boots were de rigueur for this visit to the Princess. Her flames, of course, were not.

Her flames were nothing if not reliable. Whenever a problem presented itself, those flames would command her. If she let them, that is. But she'd not let them. Not today, not tomorrow, not ever again. That was the purpose of three long years at school, wasn't it?

Except, perhaps, for this current problem. A horse. And someone else's horse to boot.

The day's heat compounded it all, the sweltering trade winds scouring down from the high ranchlands to the sea. A fingertip of sweat traced down Letty's spine as her compulsion to act, to do something—anything—flared.

She had learned a trick or two while away. Perhaps she'd count to keep herself in check. The Fibonacci sequence generally worked. *One, two, three, five, eight.*

Somehow it always came back to a horse. Or a dog or a cow or a goat or some other animal in distress. This creature's name was Diablo; she'd gleaned that much from the nameplate on his halter. Now all she could think about was how to help the poor devil. And keep herself from doing anything foolhardy along the way. *Thirteen, twenty-one, thirty-four.*

Her recitation of the sequence of integers was made all the more difficult by tendrils of fire furling and unfurling at the base of her spine. Prodding her to action. Which. She. Would. Not. Take. *Fifty-five.*

Letty thought to be one of the last off the ship. She stood side by side with Captain Gibson at the upper rail, taking in the scene below. The good captain craned his head to look up at her. "Here to visit our princess again, are ye? What has it been, a few years?"

She prayed the sound of pounding hooves provided an adequate distraction from the inevitable discussion of her whereabouts for the past three years. She'd loved her time at the Redwood School, but it did not bear discussing. No one would understand. No one would believe a woman might take on the vocation she now had planned.

Another tat-tat-tat of hooves was followed by the crack of breaking wood. The hoped-for distraction had arrived.

"I can't wait to get that demon off my ship," the captain scowled. "That horse is a bad one."

"Oh no, he's not! It's just his groom! That Mr. Smith! We were on the same ship from San Francisco." Letty bit back the urge to say more, to decry the cruelty she had witnessed. That was why she'd been sent away, after all. To learn a bit of circumspection. Among other things.

At any rate, there was nothing she could say that would matter. At least not yet.

Smith led the big blood-bay stallion out on deck. Letty gasped. The poor horse was not only blindfolded but hobbled too.

Smith shoved the horse toward the winch platform, poking him viciously with the butt of a carriage whip. Once secured in the bellyband, Diablo would be lowered overboard. There the sailors would tie him alongside one of the waiting longboats to swim him to shore. This was the customary way to unload a horse in a harbor with no docks, but she'd never seen it done with a struggling horse. A horse of such obvious value. One both blindfolded and hobbled.

Eighty-nine . . .

How could he swim?

The stallion crow-hopped along the deck; a hobble rope tied too tight cut into his pasterns. A lather born of sheer terror dripped from Diablo's neck and hind legs. Even ten feet above the scene, the rank stench of wrongness burned her nose. *One hundred forty-four . . .*

Letty's fingernails bit into her palms, hands clenched against the urge to act. One by one she beat back the flames. No, she would not hop the rail to end this travesty. Not this time. But she would see this sort of treatment of animals ended. It must.

It would. Once she had "Doctor" in front of her name.

The winch creaked with the rocking of the ship. The stallion's next crow-hop became an attempt to rear. Only then she saw he was bridled too. The groom, the odious Mr. Smith, gave a vicious yank down and back, engaging what looked to be a heavy snaffle bit. Bloody froth dripped from the horse's mouth. Letty clamped her own mouth shut. Again. *Two hundred thirty-three, three hundred seventy-seven . . .*

Two burly deckhands stood back.

"Well, load him up. That's what you damned *kānaka* get paid for, isn't it? Lazy bastards."

Captain Gibson stiffened beside her. "No need for such language, Mr. Smith. We will get this done."

One of the men came forward, reaching to take the reins out of Smith's hands. With a move surely intended to appear accidental, the deckhand knocked Smith back with his elbow. "Oh, I am so sorry, sir."

Smith stood aside, muttering.

Her flames cheered.

The deckhands scooted the big horse closer to where the ship's railing stood open. They slipped the stained canvas sling under Diablo's belly, adjusting the chain for his weight. One raised a hand to signal the winchman to haul it up. As soon as the sling was tight, but before guiding the winch arm over the side, the big man laid a gentling hand on the stallion's neck. He unbuckled the bridle.

"No need to waste Lord Rowley's fine leather, right, sir?" He tossed the bridle to Smith's feet. Well, she must certainly agree with that sentiment. Leather was leather. No matter how rich this Lord Rowley might be. *Six hundred ten . . .*

The winch issued a high-pitched scream as the heavy horse was lifted up and over the side to dangle above the open water. Diablo answered with a scream of his own. And began to fight, his back arching with the force of his fear. First a creak. Then, with a sound like a rifle shot, the belly band split.

The horse dropped into the ocean like a stone.

Nine hundred eighty-seven . . .

Captain Gibson cursed in at least three languages.

Letty rushed along the rail, leaning over in horror to see what had happened. Diablo's head quickly appeared above water, still blindfolded. His front legs swam hard; he'd lost the hobble, thank goodness. But he headed in the wrong direction—straight out to open ocean.

The men stood frozen on the deck. The sailors in the waiting longboat rowed frantically backward as the heavy winch chain rattled down into the sea. The longboat was missed, but barely.

She was done with counting.

Letty shucked off her heavy riding skirt, tossing porkpie hat and boots aside. Over the rail she went, balancing on the outside ledge, toes clinging until the very last moment. Her unruly hair began its escape. Taking a breath to gather her strength, she pushed off, her dive arcing out to clear the ship. In that brief moment before she hit the water, she wondered. She'd made cliff dives higher than this . . . hadn't she?

Embraced by the ocean's cool arms, Letty pulled hard to arrest her descent, then popped to the surface with a mouthful of water. Spitting and shaking the hair out of her eyes, she twirled to find Diablo. Good. He was close, very close.

The stallion's legs flailed madly, his breath coming in great gasps through red-rimmed nostrils. Letty pulled near enough to hook an arm around his neck. Leaning forward, she loosed the blindfold in a quick yank. Twining the fingers of one hand in his mane, she ran the other hand along his neck to guide him, but the horse was too panicked. She kicked hard, bumping into his side to turn him. It worked.

Once Diablo saw land, he headed there willingly. Shoving her mass of hair off her face, Letty pulled herself onto his back. Rivulets of salty water burned into her eyes, her many hairpins long gone.

Clinging to the stallion as he swam, Letty surrendered to her flames; the elation of the rescue fanned the conflagration.

Diablo found his footing on the rocky beach to stand head down, winded and blowing. Letty slipped off his back, wrapping her arms around his neck, her own breath ragged. Her knees betrayed her and buckled. This weakness always came after she gave in to her boldness; it was worse since she'd been at school. Her flames had their price.

A crowd gathered, but no one approached. A tall figure on a big dun horse came pounding down to the harbor. The man flung himself off his mount to limp in her direction. "That's my horse," he said.

Letty yanked her head up from Diablo's neck to stare straight at the man. "You!" Shoving her body between the man and the stallion, her weakness evaporated. This time anger held her upright. "You don't deserve this horse. You and your fool groom just nearly got him killed. You are an ass and a moron, and you shall not have him."

"Leticia Lili'uokalani Lang! PLEASE! Give the poor man his horse!" Bull's deep voice lashed out like the whip he always carried.

She jolted to attention. Here she was, standing in front of an open-mouthed crowd in her dripping shirtwaist and pantaloons, making a complete spectacle of herself—just what she'd been sent away to San Francisco to stop doing. *Oh no.* The weakness took her. She swooned.

Timothy rushed forward, only to be beaten to the horse's side by Bull Jefferson, Princess Kahōkūlani's ranch foreman. The unconscious woman lay squarely between the stallion's front legs.

"Stand back, Rowley. Let me fetch her before the poor horse steps on her," Bull growled as he ran his hand calmly along the stallion's neck. Diablo stood stock-still, breathing hard, as Bull extricated the woman's limp body. Thankfully the horse remained unmoving.

"There, the horse is all yours now." Bull cradled the unconscious young woman to carry her to the waiting wagon. The red blaze of her hair nearly swept the ground.

Bull turned back to deliver Timothy a crooked smile. "Oh, by the way, I am sure the Princess will be quite amused by all this. Leticia is one of her goddaughters. She'd be a princess in her own right if we had not lost the monarchy to the damned Americans. See you soon, Rowley. At MacHenry, heh?"

Timothy stood, dazed, squinting to clear his vision as Bull moved away. He could swear he saw red lights around that woman. Grasping Diablo's halter, he was chagrined he didn't even have a proper lead rope. He really had been expecting a pig.

Behind him, a cough—then, "Your Lordship, sir, may I take him for you?"

Turning around, he saw a plainly dressed man with his hat in one hand and a horse's bridle in the other.

"Who are you?"

"Hank Smith, sir, the new groom sent to help you by your grandmother."

Gram had never mentioned anything about a groom. But then she'd not revealed much about this gift either. "Are you the one who hobbled Diablo and blindfolded him?"

Smith said nothing, instead handing Timothy a letter on his grandmother's engraved cream stationery. It clearly supported the man's tale of being sent by Grandmama. Odd. He would review it all in detail later.

For now, he just wanted to get everyone back to the ranch in good order. Then return to the plantation. He had cane to harvest. Loads and loads of sugarcane.

Chapter Two

Ahu ke pilo

A HEAP OF STINKS

ʻIolani Ranch, Hawaii Island, the 10th of June, 1909

The morning dawned crystal clear with a promise of heat to come. Princess Kahōkūlani sat in her office finishing a last bit of correspondence to be sent off on tomorrow's boat. As was his habit each morning, Bull sauntered in to consult about the day's plans.

"Have you spoken to Letty yet?"

"No," she said. "I am grasping at ways to avoid it. But I know that I shan't. What would you do in my place?"

"Hog-tie her." Kahōkūlani turned in her chair to face him. Bull stood squarely, almost seven feet tall in his boots, thumbs through his belt, looking for all the world like one tough cowboy. Except for the grin.

"Not likely! Even as a girl she ran faster than you! Now she is a woman grown and assuredly faster still. So! You leave it to me to be the villain."

"You might send her back to Honolulu," he said, scratching his chin. "I fear her presence here could turn the MacHenry Ranch dinner into a bit of a sideshow. I can tell you that her diving escapade is already the talk of the island, and it's not been twenty-four hours yet."

"That is the one thing I know I cannot do. I've spent years with Letty—and other young women too—encouraging them to embrace their convictions. How can I punish her now? How can we proclaim that we want more bold women and then the minute we have one, put a bridle on her? Sheer hypocrisy!"

"The problem," Bull said, "is that she needs to put a bridle on herself. Isn't that why you had her sent away to that fancy school your friend runs?" Bull turned back toward the door. "At any rate, I came in to tell you that she is out in the corral, scaring the hell out of the *paniolos* with her bullwhip. I fancy she is whipping herself up to face you, my dear Princess K. If I were you, I would get to her first. Want to borrow my whip?"

"No. I have one of my very own, thanks to you!"

As Kahōkūlani neared the main ranch corral, the singing snap of Letty's whip greeted her. Empty beer bottles stood in a tidy line along the fence. With fluid motions, Letty's whip picked them up, one by one, left to right, and back again. This, the very exercise that Bull taught to prove that a bullwhip properly used is a precise instrument. Letty always had that gift. Along with many others.

Princess K was dressed for her morning ride, making her decision easy. In any case, riding was her preferred medicine for every difficulty. They would ride.

"Letty, have you had breakfast?"

"No, ma'am."

"Please go to the kitchen and ask Isaac for something you can eat in the saddle. I need you ready to ride out in twenty minutes. We have much to talk about." Letty turned and ran, coiling the whip as she went. "And put your boots on."

Kahōkūlani squeezed the back of her neck with one hand. At least she had no headache. Not yet anyway. She entered the stable to get her horse. Moving from the bright sunlight to the darkness of the barn, she blinked. Familiar lights flashed at the edge of her vision. Thank goodness. Her stars were with her. This might be a difficult day, but she'd have her stars to guide her.

Kahōkūlani walked down the aisle of the airy stable, rubbing each horse's nose as she went. These animals were her biggest extravagance, yet always her greatest joy, ever since she had received her first pony on her seventh birthday. Dear old Fairy, now twenty-eight years old, heaved himself to his feet to greet her. "Now, now, old man, no need to get up!" K gave him the lump of sugar he expected. She massaged the pony's ears and under his chin. Fairy sighed in equine ecstasy. His eyes were milky, but otherwise the pony was in astonishingly good shape. She occasionally let very special small people ride him around.

Kāhili, his big head over his stall door, watched as she approached. The stallion was *hapa*, as they say in Hawaiian—a mixture of things. Part draft horse and part blood horse, he had the best characteristics of both: the high step and serene disposition of his Dutch dam, and the fleetness and intelligence of his racehorse sire. But best of all, he had glorious feathered feet that looked for all the world like the feathered standards—the *kāhili*—that accompanied the queens of old Hawaii wherever they chose to travel. How could she not call him Kāhili?

As she led Kāhili into the saddling area, Letty came running to join her. "Princess, shall I ride Malolo?" Letty slipped right into Malolo's stall as if to clinch the deal.

It had been three years since Letty had seen the horse, but Kahōkūlani was not surprised she remembered. The girl always had a special talent with horses. She and the mare had been inseparable over the summers. Malolo's answering whicker spoke volumes.

Kahōkūlani needed to remember that Letty was a girl no more. That would not be easy.

"Yes, you can ride Malolo—just please don't let me see you take her flying. Like her fishy namesake." Malolo could jump over almost anything; she lived up to that name, Hawaiian for flying fish. *Hmm*, K thought, *should I tell Letty now or later that I have been letting Timothy Rowley ride her precious Malolo?* Rowley, homesick for fox hunting in his native England, loved to jump a fence or two. Malolo was happy to oblige.

Rowley was so good with horses that Kahōkūlani had sold him one of Kāhili's daughters, Sunflower. This all made no sense. What could possibly cause Letty to make a scene about Rowley's fitness to own a horse?

The two trotted out of the gate side by side.

"Princess, where do we ride today?"

"To see the people, as we always do. To check on the homesteads, the *kuleana*." Such a powerful word, *kuleana*. The responsibility. To the land, the *'āina*, and so much more. Kahōkūlani might never be Hawaii's queen, but she would care for her people nonetheless. This was her own *kuleana*. "We'll have a lovely chance to get reacquainted, don't you think?"

Out of the corner of her eye she glimpsed Letty's nervous nod. Perhaps by the end of this ride this oddness about Rowley's horse might all be sorted out. Kahōkūlani tipped her *lauhala* hat forward to better shade her eyes. Or see her stars. Both might be needed.

The Princess relaxed into the saddle, reveling in the warmth of the afternoon sun. Already this was just the sort of day she most enjoyed. Out with the people. Her people.

Everyone everywhere offered welcome. Children came running. Adults showed off their latest, whether it be babies or new houses or piglets. Kahōkūlani and Letty admired them all. When her people asked for help with their problems, she did whatever she could to solve them. This was her life now. Her *kuleana*.

Letty had been unusually quiet, no doubt dreading the conversation yet to come.

Kahōkūlani had purposely chosen visits near to the Moran Sugar Plantation. From the lips of the people, that would be the best way for Letty to learn what kind of man Timothy Rowley was, straight from the people. On the last visit of the day, Kahōkūlani and Letty rode into a village nestled among Moran Sugar's cane fields.

The Princess would not be disappointed.

"Kerala," she said, swinging down to greet the headman, a beaming Hawaiian *kupuna*. "How are our piggies?"

"We show you, Princess!" the man said. "And Mr. Tim, he builds us a piggy palace!"

Ah yes, of course he did.

The women walked with their horses toward the last house in the village. Around the back, a substantial pig shelter came into view.

"Mr. Tim built this, you say? But Kerala, he knows we will soon file the proper deeds to protect your homesteads, all your *kuleana*. This is not his land. I told him this myself."

"Yes, Mr. Tim, he very good with that. He say that if we have land next to his land, it smart to make things better for everyone. Good neighbors, he say."

"This I am glad to hear."

"Mr. Tim, he know *aloha*, he pay fair. Hawaiian, Portuguese, Japanese all get same pay. Not like others. He cut cane. He like pigs too."

Princess K could not contain her smile. "You have that right, Kerala!"

As Kahōkūlani and Letty rode back to the ranch, the late-afternoon sun made eye contact difficult. This was a good thing given the discussion at hand. But first, business.

"Letty, do you understand how important this dinner at MacHenry Ranch is? Many of the big landowners fear the work we do to help the people get proper deeds to their *kuleana*. They refuse to believe there is no plot to gain the crown back! This dinner is to reassure them that we have no such designs. Your comportment will be scrutinized. Are you prepared for this?"

"Yes, Princess. I studied diplomacy with your friend, Miss Fred. At Redwood."

I hope so. The Princess kept this thought to herself.

"Now, Letty, I am ready. Do you want to tell me what happened yesterday?"

First, silence. Then her goddaughter rode up beside her to unleash a torrent of words. Kahōkūlani let the stream just flow until finally she said, "Wait, Letty, I think you must go back to the beginning if I am ever to understand all this."

Letty knew she'd need to tell the tale in its entirety. Calmly. Or her leap into the sea would make no sense. She tamped down her eager flames and began again.

"It started when I left California. Just days ago. I was standing at the rail of the *Columbia*, waving." At this, Letty smiled. "I'd had quite the wild ride to the harbor with my friend Irene Stansfield and her father. In his latest motorcar. Mr. Stansfield sells the things, so he is quite keen on them."

"Yes, I remember Irene from your letters. But let's stick to the story, shall we? I shall hear about Mr. Stansfield's motorcars later."

So much for Letty's gambit to distract the Princess. And, more importantly, herself. At least the detour had quenched her flames a bit.

"At any rate, my cabin wasn't ready so I stayed at the ship's rail. I watched a big horse-drawn wagon pull up next to the ship. You know the kind, the ones used to haul prize cattle?

"The delivery men pull down the wagon's gate, bringing out a horse that took my breath away." She tipped her head back at the recollection. "Wait until you see him. Diablo. Huge. Very well bred. Deep red with a mane and tail of coal black. A true blood bay with not a single white marking. Glorious."

Letty leaned forward, toying with Malolo's mane with the fingers of one hand.

"Then the man who was to take him aboard—I learned later this was his groom—grabs the lead rope, yanking the horse behind him toward the ship. The horse stalled until the man hit him. Hit him! The horse moved up the gangplank, stopping again and again, only to be hit every time. Right then I knew I'd ask the captain for permission to go below to check on the horse during the voyage. And I did.

"The first few days, the seas were rough. My stomach is strong so I was up and about, but many others were not. It wasn't hard for me to visit the horse in the ship's hold. Someone kept the horse fed, but not clean. What was wrong with his groom? Still, the talk of the dining salon was that the horse was destined for some English lord on Hawaii Island. All I could think of was how little he cared for this fine horse!

"The fourth day out, the seas began to calm. This time, as I climbed down for my visit, I heard blows and then a whinny. I could see the groom yanking on Diablo's halter.

"My first instinct was to push the man away. But truly, I *did* study diplomacy. Miss Fred always claimed good cheer to be your best line of defense. 'Good cheer before war.' Surely you've heard her say that?"

Kahōkūlani nodded. "Oh yes, I have. Dora and I put up with some shenanigans at Stanford. We 'good cheered' away any number of annoying young men. Although I must say Dora possesses more capacity for good cheer than I! Go on."

"So, I say, 'I have come to visit this very nice horse. May I help you with him?' With that, the groom backs away. Splendid! I think. The diplomacy is working! I step forward to offer Diablo a carrot.

"Then the man moved back in so close I smelled the liquor on his breath. 'No, I don't need no help with the horse,' he said. 'But maybe I've other things you can help me with . . .'"

Letty's hand flew to her face, her revulsion still vivid.

"I beat a swift retreat. So much for the diplomacy."

Kahōkūlani nodded. "Very wise."

"The next day I waited until evening, thinking to avoid Mr. Smith. But when I went below, I heard cursing. And the sounds of blows.

"The horse fought, but the groom hit him again and again. This time I ran at the man. I yelled. He jumped back. I must have startled him."

Letty gulped, then spit it out.

"Then he turns to me. 'Well, aren't you the fiery one.' That's just what he said. Something about it made the hair prickle on the back of my neck. He came very close. 'I like my women fiery . . . and dark.' I hurried off, but afterward I felt as though I ought to bathe to put the moment behind me."

Letty stopped Malolo and just sat for a moment, snapping herself back into the present before she went on. And to let her flames quiet.

"Once we landed in Honolulu, I went home for a few days to be with my family. I did not see the horse or the groom again until I boarded the *Pele* to come here. You must know all the rest. I am sure Bull told you."

The Princess said nothing for a moment, sitting still as a statue on Kāhili. "Of course, I understand. I too would struggle to witness that kind of cruelty. And for you it is especially tough when it comes to animals." She reached over to touch Letty's hand. "But I need your help, Letty. It's about that little speech you gave before you fainted on the beach . . ."

"You mean the one where I called Rowley an ass and a moron?"

"The very one. And now what is your opinion concerning Mr. Rowley?"

"I may have made a mistake." Letty tipped her head to look at the sky to avoid swearing. That would be one of the less fortunate things she had learned at Redwood. "Does the man really cut cane? I have never heard of any *haole* cutting cane."

"Yes, yes, he does. And he has the scars on his arms to prove it. Although I can tell you the rest of the sugarmen find it most peculiar. Not that Rowley cares!" Kahōkūlani chuckled.

"I witnessed one foolish gentleman inform Timothy such work was 'beneath his Lordship's dignity.' Hah! Rowley dished it right back. That honest work was never, NEVER beneath anyone's dignity. That he's seen his own grandmama, the dowager countess, wield a scythe. And that, like all his family, he was handy with sharp things. I was never clear if it was the word 'countess' or the word 'sharp' that shut the man up."

Drat, her concern for the horse had her jump to conclusions. Quite bad ones, it seems. Worse than simply jumping into the sea.

"It might have been best had my rescue ended in a slightly less dramatic fashion."

"Well, no more such speeches, please. Or mad escapades. Lord Rowley's grandmama is a great friend from my time in England. Philomena is almost a mother to me. Timothy can be a bit stiff-necked and old-fashioned, but he is a good man. He supports our work on land rights for our people." Kahōkūlani chuckled again. "He claims he has not yet made up his mind about votes for women, but I suspect we shall persuade him in good time. And if I don't, Philomena will.

"Here is the thing, my dear: I am proud of you for taking bold action to save the horse's life. Even more so now that I understand all that happened. But you made such a scene at the harbor . . ."

Letty swallowed the embarrassed self-recrimination she was about to deliver as Kahōkūlani continued.

"I will ask our hosts to seat you next to him at the dinner. That may forestall a bit of the gossip. You have until then to perfect your apology. You just said you learned something about diplomacy at Redwood? This will be the time to employ those lessons. Good cheer and all that."

And better yet, give Letty the perfect opportunity to plead Diablo's case.

The Hawaiian twilight deepened rapidly into dark blue velvet, so different from the lingering twilights of summer evenings during her exile in Britain. Now one of Kahōkūlani's favorite things was sitting in her study of an evening, reading. In Honolulu her home had electric lights, but not yet here at her

high mountain ranch. Here, she read to the soft glow of a ker-
osene lamp. She always found it rather romantic.

Bull appeared at the door. "How did it go?" He angled
his big body down into one of the delicate Victorian chairs
Princess K inherited from her mother. *I must not wince when
the chair creaks,* she thought. It creaked. She winced.

"Better than I expected."

Bull lounged back. His extremely large and dusty bare feet
rested on her Chinese silk rug. The chair creaked again. "Are
you prepared to let her go to the dinner?"

"It is a risk we must take. I told you, I refuse to hide her
away." Kahōkūlani looked pointedly at his feet. "Have you been
consulting with the *'āina* on the matter? You have certainly
brought enough dirt in . . ."

"Does her hair look redder to you?"

Startled, Kahōkūlani peered at Bull over the top of her
reading glasses. "Do you mean what I think you mean?"

"Let me say this: she is the proper age for her gifts to mani-
fest. When she hauled up on the beach with that horse, I could
have sworn I saw a red flash around her before she fell. When I
carried her to the wagon, there was so much heat rising off her
body I almost dropped her. We need to be careful."

"Point taken. I shall invite your sister to join us for a few
days. Esther is the best person to deal with this."

"I've already sent for her. It's my job as *kahu* to think ahead."

He stood, nonchalantly shaking a bit more dirt onto the
rug. "Here, I am leaving you the wisdom of the land. I know
you can use it!" Grinning at his own joke, he headed for the
door.

"However did I get stuck with a *kahu* that fancies himself
a vaudevillian? Your wife is a saint to put up with you." She
laughed in spite of herself.

At the door he turned, serious once more. "Sleep well, my
lady. I think you are going to need it."

All she could do was nod as she turned her attention to the letter Letty had delivered.

My dear friend K,

This missive will be coming to you in a packet of books I have asked Letty to bring to you. Along with a bit of Brundidge's fine tea! I hope you find it early on so that you may consider what can be done to help this fine young woman.

Letty is the brightest student I have taught. She masters everything she touches, but most particularly mathematics and the sciences. Her impetuous nature is the only thing holding her back. If she can learn to master herself, who knows what she can accomplish?

You must know how much she loves animals. Last summer I arranged for her to assist a Doctor of Veterinary Medicine, a Dr. Feeney. He has opened a college for animal doctors in San Francisco. The good doctor believes our Letty has all the makings of a fine practitioner. She has the "fire in her belly," as he says. With another eighteen months under his tutelage she can obtain her veterinary certificate. She would be the first woman in California to do so. I dare say she might be one of the first women anywhere to do so.

Letty has told me that she is expected to work in the family business. A further challenge is the tuition. It is a bit steep. Because the program of study is demanding, Letty will not be able to work to defray costs as she has all through her time at Redwood. The one bit of good news is that a friend's family, the Stansfields, have offered her room and board in exchange for the occasional tutoring of their youngest child.

I've a feeling she may need an advocate to convince her own family to allow her to attend. Perhaps you can help her realize this dream, as you so graciously helped me realize mine? There is no better champion than you!

All my very best,
Dora

Kahōkūlani ran her finger along the deckle edge of Dora's letter. Yes, of course she'd be Letty's champion. But if Bull's observations were correct, the young woman might have more obstacles to surmount than her *'ohana*. Many more.

Chapter Three

Ulumāhiehie

TO MAKE A FINE
APPEARANCE

'Iolani Ranch, Hawaii Island,
the 11th of June, 1909

"You no look yet." Letty ached with impatience, her back to the huge mirror, another piece of the Princess's royal inheritance. Extravagant gold curlicues framed the vast expanse of glass necessary to showcase Kahōkūlani's aunties and *tūtūs*, the *ali'i wāhine*, Hawaii's tall princesses, in formal court dress. Today was Letty's turn, standing tall as Miyako, Kahōkūlani's dressmaker and Bull's eternally patient wife, fussed and pinned. This gown was to be her birthday gift from the Princess.

"You turn around now."

Letty turned slowly as the pins prickled under her breasts. Of course the dress must be lengthened, eased in the bosom too. She had grown to such an Amazonian proportion since the last time Miyako took her measure.

Her breath went out in a whoosh as she caught sight of herself. Her slack jaws snapped shut, but her eyes continued to betray her shock, as her hands smoothed the delicate silk against her hips.

"This right color for you," Miyako purred. "Princess say green, but this better." She had draped Letty in the deep, deep turquoise blue of the island's ocean.

The dress was a *holokū*, the gown worn by generations of Hawaiian women. When the missionaries arrived in 1803, they urged Hawaiian women to cover up, and the loose *holokū* was born. Now, in Miyako's capable hands, the style took on new life. Slim and fitted up above, flowing down below and sporting a waterfall train, the *holokū* gowns became Kahōkūlani's signature. If the missionaries could see the dresses now, they'd hide their eyes.

For the very first time, Letty would have her own formal *holokū*, thanks to the Princess.

"You like the flowers?" Miyako pinned furiously as she talked, extra pins dangling at the side of her mouth. "If you look ova heah, I put little bird in, too, because I know you love all the animals."

Over Letty's left shoulder and down and around the base of the gown flowed embroidered sprigs of the fire-red flowers known as *lehua*. "I see the little bird, Miyako! A honeycreeper!" She leaned forward to touch the tiny bird at the hem in wonderment, running her finger over stitches almost too delicate to be real.

"You stand up and stop wiggling, girl, so I can finish for party!" Miyako carefully helped Letty slip out of the gown, neatly avoiding the pins.

"*Mahalo*, Miyako! I feel like a princess myself in this dress!" She leaned down to give the tiny woman a hug.

"You princess now, girl. I watch you grow." Miyako reached up to put her hand over Letty's heart. "Princess is here, inside.

You act like princess, you be princess, because princess in your heart." She pulled Letty's shoulder down to deliver a quick peck on the cheek and glided out of the room.

A single tear escaped to slide down Letty's nose. Her own mother had been a princess; if only Letty could remember her, perhaps the pain would not be so great.

ʻIolani Ranch, Hawaii Island, the 13th of June, 1909

The rituals of female preparation began. Letty perched in a chair as Tomiko, Kahōkūlani's maid, attempted to tame her unruly mass of hair. Miyako arrived, cradling the sea-blue gown in protective muslin.

"We want everyone to know what real *aliʻi wāhine* look like! Yes?"

Kahōkūlani swept into the room. She wore black, this time a *holokū* of voile embroidered with white star jasmine. Called *pīkake*, or peacock flowers, they were the Princess's favorite, just as she favored the peacock bird. With her hair piled on top of her head like a crown, the white strands peppering her temples drew up like rays of starlight to ring her face. Real *pīkake* was braided throughout. Around her neck was a simple pearl necklace with a diamond pendant. Letty gulped. Kahōkūlani looked every bit the queen she was born to be.

"All right, young one—your turn." The Princess reached for Letty's dress draped over Miyako's arm, folding back the muslin. Her finger traced the embroidery. "My, my, Pele's flower, the *lehua*. You've outdone yourself, Miyako!"

She turned back to Letty. "Do you know some believe *lehua* means 'twisted by fire,' Letty? It denotes courage. And courage is something we know you have to spare."

She handed Letty a blue velvet box. "I've some diamond clips that might be very becoming on you. These were my mother's. Wear them well."

Kahōkūlani swept back out the door. "Come to the lawn to drape your *pā'ū* as soon as you are ready."

Letty turned to face the mirror. She did not hold much hope for her hair. There was just too much of it. Tomiko put a photograph of a woman with beautifully braided hair in Letty's hands. "This is Princess Victoria Kamāmalu. Our princess thought her hairstyle might be right for you. Very good, yes? I show you how to do it."

"Oh yes, very good." Letty sat still, letting Tomiko's skillful fingers move rapidly through her tresses. She rarely had someone dress her hair. It felt pleasant . . . almost familiar . . . Her throat caught as a wispy, distant memory of her mother brushing her hair flitted through her mind. She wished so much that she could remember more.

Almost too soon, she was ready for Miyako to help her into the dress. Her back was again to the mirror. Miyako insisted on it. Once the dressmaker fastened the last of the tiny buttons, she tapped Letty's arm.

"Letty, do not forget that *holokū* is special. This kind of dress, it shows you a true daughter of old Hawaii. Some say it old-fashioned, but Princess believe *holokū* send a message about the old ways. You wear with pride, yes? Turn around now."

Letty gasped—a beautiful stranger looked back at her. Well, perhaps not beautiful, but the best she had ever looked. All her life, her clothes had been ruled by the practical. Nothing had prepared her to look—or feel—like this.

"Miyako . . . Tomiko . . . *mahalo . . . mahalo nui.*" Letty's voice cracked with emotion.

Miyako squeezed her hand. "You make us proud, girl! And no jumping in water or anything!"

Just as the sun set, Letty and Kahōkūlani rode through the gate
of Kauluwehi, the big house at MacHenry Ranch. *Paniolos* and
the house staff rushed forward to help the ladies. Doing her
best to look accustomed to such treatment, Letty dismounted,
her *pāʻū* wrappings gathered to be used again to protect her
dress on the moonlit ride home. Letty trailed the Princess
toward the gay swirling crowd on the front lawn.

A long table covered with damask, fancy dishes, and crystal
filled the lānai. Silver candelabra waited to be lit. Thankfully,
Miss Fred insisted all Redwood ladies learn the manners
expected for a formal dinner. At least she need not fret over
what fork to choose! Still she had a bit of the chicken skin in
her excitement.

Princess K floated through the crowd like a sailing ship
with landfall in sight. Letty contented herself with bobbing along in her wake. Kahōkūlani's intended target, A. J.
Chartwell, the MacHenry Ranch trustee, stood at the center of
the maelstrom, holding court. The Princess made short work
of getting to him; only someone who knew her well could tell
she was on a mission. Otherwise, she seemed to be graciously
greeting everyone.

"My dear Judge Chartwell, what a lovely evening for a
party." Kahōkūlani glided to his side. "It seems everybody who
is anybody on this island is here tonight."

Chartwell was one of the few men in attendance tall
enough to look down at Kahōkūlani. He leaned toward the
Princess conspiratorially. "This is what you wanted, is it not,
K? A chance for everyone to see you are neither a villainess nor
a Bolshevik?"

The Princess delivered a brilliant smile. "Thank you for
this, A. J. We are at a critical point in our work with the families who need deeds to their homesteads. The *kuleana* lands

are the foundation of economic security for our people; it is just that simple. The big landowners have nothing to fear."

"It is not 'nothing' they are worried about, my dear. You have become enormously popular among the people, we are in a time of much political uncertainty, and they fear an attempt to reinstate the monarchy. I'm not surprised they distrust your motives. I would be suspicious myself if I did not know you better." Chartwell added quietly, "Sensible of you not to wear your tiara tonight."

Letty stood stock-still, feeling quite the fly on the wall for this conversation.

Princess K gave a ladylike snort. "You of all people, A J, know how I feel about any attempt to regain the crown. It would be fruitless and brutal. The Americans will never let us go. These islands are too valuable."

Another snort, much less ladylike. "Yes, Hawaii has been well and truly captured. What's done is done. We must fight our battles in other ways."

"You know I agree, but not everyone here understands; be careful tonight."

Kahōkūlani inclined her head in acknowledgment, giving Letty a wink from under her lashes. Perhaps she had meant for Letty to hear this conversation.

Chartwell turned his gaze to Letty. "And who is this glamorous young Amazon? Another of your suffragists on horseback? Not the brave soul who saved Rowley's horse from drowning? Leticia Liliʻuokalani Lang, I presume?"

Letty held out her hand in greeting, smiling though her tummy was jelly. Judge Chartwell was a legend among Hawaii's ranchers. "I am honored to meet you, sir. Thank you for including me in this lovely evening."

"I have worked with your father and grandfather for many, many years. Extraordinary judges of good horseflesh, and honest traders as well. Might I assume that you inherited the skill with horses?"

"Oh, yes sir." Letty was breathless. "I hope to one day become a veterinarian. I am training—"

Chartwell had already turned away as his eye sought another person in the crowd. "There is Timothy Rowley now. Have you been properly introduced? This is a perfect opportunity for you to receive his thanks for your daring rescue, and"—he leaned in toward Letty, his eyes twinkling—"you might also apologize for making him a laughingstock at the harbor. Just a thought."

Letty gulped as the Princess grabbed her hand, drawing her toward a tall, sandy-haired man in full evening dress. Very tall—he easily had a good three or four inches on her and here she was almost six feet. Slim and broad shouldered, he presented an arresting profile. Not handsome exactly, or at least not what she usually thought of as handsome. But interesting, strong like a hawk. He turned when Princess K tapped him on the shoulder, cool gray eyes widening when he saw Letty.

"Timothy Moran Rowley, may I present Leticia Lili'uokalani Lang, my godchild and erstwhile protector of all creatures great and small. I am certain you have much to talk about."

Timothy grasped Letty's hand, then dropped it as if it were a hot stone. Her flames rendered an immediate jolt at his touch. Might he have felt it? "My pleasure, Miss Lang. May I help you to a glass of punch, and then perhaps we could chat about Diablo?"

Letty glanced to Princess K, received a nod, and then smiled at Timothy. "Why yes, sir, that would be most welcome." Out of the corner of her eye, she caught people staring. Yes, her manners were definitely on display tonight.

Timothy offered his arm on the way to the refreshments table. Letty grasped a punch cup, carefully choosing one not too full. One of Miss Fred's little secrets for not spilling the sticky stuff. Then the man gracefully drew her to a bench at the side of the gathering.

"First, let me apologize—" he began.

"No, the one who needs to apologize is me—"

"Not true." His face was intent. "To begin with, your quick thinking and brave actions saved Diablo's life. I ought to have come to the ranch immediately to offer my thanks, but the cane harvest intervened. Please tell me what happened."

"Well, I first saw Diablo on the docks in San Francisco. Mr. Smith was leading him aboard the steamer. The horse was obviously frightened, but Smith kept pulling him and striking him. By the time he was loaded, we could hear Diablo kicking the stall. He only quieted when the steamer sailed."

She took a deep breath; how to tell him nicely that his groom was cruel? "Over our time at sea, I visited Diablo with tidbits from the table. By the way, he particularly loves green beans; you must be sure to give him some. When I was by myself with the horse, he was calm and even gentle. Yet whenever Mr. Smith appeared, Diablo would shy and move as far back into his box as he could. Once we arrived in Honolulu, they disembarked. I did not see the horse and groom again until three days later. That was when we boarded the steamship to come here. You know what happened then."

Timothy reached for her hand as it rested on the bench between them, then pulled back. What was that about?

"Miss Lang, something is amiss here, but I cannot put my finger on it. Mr. Smith was sent by my grandmother with a personal recommendation. Grandmama is an ardent horsewoman and cannot abide cruelty in any form. There must be more to the story."

Letty crossed her hands on her lap to avoid any more awkwardness. "I don't know what more to tell you. What I do know is this: when an animal visibly fears someone, very bad things most certainly have happened."

"Well, you have my heartfelt thanks for rescuing Diablo. Thank you for this information about Mr. Smith as well. It gives me much to ponder." Timothy inclined his head toward Letty. "Tomorrow I will be back at my stables and get my first chance to work with Diablo . . . and his groom. Perhaps the answers will appear then."

"Oh, by the way, Mr. Rowley, I have decided you may keep the horse." Letty let the mischief get the better of her. Her flames gave a laughing tickle.

"I am most relieved to hear that, as I have already had a request to put him out to stud," Timothy responded with a smile and another little bow as he stood to take his leave. My, he was good to look at.

Just then, a florid and sweating matron in a ruffly pink dress bustled up to Timothy. Behind her trotted a blond young woman of an age with Letty, who looked rather nice despite another overwrought dress, this one of pale green.

"My dear Mr. Rowley," the woman simpered, "or do I say *Lord* Rowley? Adele and I are very much looking forward to your company this evening." She pointedly ignored Letty, a fact not lost on Letty at all.

"Mrs. Simmons, what a pleasure! Might I introduce Miss Leticia Lang to you and Adele? She very graciously saved the life of one of my horses a few days ago."

The corpulent Mrs. Simmons looked at Letty, her ill will palpable. "Oh, my dear, are you native?" Timothy stiffened.

"And your dress, how quaint . . ." Her daughter had the good grace to glance away in embarrassment. But Letty had dealt with people like the Simmonses before. She rose up from the bench to her full height, enjoying the expression of astonishment on Mrs. Simmons's face. Flames danced up her back with amusement.

Letty turned her head in the hope the diamond hair clips might flash in the lights. "My pleasure to meet you both. I trust

you will find our islands much to your liking." Out of the corner of her eye she noted Timothy's gulp of relief. Perhaps he
had been expecting a scene. Well, not tonight; she had promised the Princess her best behavior. Even her flames agreed.

Still she was not through. "Oh, Mr. Rowley," she said,
reaching out to tap Timothy with her fan, "I believe we are to
be seated together at dinner. We can continue our equine conversation then." Letty glided off into the crowd.

Timothy watched Miss Lang sway away, wondering at how
a woman so big moved with such grace. Her skin seemed to
glow from within, a deep bronze against the ocean's blue of
her dress. And the hair, again he could swear he saw it reflect a
warm light, sparkling red, just as he'd seen on the beach. He'd
wanted to reach out to take her hand and ask her to stay. Hell,
he'd wanted to reach out to touch that hair. *Whoa, steady, back
to the business at hand.*

Timothy turned to level his attention on Mrs. Simmons
and her very eligible daughter, Adele. Now, this was an heiress. Just the sort that his father might approve. Oil money, if
the gossips were to be believed. Yes, Adele Simmons might fit
nicely into his plans.

Mr. Chartwell appeared at Letty's elbow with a smiling older
woman in tow. "Letty, have you met my sister, Angeline
Chartwell Bliss? She is just returned to Hawaii from many
years on the mainland. I informed her that you are a great lover
of animals, and she professes a desire to be introduced."

"My pleasure, I am sure." Letty smiled.

The houseman rang the chimes for dinner. "My dear," Mrs. Bliss exclaimed, "we must head to the table, it appears. But perhaps later"—she leaned in, her tone lowering in anticipation— "you will regale me with your amazing diving rescue. I am quite taken with what I have heard thus far! In the open ocean! In your pantaloons and shirtwaist! Such bravery!"

Letty swallowed. It would have taken a miracle to make it through the entire evening with no mention of the incident. That miracle would not occur. "Why, thank you for your kind words."

As they approached the long table, Letty found she was indeed seated next to Rowley, Adele Simmons on his other side. Despite her mama, Adele herself seemed quite nice. At least that is what Letty would choose to think. To quote Miss Fred, a lady always extends the benefit of the doubt. If only she'd done that with Rowley in the first place.

Dinner was exquisite, conversation flowing. Letty held her own; she might be behind on the local gossip, but she was certainly up to date on world affairs. She had Miss Fred to thank for that. To her left sat one of the new plantation managers, an earnest young man of Dutch extraction who had just moved to Hawaii from Jakarta. He seemed eager to learn about the political climate in the United States.

"Tell me," he said, "what is your stance on women's suffrage?" As luck would have it, most conversation around the table ebbed at that very moment. In such an opening, where all could hear, Letty's voice rang out like a bell.

"Why, I am all for it. Women *must* get the vote. I read the suffragist paper, the *Yellow Ribbon*. Have you heard of it? I wear the yellow ribbon too. In San Francisco, I met Maud Younger! She is so inspiring—she drives her own motorcar!" Letty suddenly felt all eyes on her. *Uh-oh . . . not again.*

Across the table a red-faced Mrs. Simmons turned to her dinner partner, a Mr. Owen Cameron, and spat, "How uncouth!

The girl is clearly a hoyden. No daughter of mine would be mingling with those classes. Jews and labor unionists! What must her mother be thinking?"

Letty looked down at her plate. If only she could slip through the floor.

Mr. Cameron, an old friend of Letty's father, replied, "Her mother is no longer with us, but her godmother, our Princess K, stands in her stead here tonight. If you have issues, you may take them there." He gestured to the Princess at the head of the table. "I'd like to see that, actually . . ." He turned to give Letty a wink.

From the end of the table, Kahōkūlani's voice rang out. Laden with good cheer. The war might come later. "Why, Mrs. Simmons, I should be delighted to debate you on these matters. Shall we set a time, choose our weapons, and name our seconds?" Mrs. Simmons's nervous titter was her only response. Conversation around the table resumed.

Letty swallowed. Best to get back on safe ground quickly. "And, sir, how did you determine to come to Hawaii?"

The gentleman from Jakarta launched into his own tale. "I have spent many years in the sugar business . . ."

Letty smoothed her face into a look of sincerest interest. She simply must make it through the rest of the evening without further incident. Mrs. Simmons was to be avoided at all costs.

The next morning, Timothy entered the stable, only to be greeted by a torrent of swearing and the sound of blows. Rounding the corner, he found Diablo cross-tied in the grooming area, struggling to break free while Hank Smith struck him with an open palm. Timothy rushed in, yanking the groom away.

"The son of a bitch stepped on my foot!" Hank snarled. "I'm going to teach him a lesson."

Timothy pushed the man up against the wall. "No, you will not. Miss Lang was right about you. Get your things and wait for me outside my office. I will settle your pay."

The man limped off toward the bunkhouse. Timothy went to Diablo to soothe him. The stallion's eyes rimmed with white as he shied away from Timothy's hand. "I'm sorry, big fellow," Timothy whispered. "I should have been paying attention. You will not be seeing the likes of him again."

At the office, Hank was unrepentant. "So that little bitch complained about me, did she? She is a fiery one. Be careful if you are diddling her—she bites. I know that for a fact."

Timothy slapped the final pay envelope into the man's hand. "I very much doubt that. And if you go around saying such things about the women here, you may just find yourself in an irrigation ditch with your head bashed in."

"Are you threatening me?" Hank snarled.

"I am not threatening you; I am making you a promise. Now, get off my land and don't ever come back. Joshua will take you to Hilo in the wagon. If I were you, I would get the next boat off this island." Timothy stood with his arms folded as the man headed toward the waiting wagon.

Something was not right. Why would his grandmother send this man halfway across the world? She was a better judge of character than that.

Kearny Street Hall of Justice, San Francisco, California

The man on the bed opened one eye, then closed it quickly. The ceiling spun. His head hurt too badly to even think. The noise

of metal doors banging and chains rattling eddied around him.
A key turned in the lock on his cell. He opened up an eye again
to see a large constable come in. "Get up, you rogue, there is
a fine gentleman here to see you. A Pinkerton. You must have
done wrong to someone with lots of money . . ."

A burly man in a plaid suit and fedora followed the constable through the door, apparently one of the famous Pinkerton
private detectives. The suit was a quite unfortunate shade of
purple.

"This is him, sir. We found some papers on him with his
name." The constable backed away to let the detective in closer.
"Stand up, fellow."

He obeyed but gripped the wall for support.

The Pinkerton grabbed his chin to look at his face closely.
"You have papers with the name, you say?" he asked the
constable.

"Yes, sir, and the whore that dragged him in, she called him
by that name too . . ."

"Well, officer, you have been deceived," the Pinkerton said
with notable disgust. "This is not the man I am looking for . . .
In fact, the man I seek is the most likely candidate to have
caused the big goose egg on the back of this poor gentleman's
head."

Then he asked, "Tell me, sir, what is your name?"

The man hesitated and mumbled, "I don't recall . . ." In
fact, he was doing his best not to vomit on the detective's shiny
boots.

The Pinkerton cocked his head.

"Well, the sooner you can remember, the sooner you can
help me track the man who put you in this position. His real
name is Frank Allerton, and he has a nasty history of turning
himself into other people whenever it suits him. Let me guess:
a nice gentleman bought you a beer or two and then you don't
remember much after that, do you?"

The man slumped back down on the bed. Suddenly things came back to him. He patted his chest pocket where the dowager countess's letter of credential was supposed to be . . . Gone. "I am Hank Smith," he stammered. "I am here to pick up a horse."

"I am sorry to tell you, sir, that Allerton is probably long gone with the horse and now styling himself as Hank Smith. I have been tailing him for six months, and this is his modus operandi." Turning back to the constable, he asked, "How long has he been like this?"

"Three days, sir."

"Well, Mr. Smith, Allerton has a bit of a head start, but we shall be right on his trail. You help me and we will find your horse." He turned back to the jailer. "Constable, can you release this man to my care? It looks to me like a bath and some sleep would make him a much better traveling partner."

Hank Smith struggled to his feet and grabbed the hand of the Pinkerton. "Thank you, sir. The horse, well, the horse is very special. The countess, she trusted me . . . I cannot fail her."

CHAPTER FOUR

Huikau

COMPLICATED

'Iolani Ranch, Hawaii Island, the 14th of June, 1909

Kahōkūlani stood warming her hands in front of the kitchen woodstove. At the ranch's high altitude, mornings dawned crisp and cool. Isaac had sweet coffee, biscuits, and sage advice waiting. Perhaps she would take a second cup. But no more advice.

Letty swooped in to grab a third biscuit. Isaac slapped her hand. "Save some for Bull, hey? He even bigger than you!" His grin filled his seamed face.

Letty laughed as she gave the beloved old man a hug.

Isaac had been with the family as long as Kahōkūlani could remember. Even when she was a little girl with a skinned knee, Isaac knew just what to say. And what cookie might soothe it. He'd done the same for Letty and the other girls who came every summer. Or used to. They were all grown up now.

"You stay out of trouble today, Missy Letty—need time to get over late-night big party, you get?" Isaac also knew how to put someone in her place.

Letty nodded, her mouth full. Kahōkūlani glanced at the big clock Isaac kept to time his baking. It was later than she'd realized. "I'm off, Isaac. It will be a long day, so no need to prepare a tea this afternoon."

Out in the yard, Bull had the horses waiting.

The Princess swung up. Kāhili danced a few steps, feathered feet flying, and then settled under her hands. As he tossed his head, she fancied Kāhili looked just like the war horse some valiant warrior queen might ride in days of yore. Well, she was off to do battle for her people. Today land rights, tomorrow votes for women. Tally ho! Enough fanciful thoughts; a day of legal wrangling lay ahead. It was well that she could wield the law better than any sword.

"Tako, pull that bunch of cows and calves off the mountain today." Bull sat easily on his big pinto as he gave out the day's orders. "Then Rowley is expecting you to help with his two colts in the afternoon."

"Letty come with me, boss? She good help."

Letty stood quiet against the fence. Kahōkūlani wondered if a day out with the *paniolos* might be just what she had in mind. And seeing Mr. Rowley again. Kahōkūlani had not missed the way Rowley stared at Letty. Hopefully that was just her imagination. Still, the young one deserved a bit of fun. Her mind made up, the Princess nodded to Bull. There would be plenty of serious business for Letty to deal with tomorrow once Esther arrived.

"I guess." Bull sounded more than a bit dubious. "Letty, please don't forget that Tako is in charge. Follow his orders. You've had a couple of years to forget your way around the mountain."

"Yes, sir."

Princess K gathered her reins.

"Letty, remember that tomorrow Esther comes for a visit. There are some bits of history we'd like to share before you head back to Honolulu. Some old legends."

"I enjoy hearing the old history!"

"Of course. I am sure you will enjoy it."

Princess K rode off without further comment. She'd keep her unease to herself. How might practical, scientific Letty take to discovering that she was the subject of one of those legends? That remained to be seen.

As they approached the upland trail, Bull pulled alongside Kahōkūlani, "You look tired. Have you been seeing stars again?"

"Yes, I have, and I am glad of it. But I still do not yet see the way forward for Letty."

"Tomorrow will be a challenge, even with Esther to help you. We may all need the wisdom of your stars. There is more to this story. I can feel it." He slapped his own cheek with one meaty hand. "Now, if Tako can just keep her out of mischief today, I will count it a blessing."

Up on the slope of Mauna Kea, calves and mamas grazed peacefully, spread out between clumps of scrub trees and outcroppings of lava rock. Three thousand feet below, the misty blue Pacific tumbled and rolled. The morning sun made Letty glad of her broad-brimmed hat. Later the day would be hot, but right now—up at mountain altitude—the temperature was delicious. She relaxed into the saddle with pleasure at both the day and the task. Not to mention the prospect of seeing Mr. Rowley again. Malolo, sensing her mood, gave a little hop of joy.

Tako led the *paniolos* upwind so as not to disturb the cattle. "Here is the plan," he said as the group gathered around. "We spread out and push herd downhill slow. Better don't run—less bad to calves. Letty, you stay uphill, look for stragglers."

"You got it, boss." The game was on.

The *paniolos* fanned out and gently pushed the cows down the hill. Everything went as planned. That is, of course, until one crafty mama decided to make a break for it, tail in the air, little one trotting close behind.

Tako was right there. He roped the cow easily, returning her to the herd. Letty sat back as she was told. She loved to watch the old cowboy work.

Letty nudged Malolo to follow the herd downhill but stopped when she heard the crack of brush breaking to her right. And snuffling. A wild longhorn bull pushed his nose through the underbrush, so close she could see his nostrils flaring as he took in the scene. How could she have not known he was there? The beast turned his head to consider the closest target. Herself.

Letty loosened her bullwhip, turning Malolo to face the beast, and slowly backed the horse away. A fiery curl tickled up her spine.

The bull gazed down the hill at the *paniolos*, then turned back to Letty, still pawing. If she yelled for help, he would most certainly charge. Besides, her throat had gone completely dry. Her flames buzzed up and down her back in uncertainty. She kept backing Malolo slowly away, hoping against hope the bull would lose interest. She'd never used her whip from a horse's back before. Even if she startled the bull away, Malolo might bolt in the process. There were no good choices.

The bull made up her mind for her, letting out a deep bellow as he charged. Her fire arced up her spine. She rode Malolo hard right at the beast, lashing her whip into his eyes. The bull fell to his knees. Just long enough for Malolo to make a flying leap over, somehow avoiding taking a horn in her belly. Letty slipped a bit, dropping her bullwhip, but clung to the saddle and kept on riding.

Tako spurred his horse up the hill, his lariat loosened and ready to fly, Kaneoka right behind him.

Letty did not turn around until she was well past. By that time the men had lassoed the bull, pulling him sideways to a nearby tree.

Honi, the only remaining *paniolo*, hustled to keep the cows from scattering. Letty trotted back down the hill to help him.

Moments later, Tako rode up beside her. "You all right? That some fancy footwork," he said. He handed her whip back to her.

Letty, still breathless from the fright, nodded she was fine.

"How you know what to do? That Malolo jump look like a miracle."

"I can't explain, really—I just seemed to know." Or at least her flames did.

"This my fault." Tako was gruff. "Should have checked perimeter for wild ones. That old man trouble us a while now. Our Bull, he have my hide that I put you in danger."

Letty caught her breath enough to laugh. "I won't tell him if you don't," she said.

With the cows now safely grazing in the lower pasture, Tako and Letty set off again. This time to Rowley's ranch to help with the colts. Letty had not visited the property for some years. Back then the place belonged to Rawhide John Carver, a crotchety old cowboy who had taken a shine to the Princess. Letty was curious to see what Rowley was doing to the place.

Approaching the big gate in the late-afternoon sun, Letty pushed back her hat to wipe away the sweat. Her breathing had finally settled after the fright with the bull. She looked forward to a quiet afternoon with a couple of unbroken horses.

The gate, at least, was as she remembered. As were the big trees. And the hitching rack, where she and Tako dismounted. A horse hitched to a pony cart stood nearby lazing in the shade, one foot cocked up. But for the rest, clearly Lord Rowley had been hard at work.

She loosened Malolo's girth as Timothy came out of the refurbished stable, dusting off his hands. "Tako, old man, good to see you! I need your wise words today with these two young ones! And who is your assistant?" Timothy took a closer look; his jaw dropped. "Miss Lang?" This in a strangled whisper. "Are you wearing . . . *trousers*?"

She was about to launch a retort when she spied Mrs. Simmons, with Adele at her side, at the stable door taking in the scene. Mrs. Bliss right behind. This would not go well.

Mrs. Simmons was nothing if not predictable.

"Is this Miss Lang? The suffragist? In *trousers*? Well, we were just preparing to leave, thank goodness. I am sure we would not want to witness any such vulgar spectacle!"

Mrs. Simmons blew herself up with indignation, looking quite like an angry chicken. "Come, Adele. Avert your eyes— let us get to our carriage. Good afternoon, Lord Rowley."

Letty thought it wise not to point out to Mrs. Simmons that the carriage was actually only a pony cart. As Adele floated by, she gave Letty an apologetic look. She must have to do that rather often.

Mrs. Bliss was the last to head toward the conveyance. "Timothy, thank you for the tour of the stables. You were quite gracious to give us your time. We dropped in on you *so* unexpectedly." The woman checked to see that Mrs. Simmons had her back turned, then gave Letty a discreet thumbs-up.

Mrs. Bliss expertly guided the pony cart out of the gate and back toward MacHenry Ranch. Timothy waved politely as the three ladies spun out of sight, then turned to Letty with a grimace. "Must you always make such a controversial entrance? *Trousers?*"

Tako doubled over laughing. Letty stood stiff, completely mortified. "I am here to break horses—what *should* I be wearing?" she announced with as much dignity as she could muster.

"Oh, of course, you are here to help." Timothy's voice dripped with sarcasm. "I don't recall inviting you, just Tako and one of his men . . ."

Tako recovered swiftly from his fit of hilarity. "Mr. Tim, she best horse breaker we got—that is why I bring. You see soon."

"No, I won't see! Miss Lang, you may think me 'an ass and a moron,' but I am not a fool. No woman is risking injury in my corral, even if she is wearing trousers!" Timothy stood, arms crossed, gray eyes flashing the warnings of a storm, his chin in a stubborn set, the white scars of his work in the cane fields visible on his tanned arms.

Letty was quick to notice them. And the underplay of muscles as he tensed. She'd never heard of a *haole* cutting cane. Somebody just needed to tell this man to keep his sleeves down. And to calm down.

"Look, Mr. Rowley, let me apologize again for the things I said on the beach. I spoke in the heat of the moment. But, today I'm already here and—like it or not—dressed to help. Perhaps you and Tako might get started? I will just hang here on the fence in case you need me. Would that be all right?"

"No. I am afraid that won't do."

Letty cocked her head in surprise. Maybe she'd been right about this man in the first place. An ass and a moron indeed. "Well then, I suppose I shall be riding out."

Tako grabbed her arm as she turned. "Then I go with you." He turned back to Timothy. "Maybe some other day."

Timothy grimaced and extended a hand to Letty. "My apologies—I am at my worst with surprises. First the ladies and now you. I mean, not that you aren't a lady too, you are just another surprise."

He blithered. That was amusing. Almost.

"Clearly my manners have failed me. I am honored to have you here. Please stay."

Letty reached to shake Timothy's outstretched hand. "Apology accepted. And please call me Letty. We came here to work; shall we get to it?" She started marching purposefully toward the corral, the fat braid of her hair bouncing right and left on her back. So much for a quiet afternoon.

Tako slapped Timothy on the back. "Hey, Mr. Tim, she already face one angry bull today. So, you fussy? It nothing!" Then in a quieter tone he added, "You should know, when it come to horses, Miss Letty, she worth two of us. Maybe three. You see soon."

Timothy had no doubt he would see, whether he liked it or not. That woman was trouble.

Two hours later, dusty and tired, the colts had completed their first lessons. Everyone was ready to call it an afternoon.

Timothy chewed on the inside of his lip. He'd made a fool of himself to begin with, then spent the next two hours trying not to stare at those long legs. In trousers. To make matters worse, Letty had been truly helpful—if a bit bossy. And a joy to watch. The horses simply seemed to trust her. Now what? And he should tell Letty he'd fired that nasty groom. She'd been right. He just didn't know how much humiliation he could stomach in one day.

He stood irresolute as Letty and Tako adjusted the girths on their horses and prepared to saddle up. "I thank you both again. I truly needed your help today. I am sorry I was so inhospitable earlier." Damnation, he still sounded like an idiot. Well, he *was* an idiot. Just add that to what she called him at the harbor—an ass and a moron and now an idiot . . . perhaps she had a point.

Something about this woman threw him off balance. Her striking appearance made it worse. He found her . . . perhaps compelling was the word? Not that she was his type. Far from it. Blond and petite had always been his cup of tea, not auburn-haired, bronzed giantesses. Still . . .

He moved to stand awkwardly by Letty's horse. He'd thought to help her mount, clearly a futile idea. Of course this woman would mount on her own. Perhaps that was what so unnerved him; she just did not seem to need help from anyone. Annoyingly competent, that was it. Or perhaps it was her impossibly long legs. In those damned trousers. He kept coming back to that thought . . .

A commotion erupted from the stable door. "Mr. Tim, Mr. Tim! Sunflower, she having baby and it look like trouble!" Timothy waved goodbye, turning to go.

Somehow he was not surprised to find Letty already off her horse and jogging behind him. "I know a lot about this," she said.

Timothy sighed. "Of course you do."

The mare shivered with the strain. Letty placed a comforting hand along her neck. Most likely her labor came on quickly, too quickly. That was the way of these things, Letty knew that much. One tiny hoof protruded from Sunflower's birth canal.

The stable boy pointed. "Look, boss, only one hoof. I think leg bent, maybe can't come out. She need help."

Timothy stood back, arms crossed, and looked at Letty. "Freitas, the head groom at MacHenry Ranch, should be here in an hour or two. Or perhaps sooner. Surely, Miss Lang, you know Freitas? If your family deals in horses you must. He agreed to come this afternoon to check on her." Timothy's tone was firm. "We will wait for him."

She doubted they had an hour to wait. Letty slipped out to check the tack room. Thankfully, the shelves were well stocked. She grabbed a few clean-looking rags and a can of soft soap. All she needed was hot water. Heading back to the little mare's stall, she met Timothy coming out, his face grim.

"Is she worse?"

"Yes. Did you say in your veterinary studies you helped with births like this?"

"Yes," Letty said, "of course." She'd assisted only a couple of times. But she'd seen such births before. Her grandfather delivered foals all the time. And she'd studied the techniques. Read about them. That would be enough, certainly. The mare needed help now, right now. Didn't she? Didn't she? The flames began a slow, insistent curl up her spine.

"Well then, I need hot water and . . ." Entering the stall, Letty found the mare even more distressed. Still in active labor, yet she appeared to be weakening. The foal must be repositioned now while Sunflower still had the strength to deliver it.

Letty pulled off her work shirt, leaving both arms bare. Thank goodness her camisole was on the modest side. The stable boy appeared with a steaming bucket of water. Carefully, she cleaned her hands and smeared soft soap all over her right arm. "Timothy, the mare trusts you. Go hold her head. Talk to her." Letty's voice conveyed more assurance than she felt.

With infinite care, she slipped her arm into the birth canal. Letty shut her eyes to concentrate only on what she could feel, running her fingers along the foal's leg. Both knobby little knees fit in one hand, but one leg was turned under. Slowly and deliberately she pushed the little one back into the womb, coaxing the second leg fully forward. Now the legs could lead the baby out into the world.

Letty stood back. Both hooves appeared, side by side, and all seemed well. That is until everything just stopped again. Sunflower trembled with fatigue.

"I am going back in," said Letty.

"*No,*" said Timothy. "Please, we must wait for Freitas."

The mare gave a huge shudder. A wave of urgent fire rolled up Letty's spine.

"I'm not waiting." Letty stepped back into position, beginning again to feel her way. A surge of energy and heat enveloped her. Her breath steadied. Eyes again shut, with absolute attention on what her fingers could discern, she reached beyond the foal's legs to its shoulders.

"Oh my," she whispered, "it's bad. The neck is bent. There is no way Sunflower can deliver unless we get the foal's neck straight. Both will die if we don't. I am going to try." She met Timothy's eyes, prepared to argue if he tried to call her off. Instead, he nodded.

Gently, Letty pushed the foal back into the womb, keeping her hand on the tiny shoulder. Eyes squeezed tight, she willed herself to see with her fingertips. Her hand crawled up the shoulder to the neck, finger by cautious finger. The contractions were weaker now. Angling her hand, she grasped the neck to ease the head forward. Progress. But another contraction, and the foal's neck slipped away. She found it again, panting with the effort. This time she almost had it. Almost.

Letty sucked in a deep breath, tears of effort running down her face.

Sunflower let out a sudden deep groan and fell to her knees. Knowing there was little time, Letty stretched. This was as far as her arm would go. She gulped in desperation. Again, a surge of warmth and energy, this time her fire running through her

hand. Sunflower contracted sharply, the birth canal squeez-
ing Letty's arm like a vise. The foal pushed near enough that
she could grab the tiny head and move it forward. Quickly she
aligned it with the front legs—she always thought it looked like
any foal about to be born was prepared for a high dive—and
hoped for more contractions to come. But Sunflower was too
weak.

"Timothy! You need to massage her. I will start pulling, but
see if you can get her to contract."

Letty grasped the two little front legs and pulled. Sunflower,
as if taking her strength from Timothy, gave another huge push
and the baby popped out. But not breathing.

Quickly wiping off the nostrils, Letty went down on her
knees to give the foal her own breath. With a start, the little
one began to breathe. At that same moment Sunflower chose
to heave herself up, knocking Timothy ingloriously on his butt.

Letty laughed—big, gulping, laughs of relief. Timothy
couldn't seem to help himself and started laughing too. She
stood and went to give him a hand up. Without a thought for
the slime, she gave him a hug. "We did it, boss." She pulled
away as her flames gave another zing.

Sunflower, meanwhile, was licking the colt and nudging
him to stand for his first meal. He was a gleaming little red
chestnut. Like flame.

Freitas came rushing into the stall. "Sunflower, she okay?"

"Yep. One leg and the neck were turned, but we were able
to fix that," said Letty. "There is still the umbilical cord and the
afterbirth to be handled. Can you help?"

"You some doctor, Miss Letty," said Freitas, his admiration
evident. "I will take care of the rest. Sunflower, she good horse!
You some doctor!"

"I wish, maybe someday," she said, walking straight out of
the stable back to her horse. She knew that if she didn't ride

out soon, she might wilt from the emotion. Then she'd start crying, and goodness knows what else she might do.

"Letty! Don't you want to stay? Clean up? I don't know what to say . . ." Timothy sputtered, trotting along behind her.

Letty pulled her shirt back on over the slime and blood and swung up on Malolo.

"*Mahalo*, but no—I have a princess to go see."

Halfway to the gate, Letty turned her horse around. "Please name him Lohi'au, after Pele's lover. His life is a gift from the *'āina*."

Timothy watched her ride away, Tako at her side like an honor guard. What had he gotten himself into? Nothing made sense. He could swear he saw red light swirling around Letty during the birth. Just like the lights he'd seen on the beach when she had saved Diablo. Now a part of his heart rode away with her.

Timothy shook his head to clear it. Enough nonsense; he had a baby to care for.

As Letty rode through 'Iolani's main gate, she met Princess K heading out, followed by two women on mules, saddlebags bulging.

"My goodness, Letty . . . what happened to you?" The Princess brought Kāhili right up next to her. "Is that blood I see?"

Letty attempted a smile as the rush of energy from the birth evaporated. She might slip off her horse. "Sunflower's colt came early and I helped deliver it."

"She do more than help," said Tako. "If she not turn baby, Sunflower and colt both die."

"Heavens, where was Freitas?"

"Baby came fast. They sent for him, but he arrive after it was done. Letty save lives." Tako's tone was approving.

"Well, good for you, my girl!" Princess K leaned over to touch her arm. "I can see you are exhausted. I am on my way to the Queen's Bath, and there is nothing better after a birth! Tako, have one of the hands go to Tomiko and request a change of clothes be brought down to us posthaste. And food, plenty of food! *Wikiwiki!*"

Tako touched his hat and rode off.

Letty did not have the strength to argue. She turned to follow K, slumping in her saddle. Malolo would get her there.

Half an hour later, she trailed Kahōkūlani into a palm grove surrounding brackish ponds near the sea. Over centuries, the royal women of Hawaii, the *wāhine ali'i*, came here, to the Queen's Bath, to be refreshed. Some believed the waters to be healing. Letty knew the Princess came here often, but she had never been invited before.

The women pulled bundles from their saddlebags. Letty recognized them now, *kāhuna* from the village near Hawi. Letty slid off Malolo, nearly boneless in her fatigue.

Princess K removed her clothing, gesturing to Letty to do the same. "First, we bathe." Letty was too tired to do anything but obey. Moving carefully to keep from slipping, she followed Kahōkūlani into the rock-rimmed pool. The *kāhuna* began soft chanting.

Crystal-clear, slightly salty, and pleasantly lukewarm water cradled her. Letty scrubbed the birth slime off and submerged to cleanse her hair. Then she just floated. Tiny fish tickled her toes. She was so relaxed, she almost fell asleep.

"Do you feel it?" Princess K whispered.

"Feel what?"

"Well, perhaps it is just me . . ."

Suddenly a tingling sensation, almost electrical, yet entirely pleasant, surrounded her. Letty's exhaustion lifted away, replaced by a sense of profound well-being.

"What is that?"

"I don't know, but I choose to think it is Pele's way of sharing her sweet fire with us, the power of the living land, our *ʻāina*. I come here when I need to be reborn." The Princess moved her hands slowly through the water, creating gentle ripples. "You know I almost died in 1899, don't you?"

"Yes, but you got better and went to the university . . ."

"Well, I almost didn't get better. I was very ill. I had lost my desire to live. Who wants to be the princess of no country?"

Kahōkūlani sat up and pushed her hair back, settling comfortably on a submerged rock, legs crossed. "We were staying up at MacHenry Ranch. No one knew what was wrong with me. I was trembling and had trouble breathing. My father wanted to take me back to Honolulu, where I surely would have died. He put me in a litter to be carried to the harbor. Esther and her women blocked the roadway and would not allow the men to pass. She insisted we come here first. I don't remember much, but I do know one thing. This"—she swept her arm to encompass the pool and its surroundings—"this place has power.

"I believe that the *ʻāina* brought me back, brought me back to do something important. It was here I began to understand that I had a new destiny."

The Princess got out of the pool; the women wrapped her in a kapa cloth. She went to a cushion of mats the women had prepared.

"Come, Letty, now we have *lomilomi*. You saved two lives today. You have earned it."

Chapter Five

Makana

GIFTS

'Iolani Ranch, Hawaii Island, the 15th of June, 1909

Letty closed her valise with a snap. Tomorrow morning she'd head back to Honolulu.

She looked forward to time at home. Was it just three years ago when it seemed she and her Australian stepmother might never make peace? Now, she was at a loss to remember what triggered her wrath. Somehow she'd fallen under Agnes's fierce and loving spell. The woman was even throwing a party for Letty's soon-to-be nineteenth birthday. A full-on *lū'au*. With *hula*.

She must remember to ask Isaac for a jar of his prize guava jelly to take to her stepmother. Agnes loved all sweets.

Princess K stuck her head in. "Esther is here. Where should we meet with her? The back lānai might be nice. Under the *hau* tree. There will be food."

"That sounds lovely. I will be right out." Letty set the box containing her *holokū* on top of her valise, now ready for her last afternoon at the ranch. Whatever could Esther have to talk about that would take long?

Kahōkūlani's lānai was big even by Hawaiian standards, a breezy, shady place to linger, with a doorway to Isaac's kitchen for provisioning. Esther sat, settled in a chair with a cup of tea, a tray of the cook's cream scones beside her, with guava jelly and fresh mangoes to slice. Letty's nose filled with the warm scent of things freshly baked.

"*Kupuna, mahalo* for coming to see me." Letty chose a chair directly across from the mountainous woman. Esther was nearly as tall as her brother, Bull, and nearly as wide too, emanating a quiet strength. Esther had been Kahōkūlani's childhood bodyguard; Letty knew her from past summers. Now she knew that it was Esther who saved Kahōkūlani's life seven years ago. No wonder the Princess trusted her.

As she settled in, two of Princess K's cats came to wind around her ankles. Letty leaned down to scratch their ears.

She looked up to find Esther staring at her silently. No, not staring, studying her, as if she were a bug under a microscope. Esther had always made her a little nervous, with her ageless face and uncanny streak of white hair. Now Letty wondered if she would have the stomach for the generous helping of scones already piled on her plate.

"I see you have an appetite, my daughter. This is good given the day you had yesterday. You must get your strength back."

"Oh, I am fine really—this is what I have been studying to do. I hope to become a doctor of animal medicine. Science is my best subject . . . and mathematics, of course." Letty's words ran out in the face of the woman's intense gaze.

"What is it you wanted to tell me?" Letty said with a gulp.

"I have questions for you first. Tell me about the birth."

Letty shifted in her chair. "Well, there is not that much to tell, really. It seemed like it took forever. But once we intervened, it was perhaps half an hour until Sunflower gave birth."

"That is not what I am asking. What was it like? How did you feel?"

Letty looked down to see her scones cooling as she considered her answer.

"Eat, child—maybe that guava jelly will help you tell the story!"

Letty was ravenous. She'd had breakfast, but her body seemed to demand more. Never had scones and jelly tasted more delicious. Not to mention the mangoes. As she mopped up the last few crumbs with her finger, Princess K settled into the other chair facing Letty. What was this, the Inquisition?

"Replenishing our strength, very good. Do I need to ring Isaac for more?" Princess K smiled, but Letty could not escape the sense that she was somehow in trouble.

"No, thank you, ma'am. I am feeling much better." And, in truth, she was.

"Now, let me ask again, about the birth . . ."

More than a bit defensive now, Letty forged ahead. "All right, perhaps I embroidered my training a little bit. Maybe I did not know quite as much as I told Timothy I did. But if I had done nothing, Sunflower and the colt would have been lost. It all worked out fine." Both women stared at her now as if she truly were a bug.

For a moment that seemed like an eternity, no one spoke.

Princess K sighed. "That is exactly right, my dear. It all worked out, but for reasons we believe have nothing to do with your training in San Francisco."

"Letty, I ask again, what did you feel during the birth?" Esther leaned forward.

"It is hard to describe. I just knew what was right. I mean it was obvious, really, the colt had to be turned or Sunflower could not deliver him."

"Again, what did you *feel*?" There was a slight rise in Esther's voice. Letty wondered what she might be saying wrong. Her flames made an uneasy lurch.

"Well, I just told you . . ."

"Bah, you have told me nothing yet, girl!"

Princess K put her hand on Esther's arm. "Perhaps, *kupuna*, we must be more specific. Letty, what physical sensations did you experience?"

Letty rubbed her hands together, unsure of what to say, how much to say. She'd like to keep her flames out of it. Plus, this had been different, she had felt something more. "I felt warm . . . no, really sometimes hot . . . like fire ran right through me. Somehow it made me feel confident . . . strong. When I felt the fire, I knew just what to do. And then I just did it." There it was. She admitted she felt flames. Let them make of it what they will.

"Exactly when did you feel fire the most?" Kahōkūlani did the asking. Esther kept silent, her eyes searching Letty's face.

"I had to turn the colt twice. The first time I did not feel much . . . fire. But the second time, it was bad—his head was bent back. I thought we were lost. Then it came again, like fire in my veins, and I turned him." Letty glanced up at the two older women. Both looked at her, but not like a bug, not anymore.

She sat up straight. "Well, this is silly. I was very excited and frightened, that is all." The tendrils of her own uneasy flames licked up her spine.

Esther began again, more gently now. "Letty, have you noticed any changes in the color of your hair?"

"Well, yes, there must be something in the water in San Francisco. It makes my hair redder. I think it's iron."

"Sweet girl, what if that is not what it is? What if it is . . . magic? Power?" Princess K spoke with an air of nonchalance, but Letty could tell she was serious.

"Come on, we are educated people; we know better. There is no magic."

"But what if there is? What if you have gifts from the *'āina*?"

Letty shook her head vehemently. "I don't believe that." The flames flared higher. She began reciting the Fibonacci sequence to herself. The Fibonacci always calmed her down. Always. Well, mostly.

The Princess spoke softly. "Letty, look at me—look at me carefully, and do not take your eyes away."

Letty put her hands under her knees and did as she was told. Suddenly, around Princess K's head and then all around her body she saw a white light, a corona that flickered, then faded.

"What did you see?"

"It must have been a trick of the sun . . . a reflection like a halo around you."

"No, Letty, that is what my gift, my power, looks like."

Letty's heart constricted. Even the Fibonacci would not help this. "*No*, that is not it . . ."

"Enough of this nonsense!" Esther grabbed the sharp little fruit knife Isaac had provided for the mangoes and stabbed it into Kahōkūlani's arm. Blood gushed.

"*NOOOO!*" Letty grabbed the wound, wrapping her hands around Kahōkūlani's arm to stanch the bleeding. Her flames engulfed her, coursing through her hands. A red glow seeped from between her fingers. Her hands were so hot she wondered if she might be burning Kahōkūlani.

Esther rocked back, crossing her arms. "Very good, my daughter. Do you see the light? Now take your hands away to see what you have done."

All this time Kahōkūlani sat as if nothing were amiss.

Trembling, Letty pulled her hands away to see a scabbed-over wound on the Princess's arm where only moments before blood flowed.

Esther sucked in her breath. "She is strong, even stronger than I may have hoped."

"You saw the light, my dear?" Kahōkūlani reached out with her uninjured arm to grasp Letty's hand. "That beautiful red light is the sign of your power. It is your own gift from the *'āina*."

"No, it is not. I don't know what this is, but I refuse to believe it. It cannot be true. I am a scientist and a mathematician, and I am going to school to be a doctor. You sent me away to learn to control myself, and I have. You are playing a mad game with me." Letty stood and backed away, throwing down the Princess's hand. Panic overwhelmed her. She would not be a slave to the flames. Not now, not ever. Except when she was.

"Enough of this—I am going to my room now. I need to pack."

Esther and the Princess watched in silence as Letty marched stiffly away.

Kahōkūlani turned to Esther. "That poor child—I thought we agreed to break it to her gently. Now she's in shock and she is leaving tomorrow. What were you thinking, *kupuna*?"

"She is no child. Her gift is great; we do not have time for niceties. She must accept who she is and do so soon. Otherwise, she is a danger to herself and others. You know that those who can heal can also do great harm. And that dangers just seem to find them. She will need a *kahu*, and soon."

Kahōkūlani stood at the doorway, watching Letty. The young woman sat on her bed, staring at the wall, silently rocking. Her shoulders hunched up to her ears, and if it wasn't so hot, Kahōkūlani would have sworn she shivered too.

Poor child, the thought came to her again unbidden . . . Esther was right; you could not call a very tall young woman with healing fire at her fingertips a child anymore! Still Kahōkūlani remembered the difficulties of her own transition. One felt like a child in the face of such unknowns.

Kahōkūlani had been older when she came into her gift: twenty-three. But she never forgot the shock of the discovery that she was not like other people . . . that nothing in her schoolbooks could explain who she was. And that her life might never again be her own.

She cleared her throat. Letty started at the sound. "Go away. I want nothing to do with you and that crazy woman."

"What are you thinking right now?"

"I am not thinking, I am counting. A series of integers, to be precise. This one is called the Fibonacci sequence. You sent me away to school to learn to control myself? Well, I did. When the impulses take over, I count. It works rather well."

Kahōkūlani moved farther into the room and settled herself into a chair. "I am going to tell you a story, and I will not leave until it is done. Do you know how my mother died?"

Letty, still facing the wall, gave her head a stiff shake.

"Well, the doctors never knew either. One day she just stopped wanting to live and slowly wasted away. I was only eleven."

Letty leaned toward her; the motion was slight, but perhaps she was listening.

"On her deathbed, she said to me, 'Oh my daughter, you will be sent far, far away . . . You will never marry . . . You will never be queen.' She was right, of course. But there is no rational scientific way to explain how she knew."

She paused to let that sink in. "Just as there is no rational way to explain why I glow white with truth and you glow red with healing. It defies everything we have been taught to believe about the modern, explainable world. But there it is."

Letty said again, "Go away." But this time to Kahōkūlani's ear it lacked conviction.

"Here is what I know. In all the history of Hawaii, our people have believed in the power of intentions. If you seek for good to happen or if you wish bad to happen, your intentions matter. You know this from how we seek reconciliation with *ho'oponopono*. The first thing we do is understand our own intentions and those of others. Because they matter.

"What we call magic, your gift, is simply your intention. Nothing more, nothing less. It is about what you think. *Mana'o.* You intended to save the mare and colt, and so you did.

"Everyone has intentions. But for a rare few of us, our intentions come with a flow of energy, a gift of power from the *'āina*. Some people, but only special people, only those who are bound to you in some way, can see the energy when you wield it. It is called an aura. That is why you saw my white light down on the lānai. Because we are bound together, you and me. As Gates.

"Look at me now and tell me what you see."

Letty's head turned as if invisible hands forced her, staring straight at Kahōkūlani.

"I am speaking the truth right now. You see it again, the white aura, don't you?"

Letty's eyes widened as she whipped her head back around to face the wall. "I do not believe this. This is insanity."

"How my mother died remains a mystery. But I cannot help thinking she may have been the victim of bad intentions. Why else would a healthy woman waste away? Many of our people believed that she was despised by the old *kāhuna*. Because she had chosen a *haole* father for her royal child, the old men wished to punish her. They intended her dead and so she died. That was the power of their intention, the *mana'o*."

Kahōkūlani began to pace. "What do you remember about your own mother's death? Oh, I forgot—you are not speaking to me."

Letty turned again slightly. "I am listening."

Kahōkūlani stopped for a moment and looked at the girl's tense back. "I have an idea: I'll have the horses saddled. We are going for a ride, you and me. And while we ride, I will tell you a few more stories. You would like a last ride on Malolo, I think."

Wooden, that might be the best way to explain how she felt. Wooden. Her mind ran in an endless rut of disbelief. This could not be happening. It just couldn't.

She sat unmoving in the saddle as Malolo followed Kāhili nose to tail up the trail to the lookout on the *pu'u* at the top of the ranch. The old cinder cone was all covered in grass, but you still knew that once it had been a gateway to the power of the living land, the *'āina*. A relic of some ancient eruption. A sacred place where the heart of the earth came near. Kahōkūlani kept a bench up there, overlooking the sea.

As they crested the *pu'u*, wind caught Kāhili's mane and feathers. Letty watched as the Princess threw back her head, tossing her hat off and releasing her hair to the wind's wild ministrations. Kahōkūlani halted Kāhili behind the bench, tossing her leg easily over the front of her saddle to slip down.

Her look back to Letty framed a command. Letty recognized an order from an *ali'i* when she got it, however unspoken. Slipping off Malolo, she loosed her own hair, which in her case went even wilder.

"Shoes off too. We must touch the *'āina*."

Letty pulled a bit of windswept hair from her mouth.

"Now we talk." Kahōkūlani moved to the bench and patted the place next to her. Letty sat, upright and stiff.

"When was the first time you felt the flames?"

Her breath went out in a woof. She could not deny it. Not in this place.

"I think I was seven."

"What happened?"

"I saw two boys laughing on the side of the road. They had a bag. They were poking and hitting it with sticks. The bag moved, and I heard little cries."

"Oh no." The Princess placed her hand over Letty's on the bench. Letty pulled it back onto her lap.

"Oh, I said no, all right. I screamed it at the top of my lungs. No! No! No! I ran at them and knocked over the bigger one. He laughed and got up. I kicked his shins. He and the other boy hit the bag again. Harder." Letty stopped; a tight band squeezed her chest.

"And?"

"It happened. The flames took me. I yelled again. This time it was NOOOOO. The boys looked at me, eyes big as saucers. I swear I saw my fire reflected in their eyes. Then they ran." Her mouth went dry as a wave of nausea rose.

"They had puppies in that bag. They were beating puppies."

Kahōkūlani's arm slipped around to pull her close. Letty let her head drop to Kahōkūlani's shoulder. "I carried that bag of puppies home to Mālama. There were five. One was already dead. Two had broken legs, one a busted eye. Mālama watched me give them my fire." Kahōkūlani rocked her. "They survived. Two of those dogs still live up at my grandfather's ranch." Tears welled. "I did what I could to save the puppies." Now the tears flowed as Kahōkūlani rocked her harder, the two women surrounded by a curtain of windblown hair.

"Sweetheart, you will always save the puppies. That is who you are."

"Never tell anyone. That's what Mālama told me. Never tell anyone. The *haoles* will take you away."

Letty shivered, suddenly feeling the ocean wind as a chill nip. "I never told."

"Of course you didn't." Kahōkūlani released her, shoving back her hair as she continued.

"Mālama was wise, you know? She told you true. People fear the things they do not understand. If they'd found you out, they would have feared you. They would have taken you away. The *haoles* have made the old magic illegal now, saying it is all a trick. As if the *ʻāina* cares what they think.

"Me? I was not so clever. I told people about my stars. How they showed the way. So I was sent away. For eight years. To a foreign place where no one believed in *aloha* or magic. To a place where the *ʻāina* is old, where you can barely feel its beating heart.

"I remember it all like it was yesterday. I was standing outside the parlor at ʻĀinahau. There were three men in with Papa, speaking low and harsh. I heard Papa say, 'She will outgrow it, certainly she will outgrow it.' And then another voice. 'She must or she will never return.'"

Letty straightened up. "This is ridiculous. I just want to go back to San Francisco and study."

"I did not want the gift either, but it took me. That is what happens, you know? The land, the *ʻāina*, takes you, binds you."

"I don't believe it. I don't want to believe it."

"Whether or not you do doesn't make it any less real. Nor does it change the price you will pay."

"I'm listening."

"There is so much we do not know . . ."

The next morning, Kahōkūlani found herself leaning against one of the big verandah pillars with Esther standing like a statue by her side. Bull pulled up in the wagon, ready to take Letty to the harbor. Kahōkūlani had done her best to tell Letty what she knew, everything she knew, but in the end the young woman had retreated to her room in silence. Isaac sent in trays of food, but Letty did not appear again.

Until this morning. For scones. Now Letty emerged from the house, gaze downcast, carrying her luggage in a death grip. Esther gave a deep chuckle. "Say goodbye to your elders, girl." Letty tipped her hat and mumbled.

Glaring up at Bull, Letty tossed her valise and Miyako's dress box into the wagon. "Now I know you are just as crazy as they are. The Princess told me all about you. Her *kahu*?" She climbed up with a muffled grunt.

Bull gave a wide smile. "Yes, crazy, that's me!" He reached over and grasped her hand. "And I am here for you too. For all the Gates. Anything you need, just ask. Now, say goodbye nicely."

Letty turned and gave another reluctant salute to the two women on the porch. Esther inclined her head in acknowledgment. Bull's sister always was a woman of few words. It was left to Kahōkūlani to say something. *"A hui hou . . . mālama pono!"* Come again and take care. Trite, but Kahōkūlani meant it. A tingle of heat signaled her aura was active. Letty's head snapped around to avoid the sight. The wagon pulled away.

"Does she understand that she must be careful? That danger will surely find her?" Esther paused, her brow furrowed. "If only Bull could be in two places at once. She will need her own *kahu*." Another pause. "I pity the man who gets that task."

"I don't know, I tried. I told her how little we know. And that there is always a price to pay. A lonely price."

"Did she believe any of it?"

"She told me none of it mattered. Because she's already a suffragist, so that makes her fearless. And she intends to be a veterinarian. She says lady doctors are a lonely bunch anyway."

At this, Esther smacked her forehead. "Well, well. She has all the answers. Why am I not surprised? At least she'll be speechless when you show up for her birthday."

Now Kahōkūlani smiled. "One can only hope."

Letty sat in silence most of the way down to the harbor, watching the blue sea edge closer and closer. A little way out, Bull broke the chill. "So, are you scared?" She gave him a look that she hoped resembled skepticism. What she felt was more like fear.

"Why? This is all the ramblings of a couple of old women who have stayed too long in the sun." She turned to stare straight ahead, her chest constricting all the while. "I will be glad to get back to Honolulu. And at the end of the summer, I intend to return to San Francisco to continue my veterinary studies. I am a scientist and a mathematician, for heaven's sake!" If only she still believed it could be so simple. If only her own flames did not put it to the lie.

"I promise not to tell K you called her old!" Bull chuckled. "I can tell you I was frightened when I first found out about all this. That I had a role to play. Being *kahu* for the most powerful *ali'i wahine* in twenty generations is not what I thought my life would be. I just wanted to be a *paniolo*."

He slapped at a fly on his neck. "Sometimes you must accept that life controls you, not the other way around."

"Bull, I love you and Princess K like my family. You *are* part of my family, my *'ohana*. Just don't expect me to swallow all this. It's too preposterous. I can't do it. I refuse."

"All I ask is that you keep an open mind. I have been with K almost constantly since she came back to the islands in 1898. She is one of the wisest people I know. And she speaks the truth as she sees it. I'm not sure how best to explain it, but she knows the way. You saw her white light."

"Maybe I did and maybe I didn't . . ."

Bull reached over to pat her hand. "'Maybe' sounds good to me; at least that is progress."

They turned down the last part of the road to the beach, the wagon jouncing over a particularly rough patch. The boats were busy unloading people and cargo. Letty jumped down.

"I will see you at the end of summer for the Cup." She pulled her luggage from the back of the wagon. Bull waved and the wagon moved on to the harbormaster to pick up supplies.

As she lugged her gear to the shore, she noticed an odd pair getting out of one of the longboats. A stout man in an awful purple plaid suit accompanied by a small, quite bowlegged fellow who seemed a workman of some kind. They stood looking around, but clearly no one was there to meet them. Strange. Not many visitors came unexpected to the west side of Hawaii Island; usually you only saw folks you knew. Well, the harbormaster would take care of it. Letty had a *lūʻau* to attend and magic to avoid.

Chapter Six

Huina alanui

CROSSROADS

Rowley Ranch, Hawaii Island, the 16th of June, 1909

Timothy stood with one foot up on the pasture fence watching Sunflower's colt explore his new world. Baby horses always amazed him. Just a few days old and already running and kicking. Lohi'au, was it? The handsome lover of Pele? The name seemed just right. Still, he'd best stop thinking about the fire goddess who had delivered the baby. An heiress must be in his future. Not some woman who fancied herself a doctor of animals. And seemed to need no one.

A commotion erupted out front. Walking back through the wide stable door he saw his cook, Inoli, talking to two men standing with mules. Inoli jabbered away in pidgin, waving a big spoon. The strangers looked comically confused. One was a portly man in a preposterous purple plaid suit, the other a short man with bowlegs, perhaps a jockey.

"May I help you?"

"Yes, sir, we are looking for a Lord Timothy Rowley."

"That would be me."

The smaller man spoke up. "I am Hank Smith, sir. I was sent by your grandmother to accompany a stallion to be delivered to you, and then work for you for a year."

Timothy took a step back, his breath catching with the gut punch of shock.

"Can you prove it?"

The man in the purple suit pulled out a wallet to display his credentials. "Pinkerton Detective Agency, sir. The name is Williams. If you could please tell us, has anyone else been here calling himself Hank Smith? I am seeking him, sir—he is a murderer and a con man. Very dangerous. His real name is Frank Allerton."

Timothy looked to the sky and swore softly. "I knew something was up. Gentlemen, come to the cottage for a cup of tea. We clearly have much to discuss."

An hour later, after several cups of tea augmented by a glass or two of sherry, the story unfolded. The real Hank stood up and touched his cap.

"Would you mind, sir, if I went to see Diablo? I never got to meet him, you see. I was to collect him from the seller's people right before we took ship. By that time, I was lying in a gutter, not knowing which way was up."

Once in the stable, Timothy stood with the detective as the little groom headed unerringly to the big stallion's stall. Diablo's head hung over the door, but he rolled the whites of his eyes as he saw the man approach. Hank paused, stock-still, until the stallion whuffled for him to come closer. After a few moments of sniffing, Diablo let his head come down for a good ear rub. Amazing.

"That was neatly done. He is clearly the horseman he claims he is." Timothy turned to Williams.

"Yes, sir, I have every reason to believe he is telling the truth. He is lucky to be alive. Allerton is slick and moves quickly. If what you say is right, we must be back on that boat to Honolulu tomorrow. He may already have fled the islands altogether."

"I will be heading to Honolulu tomorrow on the Hilo boat myself. Diablo has a date with the ladies at one of the ranches. I am happy to have you join me, and you can rest here tonight."

Williams rubbed his toe in the dirt. "Hmmmm. How to say this . . . Did Allerton have any contact with women that you know about? He is particularly vicious with women."

"Actually, it was a young woman who alerted me about him. She'd sailed with him from San Francisco and noted his cruelty to Diablo. He cursed her when I fired him."

"Where is she now?"

"Honolulu . . ."

"Then we need to get there quickly."

Letty stood at the rail of the steamer, watching Honolulu come into view in the late-afternoon sun. So different from San Francisco, that harbor dominated by big ships. Here canoes and sampans danced around the interisland steamers and oceangoing ships in a sparkling display.

Every arrival in Honolulu was a celebration. Even today, when she was simply coming home from another island. Throngs of brightly clad people eagerly awaited what each ship might bring. Musicians strummed ukuleles. Everyone wearing or carrying flowers—or both.

The steamer eased up to the dock. She spotted Agnes with Johnny in the crowd, both waving madly. Now that Johnny, her stepbrother, was seven, he thought himself quite the grown man—but not so grown up apparently that he could not jiggle from foot to foot as he waved. Letty suppressed a laugh.

Moments later, Letty found herself swept along in the current of bodies heading down the gangplank into the arms of waiting family.

"Letty, Letty!" shrieked Johnny. "Wait until you see what we have for you!"

Agnes moved forward to put a lei around Letty's neck. Letty leaned down so the petite woman might kiss her on both cheeks. "Welcome home again, my dear. We have quite a birthday *lūʻau* planned for you! I drove the carriage here myself because I cannot wait for you to see how accomplished I have become." She took Letty's arm to guide her through the crowd to the small carriage. Letty could see Tanaka, her father's head stable man, holding the horses.

"Mama, Mama, show her now, *pleeeze.*"

A small cry emerged from a basket on her stepmother's arm. "Goodness, Agnes, is that a baby in there?"

Agnes dimpled. "Well, you might say that . . ." she said as she pulled back the lid, revealing one of the most adorable puppies of all time. "Happy birthday, dear. This little lass is from Johnny and me. We could not wait to give her to you because she made such a ruckus in the house! She is a Chinese lion dog."

"I found her, I found her!" Johnny danced about. "Mama and I went to Chinatown to buy herbs. We met people and they sold us this puppy."

"Shush, honey. Let's get in the carriage, and you can tell Letty the whole story on the way home."

Tanaka took Letty's bag and box to stow in the back of the carriage. Johnny flew into the back to ride with Tanaka. Agnes handed the puppy basket to Letty and stepped up to take the driver's seat.

"Oh no!" Letty burst out in a wave of giggles as a thin yellow stream flowed out of the bottom of the basket, hitting the ground. "Tanaka, do you have an old feed sack in the back? It looks like we really do have a baby on our hands."

Agnes's eyes widened, then she laughed too. "Oh my! I'm sorry—I should have thought of that."

Letty put the burlap under the basket, then settled it on the carriage floor. She reached in to pet the little one, who responded with eager licking and a touch of tiny teeth. "Thank you, Agnes—this is the best gift you could give me."

The puppy's face looked up at her, quite like a little flower. "I think her name must be Rosebud. Perhaps she will be a lady and live up to that name." Letty grinned wickedly at Agnes, adding, "Since I have so much trouble doing that!"

Agnes tapped her arm with a smile. "I still have high hopes, my dear!"

The carriage moved quickly, threading its way through the maelstrom of downtown Honolulu. New motorcars roared by, kicking up dust and noise. Chinese wagons loaded with goods pulled by sweating men. But most joyous of all, women on horseback in the brilliant swirling colors of *pāʻū*, laughing gaily as they trotted along, skirts flowing behind.

"Sophia!" Letty shouted and waved at one of the passing riders. "Agnes, that is one of my friends from Sacred Heart." Sophia waved back.

Agnes patted her hand. "I know, dear—I think everyone in Honolulu knows that you are home. We expect quite a parade of people through the house for your birthday *lūʻau*. How was your time with the Princess?"

Letty paused and looked down at her hands. What could she say? The last person she wanted to discuss magical gifts with was this practical little woman from Down Under. "It was interesting. I attended my first formal dinner. Wait until you see my dress!"

Fashion, as always, was a great distraction from the realities of life.

The carriage rolled into the Lang's Livery yard. Letty found herself awash in the smells and sounds of home. The horses in the paddock came pounding up to the fence. The three stable dogs—Johnny's three musketeers—ran barking to the gate. The plumeria hedge lining the gateway rioted in full summer bloom, its fragrance heavy and sweet.

Her father appeared, carrying Hannah, whose screams of "Yetty! Yetty!" might possibly be heard up to Diamond Head. The child's ginger curls and rosy cheeks played counterpoint to George's own Hawaiian looks. Both Agnes's Australian and the Lang family's Irish could be seen in this one. Letty was charmed the child remembered her. The little girl's outstretched arms presented an invitation Letty did not resist. Bouncing and kissing her little sister, she turned to see the stable dogs jump up on the carriage floor to surround Rosebud's basket like some sort of a gang.

Letty perched Hannah on her hip to rush to the rescue. Agnes held up a hand.

"Watch this."

Agnes leaned over, lifting the lid of the basket. One of the dogs stuck his nose right in it, only to back off howling. Rosebud reared up to put her front paws on the basket's edge, delivering the evil eye to the other two, punctuated by an elegant little snarl. All three older dogs began to slink away.

"This one will be queen of the place, I think." Agnes scooped up the basket and jumped down, carefully holding it away from her dress. "If we can just get her to mind her manners!"

Her father put his arm around Letty and gave a squeeze. "I am glad to have you back. We are looking forward to keeping you to ourselves for a while!"

Arm in arm they trailed into the house, little Hannah planting slobbering kisses on Letty's neck. Surrounded by the warmth of her *'ohana*, Letty felt the clouds of the past few days blow off into the distance. Perhaps tomorrow they'd be gone.

CHAPTER SEVEN

'*Owe sanana*

MAKE MERRY

Lang's Livery, Oahu, the 18th of June, 1909

"Papa, may I speak with you?"

Letty paused at the door to the study, looking at her father bent over the accounting books. He waved her in without looking up. His shoulders slumped. Somehow he seemed older. Well, of course he was older, but this was *older*. She crossed to the "visitor's chair" beside his desk. She'd sat here many times. Mostly when she was in trouble, sometimes when she needed advice, and always when she had a big request to make. Today might be the most important sitting yet.

He pushed his glasses back up his nose as he turned to her. New lines etched his bronze forehead and a dusting of gray frosted his thick dark hair. "What can I do for you, princess?"

She hardly knew where to begin. Perhaps the most straightforward approach was best. "Papa, I want to become a doctor for animals, a veterinarian. I have a gift for this . . ."

She tapered off as he raised a hand to stop the torrent of her words. Now he looked even more tired. He turned to fully face her.

"My dear, I know. I have heard about your talent from every corner—your teacher, your friends in San Francisco, and Princess K have all weighed in as to your abilities. I have seen it myself over the years. That makes what I am about to say all the more difficult." He took a deep breath before muttering, "Coward that I am, I was hoping to avoid this conversation until after your party."

Letty sat stone still. Even in the afternoon heat, her body chilled.

"I need you right now, Letty. Our business is failing. The horseless carriage is here to stay, and we must figure out what to do about it. In the years you have been at school, our profits from horses have plummeted. No one buys horses anymore. Haven't you noticed that the stable is half empty? We've not sold a coaching pair or even a draft horse for the last four months.

"I need your good sense and hard work here beside me to carry us through. And even if I didn't need you, we just don't have money for more schooling. I have been borrowing money for the last couple of years. There is a mortgage on this place . . ." He slumped forward, his head in his hands. "I am so very sorry to have to tell you no."

The beginning of tears gathered in the corner of her eyes. It would not do to carry on in front of her father. Tendrils of flame tickled up her spine. In the back of her mind she began a slow, calming count.

"Papa, I understand." She rose to go.

"Letty, please do not tell Agnes about this. I have not told her my worries."

"Don't fret, Papa, I won't." Letty quietly left the room and shut the door behind her.

From the far end of the hall, Rosebud came scampering, skittering to a stop right in front of Letty. Gazing up at her mistress in delight, tongue hanging out, the pup peed on the floor like it was a wondrous gift. Letty found herself smiling despite the answer she'd just been given, her tears averted by the silliness of the dog.

She scooped up Rosebud and headed off for a cleanup rag, wriggling puppy under her arm.

Letty slipped into the hustle and bustle of the kitchen determined not to get in anyone's way. Cook had been at work since well before sunrise. Horse carts delivering fresh poi and fish rolled through the front gate. A table big enough for dozens of people, simply boards on sawhorses, stretched across the lānai. Colored paper lanterns dangled from the trees. You could see Agnes's steady hand in all of it.

Letty grabbed an old rag, Rosebud still safely tucked under her arm. Agnes turned and saw her. "Is that little demon making messes again? We are going to have to get her a real cage! And Letty, come right back, will you?"

Cleanup completed, Letty reappeared.

"Letty, I need you to run an errand for me. There is a parcel to pick up at Takata's store. Would you mind going to town?" Agnes did not meet her stepdaughter's eyes as she said this.

Letty did her best not to smile. This, the oldest trick in the book . . . distract the guest of honor while her 'ohana set up some surprise. Well, the least Letty could do was play along. "Of course, I think Sheba is probably due for a ride."

"Oh, I had them saddle Captain for you; that way you will be home sooner. Now run along." Settling Rosebud in her little playpen, Letty trooped out of the kitchen to the stable.

As promised, Captain was saddled and ready. A big, rangy thoroughbred, her father's horse had beautiful manners, but something of a sense of humor. Captain was always out to see if you were paying attention. Not everyone could ride him.

From some corner of her mind came the thought: Rowley most likely could, he was that much of a horseman. She'd seen his skill on that day at his ranch. Goodness, that seemed a lifetime ago. She wondered when she might see the man again. Perhaps he'd race Diablo in the Cup?

Well, now she had other distractions. Magic to ignore. A package to pick up. And school to finish. Somehow. Some way.

Captain turned his head toward her foot in the stirrup to attempt a quick nip. Ever vigilant, she poked his nose with her whip before he got very close. "You can't fool me, old man, so don't even try."

They pranced out of the livery yard toward town.

A sudden wild hullabaloo as horses raced toward her. *What?*

Sophia was the first to reach her. "Did you think you could have a birthday without a *pāʻū* ride with your friends?" Now, amid the brilliant colors . . . blue, pink, yellow, green, purple, rust . . . Letty scanned dear faces . . . Eva, Therese, Leilani, Maleah, Rebecca . . . and Irene? How could Irene be here?

"Irene, what are you doing here? When did you arrive?"

"I am here for your birthday, silly goose. Papa must come next week to Kauai on his fertilizer business, so Mama and I came ahead. We will go on to meet him there. Your stepmother was ever so helpful . . ."

Laughing women surrounded her as she dismounted. Sophia waved a mass of red fabric. "And we knew you would underdress! We are here to wrap your *pāʻū*!"

Letty stood still, arms upraised, as Sophia draped her in yards of calico. First fabric around her waist, secured tight with rope. Then another sweep between her legs before the final wrapping. She always thought of her *pāʻū* as pantaloons that fly. Once mounted, this red *pāʻū* overskirt would float behind her like wings of fire. Thank goodness no one here knew how appropriate that was.

Behind her, more hoofbeats. Irene's mother, Imogene Stansfield, and Princess K joined the throng, all in *pāʻū*. The Princess was here too? "Letty, we shall have a real Ladies' Ride, just like the old queens. Up and down Beretania, and let the horseless carriages beware! *Nā wāhine holo lio!*"

Letty swung back up on Captain as he sidestepped, pretending to spook at the billowing overskirt. She laid a calming hand on his shoulder. Princess K rode closer to put a big lei around Letty's neck with a kiss. Each rider did the same until Letty was covered in flowers. Sophia unfurled the Hawaiian Ladies' Riding Society banner. Maleah slung a "Votes for Women" blanket across Captain's rear, fastening it to her saddle.

"Are you ready, my dear?"

"Yes, Princess, let's ride!"

Everyone bunched up with Letty and began to trot. Once they were all together, she waved the way forward. The group took up a rocking canter, overskirts billowing back, banner flying, looking for all the world like a rainbow on horseback.

People on the street stopped to stare. Cars pulled over. Cart horses shied. Passersby yelled encouragement. *"Nā wāhine holo lio!!!"* And then, "Princess, Princess!" A few "Votes for Women!" too.

Captain was in his element; his pleasure telegraphed to her through the reins. Letty gave herself over to the exhilaration of the moment, the riders moving together as if one being. Without words, the ladies navigated traffic and circumvented obstacles, all while waving to those not fortunate enough to be on horseback. Laughing out loud with the sheer joy of the ride, now they traveled at a full gallop.

At the end of the street, they wheeled around the statue of Kamehameha I to head back.

Letty yanked Captain to a stop. "Wait! Didn't someone tell me I have to go to Takata's to pick something up?" Her grin could have split her face. A wave of laughter gave the answer.

Letty raised her hand again. The long, straight avenue lined with palm trees beckoned in the afternoon sun. "Let's show them how this is done! Hawaiian Ladies! Ride!"

Letty breezed back into the kitchen. Invigorated by her ride, she determined to put the dark cloud of the conversation with her father behind her. This was helped immeasurably by a barrage of delicious smells. Ginger, pineapple, and her favorite Chinese five-spice pork.

Agnes bent over something, while little Hannah clung to her leg and reached up to try to grab at the spoon in her hand. "*No!* You can't have that! Don't make me ruin it!" Agnes sighed. Hannah screamed in frustration.

Letty headed straight to Rosebud's little pen in the corner. The tiny dog danced on her hind legs, eager to gain her freedom.

"Letty, how was your ride?"

She lifted the wriggling Rosebud into her arms. "Just lovely."

"I am quite proud of myself, I must say. You are not an easy person to bamboozle!"

Agnes straightened up and turned carefully, trying to shield her work from Letty's view. This attempt was not entirely successful, as Letty spied a rather lopsided cake, partially frosted, peeking out from behind her. And a pile of coconut waiting to be added.

"*Kaikuahine!* Lanky! Pumpkin head!"

The cyclone of energy that was her brother burst into the room. Letty rushed to hug him, puppy and all. He'd grown. Liam now topped her height by a good six inches. And so broad shouldered that she could barely reach around him. He hugged her back with the intensity he brought to all of life.

"*Hauʻoli lā hānau!* Too bad you are getting old, but hey, we party!"

Letty stepped back to look him in the eye. "How is Maui? Are you learning anything, or just breaking the hearts of all the girls?"

Liam's smile always lit up any room. "Mr. Bartlett is a genius with machines. I'll be able to fix almost anything, even motorcars!"

"Well, thank you for putting your tools down long enough to come home for my birthday. That *is* why you are here, isn't it?" Letty arched one brow, awaiting Liam's answer.

Liam looked down and shuffled his feet; this, a mannerism from childhood. He was avoiding something. A "tell," as they say in poker, not that she was admitting to anyone that she had learned to play poker at Redwood . . .

"Well, I will see Sophia while I am here."

Hmm, just as I thought.

"And I heard that Irene was coming to surprise you. I enjoyed her company in San Francisco last fall."

My goodness, I must give Irene fair warning.

"Besides," Liam looked back up with mischief-filled eyes, "it is the birthday of my one and only *oldest* sister!"

"Of course, it is. I am beyond honored that you remembered."

Rosebud whined, so Letty rushed her outside. Best to get the puppy settled so that she might dress. Her beautiful *holokū* was laid out on her bed, ready to put on. She just needed to figure out what to do with her hair . . . Maybe she'd attempt the fancy braid Tomiko had showed her?

Chapter Eight

Hoʻolauleʻa

CELEBRATION

Lang's Livery, Oahu, the 18th of June, 1909, evening

Letty's *lūʻau* was in full swing. K sat as close to a window as she could, gently fanning herself in the humid air of the summer evening. She always carried a hand fan. A bit old-fashioned, but she'd inherited many from her mother. The irony that she—a princess of Hawaii—was sensitive to heat was not lost on her. Eight years of exile in Britain had seen to that. The heat of her own gift as a Gate only made matters worse.

Imogene Stansfield and Agnes completed her little group. Hmm, quite a stately group of matrons . . . except she was a spinster herself. And always would be. Her power made certain of that.

Across the room, a knot of men surrounded Timothy Rowley. Letty's father, George, and her grandfather, Lot, stood next to him, looking grave. Tom Kalama, his arms folded, peppered Rowley with questions. Dear Tom, of course he'd be concerned. The *Pele* was one of his ships. Letty's brother, Liam, stood there too, hands behind his back, eyes moving from man to man.

She wondered how Timothy held up to this interrogation. And if he was still glad she'd convinced him to come along to the party.

And now, another mystery, about the groom. Or more precisely, the man who wasn't a groom after all. Letty would be distressed about it all once she knew.

"Princess, I see you are indulging in the view of fine male pulchritude in the far corner." K turned to see Agnes, eyes alight with mischief. "And when are you going to put our Captain Kalama out of his misery? At least you might ask him for a dance."

"Well, my dear, as I am the subject of a prophecy that decrees I shall never marry, that would be rather pointless, would it not?"

Imogene's response might best be described as a harrumph. "What has marriage got to do with it? We are modern women! It is not just the right to vote we want, it is all the rights men have, including the rights of pleasure!"

Agnes blushed, ducking her head. "Well, sometimes in a marriage you have pleasure too."

K gave in to the laughter. "You are out of my league, ladies. Shall we just disport ourselves with a bit of womanly gossip? Looking across the room, I am guessing the men are dissecting Letty's jump into the sea. How typical that they have not invited the female at the heart of it all to join them!"

At that moment George slapped his forehead as Tom shook his head incredulously. Letty's jump would be "talk story" for generations.

"Princess, I understand you met Elizabeth Simmons on her recent visit to Hawaii Island." Imogene arched an eyebrow. "You have heard her story, have you not?"

"No, I know nothing," said the Princess.

Agnes jumped in, "Well, all I have heard are tidbits—some very tasty!"

"Yes, I might call this tasty. Here is what I know. When Mrs. Simmons came west—as a young widow with a daughter to support—she caught oil fever. They say she invested everything she had in the Los Angeles oil fields. At one point, she owned most of the oil wells in California. The newspapers dubbed her 'Oilpatch Lizzie.' It was not a compliment. But then, that is how women in commerce are always treated."

"An accomplished woman indeed." K grimaced. "I must admit, after meeting her, I find that a surprise."

"And savvy. She sold everything right before the oil crash. She'd have been penniless if she had not sold. Instead, she is an astonishingly wealthy woman."

Agnes clapped her hands. "Of course, the tales I heard included none of this! The woman was in Honolulu for a few weeks, throwing her daughter at every wealthy plantation owner's son. Once she heard there was an English lord on the Big Island, she hauled the poor girl off there. Such obvious husband hunting is not done. It was quite the talk of the town."

"I can only imagine." Imogene grew quieter. "I met her when she moved to San Francisco. She was dogged by rumors that there was never a Mr. Simmons. So, when she tried to force her way into San Francisco society, it was not well received. There are things even money can't buy."

"Of course," K said, "that means Adele is quite the heiress."

"Yes, it does. At any rate, since Irene and Adele attended the same primary school, I thought to enlist Mrs. Simmons in the suffragist cause. I paid a call. Wouldn't you think her success in a man's world might predispose her to our views? But no! She practically threw me out of her house!"

K fanned herself a bit harder. "Well then, that explains a few things. At an inauspicious moment during dinner at MacHenry Ranch, Letty proceeded to announce her suffragist sympathies. Mrs. Simmons effectively called her a hussy to the whole party. Thankfully, Owen Cameron was there and spoke up. As did I. But still . . ."

Agnes looked at her sharply. "Letty is a suffragist? When were George and I to learn of this?"

K took that moment to drop her fan as a distraction. Blessedly, the music began again. There was much about Letty that she was not prepared to discuss with Agnes and George. At least not yet.

The air came alive again with music, beloved old songs and new, this one a *paniolo* waltz. George appeared to ask Agnes for a dance and the awkward moment passed. K watched Timothy laughing with Letty and her friends next to the cake table, happy to see him enjoying himself. The lad was marooned with too many old-timers on Hawaii Island.

Johnny was good with parties, at least for a while, particularly when it was his own birthday. But once he was full of food and sweets, he always got bored. Even if the party was for his beloved stepsister. No one had much time for him. This time was surely the worst . . . because, when no one was looking, he'd downed a cup of Mama's special "grownups only" punch. And then another one.

Now he was sleepy. So, so sleepy. He wanted to go up to bed, but the music was too loud. People's voices made his head hurt. Maybe the barn would be the best place. Up in the loft with the cat; that might be very nice.

As he walked to the barn, the cat came out to greet him, weaving his way in and out of Johnny's unsteady legs. Once inside, the soft rustling of the horses reached out to him like a lullaby. The sounds of the *lū'au* faded off into the night. Up the ladder he headed, right toward a pile of old blankets, and *ahhhhhh . . .* no one would even notice he was gone.

Here and there people packed up sleepy children as guests began to trickle off home.

Bull went to one of the musicians and asked for his ukulele. Moving to the front of the room, he gave K a nod as he plucked the opening bars. "Wahine Holo Lio"—the *mele* honoring Queen Emma, the beloved "horseback-riding lady of Hawaii," filled the air. K glided out to the middle of the room, losing herself in the music, using her hands and heart to tell the story of the lovely queen as she went riding.

K drew Letty out to join her in the dance. Timothy stood to the side, wide-eyed. Likely he'd never seen much *hula*, and certainly not this kind—*'auana*—elegant and flowing.

Side by side, Letty and K swayed the song to life. As the music waned, Letty gave the Princess a fierce hug. Touched, K kissed her cheek and whispered, "Never forget who you are, no matter how much it frightens you."

Letty said nothing, instead hurrying back to receive the accolades of her friends. And Timothy. Interesting, that.

With rounds of *aloha*, more guests drifted out, leaving in a mixture of carriages, both horsed and horseless. Irene and her mother among them. As K took her place back near the window, she watched Letty embrace her friend. A motorcar from the hotel was there to whisk them away. Next time K would insist the Stansfields stay at 'Āinahau.

Letty stood in the lane, waving as they sped off.

Inside, the family music began again in earnest. Almost every member of the extended Lang *'ohana* played some kind of instrument. They would play until dawn if Agnes let them. K sat back to enjoy the spectacle.

Bull suddenly tensed, putting down the borrowed ukulele. He looked around and then came over to her side.

"What is it?"

"I don't know, but I am going to take a look around."

With many of the guests gone, Letty thought to slip out to the barn. Back in the house the music began again in earnest, but for Letty the fragrant night beckoned. And she carried a few green beans for Diablo.

Letty always loved the peace of the dimly lit barn at night. Moving stall to stall, she rubbed noses and dispensed little treats as she went. How had she not noticed that the big barn was almost empty? She'd been so wrapped up in her own dreams, she'd missed what was happening with her family.

Captain put a sleepy head over the door of his stall and whuffled a welcome. Letty stopped to give his ears a massage. Diablo leaned out from one of the stalls at the back of the barn. How lovely that K had thought to bring Timothy for the *lū'au*. The poor man appeared to have survived her father's grilling about her jump into the ocean. That took stamina.

Timothy said he had more news for her, but it would wait until tomorrow.

One thing she knew already. The word was out about Diablo. That's why Timothy was here on Oahu tonight, and the big horse with him. Doc Willingham offered a substantial stud fee; Timothy accepted. Tomorrow he would ride up to the Willinghams' place, and he'd invited Letty to join him. She looked forward to the chance to become a bit more acquainted. She'd hear all the news then.

"I have your green beans, dear one." She opened her hand to let Diablo see the treat as she neared his stall. Then stumbled. Diablo shied, nostrils flaring. Her head was wrenched back, even as she was thrown forward. The green beans flew from her hand. Something cold and sharp pressed against her throat.

"Hello, sweetheart. How convenient that your noisy relatives will cover any sounds that you might make."

She knew the voice. The man who'd hurt Diablo. Her head was yanked farther back. "Just to let you know I am serious . . ." She felt the quick sting of a cut at her throat, followed by a warm trickle of blood. "This blade is very sharp, so don't try anything . . ." He moved the knife from her neck and sliced the bodice of her dress, forcing her down almost to her knees.

"You let her go! That's my sister!"

"Johnny, run! Get Papa!" She gasped as the man's knife nicked her again. Before she thought to struggle, he'd shoved her hard up against the wooden door of Diablo's stall. Slivers from the raw wood of the door pressed into her arm and cheek like tiny razors.

Diablo, in the back of his stall, squealed and paced in fear.

His arm forced her head against the stall door. She could not turn it. Just out of the corner of her eye Johnny wavered. "Come on, kid, don't you want to help your sister? Come and stop me," the man taunted.

Her knees went to jelly as Johnny made a flying leap, the man easily delivering a vicious kick that sent the small boy airborne. Johnny struck a post and slumped to the ground, unnaturally still.

"No!" Letty panted. Her flames raced up and down her spine.

The man just laughed, cranking her head even farther. Now she struggled to breathe. "Actually, what I think you meant to say was yes . . ."

Her flames rose and a red mist filled her eyes. She was frantic to get to Johnny. She struggled against the man's grasp, but he cut her again. This time the metallic scent of the blood gagged her.

Suddenly the man was flung back; his weight no longer pinned her against the stall. He screamed. She spun away to see Diablo's teeth sunk deep into the man's shoulder. Somehow the stallion had overcome his fear, reaching over the stall door to make the grab. He'd taken a fierce hold, shaking the man like a dog with a bone.

Letty screamed too, only hers was the scream of a woman aflame. She yanked the latch on Diablo's stall door to set him free. The stallion dropped the man, but pushed through the stall door, charging at him, rearing.

Letty grabbed the only thing she could find, a lead rope with a heavy brass toggle.

With his left arm dangling uselessly at his side, the man still waved the knife in his right hand. It glinted as he sliced up at Diablo's throat. Letty swung the lead like she might her whip, overhand, her flames impelling her arm forward. The toggle wrapped around the man's wrist. She yanked. The man screamed again. The knife flew away as Diablo renewed his attack, hooves flashing like knives of his own.

From behind, a real whip sang out. Diablo backed off. The man lay on the ground, writhing and crying. As the red madness cleared from Letty's brain, Bull's voice came as if from a distance. "Don't move, you son of a bitch. Don't tempt me to kill you. That horse will do it for me if I let him."

Now the sound of running footsteps, followed by Agnes's terrified cry. "Johnny!"

Letty found herself oddly calm. She leaned over and gently pulled Agnes away from the small boy's limp body.

"Please, I can help him."

Her flames rose again, softly now, this time to heal. Her intention washed over her as she touched the child . . . a bad bump on the head and maybe bruised ribs. She had no notion of how she might know this. She lay down on the stable floor, encircling him with her arms, lending her heat to him in every way she could. Agnes sobbed quietly in the background.

Johnny shuddered, then looked right at her, eyes bright. "What are you doing? I am too old to cuddle! That's for babies!"

Letty rolled away slightly so the boy could hop up. "Mama, did you see that? I helped stop the bad man!"

In the corner of the stable, Bull had the attacker hog-tied. The man moaned with the pain of his dislocated shoulder. Diablo, for his part, stood in his stall, calmly munching hay, as the remainder of the party rushed in.

George grabbed Letty and helped her up. Agnes clung to Johnny as if she would never let him go, staring at Letty over the top of his head.

"I don't know what just happened here, but you brought him back. Thank you." She ruffled Johnny's hair. "And I saw red lights around you while you were doing it."

Letty brushed herself off and looked at the gathered faces. "Oh, that was just my hair shining in the moonlight."

Then she collapsed.

K nearly buckled too as Letty crumpled to the stable floor. How had she not foreseen this? Liam rushed to his sister and lifted her up tenderly. Timothy touched his arm.

"What can I do to help?"

Liam turned with a snarl. "Haven't you done enough? That is the man you told us about, isn't it? You brought that monster into our lives. Just be very glad she is still with us."

"Liam!" George admonished.

"I will see you in the house, Father." Liam moved away, cradling his sister even as his own shoulders shook. The crowd of the few remaining guests parted to let him through.

The Princess understood Liam's feelings, however misplaced. Timothy was not the villain here. The real villain lay on the barn floor, next to Bull's booted foot. Moaning. If this were two hundred years ago, the man would be shark bait. Tonight. By her own command. Once an *ali'i*, always an *ali'i*. She could not help herself.

Sometimes she missed the old days.

Bull pulled the whimpering assailant to his feet. "Rowley, can you ride to fetch the police? And Lang, have you got a gun? I would prefer to have a bullet handy in case he tries anything."

"Agnes has one."

Headlights cut through the velvet night air.

A dapper man with his hair in a long braid stepped out of a black Model A truck with barred windows. Trust Detective Chen Zhou to have all the modern conveniences. Another man, in a suit so purple K thought it glowed in the dark, followed close behind.

Zhou came forward to stand next to Bull, fingering his own bullwhip. "Looks like you cheated me out of this one, bruddah. Did he hurt anyone?"

"Not seriously, thank goodness. He tried, though. Letty Lang. Rowley's horse attacked him, and that's how Letty escaped." Bull grinned at his childhood friend in apparent relief. "What brings you here at this time of night? Not that I am complaining . . ." K could concur with that sentiment.

"We went into Chinatown to try to find this man. Name's Allerton. Williams here knows he is a gambler; it seemed a likely place he would go to ground. Took us a while to get people to talk, but talk they did. He killed a girl yesterday—filleted her like a fish in a bathtub. Then disappeared. Finally, someone told us he'd been yammering about a very tall girl who had done him wrong after a horse jumped in the ocean. It could only be your Letty, so we came here *wikiwiki*."

Zhou walked over to the man and poked him with the butt of his whip. Allerton grunted. "I saw what you did to that girl in Chinatown, you pig. And my friend in plaid here says you have done it before. Rest assured, this time you will pay—dearly."

"Bull, I will take this from here. Please let the family know that I'll be back tomorrow to collect statements."

Zhou turned to Timothy, who still stood at Diablo's stall, ashen gray. "Well, your Lordship, it seems everything comes full circle: she saves the horse and then the horse saves her. Life is always interesting."

K trotted after Agnes as she headed into the house.

"Agnes, wait!"

Agnes looked back, her face a stone mask.

"Please, Letty may not want to eat, but it is important that she eat right away . . ." K trailed off at the flush of anger rising in Agnes's countenance.

"Do you think I am an idiot?" This came out in a hiss. "Don't forget that I grew up in the outback. I have seen my share of things that cannot be explained."

Agnes took a step toward the Princess. The woman's rage battered into her, yet K held her ground. She had her own responsibility here.

"She glowed red; she brought Johnny back. What have you bewitched her with?"

Another step and the smaller woman was looking right up at her. "Well, it is over, *pau*. Just leave us alone." She turned and fled into the house.

Behind her, K heard a male throat clearing. Letty's grandfather's gruff voice came next.

"She will get over it. I'll talk to her. We have all discovered that George's sweet little Agnes is quite a lioness. Some days I wonder if we should let her run the business."

"This is my fault." K swallowed hard against the moisture gathering in her eyes. "Too much, too soon. I put the dear girl in danger, and on top of that, danger just seems to find her. I can only hope that she won't turn away from what blooms inside her." Now she looked straight at Lot. "Because if that happens, I shall never forgive myself."

CHAPTER NINE

Uhiwai

FOGGED

Letty slitted one eye open to see the light. Yes, it was morning. A tiny ball of fur, rolled up tight against her stomach, gave off little dog snores. She moved to pet the beast, wincing at how her muscles ached. The events of the night came back in a rush.

Johnny jiggled into view through her barely opened eyes, peering at her. "You woke up. Mama said I must call her straightaway when you woke up." His face swam out of sight, then reappeared. "And I am to take Rosebud, so she doesn't mess. Mama said." He carefully grasped the sleepy little dog to carry her out.

Letty pulled the blanket over her head.

She woke again to the rattle of china. Peering out from under the covers, she watched her stepmother set down a steaming tray. Agnes looked like she had not slept. Maybe she hadn't.

Letty scooted herself up in bed. "I will get up and get dressed."

"No, my dear, you will not. Not until I am certain that you are well. We all had quite a night last night. What do you remember?"

Letty looked over to see her beautiful sea-blue *holokū* ripped and dirty on her bedside chair. "Everything, I think."

"Well, first you eat. Then I want to hear it all from your perspective. I have a lot to learn."

Without warning, tears coursed down Letty's cheeks. "I am so afraid . . ."

Agnes sat down on the edge of the bed and scooped her close. Hungry for the comfort, Letty leaned in. Her stepmother smelled of lavender and safety. Rocking her from side to side, Agnes crooned shushing noises. "Hush, sweetheart, it is all over now."

"No, Agnes. I think it may be just beginning."

Agnes said nothing but held on tight. They both knew the truth when it was spoken.

Two hours later, Letty found herself still in bed, food tray barely touched. She understood she must eat, but she couldn't quite bring herself to do it.

She stood up, wrapping a blanket around her nightgown. It was crazy how chilled she felt. Perhaps she'd just get moving. Do something normal. Her trunk needed unpacking. She'd begin with that.

With a bit of rummaging, Letty unearthed the box containing her microscope. She grabbed the knife from her food tray to pry it open. If she was not going to eat, she might as well use the knife for something. Although she preferred not to think about knives too much. Not after last night.

She lifted the lid, happy to see her care in packing rewarded. The leather instrument case within hadn't even moved during its long journey. Putting the cotton wool and stabilizing sticks aside, she placed the case on the table. It had taken her two years of work—exercising polo ponies and cleaning houses—to buy it.

Letty unbuckled the case, sliding the scope out of its special fittings. She found it an object of beauty, gleaming black and brass in the filtered sunlight, calling her to a future that now might never be.

Back to the trunk, she pulled out her slides and the bottles of fixative. She had a reasonable collection of interesting things already mounted. There was nothing like a session of science to settle the unquiet mind. And to put a lie to any notions of magic.

Letty could hear her stepbrother down the hall. "Johnny, want me to show you something amazing?"

The boy came racing into her room with Rosebud bouncing behind. "Is it odd? Or disgusting? That's my favorite!"

"Odd and disgusting and amazing, I promise."

Half an hour later, Letty reached her limit, having trotted out all her best ideas. Johnny was getting rather wiggly. Thus far, his favorite was scraping his teeth to see the bugs floating around on the slide. Although the preserved tadpoles had been a hit as well.

"Letty, next time can we get stuff from Annabelle the goat's mouth? And maybe one of the dog's ears too? They stink." He slipped off her lap in the midst of this proposal.

"Of course." She kissed him on his cheek before he ran to the kitchen.

Letty leaned back in the chair, weary to the bone. The interlude with Johnny had been a pleasant distraction, nothing more. The reality of her present situation came cascading back. She felt no flames now.

Only ashes.

Timothy walked through the gardens, mesmerized. 'Āinahau, the place of coolness—Kahōkūlani's father had created this oasis just for her. There was nothing else quite like it in all the islands. Whenever he had business in Honolulu, K pressed him to stay here.

"'Āinahau is in need of use," K would say. That was true; she'd avoided the place since her father's death. "Please humor me by thinking of it as your own home. As your grandmother welcomed me to your family's manor." He had not resisted, as he found the beautiful place almost alive in its own way.

As he stepped into the stable, Diablo's head emerged from the top of the stall door. The horse nickered, ears twitching. Incredibly the stallion showed no nerves after the previous night's incident. He'd even been stone-cold calm on the late-night ride back to 'Āinahau.

Timothy walked unevenly toward him. Funny, he rarely limped much since coming to Hawaii, but today was different, his sense of guilt overpowering. Williams told him that Allerton was dangerous. To women. Why had he waited to tell Letty? Why had they all waited? He'd been so certain that they should not worry her, that the news could wait, that she should enjoy her party. He had failed her. And perhaps himself as well.

Bull came out of the tack room carrying two saddles. "K and I are going to the Langs. Last night Agnes told her not to show her face again, but you know K—she never takes no for an answer."

"If anyone needs to make amends, it's me. If I had only insisted on telling her sooner, maybe this whole thing would not have happened."

Bull clapped him on the shoulder. "Useless thought. One could argue that if your horse had not been there, the worst would surely have happened."

Bull walked down to the two stalls where the extra riding horses were kept, put the saddles down, and turned back to Timothy. "Weren't you going to see Willingham this morning? To negotiate?"

Timothy nodded; he did not trust his voice. He'd been planning to ask Letty for her opinions on the deal as they rode together. She'd said last night she had ideas. He'd already learned that the woman *always* had ideas. Like the day she saved Sunflower's colt. "I know a bit about this" she'd said. And she did. And how had he repaid her? With Allerton.

"Then saddle up. Lang's Livery is right on your way. I think we all have some *ho'oponopono* to do."

Letty peeped out the window at the dogs' furious barking only to see Agnes fending off Timothy, Bull, and Kahōkūlani. Her stepmother's vehement pointing needed no translation. As the trio turned to ride out, Timothy swiveled to look back. Letty hurriedly put the curtain down.

She had just settled back in her chair to reopen her book when the sound of a motorcar reverberated from the yard. Who now?

The detective, Chen Zhou, stepped down from the shiny vehicle with the Honolulu Police logo on the door. Agnes and George ushered him in. She had best put something on and try to get her hair together. She doubted she'd be able to avoid this meeting.

Letty entered the parlor. She had mustered an old-style loose cotton muumuu and braided her hair, if barely. Nothing could be done about her exhaustion . . . or her nausea or the flames of warning tickling up her back.

"Here you are, my dear. Detective Zhou must take a statement from you. He understands this is distressing so won't question you for too long. Isn't that right, Detective?" This was an extraordinarily long speech for her father. It was fortified by Agnes giving Zhou a hard look, the sort that turned most mere mortals to stone. Well, at least her family wanted to spare her. She could be grateful for that.

"I understand. However, a crime has been committed and I must investigate."

"I will be fine. Let's get on with this." Letty lowered herself into the closest chair. This could all be explained with no mention of magic.

"Can you first tell me how the little boy came to be in the barn?"

"He told me he was tired and the house was noisy. He went out to the barn to sleep." Agnes frowned. "Certainly you will not need to question him."

This became moot the moment Johnny came barreling through the door with Rosebud in hot pursuit. "Are you the famous detective? *Wow!* I love your motorcar! Can I shake your hand?"

"Well, since we are all here, let's begin with the lad. Can you tell me what you saw?"

"I was up in the loft sleeping, then I heard Letty talking to someone. He had a big knife and he was going to hurt her. So, I came down to save her. He kicked me, and that is all I remember. But I saved Letty!" This said with the confidence of a seven-year-old.

Zhou leaned forward. "A knife, you say?"

"Yes, a big, scary knife like a pirate."

"Do we know where this knife might be?"

The family looked at each other in consternation. George ventured, "It was quite chaotic last night. So, no."

"Well, I hope we find it. Allerton is accused of a murder in town two days ago. With a knife. He stands convicted of two similar murders in Chicago. That's why a Pinkerton was after him; Williams was hired by the father of the two deceased young ladies. If I can find the knife, we can make sure he pays for all his crimes."

"Let me take you to the barn—it must be there."

Zhou stood to head toward the barn. "Letty, can you accompany us while we look? Your memory of what happened will be most helpful."

Letty rose obediently to follow.

Zhou questioned her as they searched for the knife. Letty answered as best she could. Much of what the detective wanted to know—like where Allerton had been hidden in the barn—she could not answer, her memory a jumble. She was so exhausted she barely noticed how deeply he was probing until her father said, "Chen, is this necessary?"

The detective scratched his head. "The thing that really puzzles me is the horse. In all my years investigating animal cruelty cases, I never heard of a horse defending himself like that."

Letty turned from the hay bale she was shaking in the search for the knife, so far fruitless. "That's because he wasn't defending himself; he was defending me."

"Then you must be something special, my girl. Something special indeed."

Letty gave the hay bale one last good shake. The knife came clattering out. Fragments of hay stuck to dried blood along the slender blade. This knife was meant for no other purpose than to harm.

Zhou wrapped it in a cloth. "Thank you. This is essential to the case. I won't bother you for more right now but may have questions later."

He bowed to Letty and George and returned to his car. George took Letty by the arm to lead her gently back to the house. As they climbed the steps, he leaned in to kiss her cheek. "I am very glad you are all right."

"I am too, Papa."

She was all right. Wasn't she?

The next morning Letty found herself on the big porch, wrapped in a blanket, neglected book beside her, staring blankly out over the pasture. It was as if she had descended into such a deep, foggy valley that she would need a machete to cut her way out. She couldn't even bestir herself to read. Even her flames remained idle.

The only things that seemed real were Rosebud on her lap and the fierce protectiveness that emanated from Agnes every time she came out to adjust Letty's blanket. Or to try to force her to eat. Letty had eaten almost nothing since the night of the "incident," as everyone circumspectly called it.

Confused and sick, that's how she felt. Waves of remembrance tumbled over her. Never in her life had she thought to be harmed by another human being. The experience was unshakable. She would bear the mark forever, just as the cuts on her neck showed every sign of scarring.

Rosebud chose that moment to climb up Letty's chest and give her a big, wet kiss. "Eww. I know where that mouth has been. But I appreciate the thought, Rosebud." She leaned over to put the little golden ball of fluff on the floor. Maybe she would feel better if she stood up.

The sound of booted feet rounded the corner of the porch. Her father and grandfather must be heading her way.

"How now, princess?" Lot cocked his head to take in the scene. Rosebud ran from man to man, dancing and yipping.

"I don't feel like a princess—at least not anymore."

George settled one hip on the porch rail. "We have a job for you. Doc Willingham has offered us a proposition, but we need your help."

Agnes appeared at the screen door. "She is not doing anything until she eats."

"You are not eating?" Lot's face became grim.

"I just don't feel like it."

"I don't care. You will eat, and now."

"I'll get another tray." Agnes hustled back inside, returning with a plate of sandwiches and fresh fruit. "Cook already had this prepared. It's your favorite, roast pork."

Letty glanced from her stepmother to her father to her grandfather. Clearly, all must be appeased. She kept her eye on George as she chewed. "What is this deal, Papa?"

"In six weeks the Willinghams will host a polo match at Kapiʻolani Park. Doc's boys took up the sport at Yale and are quite keen. Players will be coming from the mainland. Needless to say, they require polo ponies. Willingham knows we have some fine young horses that have not been selling. He is offering a good price if we can deliver a string of six, trained and ready to play in the tournament."

George began to pace. "We have no one qualified to do the training except you. I know you've played *paniolo* polo here and that you exercised ponies in California." He paused and looked straight at Letty. "We need the money."

At that, Agnes swiveled her attention to George.

Letty stopped chewing long enough to swallow. The sandwich tasted like sawdust, but she was determined to finish it. "Of course, if you need me, I will do it."

Lot watched her eat. Slowly. "Letty, finish that sandwich and maybe another one. It's time for you to get moving; I will be back for you in an hour. Be ready to ride up to the ranch to look at the prospects."

"As you wish, *Tūtū kāne*. Perhaps that will clear my head."

Exactly one hour later, Lot stood by the front porch with two saddled horses. Letty emerged with Agnes pressing a bag of extra food on her.

"You already look much better," Agnes said. "There are cookies in this bag and dried mangoes. Please keep eating!"

"I'll eat the cookies if she won't!" Lot chuckled. They were off.

Riding was just the thing. The sun shone warm on her back and her grandfather sang, his beautiful tenor rising and falling like the waves. She was even a bit hungry again and turned in her saddle to reach her saddlebag.

"Hey, give me a cookie too!" Lot said.

They shared a laugh and several cookies while trotting down the road. The dark clouds parted. At least a bit. At least for now.

Wu, Lang's head wrangler, had the three- and four-year-olds corralled. There were ten in all. The Langs' signature stock descended from the original Spanish barbs, horses that came to the islands more than one hundred years earlier as a gift to the king. Always intelligent, nimble, and muscular, but with a flair for drama; this bunch was no exception. Right now the horses circled the pasture, bucking and kicking in high spirits for no reason other than the joy of it. She'd need a miracle to get six trained polo ponies out of this crew. But maybe miracles were to be part of Letty's life now. Or not.

"Wu, how many of them are broken to saddle?"

"Well, you know how it is, Missy Letty. We break all at two years, but if no sell . . ." The man gave a shrug. "They just go wild. We no sell in big while because of the demon machines."

"I see. We have work to do." Her appetite awakened with a sudden growl from her stomach. "I am having another cookie. Anybody else want one?"

Agnes leaned nonchalantly on the door to George's study. "I hope all goes well with Letty up at the ranch. Her color improved just from those two sandwiches."

"My father holds more sway over Letty and her brother than I ever have. She just needed someone to tell her to eat."

"I wish I thought it was that simple. I want to tell you before you hear it from someone else. Princess K, her man Bull, and that Rowley came by yesterday."

"Yes, and?"

"I threw them off the property. Something is amiss here, something that we don't fully understand. I saw Letty glow red as she healed Johnny."

"I am sure that was a trick of light. And she didn't heal him, she just comforted him, and he woke up."

"Well, I don't agree." She pulled herself up tall and walked forward.

He turned to face her. "You can't throw people like that off the property. We need the business."

"I can, and I did. Now, you tell me, what did it mean when you looked Letty in the eye and said, 'We need the money' with such emphasis? What does she know that I don't?"

"Agnes, we always need the money—you know how it is."

Agnes swept out of the room, unwilling to start yet another fight. She was not blind; the new horseless carriages were decimating their livery business. She told George time and again she might economize in the household or even help him with the business books, but he always rebuffed her. "I have it in hand," he'd say. Or she'd offer to do with fewer servants. But George always pointed out that most had been with the family for years. They were *'ohana*. "Where will they go?" he'd say. And he was right.

This thing was not over yet. She would find a way to figure out what was really going on, including this mystery with Letty. Especially this mystery with Letty. She knew what she'd seen.

Flames.

CHAPTER TEN

Nīnau

INQUIRE

Agnes kissed Hannah on the top of her head, drinking in her sweet baby smell, before releasing her into her nurse's waiting arms. Dear Mālama. The woman was one of the family, having been with the Langs since a few years after Letty and Liam lost their mother. Part of that *'ohana* that George was so determined to protect.

"Enjoy the day, you two! With everyone else gone you will have the house to yourselves."

"All better to play hide-and-seek, missy! We be good." Slung on Mālama's comfortable hip, Hannah was doing her best to swallow her own fist. Adorable. Well, off to business.

"I will be back before teatime." Agnes went to the mounting block to jump up on sweet Sheba. While her riding had improved, she still took the gentlest of horses.

In what seemed no time at all, she trotted through the gates of 'Āinahau. The house—a grand Victorian pile built by the Princess's father back when everyone thought she would be the queen—loomed up before her. A gigantic banyan tree at the center of the lush gardens beckoned all to sit within its dappled shade. K sat with Letty's friend Irene Stansfield and her mother, Imogene. And another woman Agnes did not recognize.

One of the Princess's stable lads appeared to take Sheba as she dismounted.

"Agnes!" K leaped up and rushed to grab her hand. "Delightful to see you. Does this mean I am forgiven?"

Agnes smiled. It was hard to stay angry at this woman; there was something so honest about Kahōkūlani, even if she was rather bossy.

"Possibly. At any rate, I am here to discuss it. Perhaps if you offer me a cool drink in the shade of this lovely tree, I can be more easily persuaded."

"Done, my dear. Matteo, please bring us a fresh tray?"

Arm in arm, the two women headed to seats under the tree. "Agnes, you already know Irene and Imogene." Both smiled. "We are all longing to hear how Letty is doing. But might I also introduce you to a dear old friend, Angeline Chartwell Bliss? Her brother is A. J. Chartwell of MacHenry Ranch, one of your best customers. She has just come off a most exhausting tour of duty squiring Elizabeth Simmons and her daughter, Adele, around the islands."

"Yes, they are on a mission to find Adele a most magnificent husband," Angeline said.

"Is Timothy Rowley still the prime target? Rumor has it he is looking to marry an heiress of some sort. It seems his family expects it." Agnes could scarcely contain her curiosity.

"Well, he was until a few hours ago. I just put them aboard the steamer back to Los Angeles. Captain Kalama welcomed them right on the gangplank displaying his customary charm and gorgeous physique. Mrs. Simmons took me aside to inquire if he was single. I fear Tom is in for a barrage of flirtation at the captain's table on this voyage. And not by Adele."

K settled back into her seat with a sigh. "Tom Kalama I do not worry about—he always enjoys being the center of attention."

"And the truth is, he only has eyes for you." Angeline was insistent.

"We are good friends—that is all."

"That will be true when Rowley's pigs fly."

At that very moment, the man known for his pigs strode around the base of the huge tree. "Those pigs do not fly, at least to best of my knowledge. However, they are extraordinary in every other way." Rowley delivered a rather lopsided grin. Until he saw Agnes. A shadow flickered over his mien. "Mrs. Lang, might I enquire how Miss Lang is faring?"

Agnes did not hesitate. If she was on a mission to discover the truth, she must leap. "Let me see. Since she has twice saved your horses *and* your horse saved her, she may prefer you call her Letty. If you care to visit, you can discover for yourself. Perhaps tomorrow?"

"Thank you. I shall." She watched as a slow, relieved smile spread across his face.

Irene had been silent but spoke up now. "Might I come too? We have been so worried about Letty."

"Of course, Letty is so determined she is already back at work. I know she would be delighted to have visitors. I will let this be a surprise."

Agnes returned to the purpose of her call. "Princess, I must head home shortly. Might we walk in the gardens for a few moments?"

"Of course."

As they strolled, the Princess named each rare plant along the path. "My father wanted very much for this to be a place fit for royalty. But that was not to be my destiny."

Agnes blurted, "We need to talk about Letty. I must understand what is going on if I am to help her."

"Well, if I may again set foot on your property . . ."

"Please, Princess, I am sorry about that. I was frightened . . . I am still frightened. I lived much of my young life in a mining camp in the far outback of Australia. I saw things there that could not be explained, some very dangerous. Now such a mystery is right in my own family." She looked away. "George says I am imagining things, but I know what I saw."

"And what did you see?"

"I saw red lights around her. Then she brought Johnny back to us."

K clutched her arm. Agnes found the Princess's hand unaccountably warm. "You are right to be fearful, but not of Letty. I am uncomfortable talking about any of this behind her back. She is a woman grown. She must make her own choices in her own time. She scarcely understands this herself. So much of this remains a mystery. Even to me. Might I come for tea tomorrow to have a conversation with you and Letty? And perhaps George as well?"

"Yes. Thank you." Agnes patted her hand in return. "You must forgive me for feeling so protective of Letty. I have no more of my Australian family, only Johnny. Letty and all the Langs came into my life like gifts from heaven. I cherish her. Do you understand?"

"Completely."

The Princess paused a moment before adding, "And my thanks to you for your invitation to Timothy Rowley to visit. If you can bring yourself to forgive Rowley for his part in all this, that would be most kind. He is so concerned about Letty. They formed a bit of a bond over the two horses she saved."

"Of course. That is what I expected. There are few things Letty cares more about than horses. And she can use a distraction right now."

"Quite."

CHAPTER ELEVEN

Kau Lio

RIDE HORSEBACK

Buoyed by the sunlit morning, Letty let Captain pick his pace. He responded with a rolling canter smooth as the summer sea. The trees lining the road leaned over to form arches, almost like a cathedral.

Letty tried to leave the puppy home, but Rosebud raised a ruckus. Letty capitulated. Now Rosebud nestled against her chest in a fabric sling. Her tiny nose pointed into the wind, drinking up the scents as they passed.

"You like this, don't you, scalawag. Am I going to be stuck taking you to class with me next year?" At least she hoped to be back in class by then. She'd not give up her plan of veterinary school without a fight, that was certain. Letty tried to talk to her father again, but he brushed her off. And she refused to think about her gift, if such it was. In the bright light of day, she chose to believe that K was delusional. Esther too. Letty had no plans to be sucked in by those delusions. Unfortunately the flames tickling her spine told her differently.

There was nothing left to do but sing. Yes, sing, to celebrate it all—her horse, the day, the clouds, the earth, and the little beating heart nestled close to her in the sling. The pup might like that. A song. "Hawai'i Aloha." Sung at full throat, of course.

She had just reached the chorus when hoofbeats came up from behind. Two voices joined in, one surely her brother Liam's baritone? And she would recognize Irene Stansfield's soprano anywhere after three years of singing side by side at Redwood.

Then a third voice Letty did not recognize. A tenor. She turned to see Timothy on Diablo. It was now a full chorale:

> *E Hawai'i, aloha e*
> *E hau'oli e nā 'ōpio o Hawai'i nei*
> *Oli e!*
> *Oli e!*

Rosebud provided a chorus of yips.

Laughing, she reined up. "Good morning, all! What brings everyone out so early on this fine day?"

Captain tried dancing a half step closer to Diablo for a nip, but Letty pulled him back. The big bay stallion trotted calmly, not caring one whit about Captain's attempt to spark an altercation. Timothy rode with such grace.

"Timothy, he looks good," Letty commented. That seemed a safe thing to say. Since blurting out something like, "My, don't you have very broad shoulders" would be unfortunate. Quite unfortunate.

"Well, I am finding that he is quite the rock once he is among people he trusts. I was expecting him to be skittish for a few days after the contretemps the night of your birthday, but no such thing. He is ready to get down to business with

Mr. Willingham's fine mares." His voice lowered. "Are you all right?"

She nodded.

"Agnes invited me to visit. I wanted to tell you . . ." Timothy might have said more, but Liam rode up on her other side. Letty was grateful for the change of subject.

"So, sister mine, what can this merry band do to help?"

"I hate to ask this, but does Agnes know you are here?"

"Oh, absolutely. Since the Princess is coming to tea this afternoon, she was glad to have me gone." He waved his arm to include his companions. "Irene and Timothy magically appeared in the yard, and here we are." His grin took on an edge of wickedness. "And I am not so foolish as to invite the ire of the lioness that is our stepmother."

"Liam!"

"That is what *Tūtū kāne* calls her! Not my idea! Anyway, we need another song!" Liam launched into a rollicking version of "What Shall We Do with a Drunken Sailor?" Letty's chest bubbled with laughter, but she maintained decorum—that is until Irene and Timothy joined. In harmony. Then her laugh exploded.

Was it only three days ago she thought she might never laugh again?

They rounded the corner into the Lang Ranch corrals. Wu was there, and Jacko. All ten of the polo prospects were milling around in the main corral. A long and dusty day of horse wrangling loomed. Letty had to admit she was glad of the proffered help.

She swung down and took Rosebud to the little shelter that Wu built for her.

"No want little one kicked, hey, missy? She fly far." That would be the truth. She was glad that Wu had a thought for the dog's safety.

"Shall we get to work? I need to see if any of these wild things remembers what a saddle feels like."

Exhausted and dirty by early afternoon, Letty ordered a break. Agnes, bless her, had sent massive amounts of food. There were even cookies left to share. Letty always seemed to find herself hungry now.

"I think this is the final six, Wu. Once we are done here, leave them in the corral tonight and let the others go. I want to talk to my grandfather about my plans before we move them into the stable."

Liam sprawled on the ground like a dead bug. Timothy sat, upright at least, shaking his too-long curls out of his eyes and unconsciously rubbing his leg. One day she would ask him about that limp of his.

Irene settled herself next to Rosebud's pen to give the little dog an ear massage.

"Do you think Leonardo would be pleased if I found another one of these puppies to bring home?" she asked.

"Hmm, probably not . . ." Letty was not going to mention her own hopes of taking Rosebud to San Francisco. No sense in jinxing the future.

"Who is Leonardo? Your beau?" Liam propped himself up on one elbow. Irene's mention of a male got his attention.

"No, silly. Leonardo is my cat."

Letty simply observed the exchange. It took work to keep track of Liam's interests.

Timothy stood up to stretch, those mesmerizing shoulders flexing under his formerly immaculate white shirt. Then there were the thighs encased in tan breeches . . . he moved like a big cat. And not a house cat. She mustn't stare, or Liam would tease her unmercifully. Besides, the man was after an heiress, wasn't he?

Timothy turned her way.

"You have only six weeks to do this? It's going to take a bit of magic and maybe a couple of miracles."

"Well, I am just the magician to pull it off."

Letty wanted to swallow her tongue. What had she just said? Flames danced at the base of her spine. She blushed for sure. Silly, since no one else knew the reason. Thank goodness for the big hat shading her face.

"I will be back to pick up Diablo in a few weeks. If you don't mind, I owe you for a couple of your miracles. I'd be pleased to help. And I've been asked to play on the Willingham polo team. That means I'll likely ride a few of these ponies in the match."

"Accept his offer, sister mine, before he realizes this is lunacy and says he wants no part of it."

"Thank you, Timothy. Offer accepted."

Irene stood, rubbing her back. "And I shall be back at the very end of summer with Papa as well. He is bringing over some new automobiles to gauge the interest here in sales. One will be an Oldsmobile Limited."

Liam's head practically flew off his neck as he turned to stare at Irene. "The Limited? The fastest car in America? The one they race against trains?"

"The very one." Irene was visibly smug. "Maybe if you are nice to me, I will take you for a ride in it. I am quite an excellent driver."

Chapter Twelve

Kaumaha Loa

HEAVILY BURDENED

Agnes studied the man as he walked back to his automobile. Stout and well dressed, with longish, slicked-back hair and old-fashioned muttonchop whiskers. She had made it her business to know everyone who was anyone in Honolulu, but this gentleman was not familiar.

Her husband stood to the side of the automobile, talking as the man settled into the driver's seat. George's shoulders were unaccountably hunched. He kept looking down at his feet as he spoke. The man waved his hand at George dismissively, then drove away.

Agnes went out on the porch to face George as he came up the steps. Her husband's expression was leaden. "Who was that, my dear? I don't recall seeing that gentleman before."

George stepped around her to head to his office. Not meeting her eyes, he mumbled, "Just a customer."

A man coming to buy a horse arriving in a horseless carriage? Not likely.

She trailed him down the hall, her shorter legs doing double time to keep up with his long-legged Lang family stride. Truly, she hated being almost the shortest person in a household of giants. Even Johnny would top her soon.

As she walked through the office door, George was already easing himself into his chair. She stiffened her spine in preparation. George had wooed her with the promise of a marriage of equals. Agnes did not intend to settle for anything less.

Making a beeline right for his beloved fern in the blue-figured Chinese pot, she reached in to grasp a small key. The desk chair squeaked as George swiveled to look at her.

"Oh, look what we have here—the key to your files. Now, George, I am going to give you a choice: either you tell me what is going on right now, or I will use this key to search the files at my leisure."

With a firm grip on the key, she moved to sit in the chair beside his desk. "I am listening."

George looked away, swiveling back to his desk. "It is none of your business."

"That is not the sort of arrangement we have. If my business is your business . . . then most certainly your business must be mine. For richer, for poorer—or at least that is the way I remember it."

"Really, it is nothing."

"George, stop this nonsense. I know full well that things are amiss."

He leaned forward to rest his head in his hands on the desktop. "We are in debt." His words were muffled as if they came from the bottom of a barrel. "I cannot make the payments."

She gripped the key so hard she felt its imprint on the palm of her hand. "Is that why we just had a visitor?"

"Yes. That was Jesse Gannon. He loans money to lots of people. Thus, he owns lots of land—land that he gets when people cannot pay. I thought I was smarter than everyone else. It seems I am not."

"When do we need to make the payment, and how much?" She thought of her inheritance sitting safely in the bank.

George lifted his head, but still did not look at her, instead staring straight at the wall.

"It is too late. Apparently, I missed the fine print on the note I signed. Once a payment is late, a penalty ensues. To pay him off now will take more than this property is even worth."

"This property, George? This house? The livery? We have debt on our home? Our business?"

Agnes struggled to keep the anguish out of her voice.

"Gannon was here to threaten me. He says he'll take the property if we do not follow the letter of the agreement."

She lost her struggle for composure. "And exactly when were you going to tell me this, fine sir? That you have gambled our home and you lost?"

He looked at her in desperation. "Agnes, it is not like that—I just thought we were in a temporary lull in the business. I thought things would surely turn around. Lang's Livery has been here for years."

"Well, I hope the irony is not lost on you that this gentleman came to deliver the news in his *horseless* carriage. The world is changing, George, and we must change with it!"

She stood and dropped the key on his desk. "Now I will head back to the kitchen to prepare for the main event of the day, a confabulation with dear Princess K to find out why *our* daughter glows in the dark. Did you hear what I said, George? *Our?* We are in all of this together, and it is time you start acting like it."

Already in the hallway, she turned back for one last word. "And you can tell that Mr. Gannon he had better bring an army if he wants to move me out of this house. I have a gun and I know how to use it."

She marched toward the kitchen. Back at the end of the hallway, she heard George emerge from his office.

"Letty does not glow in the dark."

"Yes, she does. I love you, George."

Despite the day's hard work, the ride home was merry. More singing and silly jokes. Rosebud happily snuggled in her little sling. Letty had forgotten how much she relished the company of friends. And her irrepressible brother. And the intrigue of the Englishman.

Liam was over the moon about the motorcar arriving at the end of the summer.

And now he sang that automobile song, like a crooner, right to Irene:

> *Come away with me, Lucille,*
> *In my merry Oldsmobile.*
> *Down the road of life we'll fly*
> *Automobubbling, you and I.*

"Wait, no, that is not right." He began again:

> *Come away with me, Irene,*
> *In my magnificent driving machine . . .*

A laughing Irene grabbed her canteen, dashing Liam with water. "You need to cool down, mister."

Twenty jolly minutes later, the group reached the fork in the road that led back to 'Āinahau. "We part here. Thanks for all your help," Letty said. "Timothy, when do you head home?"

"Tomorrow. I'll deliver Diablo to Willingham's stables, then catch the night boat to Hilo."

"Have safe travels!"

Letty and Liam waved as Timothy and Irene trotted out of sight.

"Well, sister mine, are you ready for what lies ahead? The Princess and the Lioness. I can hardly wait."

"Oh, shut up, Liam."

She urged Captain into a canter for the rest of the trip.

Letty trudged down the back stairs, scrubbed and ready for whatever awaited. She'd chosen the comfort of wearing one of her most old-fashioned *holokū*, loose and high-necked. And white, the color of innocence. Just in case anyone thought this lunacy might be her fault. She walked down the hall with the voluminous fabric swishing cool air next to her skin. No wonder Kahōkūlani wore old-style *holokū* all the time.

She preferred not to contemplate what this afternoon "tea" might bring. Agnes had been less than forthcoming, saying simply that the Princess was visiting today to talk about "Letty's recent adventures."

Letty tucked Rosebud under her arm and wandered down to George's office. There she found her father sitting at his desk, sketching furiously. A bad sign. Papa always sketched engineering projects when he was upset. It calmed him. Rather like her counting.

Letty maneuvered herself into the chair next to the desk, hanging on to Rosebud as the little dog tried madly to climb up on the desktop. That would be all they needed: a spilled ink pot and blue paw prints all over everything.

"Papa, do you know why the Princess is coming? Agnes turned her away after my birthday and said she was never to come back. What has changed?"

Her father turned his chair to face her squarely. "There is something you need to understand about Agnes. Once she decides something belongs to her, she never, *never* lets go. She has opened her heart to take you in—lock, stock, and barrel. To her, you are as much her own daughter as if she birthed you.

"And now she believes something strange might be going on with you. She claims to see red lights. She thinks the Princess has the key. What do you think?"

Letty lowered her head, looking down at her bare feet peeking out from the ruffled hem of her *holokū*. The feet that K told her needed to walk on the *'āina* to keep Letty strong.

"I'm sure I don't know, Papa. The princess always has her own views. All I want is to go back to San Francisco to veterinary school."

"Sweetheart, you must let that go."

"Papa, I just can't. I will find a way somehow."

His voice edged on bitterness. "Letty, I am afraid you will learn that life has its own way of robbing you of your dreams."

"Maybe you lost a dream, Papa. I am sorry, but I will not give up."

He squeezed her hand. "I hope I am wrong."

She tucked Rosebud back under her arm and headed to the parlor.

Princess Kahōkūlani took a deep breath, more to keep her own nerves in check than anything else. Much rode on this conversation. At least all the right people seemed to be in the room: Letty, Agnes, George, and Lot. Liam too. And herself, of course. She had her own stake in all this.

Letty looked calm, almost disinterested. The white *holokū* she wore only enhanced the redness of her hair. The color shimmered in the dappled sunlight coming through the parlor windows as the girl leaned forward pouring cups of tea.

Agnes's voice cut through Kahōkūlani's introspection. "Well, let's get down to business, shall we? Princess, where should we start?"

"At the very beginning, perhaps. With a bit of history. Even before Letty. If I may?"

Agnes nodded. The men froze. Letty looked out the window. K would take all of that for a yes.

"As you know, in our Hawaiian tradition we believe the *'āina* has power . . . and through our connection to the *'āina* our own intentions have power . . . that what you intend can become real if only your intention is strong enough.

"In ancient times, we believed it possible to think someone to death with strong intentions, the *pule 'anā'anā*. Some believe that is still possible; in fact, they blame my mother's own mysterious death on such dark thinking.

"What seemed lost was the power of good intention. *Mana'o pono*, righteous thinking."

K paused. No one said a word. Or even blinked. She swallowed. All right, if this became a lecture, so be it.

"There are prophecies, old ones. They say women with the gift of *mana'o pono* will come again. Women come to guide our people into the future. Nine women. Called the *mākāhā*, the Gates, because they open the way for the power of the *'āina* to come back into the world."

Her next words came out in a rush. "These Gates will be the new *wāhine ali'i nui*, women who lead the people. I believe that Letty will be one of these women."

Letty sank down into her chair as if to escape notice. Not an easy feat for someone of her stature.

Agnes leaned forward. "I don't understand. What does this have to do with Letty glowing red and bringing back Johnny?"

George slapped his hand down on a side table so hard the table jumped. "Enough—none of this has to do with old prophecies! Letty was in a very dangerous situation, but she escaped. Anything we all thought we saw was a result of high emotion. Nothing more."

Clearly something beyond a lecture would be required. Kahōkūlani walked over to the tea table, pushed up her sleeve, and picked up a pointed fruit knife. This again. With a quick stab, blood gushed from her own arm. Utter calm engulfed Kahōkūlani as she watched Letty helplessly propel herself across the room, red lights flaring, to seize Kahōkūlani's arm. The heat of the girl's touch was almost painful. The wound closed just as she knew it would.

"Damnation!" Lot, Liam, and George swore in tandem. Agnes leaped up, running to Letty as the girl slumped to the floor.

"Princess, that was not fair!" Letty's eyes brimmed with betrayal. She panted as the tears slipped down her face.

Agnes knelt at Letty's side to place a comforting arm around her. She looked up at K with an intensity burning like Letty's own fire.

"There are others?"

"Yes, but we have not yet found them all. Possibly nine if the prophecies are to be believed."

"Why? Why now?"

"I do not know for certain. So much of the old knowledge had been lost. The *kāhuna* tell me it is because the need is so great. Our world is changed. And because of the mixing of the blood. All the young women we have found with potential are *hapa*."

K watched Letty's breathing calm, but now the girl would not meet her eyes.

"There is much we do not know . . ."

"Princess, show them your power, your aura. You owe it to me, for this . . ."

"I . . . I . . . well, I have the gift, *mana'o pono*, too. I am one of the nine. A Gate. Every Gate's gift is different. Letty's gift is a healing power, the power of fire.

"My gift is the power of truth. I am a wayfinder. I find the right path. By the stars, the same stars our people have followed since the beginning of time. Once I see the truth of a thing I cannot turn away; I must pursue it."

"Show them." Letty's words came out as a croak.

"They may not see."

"Show them anyway."

K breathed deeply, settling into a practiced rhythm. Then she extended her hands as if in welcome. In some odd way, this was a welcome. "Believe these gifts are real." Heat suffused her body as if she stood at the volcano's rim on the hottest of days. She must not faint now, not while so much depended on Letty's *'ohana* accepting the young woman for who and what she truly was.

"*Mana'o pono* is part of who we are; we are bound by it. All of us, all of *Hawai'i nei*. It is the gift of the *'āina*. The Gates— Letty, myself, and the others—we will open new ways for our people. But our secret must be protected. The old ways are illegal now." The heat of her aura intensified and then began to fade.

They must have been able to see it. The men went slack-jawed. Agnes stared with cold calculation. Letty still did not look up, her head buried in Agnes's shoulder. Kahōkūlani had never seen her own aura in its entirety; that was not possible. Auras do not show up in anything so prosaic as a mirror. When she asked Esther, the woman described K's as a blinding white light, like the brightest star. Bull refused to describe it at all. Judging from the response here, it must be quite impressive.

"Well, well. I think we all need a spot more tea." Agnes stood up to take charge. Everyone in the room commenced breathing again.

Over tea and scones, K made the case that Letty needed a teacher, a *kumu*, to help her harness her talents. Letty tried insisting she return to San Francisco in the fall, that she needed no teacher. K gently explained it was not safe for Letty to leave the *'āina*. Not until she was trained. And had walked the *'āina* enough to fulfill her gift. Someday, perhaps soon, maybe even in the fall, but not now. Not yet. George seemed peculiarly relieved by this. K soldiered on.

"This is enough for one day—it is all so much to take in. I will consult with Esther to get you the proper *kumu*," she told Letty. "Perhaps this week is not too soon to start."

"You'd better find someone that rides, because I will be training polo ponies."

"Never fear, my dear—only someone who rides will do!"

Chapter Thirteen

Kumu

ONE WHO TEACHES

Two days later, a woman rode into the Langs' yard on an unusually tall white mule, a big, rangy dog at the mule's heels. The shade of a wide-brimmed *lauhala* hat obscured her face. Long silver hair flowed down her back. Even from this distance, Agnes could see that the hatband was made of feathers. Many strings of rare shells hung around the woman's neck. Ni'ihau shells. Fit for royalty. This woman was somebody.

As was the dogs' custom, the three musketeers came racing out, barking full tilt. But they stopped suddenly, then sat down, then lay down, almost as if they were paying their respects. Agnes shook her head in bemusement, heading out the door to greet the visitor. Could things get any stranger around here?

The mule went down on one knee to let the woman dismount, as more members of the barn menagerie came forth: first the rooster, who also sat down as if to pay court. Then the cat, who, after circling the woman and the mule, went right up to the big dog to touch noses. Unbelievable!

Agnes stood on the porch, wiping her hands on her apron. "May I help you?"

The woman turned, her face strangely young despite the white hair. "I am the *kumu*. I am here for the girl who loves animals."

Agnes stepped off the stairs and held out her hand. "Of course you are. Be welcome."

"This is not what I was expecting." Letty knew she must sound petulant but could not mask her feelings. "All we do is breathe and stand around barefoot. I am not learning anything at all!"

The woman's serene expression remained unmoved. Most of the Langs' resident menagerie lay at her feet. "Ah, but breathing is most important. Without it, you will die."

"That is not what I mean, and you know it. Why aren't you teaching me to control my gift? That is why you are here, is it not?"

"Very good, so now you admit you have a gift. This is progress. Yesterday you told me you did not."

Letty threw up her hands. "Don't try to twist my words. I can't believe that K thinks you will teach me anything. I am done here."

She stood, calling to Rosebud, "Let's go, pup!" The little dog remained in place, part of the animal circle surrounding the *kumu*. "Rosebud, let's go!" The animal swiveled her head back and forth, her distress plain. Whom should she obey?

"It is beneath you to torture the dog, Letty. She knows I have not said the lesson is over; she cannot leave. But she feels the force of your intention, so she is caught between us. Sit back down so we can finish."

"*No*, you let my dog go!"

"That I cannot do, child. I made a promise to teach you. I will hold you to your lessons, however I may."

"*Then teach me something!*" Now Rosebud sat quivering on the floor. Annabelle the goat came up on the porch to see what was amiss.

"I have taught you something; I want you to use it now. You see these poor animals agitated by the force of your intention? Just sit down and breathe as I have taught you, then watch what happens."

Letty dropped back down to begin the breathing exercise. Eyes shut, she flowed into the rhythm. *Breathe in, breathe out, hold; breathe out more, then breathe in and hold again. Breathe out slowly, then breathe in slowly and open your eyes.* Silliness. Except . . . her eyes popped open as she felt Rosebud's little tongue licking her toes. *What?*

"A gift such as you have can be very dangerous if not controlled. You saw the distress of your dog. Even the goat took notice. The breath is the key to control. It is not the mere breathing, but the conscious, *intentional* controlling of the breath. This calms you and in turn allows you to be mistress of all your intentions."

The *kumu* cocked her head as she looked at Letty. "How do you feel?"

"Better, but I am still annoyed with all of this."

"The breathing takes nothing away from your intentions. It merely gives you mastery over the storms they might create. So you are free to be as annoyed as you choose. But this way, you are not sending out waves of power that distress other beings.

"This is the warrior's way. To move forward in calmness no matter what lies ahead. You, my girl, are quite the warrior. It is only the mastery you lack."

The *kumu* stood. "I will return at this same time tomorrow. I have many ways of the breath to teach you. Be ready. Walk barefoot on the land to replenish yourself." She gathered her things and began her effortless glide toward the door. Turning back to Letty, she said, "I will no longer call you Leticia. Your true name is Lili'uokalani. It is a queen's name, and you will earn the right to bear it. Good night for now, my Lili'u."

Letty stood speechless. The *kumu* mounted her kneeling mule and rode slowly away, the giant dog ambling behind her.

Part Two

He eʻepa ke aloha, he kulaʻilua

LOVE IS PECULIAR; IT PUSHES IN OPPOSITE DIRECTIONS

CHAPTER FOURTEEN

Ho'ohohonu

GO DEEP

Lang's Ranch, Oahu, the 19th of July, 1909

Routine helped. For the last month, Letty's days had taken on a comforting sameness. She rose early to get to the ranch, then headed back home midafternoon for her studies with the *kumu*. The daily rhythm of the work with the ponies gave her a sense of firmer ground. The rhythms of all the different breathing exercises did too. The very thought that she possessed some kind of power seemed less daunting.

In the beginning she'd been terrified of her gift itself. That her flames had meaning. Now she most feared the choices she might be forced to make. Her life in San Francisco seemed so long ago. Could she ever reclaim it? Go back to the science and logic and order she craved? Or must she be content with standing barefoot on the *'āina* to keep her gift alive?

No bare feet today; she wore boots. This was the day Timothy would join her for the week of promised help. She could use it. And the chance to see him.

Letty had just settled Rosebud into her pen when she heard the hoofbeats. Timothy rode up to the hitching stand, flinging one long leg forward up and over the pommel, dismounting in a single fluid motion to land lightly on both feet. She would not stare.

The man stood, arms crossed, surveying the practice field.

"My, you have quite a setup here. Why would you want polo ponies to do obstacle courses?"

"Well, greetings to you too, on this beautiful day. Would you like me to curtsey, Lord Rowley? And then you can bow and kiss my hand?"

A slow grin crept across his tanned face. She couldn't ignore how attractive she found him. Timothy was not handsome, not in the usual way, but she felt drawn to him nonetheless.

"All right, point taken. I shall deliver a proper greeting." He pulled off his hat, sandy curls dancing in the morning breeze, and executed a sweeping bow, going down on one knee. "I salute you, my princess of polo. How can I, your poor servant, be of assistance?"

She caught herself giggling, then laughing out loud. "Oh Timothy, it is good to see you. The last month has been nothing but work. And more work." He did not even know about the daily sessions with the *kumu*. And he'd not know. Ever. "This princess finds herself in need of a laugh now and again."

"I will do what I can." He stood up with only a bit of a waver visible in his bad knee, then ambled over to Rosebud's pen. The pup danced on her hind legs for the forthcoming chin scratch.

"How can you not be laughing with this little monster in your life? My grandmother would love one of these dogs. Perhaps I shall send her one as payback for Diablo."

"Easy—she is still not housebroken. Agnes is on a tear about it even though she gave me the dog. And Rosebud has her accidents in the strangest places, like Papa's shoes. You would think she was seeking to make my life difficult on purpose."

"Well, I would not put it past the beast. But back to the work at hand. I really did come to help." Timothy moved to stand in front of her. What a pleasure to talk to someone without tilting her head down; she could actually look up at Timothy. His eyes crinkled with good humor.

"I await enlightenment, my princess. An obstacle course? For polo?"

"So here is my method; I hope it is not madness. In only six weeks I have no way to turn out a perfectly trained polo pony. Since I have never actually trained polo ponies before, who knows if I could even do it in a year? What I can do is make these ponies calm, willing, and agile. The obstacles help make them spook-proof and get them to trust their riders. I have the men move the contraptions around every day. My grandfather does something like this when he trains carriage horses."

"Ah, I see."

She never knew with Timothy whether or not he took her seriously. These obstacles might look a bit crazy, but she knew they worked. Particularly the one with the old lady's bonnet, its ribbons and feathers blowing about. She pointed. "See the scarecrow over there? With the hat waving in the wind? We call that one Gertrude. Ride your mare past that if you want to see how she handles it."

"No, thank you, I will save that pleasure for another day. I have no doubt this works."

Letty mustn't let her own feathers get so easily ruffled. Or read things into what he said. After all, the man came to help. Even so, merely standing next to Timothy threw her a bit off balance. Strangely, she fancied his approval. So did her flames, it seemed, as they danced up and down her back. "Of course. Shall we get to work?"

She walked with him over to the corral, where the six ponies lazed in the sun, and propped her elbows on the top of the fence. Timothy lounged at her side.

"Let me introduce you to the string. The little gray is Ghost. A gelding, quick but sneaky. He should live up to his name. That's Pilikia; she is one of Captain's fillies and has his sense of mischief, hence the name. Then we have Apple, the shiny red chestnut. Daisy is the dappled dun. Shadow is the roan. Then over there in the shade trying not to be noticed is Baronet Percy Blakeney. He pretends to be a lazy fop but is quite the tiger when engaged."

"Sir Percy?" Timothy barked out a laugh. "*The Scarlet Pimpernel*? That is my favorite book of all time!" He pulled himself upright to recite:

We seek him here, we seek him there.
Those Frenchies seek him everywhere!
Is he in heaven? Or is he in hell?
That demmed Elusive Pimpernel?

"But don't you dare tell anyone I can recite that. No one will take me seriously if they know I read such romances."

"Your secret is safe with me. I call him Percy for short. No one need ever know."

Timothy curled his pinky finger to his upper lip to deliver the ultimate Pimpernel bon mot: "*Sink me!*"

"You are crazy." How could she ever have thought him a stuffy bore? Well. Because sometimes he was one. Just not recently.

"Yes, but no crazier than you. Why are you fond of that book?" He quirked up one eyebrow as he asked.

"Because it isn't just the hero doing the saving. The heroine saves him right back."

"Ah, kind of like you, Princess she-who-jumps-in-the-water?"

"Naturally."

He gave her a searching look, then turned to the field. "What do we need to do today?"

Crude goals at distances approximating the polo field in Kapi'olani Park were in place. "I think we just need to hit some balls. Around the obstacles."

"Quite. Well, I'm definitely your man. Particularly if it involves a mallet."

By early afternoon, every pony had been ridden multiple times—this to approximate the on-again, off-again timing of polo. Balls had been sent careening across the field and between the ponies' legs and over the obstacles. Mallets swung in every direction taught the ponies that anything was possible.

Wu and Jacko arrived to unsaddle the string. Timothy and Letty readied their own horses to leave for the day. Letty swung up neatly with Rosebud in her riding sling, turning back to the head wrangler.

"Wu, same time tomorrow, hey? Thanks for your help today."

"Yes, missy, you do good work, me think."

"Thanks, Wu. From you, that is quite a compliment."

As they rode out, Letty admired Timothy's mount, a pretty little black mare with white feet and a star. At least that is what she told herself she was looking at, not Timothy's fine seat in the saddle. "Is that one of K's? I have not seen that mare before."

"No. Willingham's. Doc is trying to convince me to take her in exchange for Diablo's stud fees. She is a sweetheart, but I rather fancy the money. I am endeavoring to buy my own sugar mill."

"Wait, what about Moran Sugar?"

"That belongs to my grandmother, not me. I want to be her partner, not an employee."

"Hah! I understand that. How many mares has Diablo covered?"

"Well, he's been busy. Doc tells me he thinks that six of his best mares may be in foal to him."

"Are you asking for one of them as part of the fee?"

"What a grand idea! I should know enough to always get the advice of the horse trader's daughter before I clinch a deal!"

"Will you race him in the Gentleman's Cup? They offer a decent purse to the winner."

"Another grand idea. That I am already planning to do."

They rode along companionably for a mile or two, Letty appreciating someone who knew how to be silent, but not distant. She'd never had the talent for idle conversation. Still, she launched a question, one that had been on her mind for a while.

"Timothy, why don't you ever go home to see your family? Don't you miss them?"

Out of the corner of her eye, she saw his shoulders clench.

"They don't want to see me."

"*What?*" Captain stopped cold with the energy of her response. How could this happen in any *'ohana*?

Timothy turned the little mare to face her squarely. "I have been disinherited by my father and told never to darken his door again. Only my grandmother communicates with me. All because I wanted to be a *farmer.*"

He turned and started riding again. Barely controlled fury laced his voice. "Nothing, *nothing* I ever did was good enough for my father. So I decided I'd had enough of being the good son, and here I am in Hawaii."

"And where was your mother in all this?"

"She died when I was three; I barely remember her. A procession of stepmothers followed. None evil, but none interested in me. One of my father's mistresses was more kind than any one of them. Cassandra Cannondale. I still write to her;

she writes back. Rather like an extra auntie. She's in London right now, just returned from India."

Letty chose to tread lightly against his wall of bitterness. "My mother died when I was four." Her stomach clenched as it always did when she spoke of this. "Agnes is my stepmother. We got off to a rocky start but have found common ground now."

"Well, at least your father did not abandon you."

"It felt like he did. At first, he refused to hire a nursemaid, so neighbors helped out. Papa traveled to other islands all the time. Even as young as we were, Liam and I began to think the only thing we could count on was each other. Our grandfather stepped in. His cook's daughter, Mālama, came to care for us. She takes care of Hannah now. Papa and I are still not truly close, even though I love him." She took a deep breath against the constriction in her chest. "Now that I am older, I understand how much he must have grieved for my mother."

"Well, I wish I could say that about my father, but I can't. He cares for nothing but himself. Perhaps I shall marry a wealthy woman and go home in triumph. There is nothing he respects more than money."

They reached the turnoff to 'Āinahau.

"Will I see you tomorrow?" she asked.

"Most certainly—I am learning along with the ponies! Don't forget I promised you five days of help. I still have four more days before I take Diablo back. I remain at your service." He gave a jaunty wave as he turned down the track.

Curse her curiosity! She certainly never intended to dredge up painful subjects. Maybe tomorrow more talk about the Pimpernel instead of 'ohana?

Now she had a *kumu* to face. And some breathing to do.

Timothy rode on to 'Āinahau, trying to shake off the pain that any discussion of his family engendered. What he had not told Letty is that he still wrote his father every fortnight, with news of his life and requesting reports from home. His letters were never answered.

At first, they came back with "Refused" written on them. Then they stopped coming back at all. He liked to think his father cared at least enough to burn them, but he doubted that. Most likely his letters were simply consigned to the dustbin by the earl's current man of business.

Perhaps he needed to get serious about pursuit of an heiress. He'd been thinking about it for a while now. Marrying money was not only what his family expected, it was the most likely path back into his father's good graces.

Adele Simmons was quite the opportunity. If he wanted his father's approbation, that is.

"Hallo!"

Letty turned from saddling Apple to see Timothy riding in. Tomorrow was to be the last day of his help. Already she did not know what she would have done without him. Timothy knew his polo; she found he was training her as much as she was training the ponies.

She kneed Apple in the belly. The mare let out the breath she was holding so that Letty could tighten the girth. Timothy rode up next to her and dismounted.

"That one likes to blow herself up like a little balloon, doesn't she?"

"That's why we call you Apple, isn't it, sweetheart?" Letty gave the horse a little rub under her forelock. "It is not just your pretty red coat, it's your big round belly!"

Timothy laughed as he tied up his mare. "Tomorrow I will have Diablo back, so I can ride him. I think it would be sensible to do some of the drills with strange horses, more like a real match."

"Wise idea. What are you doing here so bright and early?"

As always, she'd come a bit early herself to check the ponies and make sure everything was ready to go. Only ten days remained to get the ponies ready.

Letty turned to see Timothy rummaging through his saddlebags, emerging with a carefully wrapped package.

"This is the reason I came betimes . . ." He pulled aside the wrappings to reveal six perfectly baked scones. "The cook at 'Āinahau was in her glory this morning. You know how particular the Princess is about her scones. These are still warm . . ." He grinned at her wickedly. "But of course I know you're not hungry. You never are!"

"Beast! Give me a scone!" She was torn between punching him and kissing him in gratitude. As if she'd be brave enough to kiss him.

"But of course, my lady. And what are my orders for the day?"

"Ride, ride, ride." She took a big bite of scone. He'd even brought butter. And guava jelly. She was definitely growing fond of this fellow. Her flames crackled.

"In all seriousness, while I have your help, we need to do contact drills. Polo ponies bump into each other." She took a finger to wipe a big drip of guava jelly off her chin. Then sucked it.

Timothy's eyes went wide. Quickly he turned his head to look down the line of ponies, all saddled and waiting. "Bumping it is. Shall we get on with it?"

Every day Agnes sent lunch up. When Letty called a midday halt, Timothy fully expected to see one of the houseboys arrive with saddlebags full of something delicious.

But today, Agnes herself rode through the gate. Johnny followed on his fat pony, Lau Lau. And, of course, the dogs. The three musketeers were rarely far from Johnny's side. When Johnny spied Timothy, he kicked the pony into a canter, heading straight at him.

"Whoa, soldier!" Timothy leaped to grab Lau Lau's bridle. "Are you here to help train some ponies?" The boy gazed up at him adoringly as Timothy added, "Only brave men can do that."

"And women." Agnes dismounted to unload her bulging saddlebags. "And only if they are well fed!"

"We have chicken sandwiches, Mr. Rowley. My favorite," Johnny said.

The boy's earnestness compelled immediate agreement. "Yes, chicken sandwiches are tip-top. Might I share one with you?" Timothy gazed over Johnny's head to see Letty's smile. He winked back at her.

Helping Johnny unpack the picnic seemed the order of the day. Agnes pulled Letty aside for a whispered conversation. Telling himself he was not eavesdropping, at least not on purpose, Timothy heard snatches of it.

"The *kumu* paid us a call this morning. She wants you to know that she is coming here, to the training stable, this afternoon. 'I will see the work and judge it.' That is exactly what she said."

Letty's eyes went wide with alarm. "Why didn't you tell her no?"

"Are you joking? You try to tell that woman no. I don't even know her real name. I thought it was Kumu . . . and then George explained that was just Hawaiian for 'teacher' . . ."

"My goodness, this throws a wrinkle into things. I have to get Timothy out of here."

"He doesn't know?"

"Of course not. You know what the Princess said. The fewer people that know, the better."

"Perhaps, but he seems like such a stalwart friend . . ."

"No, he just thinks he owes me for the Diablo fiasco."

They turned their backs and continued to whisper, but Timothy could no longer make out what they said.

Who in heaven's name was the *kumu*? And why did Letty want to be rid of him? Out of the corner of his eye he saw Letty turn back his way. The smile she gave him now might be the one reserved for awkward guests. Yet her face seemed haunted.

"Agnes, of course I will come home early if you need me. Timothy and I have already had a very full day, have we not? And I know Timothy is eager to retrieve Diablo."

Timothy could take a hint, but he did not mean to ignore this mystery. Not when he could almost taste Letty's anxiety. He did not know why he felt so protective of her, but he did. Perhaps it was because he had never had a sister. Yes, that must certainly be the reason.

"True. Once we have finished this sumptuous luncheon, I will be on my way."

The horses stood in a row down the center of the corral, reins dropped but not tethered. It was an old cow pony trick, standing with dropped reins; Letty had taught it on a lark. Now the ponies were lined up, looking like a platoon of soldiers waiting for review. By the supreme commander. Could that be what was happening?

Her confusion increased watching the *kumu* walk down the line. As the woman reached each horse, she held a hand out as if requesting permission to approach. Then, coming close, she let the horse bury its nose in the folds of her *holokū* near her stomach. One by one, every pony in the string did the same thing. It was almost as if they were doing the breathing exercises. Percy was the last horse in the line. As the *kumu* stroked his ears, she gave a short, barking laugh . . . or at least Letty hoped it was a laugh.

"This one, he wants me to think he is a lazy boy, but he has the fire within." The *kumu* walked back to Letty and took both her hands. "You have done your work well, my child. Each and every one is prepared for the road ahead. They bear the mark of your gift."

"I don't understand what that might be."

"It is never what you expect. But what you give is calmness, peace, and freedom from pain. Because animals often cannot understand what is happening, they suffer needlessly. You have the way to stop that."

"But what about healing?"

"I have told you. Your gift is not truly a healing power. Only one's own body can heal itself. This is true for both humans and animals. Rather, you are someone who can take what happens naturally and nudge it along."

The *kumu* looked back at the line of horses. "Our Princess played parlor tricks on you by stabbing herself. Because of her own gift, her natural healing would be swift, but with a push from your power, well, it might look impressive. I am sure this won over you and your family, but it was not well done. It made it all look too simple."

The *kumu* reached to squeeze Letty's hand. "And as you have already come to know, there is nothing simple about your gift."

"What good is all this?"

"That is for you to discover. You will find ways to help, in many things, as that is your nature. But sometimes you will find that you are powerless."

The *kumu*'s mule ambled over, the big dog right behind. The visit must be over. Letty realized she had grown accustomed to the animals reading the *kumu*'s intentions. Would nothing seem strange anymore?

"Come closer, child."

The *kumu* motioned to Letty to lean down. Touching her forehead to Letty's forehead, a hand on each cheek, she breathed deeply. Letty found her own breath naturally aligning, her nostrils filling with the sweet smell of ancient earth newly turned. Letty's eyes fluttered shut, then snapped open as she was suffused by . . . goodness. This was the traditional Hawaiian kiss, *honi*, and so much more.

"I am finished here. I have no more to teach you now. *Aloha*."

The mule went down on one knee for her to mount.

"Wait! What if I have questions? How do I find you? You have not even told me your name!"

The *kumu* picked up her reins and turned the mule to take her leave. "This you must know: Ailani, your mother, was my friend. She would be very proud of you." The mule began to trot away, the dog trailing behind. Over her shoulder the *kumu* called, "Breathe, my Lili'u, just breathe. Your breath will always save you."

Letty's legs gave out from under her. She knelt in the dust, completely bereft, and she could not even explain why. Tears flowed. She gave herself over to them.

Timothy sat Diablo's easy trot as he rode back to the training ground. He would bet any amount of money that Letty was still there.

A tiny woman on a tall white mule passed by, followed by one of the largest dogs he had ever seen. The woman did not even acknowledge him as she passed. And when he turned to take a discreet look again, she had disappeared.

So that was what the whispering was all about. This woman must be the *kumu*, the teacher Letty had been unwilling to discuss. Letty let slip that Kahōkūlani wanted her to study ancient Hawaiian arts, but he'd been unable to pry anything more out of her.

As he pulled into the training yard, he could see the horses still saddled. All of them. Letty knelt on the ground, sitting on her heels, the very picture of dejection.

"I'm back. Want me to start unsaddling?"

She nodded without looking up.

He came close to her and settled down on his haunches. She shook, the tracks of fresh tears on her cheeks. "I passed a woman on a white mule on my way here. This is about the red lights I see around you sometimes, isn't it? Want to tell me about that?"

She looked up at him, her eyes wet pools of sadness. "She knew my mother. All this time with her and she could have told me about my mother, but she didn't. I barely remember my mother. And now she says she is done with me. *Pau* . . ."

His heart contracted as though there were a fist around it. "Let's clear up and get the ponies settled, and then get you home." Letty stood as if in a stupor. He reached out a hand to steady her, but she batted it away.

"I am fine."

"No, you are not. I barely remember my mother either; I know how it feels. Like a big burning hole in your heart." He'd never admitted this to anyone.

Wu came barreling out from the back of the stable. "Missy, Jacko is here. We take care of ponies. You go with Mr. Tim."

She walked stiffly over to Captain and mounted. "Yes, let's go."

They rode in silence. This time he did not take the turnoff, riding with her right up to the Langs' gate.

"I will see you tomorrow."

She nodded but made no other response. He watched her ride slowly down the lane, back hunched. A wave of her pain washed back at him; he felt it almost as his own.

He started his ride back to 'Āinahau. Tomorrow, perhaps she might rally.

CHAPTER FIFTEEN

Ha'alele

ABANDONED

Letty woke early, Rosebud cuddled against her, in the faint light of dawn. She had that drowsy "all is right with the world" feeling one has after a good night's sleep. Since her return, she basked in how good everything smelled in Hawaii. This morning was no exception, with the scent of gardenias and ginger wafting through her window. She'd get up in a moment . . .

She was awakened next by Rosebud licking her face. The sun was fully up, and she must get going. She kissed Rosebud on the top of her head and sat up to face the day. And then she remembered: the *kumu* had abandoned her.

"Have another cup of tea." Agnes fluttered around her. "I am so sorry, sweetheart. Maybe the Princess can get the *kumu* to come back to tell you about your mother."

"I am not sure K has much sway. The *kumu* seemed almost dismissive of her. Did I tell you she called the stabbing incidents parlor tricks?"

"You did. But I also know the *kumu* came to you in the first place because K asked; she can ask again." Agnes sat down in a chair next to Letty, holding her own cup of tea. "I feel foolish that we never learned her name."

"True. Well, I must be leaving. This is my last day of help from Timothy, and I need to take full advantage of it."

From the front yard, hoofbeats could be heard. Letty turned to the window, hoping that it was the *kumu*, come back to ease her heart. Instead it was just Timothy.

Today they would take lunch along, as it was Cook's day off. Grabbing the laden saddlebags, she headed through the door. "I may be late today, since I don't have to be back here for a lesson."

She turned to face Agnes directly, fighting back angry tears. "That woman was a fraud. All she taught me to do was breathe."

Agnes came forward, hands on hips. "I have told you I saw many strange things in the outback. Things that could not be explained. Here is what I do know. The stronger the power, the simpler the key to it. I think the *kumu* has given you the key. But you must find your own way to use it."

Letty shrugged and left the room.

As she came down off the porch, Timothy greeted her with a smile. "Is there lunch in those saddlebags? I expect to work up quite an appetite today!"

"Let's get going, then." She should try to smile, but she just couldn't muster it. Even her flames were silent.

Timothy pushed his hat back to wipe the sweat off his brow. His kerchief came away filthy. He was not surprised. The morning had fulfilled its promise: long, dusty, and hot. He and Letty had ridden straight at each other with mallets raised, taking shots as close as possible. Again. And again. And yet again. He was impressed. If the ponies were this steady, they'd do well on the polo field.

They stopped at midday. Letty sank down onto the grass, her fatigue evident.

"Let me get the saddlebags—don't you get up."

She nodded.

"When do you deliver the ponies?"

"Tomorrow. The Willingham brothers want to practice before the match."

"I hope you won't think this out of line, but I suggested to Doc Willingham he hire you to drill the boys. These ponies are rock solid, but even the best can come undone with an unreliable rider."

"No rest for the wicked, apparently. I must admit I am tired. This has been more work than I could have thought."

Tired, hell, she looked absolutely exhausted to his eye.

"Make him pay well, though. You are worth it." He grinned slyly. "Though I daresay your mallet skills have been improved with my own most excellent coaching."

"If I weren't so hungry, I would throw this sandwich at you!"

"Please, no wasting of precious foodstuffs!" They sat in companionable silence as they polished off the customary large lunch. Letty was no prissy miss about food; it was one of the things he enjoyed about her. When you work hard, you need to eat.

She leaned back on her arms to better catch the breeze, her face serene. A pleasant sight, Letty relaxed, wild auburn curls escaping from under her hat, dark lashes resting on her bronzed cheeks. He'd not noticed the light dusting of freckles across her cheeks before, perhaps a gift of this sun-kissed summer. A twinge of regret that he must break the moment poked him. Now was his chance. Now or never.

"What is a *kumu*?"

She sat bolt upright. "I don't think we need to talk about that."

"Maybe if you talk about things, they will make more sense. And I am good at keeping secrets. Like the fact that I see red light around you sometimes."

She sat stock-still for a moment, then turned to face him. "You are serious about keeping secrets, right? Some of this will sound like a crazy person's ramblings. Some of it is even . . . dangerous."

"Cross my heart."

"And you must tell me one of your secrets too! Then we have a deal."

"Back to the danger . . ."

"You said you could see red around me sometimes?"

"Yes. I saw it at the colt's birth and again in the stable the night . . . the night you were attacked." He scarcely got the words out. The thought of what almost happened still gave him nightmares. "I think I may have seen lights the day you saved Diablo too, but I chalked it up to a trick of sunlight glancing off the water. Or maybe your hair!" He smiled at that happier remembrance.

"Of course, my hair." She returned his smile and then continued. "All my life I have been quite . . . impetuous. I get ideas and I just have to act. I can't stop myself. Even if it seems crazy. Especially if it seems crazy." She gave a harsh bark of a laugh. At least he hoped it was a laugh. "You know, like jumping off a ship to save a horse. Who does that?"

"You."

"Well, yes, I did. At any rate, it began when I was a child. I took care of injured animals, like puppies. Mostly they got better." She pinched the bridge of her nose; he had a faint sense she might be warding off tears. "People too. I had a schoolmate who was sickly; others bullied her. I stopped them. I wanted her to be well. The girl began to sit by me. I would hold her hand and walk her home. She got healthier, sturdier. All those times, I felt warmth inside me. Like flames. Now I am told the warmth can be seen by some people. Not everyone. That red light is my aura. It is my *mana'o pono*."

She paused, looked at her hands, then back at him. Her eyes betrayed how desperately she needed him to believe her. "You must think me mad now, right?"

"Letty, I have spent too much time with you to think you're unhinged. This week all I've seen is a practical, hardworking, and talented horsewoman. You are completely level-headed. So, mad? No." He wished he could put an arm around her to give her comfort.

"In our tradition, a person's intentions matter. If your intent is good, things may go one way; if intentions are bad, things may go another. The *kumu* told me that, long ago, women like me were common. The *'āina* gave them gifts, power. The power to make the intentions, the *mana'o*, real. And when this happened, others saw the light surrounding them. This magic, if you want to call it that, died out. No one understands why. But it is coming back."

She took a big breath as if to dive deep. "There are prophecies . . . about princesses lost and princesses found. About Gates. In Hawaiian we say *mākāhā*. Like a sluice gate that opens and closes the flow. The prophecies were thought nothing more than pretty old stories. And then K came back from near death. She is the princess found. Her aura is white like stars. She is a Gate, a *mākāhā*. She can open the power of the *'āina* to the people."

"And what does that make you?"

"I guess I am a Gate too, a gate to bring the power back."

"Are there others?"

"The prophecies say there will be. I think K knows more than I have been told." She shook her head as if to clear the cobwebs. "But to answer your original question, *kumu* means 'teacher.'"

"I knew that; it was just a gambit to startle you into talking." He rolled over on his side and propped his head up on his elbow to study her. "But back to the danger part . . ."

"Do you know what *hapa* means?"

"It means a mixture of things. Don't people mostly use it to refer to a mixture of cultures? Or blood?"

"Yes. You know that K is *hapa*, right? Hawaiian and Scottish. And me too. Hawaiian and Irish on my father's side, and even Hawaiian, Tahitian, and Scottish on my mother's. The old *kāhuna* were angry that K's mother chose a *haole* father for her royal baby, so they sought to make sure the young princess was never queen. But what they did not know is that something about being *hapa* helps bring the magic back. Roaring back, in K's case."

"The danger is the old *kāhuna*?"

"More than that. All those in power, even the *haole* ones. Perhaps most especially the *haole* ones. The men who made sure the Hawaiian kingdom was lost: they've tried to kill our traditions. For a while *hula* was outlawed. The practice of old-fashioned magic is still illegal. I could go to jail."

She turned to recline facing him, her arm supporting her head in a mirror image of his position. "So, this needs to stay my secret."

"We must make sure that no one sees you glowing red in the dark?"

"Something like that."

"Are you frightened?"

She swallowed. "Would you think less of me if I told you I was terrified?"

"I would think less of you if you were *not* terrified. Only a fool faces the unknown without fear."

She rolled over on her back to look up at the sky. "You are not just humoring me? Will you ride away from here thinking what a lunatic I am?"

"Letty, I was there. I have seen this phenomenon three times now, with my own eyes. My mind says this is not possible, but I know what I saw. I must be a believer; I just don't know exactly what it is that I now believe in."

"I don't exactly know either. All the *kumu* taught me was how to breathe. And to be careful what I say when I breathe. Intentions spoken aloud are the most powerful."

"Really? That's it?"

"That's it. No magic wand or abracadabra or anything like that." She stood up with a grace that belied her unusual height. He never tired of watching her move. "It is not even magic exactly. All I do is nudge things along that might happen naturally. Anyway." She clapped her hands together as if to punctuate that this conversation was at its end.

"Shall we train some ponies?"

He would not push for more answers.

"Yes. And I promise to return the favor with a secret or two of my own on the ride home."

The afternoon lengthened. By the time Wu and Jacko came to fetch the ponies, both Timothy and Letty were encased in dust. Timothy was beyond ready to call it a day, but he'd be damned if he let this woman outlast him. Finally Letty called a halt.

Their own horses waited patiently in the shade, tails flicking away the occasional fly. As Letty and Timothy approached,

Diablo, ears swiveling, turned his big head toward Letty. Then he nickered.

"I think he wants a word with you."

She opened her arms to the big stallion. First, he put his head flat against her chest and just leaned in. She laughed, and then lifted his nose up for what looked to be a kiss . . . but this was different. Letty and the horse were nose to nose as if they were breathing together. Then she did kiss Diablo, right in the middle of his nose. Timothy felt a stab of jealousy. Of a horse?

"What was that?"

"That was *honi*, sharing of the breath. Westerners call it kissing, but it is more important than that. You know that breath in Hawaii is sacred? Sharing of breath is a way of bonding."

"Is that something the *kumu* taught you?"

"No, it was K, actually. I stayed with her every summer whenever she came back from Stanford. She taught me the best way to tame a horse was to share its breath. And that it would make you the happiest." She mounted her own horse and settled into the saddle, ready to head out.

Her voice turned bitter. "She knew when I was just a little girl that I would have gifts. Esther and Bull knew too. But no one thought to tell me." She shook her head as if to shake away the thoughts. "Now my dreams are dust."

"Why, Letty?"

"It's a long story, Timothy, and a boring one. Suffice it to say that a woman with secret magical gifts is not likely to become a scientist or a doctor of animals."

She readjusted Rosebud in her sling. "She is getting too big for this. I am going to have to find another way of transporting her." He wanted an answer to his question, but she was clearly not about to deliver it. Maybe he could help her . . . except it was not his business.

"Enough about me. On to *your* secrets. Tell the truth, Lord Rowley: Why are you here?"

"I was hoping you had forgotten that promise."

"Not me—memory like an elephant."

"Well, then. I thought not to tell anyone this, but I will tell you." He ducked his head to buy a moment to think. Interesting that he felt so compelled to have her know the truth. Well, some of it.

"Here is the short version. As I said yesterday, I had a disagreement with my father, a rather large one.

"I am the fourth son of the twenty-second Earl of Colborne. That may not mean much to you, but in England it is quite something. My life was prescribed for me by my father's old-fashioned views: I was destined for either the military or the clergy, neither of which I cared to pursue. I quit Oxford without permission and told my father I intended to become a farmer. I even had a plan to go to agricultural school in Ireland."

Timothy slapped his own face in mock horror.

"What a naive fool I was! Papa flew into a towering rage. No Rowley has ever done anything so common! A farmer! He disowned me on the spot. That was nearly three years ago. Thank goodness my grandmother did not share his prejudices."

"Surely he must forgive you?"

"No, I rather doubt that." He sat in the saddle, looking straight ahead. "We Rowleys are not a forgiving sort."

"But you came here with pigs . . ."

"That was all my grandmother's doing. At the time I thought she was testing me. Now I know that she wanted to give me a chance at a new life away from my father. Far away."

"How old are you?"

"Isn't that a frightfully rude question?"

"May I remind you, you owe me a secret."

"I am twenty-two."

She stopped her horse. He had to turn back to see her. "Why, you are barely older than I am!"

"Yes, but I am the very model of modern maturity!" He swept off his hat, somehow slightly annoyed that she had thought him so old.

They continued down the road without further conversation.

At the turnoff to 'Āinahau, Letty gave him a snappy salute. "Thank you for all your help, kind sir!" And then more seriously, "I really could not have done this without you."

"You're welcome. This is nothing compared to what you have done for me. I have you to thank for the lives of this fine gentleman and that young one and his mama back at the ranch." He wished to say more, to thank her for the gift of her friendship, for being someone whom he trusted with the truth. He so rarely shared anything about himself.

"All in a day's work! By the way, Diablo told me he wants his own herd of mares. He had quite a good time at Willingham's but prefers to avoid steamship travel in the future."

Timothy reached forward to pat Diablo's neck. "Point taken, old man." He straightened up to turn back to Letty with a smile.

"Thanks to your good counsel, I did a bit of horse trading. I got that pretty little mare you saw me riding. Likely already in foal to Diablo, I might add. And a handsome fee. And then the pick of the foals when they arrive. Doc Willingham thinks there will be eight to choose from."

"Good for you! I'm impressed."

He basked for a moment in the warmth of the compliment. The she jerked him back to reality when she took her leave. He was going to miss her. Greatly.

"I will see you soon, Timothy. Certainly at the match! Take care."

"A hui hou!" He sat motionless, watching her canter down the lane without so much as a look back. It was ridiculous to be disappointed. Diablo pawed restively as if to follow, Timothy reining the stallion gently back. "Now, now, old man, we will see her again, I am sure." But it might never be the same. Working side by side. Like colleagues or partners or friends.

At least he could be thankful he had not blurted out more about his family. Or the accident. Good god, not the accident. Letty might never understand about the accident.

Chapter Sixteen

Hoʻokūkū

CONTEST

Kapiʻolani Park, Oahu, the 1st of August, 1909

With a hand carefully placed across her brow, Letty gazed down the field searching for Timothy. She could just make out the slashes of white that signified the players, moving to and fro. It made absolutely no sense. For polo—the messiest of sports—the players wore pure white breeches. Yes, they cut quite dashing figures as they paraded out onto the field. But the effect was only temporary. Dirt would rule the day.

A barricade made up of carriages, both horsed and horse-less, surrounded the field. Anyone and everyone who fancied themselves as anybody in Hawaiian high society attended today. And the rest of Honolulu had come out to see them. Ladies in huge feathered hats and gents in black bowlers. The Willinghams planned a fancy-dress ball this evening. Invitations were limited and highly prized. More than a few of these elegant matrons would concoct excuses why they would not be in attendance. "I wasn't invited" would never be confessed.

Letty stood with Liam, a death grip on her parasol. Agnes insisted she put on a few ladylike airs for this rarified crowd. Not to mention keeping her freckles from getting worse. Still, she wore her most discreet divided skirt, just in case the horses needed her.

Today her six ponies would prove themselves . . . or not. She'd done what she could, but the game would be the true test. Only, polo was not a game; it was more like a war.

"Sister mine, stop worrying. Your babies will make you proud. Old man Willingham has already declared them to be the best polo string he has ever seen."

"But what if he was just being nice, Liam? And isn't this the first polo string he has seen? His boys just took up the sport!"

"Doc Willingham is never that sort of 'nice,' Letty. Anyway, the game is all just crazy men racing around with sticks, trying to hit a ball. How hard is that?"

"Maybe . . ."

The Willingham boys formed the core of the Oahu team. Timothy would join them as a "guest" along with an American friend of his. The Maui players were older: the Letwin brothers from their ranch near Haleakalā, also joined by visitors to Hawaii, most likely college chums over from the mainland.

Letty took a notion to inspect the competing horseflesh, walking the tether lines. The Letwin ponies were at the far end.

"Lanky Lang!"

Letty's smiling face almost split in two as she whirled about in greeting.

"Lucky Letwin!"

The young women engaged in a most unladylike hug, then pulled apart, laughing. Letty picked her parasol back up, humming with pleasure at seeing such an old friend. Of course Lokelani was here with her family to watch her brothers play. And likely destined to be the belle of the ball tonight!

"And how have you enjoyed college?"

"Mostly very well. I hated the weather off island, but I loved my botanical studies. And those college boys!"

Lokelani must be breaking hearts. All womanly curves. A hint of her Hawaiian grandmother's dusky coloring combined with the dark blond hair and hazel eyes of her New England missionary forebears. Lokelani turned heads wherever she went. Letty had always felt like a towering, gawky giraffe next to her. She still did.

"Do you believe it? They won't let me play polo! I ride better than any of them, and always have!"

"I will be sure to write a letter to the editor of the *Honolulu Star* about the terrible injustice. Not only are women deprived of the right to vote, we can't play polo! Oh, the tragedy of it all!"

"You know they would never publish it! We must start our own newspaper!" Lokelani gave a conspiratorial grin. "By the way, I heard you trained the Willingham ponies—is that true? You have always had an amazing way with the horses. I will not forget the summer we were at Princess K's together!"

"Yes, I did train the Oahu ponies. That means we are on opposing sides for this game, methinks!"

"And you still read those awful romance novels?"

"I have branched out to include biology books, but yes."

"And still saving sorry abandoned animals?"

"Always and forever! I am hoping to become a doctor of veterinary medicine."

"Well, if anyone can pull off a big dream, it will be you. I also understand you have now taken up high diving off the interisland steamer."

Letty looked down at her hands, work worn and callused. So unlike Lokelani's soft, manicured ones.

How might she explain? "I had to do it, you know. I am not the sort of person who does crazy things, but sometimes I just feel I must act."

Lokelani grasped her hand. "I am not surprised. Even at school, you were always the one to help others." She squeezed Letty's hand before dropping it. "Enough seriousness—would you like to come over and meet our team? I know Hugh would like to see you." She scanned the crowd. "Is that Liam? He has become quite the giant."

Letty could not even form a response before Lokelani began to drag her across the tether lines. "Let's go—these men are absolutely parched for our sage advice."

"Hugh, you remember Lanky Lang, don't you?"

Hugh turned with a smile, his brother Samuel doing the same. There were two other fellows—both with dark hair and blue eyes. She was taller than either of them. Probably the mainlanders she'd heard about.

"Miss Lang! You have grown! I dare say you are even more worthy of the Lanky moniker than before! Has it been four years since we've crossed paths? Let me introduce you. This is John Tennyson, joining us from Virginia. He was my roommate at Princeton." Tennyson shook her hand, holding it a bit longer than necessary. "And this is Charles Payne Whitten. His father has a polo field in New York." Hugh appeared to relish delivering this tidbit. "Gentlemen, this is Miss Leticia Lang, otherwise known as Lanky. You can see why."

Letty held out her hand to Whitten but was ignored. Awkward, to say the least. Lokelani, however, was not deterred.

"If you lose today, you will have Letty to thank. She trained the Willingham string."

Mr. Whitten responded, Ivy League roots evident in his voice. "How nice. I wondered where they got those scrubs."

Letty might swallow an insult to herself, but not to her ponies. "Those 'scrubs,' as you call them, are descendants of King Kamehameha's horses, the royal mustangs. They will run between the legs of your big lugs. Beware."

Hugh stepped in with a grin. "You may be right, Miss Lang. We will let the ponies speak for themselves out on the field."

Lokelani took Letty's arm. "Lovely to see you, gentlemen. Play well." Sarcasm dripped from the word "gentlemen."

Strolling away, Letty still heard the voices behind. "That is just how we like 'em in Virginia: tall, dark, and fiery." Her back stiffened. Hugh replied, "Have some class, lad. How do you know she is not my cousin?" Then, laughter.

Letty knew better than to respond. She'd dealt with such idiots in California. Nothing she could say would counter their belief that because of her gender and the color of her skin they were entitled to treat her like a lesser being.

"Come meet the Oahu team," she said.

Lokelani kept her arm linked with Letty as they walked. "You are a sport, Letty. Thank you for not taking that bait. And by the way, I am most eager to meet your English lord. I have heard he is quite divine."

Timothy paced as they approached, his limp only slightly evident. Letty's heart soared at the sight of him. Had it only been a week? Rather it seemed like forever. The man looked quite dashing in his snow-white breeches. His shirt displayed the flower of Oahu, the yellow *'ilima*, on a blue background. She thought it much nicer than the Maui colors, the pink wild rose on gray. Timothy's broad shoulders only enhanced the effect.

The entire Oahu team was gathered. The Willingham brothers—Brett and Franklin—she'd known since childhood. The fourth member of the team had only recently arrived: Carleton Bourne, Timothy's American roommate from his English prep school days. A Texan, to be precise. And a renowned polo player. The Willingham boys were awestruck to be playing with him.

Timothy hurried over, grabbing both of her hands, his eyes alight. Her heart skipped a beat, her flames a happy tickle up her spine. "The boys and the ponies are ready. Really ready! You've worked miracles, Letty. Oahu can win this match!"

"I hope so! Timothy, may I introduce my friend Lokelani Letwin? We went to Sacred Heart together before I left for San Francisco."

Timothy turned to Lokelani with a smile. *Hmmmmm.* Letty's flames flared. This could not be jealousy. Could it? Those looks . . . and Lucky fit the rich heiress model Timothy said his family demanded. Nonsense. How silly to be jealous, since she and Timothy were only friends. And could only be friends.

"Miss Lang, might I have the pleasure of a dance at tonight's celebration?" Carleton's English-accented Texas drawl flowed like syrup.

"Oh, we won't be attending." She bit her tongue before she added that she was not invited.

"But you must come!" Lokelani dimpled prettily. "It will not be a party without you!"

How sweet of Lokelani. But pointless anyway, as Letty had no dress. She did not even know what had become of her beautiful gown since the "incident."

"No, truly, I'll be joining my family this evening." A commitment to your *'ohana* was always the graceful way out. "But you will join the Ladies' Ride today, won't you, Lokelani? You must see the Princess's hat! She has quite outdone herself with the feathers."

"That I will." Lokelani gave her hair a toss. "You gentlemen will see the best of island horsemanship when the Hawaiian Ladies' Riding Society takes the field!"

Letty watched the tanned creases of good humor surround his eyes as Timothy's smile deepened, his full attention focused on Lokelani. "I have seen Letty handle a horse or two, and if she is any example, the Ladies' Ride will be the best show of the day. I trust your own horsemanship is of the same caliber."

The trickle of flames reignited. Letty began a count. No, perhaps breathing might be better. There was no point in jealousy anyway, since Timothy was not for her. No one was. Ever. If Kahōkūlani was to be believed.

Carleton bowed. "Well, if you change your mind, Miss Lang, I am at your service. Timothy is hauling me off to his rancho this week. Perhaps I shall see you there."

"Play well today, gentlemen!"

CHAPTER SEVENTEEN

Paomoni

MAKE WAR

"LADIES!" Letty thought it possible Kahōkūlani's voice could be heard for miles. "For today's ride, *everyone* will wrap *pāʻū* in the traditional way. That means ropes tied *tight* around your waist, ladies! Discomfort means it is done correctly! Nothing must come loose!"

Letty's own rope cut, so it must be right. At least she knew her red overskirt was snug in place. With luck she would be able to breathe. And she knew the importance of breathing.

Princess K stalked up and down the line of women like a general marshaling her troops. Well, perhaps the women of the Hawaiian Ladies' Riding Society *were* her troops. Although no mere military man could carry off the enormous feathered hat Kahōkūlani wore today. The long peacock feathers flashed behind the Princess as she walked. Letty ducked to avoid getting whacked.

She went back to wrapping Sophia with her calico, a vibrant yellow for Oahu. After Letty gave one particularly strong tug on the rope, Sophia grunted. "That's quite tight enough. I may never get this thing untied as it is. I'd rather wear a corset."

"We are suffragists, we don't wear corsets."

"You tell my mother that."

"LADIES! MOUNT UP!" Kahōkūlani clapped for attention as Letty followed orders. There were perhaps fifty riders, not only the yellow of Oahu but in almost every other island color as well. Pink for Maui, which Lokelani wore, Letty's own red for Hawaii Island, purple for Kauai with the green *mokihana* berry, orange for Lānai, and green for Molokai. As the horses danced with impatience, the overskirts began to swirl. Letty rested her hand on Captain's shoulder to calm him, then reached back to be certain her own "Votes for Women" saddlecloth was secure.

"Today we ride for tradition! *Nā wāhine holo lio!* Just like the queens of old! And today we ride for the future! Votes for all! A strong and prosperous Hawaii for our children and our children's children! Votes for women!"

Peacock feathers bobbing, the Princess wheeled her big stallion, Kāhili, into position at the head of the cavalcade. He reared at her command, his own feathered feet flying.

"We ride! *Nā wāhine holo lio!*"

"*Nā wāhine holo lio!*" The cry was fifty female voices strong.

Kahōkūlani urged Kāhili into an immediate gallop, the Hawaiian Ladies' Riding Society right behind. A dancing wave of flowers and color erupted onto the polo grounds. The crowd went crazy.

The plan was for the Princess and her ladies to take just one turn around the field. But the exhilaration of the moment won out. The riders crossed back and forth along the spectator barricades to deafening cheers. Eager hands reached out to touch the women. If the riders had been any less skilled, this might not have gone so well.

Finally, Kahōkūlani pulled everyone up at the far end of the field, doing her best to put together a kind of line. The Princess glanced left to right, then waved the way forward. *Nā wāhine holo lio!* Kāhili leaped out again at a full gallop. A wild rainbow on horseback followed.

Letty gave herself over to whooping and hollering. She was not alone.

The ladies streamed off the field as the crowd screamed and clapped.

Was that a tiny bit of K's white aura that Letty saw gleaming?

Over on the edge of the field, one of the Maui players cornered an official. All while pointing madly toward the women.

The Princess rode over to take stock, returning with her head shaking. "Apparently, in New York, where this man claims to be an important personage, they do not allow 'peasant women' to ride hither and yon and make 'difficulties' for the men. He believes we have messed up 'his' polo field." Kahōkūlani snorted. "Yes, he said 'peasant women'—I heard it with my own ears." She dismounted and began removing her *pā'ū*. "I certainly hope they send that chap back to where he came from. Posthaste."

Letty's exhilaration faded. She'd not liked the feel of that Maui player, Whitten, when she met him. Timothy told her that his sort of polo was a game of war, rough and dangerous. She could only hope that no agitated player made it worse.

She'd be glad when the game was over.

Letty stood with Liam, George, and Agnes behind one of the wagons near the south goal. Her brother thumped her on the back so hard she could scarcely breathe. "Your ponies are doing great, old girl! They make the riders look like centaurs!" He did a little *hula* move. *Really,* she thought, *he is too old for this. But I love him for it anyway.*

"That Maui team was supposed to wipe our boys up and down the field. And look at this! Tied going into the fourth chukka. I bet we win this thing. Rowley is that stubborn."

"How would you know, Liam?"

"Oh, I just know. Men can sense these things about each other."

George snorted. "At any rate, we are likely to sell some more horses after this. Thanks to you, Letty." She appreciated the accolade from her father.

The horn sounded for the final chukka to begin. Except it didn't.

Timothy shook his head. That Maui player, the one from New York, was out of control. Whitten had been called twice for fouls. Each time he'd overridden the line of the ball in a way that nearly unseated another player. It was beyond dangerous in a sport well known for its danger.

Now the referee held up the start of the fourth and final chukka. He cornered Whitten and proceeded to give him quite a reprimand. Not that it did any good. Whitten just made a dismissive gesture as he rode back to his team.

"Timothy, I can't believe we are tied with these fellows!" Brett, the youngest of the Willingham boys, mounted on Apple, fairly levitated with excitement.

Timothy elected to ride Percy for the final chukka. The gelding bounced a bit, restive and eager for the battle. Every one of Letty's string performed well; that woman could train horses for sure. But still, this horse was special.

Carleton rode up behind him. "That Whitten chap has a hell of a temper. If we score again, I'd watch out for dirty tricks."

"Agreed." Timothy turned to take his place on the field. "I have a bad feeling about this."

The horn sounded once more; this time the chukka began. Maui took control of the ball right off but overshot. Timothy whipped Percy about to capture the ball. Quickly he slipped the ball to Carleton, who slammed it in for an Oahu goal.

The hometown cheering section exploded. Timothy readied Percy for the next play. For whatever reason, Whitten harangued the referee. Again. A nasty temper, that. Timothy shrugged and the ball came back into play.

Maui went on the offensive, but this time Brett on Apple undercut Whitten, neatly carving the ball away and passing it to Timothy.

Timothy had Maui defenders on all sides. Any shot would be tough. Maui thought they had him boxed. Behind the Maui line, Brett maneuvered Apple in a tight circle; he'd have a straight run for the goal. A whisper of space opened up between Hugh and Whitten. With a savage grin, Timothy pivoted Percy to make the unexpected pass back to Brett.

Brett and Apple went all out in a run for the goal. Whitten spurred his horse madly to try to block the attempt but failed. With a loud and satisfying crack, Brett made the goal, effectively shutting out Whitten and any chance for Maui to recover.

With a roar, Whitten rode his horse right into Brett and Apple. Only Apple's quick sidestep saved them. The crowd was silenced by the sheer audacity of this, as Whitten turned back toward Brett, mallet raised.

Timothy aimed Percy like a rocket toward Brett. He did not see Whitten's mallet drop, but heard it connect. If horses could scream, that was most assuredly the sound he heard. The melee parted. *Oh my god.* Apple was down. The bastard must have hit her. Intentionally. Brett stood clear as every other rider surrounded them. He looked dazed. Then he dropped to one knee to comfort Apple.

Everything happened all at once. A streak with flying red hair raced across the field to throw herself on the little mare. The referee put his horse chest to chest with Whitten to force him back and away. Whitten screamed, "This is a farce! He was cheating! They were all cheating!" From nowhere, Bull and Chen Zhou appeared on foot, bullwhips drawn, heading right for Whitten. A crack of one whip and then another.

"Off your horse—you are under arrest."

"I will not dismount for a darkie and a Chinaman. Hugh, help me here." Hugh turned his back on Whitten, instead moving to help Brett with Apple.

"I said dismount. I am an officer of the law." Chen walked up close to Whitten. The fool raised his mallet as if to strike at the detective.

"Don't you dare touch me!" Whitten screamed. The bullwhip cracked. Whitten hit the ground. The crowd roared its approval.

Timothy's attention flew back to Letty and Apple. The mare's left front leg was extended at an unnatural angle. A broken leg for a horse was a death sentence. The young woman lay sprawled on the ground, arms wrapped around the horse's neck, crooning to her. Letty's eyes were wild, her red aura pulsing, visible to him even in the bright sunlight. His gut clenched at Letty's anguish. Timothy leaped off Percy, tossing the reins to one of Willingham's grooms.

"I can't help her—this cannot heal!"

Timothy put a hand on each of her shoulders, heat arcing into his fingertips. He squeezed. Hard. "Remember what you told me. What the *kumu* said. Breathe. You can give comfort. *Breathe!*"

Under his hands Letty fought for control. Her breathing slowed, and somehow it translated to the little mare. She whispered her intention. "Be calm, sweet one, be at peace." Apple's struggling ceased.

Brett knelt next to Apple, openly weeping.

Doc Willingham jogged across the field dangling a pistol. Timothy leaned into Letty again. "Listen to me—you know you cannot mend this, right? Doc is here and will take her out of her misery." Timothy loosed his hands from her shoulders and stepped back.

"Her pain is so great—I can feel it." Letty's breathing remained controlled, but she shivered with the strain. Dear Apple now lay completely quiet. The mare breathed slow and deep in line with Letty's own breathing.

Willingham stood behind her. "Letty, you must move. I don't want to hit you."

Letty moved down the horse's neck but not completely away. "I need to keep my hands on her. You're a crack shot; just do it."

The bullet killed the mare instantly. Letty clung to her, still shivering, but made no sound. Her aura winked out.

The hair went up on Timothy's neck when Percy and the other ponies in the string began to neigh. Other horses joined them.

Letty stayed prostrate over Apple's body. Doc Willingham leaned down to touch her shoulder. "Get up, my dear; it is over."

Timothy slipped his hands under her arms to lift her to her feet. One of the Willingham grooms brought Timothy's jacket to wrap around her. She'd gone from flaming hot to freezing cold. He kept a hand on her elbow to keep her from falling.

"I failed. I could not heal her. I felt her die." Her voice was flat, like death itself.

Without a thought he pulled her close and rocked her like a baby. She went nearly boneless in his arms. "It's all right. You gave her comfort in the end. I know you did; I saw you breathing." Letty began shaking uncontrollably.

"Let us take her."

Timothy lifted his head as Agnes and George flanked him on either side. He was loathe to let her go. But what right had he to hold her?

Agnes freed Letty from his arms and the jacket. George stepped in to fully support her weight. "We are here, sweetheart."

Letty staggered as George led her away.

"Keep breathing, Letty!" Timothy called after her, but either she did not hear or did not care. This was not his place. So why did he feel like part of his heart was being carried across the field with her?

He turned back. One of the grooms threw a blanket over Apple's still form. More than this match was over. Much more.

Chapter Eighteen

Uwē waimaka

CRY TEARS

Letty woke up in the haze of uncertain dreams, the comforting warmth of Rosebud tucked tight up against her stomach. She stretched, only to discover something largish at the foot of her bed. Startled, she sat up to see the *kumu* calmly sitting there. The pain came rolling back in a deep wave. Failure. Apple gone. Her flames quenched.

"I thought I might come back if you needed me. I did not expect it to be so soon," the *kumu* said.

"I failed. This is no good."

"You did not fail. Sometimes life fails. Sometimes evil happens, because there are bad things in the world. But in the end, you did what you were born to do: you opened the way for the *'āina*. You gave your fire. The mare was comforted even though she could not be healed."

"How do you know?" Letty felt the rancor in her voice like acid.

"I have my ways." The *kumu* patted her foot through the blanket. "Plus I had a fine conversation with your stepmother."

The tiny woman stood and began to pace. "If anyone has failed, it is me. You will always choose to be the warrior; you cannot help yourself. I know this. Here is what I did not teach you. When you feel the flames rising, you must heed their call. Always. The *'āina* cannot be denied. Do not fight it. Begin your breathing right away. Every time. It may not change the outcome, but it will protect you."

She stopped pacing, looking straight ahead but not at Letty. "You were connected to the mare when she died, were you not?"

Letty buried her face in her hands. She recalled the pain, the sound of the bullet, the flash of the mare's awareness, then nothing. It was the nothing that was the worst part, the sense of complete absence of the bright spirit that was Apple.

"Listen to me, child. The outcome was the outcome. If the mare could have been healed, your fire would have made it so. But that was not to be. Yet you did not fail—you were there for her at the very end."

She sat back on the edge of the bed and pulled Letty's hands away from her face, holding them tight. "Breathe with me now. You can comfort yourself—did you know that?"

Letty gave herself over to the pattern of the breathing. Time seemed to suspend. Her flames lent a soothing warmth. The *kumu* dropped her hands and said softly, "How do you feel?"

Letty blinked. "Oddly better. I am still sad and angry, but somehow more peaceful."

"In ancient times, these things were part of a warrior's training. A warrior who acted from a clear mind and therefore clear intention was all the more powerful." She leaned forward and gently brushed Letty's hair from her face. "You are such a warrior, my child. All I ask is that you care for yourself as you care for others."

Then she said, "I must go."

"Aren't you going to tell me about my mother?"

"It is not time."

The *kumu* moved soundlessly from the room. Until a ruckus erupted in the kitchen when Agnes demanded she identify herself by name. Then all went quiet. Agnes came through the door with a laden tray of food. Letty found her appetite had returned.

"Did you get her name and address?"

"Of course not!" Agnes slammed the tray down so hard that the dishes rattled. "She said, 'No, that is not possible,' as if she always gets the last word. Then she stood on tiptoes to kiss me on the forehead, told me the baby was going to be a boy, and sashayed out! I was too dumbfounded to argue."

Rosebud leaped down to dance on her hind legs. "Well, at least the little beast pays attention to me," Agnes wheedled. "Here, sweet doggie, have a bite of ham. On that note, I shall head back to the kitchen."

"Stop right there. What baby will be a boy? Are you expecting?" She stood up and drew closer to Agnes.

"I have not told your father yet, as he worries, but yes, I think I am. Give me your hand."

Agnes placed Letty's hand on her belly. It was subtle, but she could feel it, the growth of new life. "I think you are too," Letty said. "Are you excited?"

"Yes." Agnes rested both hands protectively on her belly. "I wish Hannah were a little older, but you cannot always pick these things." She looked up at Letty. "Do you think she really knows? That it's a boy?"

Letty shrugged. "Well, she has at least half a chance of being right!"

A few hours later, the florist's wagon pulled up in front of the house. The driver emerged with a huge box and headed to the front door.

Johnny was first to answer. "May I help you?"

The man smiled. "I have a parcel for Miss Leticia Lang. Is this the right place?"

"Yes, sir, it is."

"Johnny, what is this?" Letty came out the door with the scampering Rosebud at her feet.

"You are getting something! In a big, big box!"

Letty signed for the parcel and then took it in her arms. "Shall we go inside and see what it is?"

The blue ribbon took a few moments to untie. All the while Johnny jiggled from foot to foot in eagerness. Pulling off the lid, Letty glimpsed a mass of flowers through the tissue paper. A letter addressed to Miss Leticia Lili'uokalani Lang in assertive masculine script lay at the top. Letty opened the letter carefully, hoping it was not another emotional shock of some kind. She already felt so empty.

Dear Letty,

I must return home early this morning, but I wanted you to have a token of my admiration for your bravery and skill. You are the best friend a horse could ever have. I hope I may count myself as your friend as well.

There are six leis here, one to honor each of the exceptional ponies you trained. Of course the red roses are for dear Apple.

Thank you for letting me be a part of their training. I am sorry that this "experiment" of yours had a sad ending. But please do not let that be all you remember.

*I know you are a warrior. You will, as they say, live to
fight another day.*

Respectfully yours,
Timothy Moran Rowley

*p.s. I bought Percy from Willingham. How could I not
have Lord Blakeney in my stables? His lei is the green
orchid...*

Letty pulled the tissue aside. As the smell of the flowers
exploded out of the box, her tears began. Ginger, *pikake*, sweet
orchid and, of course, the roses. She slipped to the ground with
great, gasping sobs.

"Mama, Mama, come quick! Flowers are making Letty
cry!"

With a swish of skirts, Agnes came into the room, surrounding Letty with the warmth of her arms. "Cry, child,
goodness knows you need it. I don't know how you have made
it so long without a good cry." Agnes began to gently rock and
croon as she held Letty tight.

"I miss my mother."

"Of course you do."

"So much is happening. I can't figure it out. I don't know
who I am anymore."

"Some people never know who they are. You will discover
it, I know."

"What if I don't like what I discover?"

"Well then, change it."

"I wish it were that simple. I wish the magic would just go
away."

Agnes stopped rocking and gave her a fierce hug. "Whatever
you discover, in the end it will only be true if it embraces all of
you. The gift is part of you now. I know you will find a way."

Agnes planted a kiss on the back of Letty's neck as she stood up. Then she reached for the box. "We need to get these leis on you." She rifled through its contents. "Somebody has very good taste. These are beautiful."

"Timothy sent them."

Letty handed the letter to Agnes, who quickly scanned it, eyebrows rising. "Rowley is a bit old for you, I think. Is there anything going on that your father and I should know?"

"That is not what this is about. We became friends working with the ponies. Anyway, he is only twenty-two."

"Certainly. Friends. If you say so . . ."

Timothy began his afternoon ride home before the steamer cleared Hilo Harbor on its way back to Honolulu. Carleton remained in Honolulu for a few more nights, then would follow for his visit. The old chap said he had to rest up from the aftermath of the polo match. Or it might have been the lovely widow from Waimanolo Carleton met at the Willinghams' ball. The Texan had not changed a bit since their days at school.

Timothy was eager to get home. Champagne, stabled with friends in town, was raring to go. Even tired as he was, Timothy loved riding west over the saddle ridge between the Mauna Kea and Mauna Loa as the day lazed toward sunset.

He longed to be home for a bit. Except that Letty was several islands away. He'd miss working by her side. More than that, he'd miss her.

As Timothy rode into the stable yard, Hank Smith—the real Hank Smith, thank goodness—came out to greet him. Sunset neared, the violet twilight deepening.

"Let me take him, sir—I am sure it has been a long journey." That was true: six hours on the steamer, then four hours for the ride over the saddle. "You might want to peek into Sunflower's stall. She is a good mother, and Lohiʻau is curled up next to her like a lamb."

As Timothy walked into the stable, Diablo's great head emerged over the stall door. "Hello, old man." Timothy went to give him a rub under his chin. Diablo sniffed his jacket like a hunting dog on the scent. Of course, this was the jacket he'd wrapped around Letty at the polo match.

"She is just fine. I promise. I took good care of her. At least I tried." He hoped that his gift of the flowers was not too presumptuous. He would do anything to ease her grief. As if anything could or would. The stallion went back to his bucket of oats.

He moved on to Sunflower's stall. The mare slept peacefully with Lohiʻau curled up next to her stomach. He struggled to think the colt was only a few months old; so much had happened. Odd, really, that it all swirled around Letty. And always because the woman could not seem to avoid heroics. Strong. He'd never met anyone like her. The memory of holding her after Apple was shot haunted him. Waves of her pain and sorrow washing into him. With heat and the sparkle of flame.

Timothy shook the memories off to head back to the bunkhouse for a glass of claret and his comfortable bed. God help him, was he becoming his father?

CHAPTER NINETEEN

Ma hope

AFTER

Letty saddled up for her morning ride to the training stables. Liam would meet her there; she was thankful for his help. Still she missed Timothy's steadfast presence. The green orchid lei had lasted the longest, and today she wore it, drinking in the rare orchid scent. Redolent of the rare man thoughtful enough to have sent it.

She'd see him once again at the Cup, that was certain. It seemed foolhardy to write to him, but so many things happened each and every day that she'd like to share. So instead she wrote sparingly, hoping at least to maintain the friendship. That was all it was, certainly, all it could ever be.

Besides, she had work to do. Word spread that the Lang polo ponies were exceptional; George received a number of inquiries. Letty was grateful to find training the perfect distraction from all the things she'd rather not think about. Like magic that had failed her. Her fantasy of veterinary school. Or a certain sandy-haired Englishman.

Clatters and a bang announced a motorcar coming into the yard. A well-dressed man with slicked-back hair alighted. He began walking around the yard as if he owned the place. Letty stepped out of the stable with the saddled Sheba behind her. "May I help you, sir?"

"Yes, is George Lang here? I will be taking over this property soon and wish to review a few things."

Letty felt as if she had been slapped. A few days ago, Papa told her that "things" had been taken care of. Not so.

Agnes appeared on the porch. "Why, Mr. Gannon, what a surprise! I will call George." She gave Letty a significant look. "Letty, you should head out—Wu and Liam will be waiting for you."

"Let me get Rosebud." Now that the dog was too big to ride in a sling, Wu had rigged up a wicker basket behind Letty's saddle. The little princess rode in style, nose out to catch every scent on the wind.

Letty took her time settling Rosebud into her basket. With her back to the scene unfolding on the porch, she could listen discreetly.

"Why, Gannon, we have three more days yet. What are you doing here?" George said.

"I just want to be sure you understand the terms, Lang. You and your family need to vacate the premises by midnight on the date in the contract. Anything you leave behind becomes my property."

"That is mighty inconvenient, Gannon, as we have horses to train for the Gentleman's Cup. We race every year. It is quite an occasion."

"I don't think you understand. This will be my property, lock, stock, and barrel. I take possession on that date."

"We'll see about that, Gannon. What I do know is you will never be invited to ride in any *gentleman's* race. You don't qualify."

Mounting up, Letty turned to watch. Her father leaned against a porch pillar with an amazing degree of nonchalance. Agnes had gone back inside.

Letty trotted out of the yard, head spinning. Her *'ohana* had been on this land for generations. She could not imagine another home.

The four ponies were saddled and ready. And five more horses Letty had not seen before in the paddock. If she had to keep up this training pace, she *really* wished Rowley would come back. For any number of reasons; some she preferred not to think too much about. She'd posted another friendly note to him this morning. Friendly, that was the key.

"Wu, what is this?" Letty asked, pointing to the extra horses.

"I bring down the two-year-olds. Mr. George say we start more ponies since people want horses Miss Letty train. Make hay while sun shines, he say!" Wu shuffled a bit then said, "Mr. George, he come this afternoon, he say."

"Okay, we will look at the young ones when he arrives. Liam, what do you think, figure-eight drills? Maybe some back and forth?"

"Yes, ma'am. At your service."

When they stopped for lunch a few hours later, Letty took the chance to talk to her brother with Wu out of earshot. "Liam, have you heard of a man by the name of Gannon?"

"He is some kind of loan shark. Why?"

"He was visiting Papa today. Papa told me he had borrowed money, but this seems serious."

"What can we do?"

"Papa will be here this afternoon; maybe we can corner him. I'd like to know what is happening."

"Me too."

The opportunity for discussion came on the ride home. Letty and Liam rode on either side of their father. Liam cleared his throat. They'd agreed he would broach the topic.

"Letty said there was a visitor at the house today. A man by the name of Gannon. I have heard a bit about him. Why was he calling?"

George looked startled, then gave Letty an angry glare. "What have you told Liam?"

"That I was worried. And that I wanted to help." Her heartbeat raced. She had never liked challenging her father.

"It is none of your business, either of you."

Liam angrily spun his horse toward his father. "With all respect, Papa, you have that wrong. Letty has worked her tail off all summer. I work in our business too. We are your partners! Your *'ohana*! We have a right!"

George stopped Captain, then looked down to collect himself. "Letty knows the essence of it. Hasn't she told you?"

"You told me not to tell, Papa, so I did not."

"Here is the thing, Liam. I borrowed some money . . . from this Gannon fellow. He turned out to be quite a sharp character. But I have now consulted with experts. It will all turn out well."

Letty exploded. "What is that supposed to mean, Papa? That we are to pretend that nothing serious is going on? I heard the man say we must move out in three days! I heard him!" This time tendrils of flame shot up her spine.

"Letty, you did not tell me that! Papa! What the hell! What do we do?"

George kicked Captain forward. "That is enough, Liam. Here is what you *will* do. You will trust me to handle it. And, *under no circumstances* will you discuss this with anyone. Either of you. Period. End of story."

As George pulled ahead, Liam began to speak, but Letty shook her head. She mouthed one word: "Home."

As they entered the yard, Mālama came flying out of the house with Hannah on her hip. "Mr. George! Come quick! Missy Agnes, she fall!"

George leaped off Captain, throwing his reins to Tanaka. Letty followed, racing into the house one step behind her father. Mālama led them down the long hall at the rear of the house. Agnes lay on the floor at the bottom of the back stairs, but she tried to lift herself up when she heard the commotion.

"Missy, no move! No move!" Mālama somehow kept hold of Hannah as she knelt beside Agnes.

"The damned stairway tripped me, George!"

George stooped down to lift her. Mālama reached out to stop him. "No move!"

At that moment, Letty noticed a dark and growing stain on Agnes's *holokū*. "Papa, back away. Let me in." Her flames flared.

"I don't want to lose him." Agnes's eyes went wide, wet with unshed tears. She grasped Letty's hand and squeezed. "Letty, you must help me! I want to keep this baby!"

"I don't know . . ." All that went through her mind was that she had failed to save dear Apple . . . that her gift was a fraud . . . that she might harm those she loved.

"Put your hands on me! Start your breathing! Stop fighting your power!"

"Take Hannah." Mālama shoved the little girl into Liam's arms. The child started to fuss as he jiggled her. "George, you hold shoulders." Mālama likely better understood what was happening than Letty did.

Kneeling next to Agnes, Letty entered one of her breathing rituals, a calming one. Instinctively she reached out to place both hands on Agnes's belly, closing her eyes. Mālama placed strong hands on the small of Letty's back. "I help. You *mākāhā*. I help." The woman's words were a soft whisper as

Letty dropped into the sensations. Chaos, redness, light. Letty pushed a wave of calmness and peace through her hands. The heat from Mālama's hands burned into her back, lending her unexpected strength. Letty's own flames burned strong and steady. *Breathe in, breathe out. Pause. Breathe in, breathe out. Pause . . .*

Agnes gave a relieved sigh. "Letty, whatever you are doing, don't stop. The pain is gone and things seem right."

A quieting flowed through her hands. The life sputtering only moments before now seemed strong and sure. Keeping her eyes closed, she continued her breathing, afraid to stop.

Mālama pulled away. "All good now. Good you come home. Good you let me help."

"I did not know you could. Thank you, Mālama."

Agnes lay still. "I can tell it's fine now. You are such a blessing, child." She reached to grasp Letty's hand on her belly. "You can stop."

Letty fell on top of her, crying and hugging. "I felt it. The baby. I love you, Agnes."

"Don't crush me, sweetheart. And I love you too." Her hand tenderly brushed Letty's cheek.

"George, take me to our room. I need to get cleaned up."

"I did not know you were expecting again." He scooped the small woman off the floor.

As he carried her toward the bedroom, she rallied. "There are lots of things you don't know, my darling." With that, she looked back to give Letty a big wink.

Liam handed Hannah back to Mālama. "On that note, I am going to go see what Cook is making for dinner." He took Letty by the arm in courtly fashion to pull her up. "And you, sister mine, are coming with me. A little bird told me you have to eat after one of these 'breathing' spells."

Letty leaned heavily on his arm. "Yes, I do."

Letty woke to find herself on the fainting couch in the parlor. A plate that formerly held a large *haupia* custard sat empty on the table beside her. An envelope peeked out from underneath. Night had fallen. Liam sat in an armchair at the other end of the room, reading.

She pulled herself up on her elbows. "Have they been out of their room?"

"No, but they've had rather loud conversations. The one thing I heard for certain was Agnes yelling, 'And who is keeping secrets now?'"

She laid back again.

"On the table next to you, you've yet *another* letter from Rowley. What are you two writing about anyway?"

"Well, aren't you a snoop. Not much, really. He tells me how he is preparing Diablo for the Gentleman's Cup. And how the colt is doing. And his latest mania for soil improvement." What she did not share with Liam is how guardedly she wrote back, afraid that she might begin to care a bit too much. And even more afraid she might begin to long for what she could never have.

The *kumu* and Kahōkūlani had both been clear: the life of a Gate was a lonely one.

Still on the couch, Letty gazed down at her toes in the soft light. As children, she and Liam had contests to see who could pick up the most things with their toes. Liam was exceptionally good at it. Sometimes he let her win. They had created endless ways to amuse themselves as their father kept his distance, wrapped in his own despair at the loss of their mother. Perhaps, even then, her bare feet had given her sustenance from the *'āina*.

"Liam, I am thinking about our old made-up games and all the things we did because Papa was so preoccupied. It seems it is the same now. Only I am no longer a child and neither are you. We need the truth."

"You heard him this afternoon . . ."

"That was before I saved the baby. I am going to check on my patient. And ask a few hard questions at the same time."

She gathered her skirts to head down the hall to her parents' room. Soft murmuring came from behind the door; she would not be waking anyone up. She rapped crisply. "I am here to check on Agnes."

Her father opened the door a crack. "We are settled in for the night."

"Fine, I can sit at your bedside while we talk."

"No . . ."

"Let her in, George. It is her right."

Letty gestured to Liam to join her. George opened the door for them. "When did you know about the baby, Letty?" Her father's face was shadowed.

"I learned the day after the polo game. When the *kumu* visited. And by the way, the *kumu* says it's a boy." George's eyes widened as she walked in without further comment.

Agnes rested in the four-poster, swathed in a white linen nightgown. Her skin color looked good, but her eyes had dark circles. She must have been exhausted from the blood loss.

"May I touch you?" Letty asked.

"Please."

Letty's hands, with a sudden sure knowledge she did not know she possessed, gently probed Agnes's belly. "I think all is well."

Agnes grasped her hand. "I know it." She continued, "I have been discussing with your father some, shall we say, current events. He had thought not to tell you about this debt mess. But we are one strong *'ohana*. We are all in this together. It is time you and Liam should know.

"Help me sit up." Letty arranged pillows behind Agnes as her stepmother shook her head. "This man Gannon is a real con artist. We are not his first victims, unfortunately. But we hope to be his last." Her next words were for her husband. "Tell them, George. Everything."

Her father looked to be swallowing a bitter pill. Letty knew he never liked letting anyone in on his plans. Or admitting he was wrong.

"We have hired a lawyer. A good one, Artemus Chang. Princess K offered her help. Together we have set a trap for this shady character. A very *large* trap."

"And?" Agnes clearly wanted all to be told.

"The jaws will snap shut in three days."

CHAPTER TWENTY

'Ūpiki

TRAP

The three days passed quickly.

Walking from stall to stall, patting noses and rubbing foreheads as she went, Letty hoped the lawyer, Artemus Chang, knew what he was doing. The stable was chock full of their best stock. Even someone like Gannon should be able to see these were very valuable horses.

Her post was in the loft, ready to bear witness. And to stay above the fray as the trap was sprung.

The roar of a motorcar approached. Letty hurriedly climbed into the loft, bullwhip in hand for moral support. Looking out one of the knotholes, she watched the car skid to a stop. Gannon got out, followed by three burly Hawaiians. She did not recognize any of them.

A horse-drawn wagon pulled into the yard next, with four more toughs. Letty panicked. In Chang's plan, Papa only had to face down Gannon. Nothing was mentioned about a line of toughs who looked like Kamehameha's warriors.

"Fan out," Gannon ordered. "If the family is still here, you will escort them off the property in any manner necessary. I will pay a bonus if it is done quickly and without noise."

One of the men slapped his chest. "We can do, boss." Another peered into the stable, announcing, "Many good horses here."

Gannon entered the stable to see for himself. Letty frantically suppressed a sneeze as she peered over the side of the loft. "Pick out four of the best. We will take them right away." Two of the men pulled saddles from the tack room.

At that moment, George ambled out on the porch, his insolence barely concealed. "Gannon! Fancy seeing you here!"

"You are trespassing now, Lang," Gannon said. "This property and everything on it became mine at midnight last night."

"Is that so? Well, I never saw any court papers filed."

"I told you at the time I loaned you money that this was a completely private deal. No court filings needed! Look, don't make this any harder than it is. Just load your family up and leave." His men gathered behind him as if waiting for a signal. "I don't want things to get . . . ugly."

"I am not planning to do any such thing. You will have to remove us bodily. Oh, and be careful—my wife is expecting." On cue, Agnes appeared, looking fragile. What a farce that was! Letty would bet Agnes carried her pistol. George had told her not to, but when had that ever stopped her?

The two men in the stable came out, each mounted on one horse and leading another behind. "We take these downtown, boss? Then come back?"

"Yes, get back here as soon as you can—we have a lot of clearing out to do." Letty practically swallowed her tongue as they rode off on Sheba and Scheherazade, leading Captain and Mr. Pickwick.

Gannon turned to his gang—that is all Letty could think to call them. "Clear them out."

The five big men advanced toward the porch, so they were facing away from the gate when the most improbable of arrivals occurred. The *kumu* on her big white mule rode right into the midst of the men, haranguing them in rapid-fire Hawaiian. Gannon was clueless, but George was not. A slow smile spread over his face at what he heard. Letty almost laughed out loud.

"Foolish men, what are you thinking? Keawe, does your *tūtū* know you are here? Manu, Wikoli, Lavi, Eli . . . I ask you all the same! You dishonor yourselves! You serve a man who steals from our people! This is the house of those who protected our queen when others ran away! Shame! Shame! *Hilahila!*"

The one named Keawe stared, fear plain on his face. "Who are you, *tūtū*? How do you know these things? How do you know our names?"

The mule knelt down so she could dismount. The tiny *kumu* swept off her hat. Dark eyes gleamed in her ageless face. "Must . . . you . . . ask?" Letty could swear she saw the air shimmer around the *kumu* as she spoke. The *kumu*'s dog issued a low, slavering growl.

The men drew back as one, muttering, "old one" and "*Menehune*." The leader, apparently Keawe, turned to Gannon. "We are done. You fight your own battles if you fight with the old ones. We are never so foolish." He and his men piled into their wagon to leave.

A motorcar roared up the lane.

"Not so fast." Pulling into the yard, Chen Zhou turned his police vehicle sideways to block the gate.

The sound of hoofbeats heralded the return of the two men who had stolen the horses. Followed by what could only be described as a posse—Artemus, Liam, and Kahōkūlani.

All eyes turned to Chen as he confronted Gannon. "You are under arrest, Gannon, for the crime of property theft. And maybe a whole lot more. Like loan fraud."

"That is ridiculous. Where are your witnesses?"

"Oh, I think you hired all of them . . . and they will be very willing to talk once they learn that they can escape jail time by testifying against you. How convenient you ordered them to leave the property with the horses. There is no question now you are a thief."

Chen turned to the men to address them in Hawaiian. The man called Keawe confirmed with a nod that they would help. And then he said, his head bowed, "Whatever the old one wants."

"What old one?" Chen sounded puzzled. Letty looked around. She could not see the *kumu* anywhere. The hair rose on the back of her neck. She started a calming breath with a susurration of gratitude.

CHAPTER TWENTY-ONE

Uku

PAYBACK

George had gone to the courthouse for Gannon's arraignment. Letty sat at the table by her bedroom window, fiddling with her microscope. A distraction was needed as all her *'ohana* waited to hear Gannon's fate. And the future of the debt on the livery. The debt that could decide her future as well.

Two unopened letters, one from Dr. Feeney and one more from Timothy, lay to the side. She'd prefer not to deal with either of them. Feeney must want a deposit on her tuition. And Timothy? This would undoubtedly be another entreaty to visit. One that would be foolish to accept no matter how much she wished it.

"Honey?"

She turned to see Agnes at the doorway. "May I come in for a chat?"

"Of course. How are you feeling?" Letty asked. "Is the baby . . ."

"I feel fine. The baby feels strong. More importantly, I am here to talk about you." Agnes came into the room but did not sit down. "Your gift is real. It is time to accept it." Her hands rested on her hips as if she was ready to defend her point of view.

Letty closed her notebook. "The price is steep, Agnes. In so many ways." She ran a finger over the letter from Timothy. There were things she'd not told Agnes yet. Maybe never would. Like that she might harm the one she loved the most.

"I honestly thought I had what it takes to be a veterinarian. But now?" Her shoulders slumped in resignation.

"I've been thinking." Agnes clasped her hands. "You really must go back to school. I can give you a loan from my inheritance. What could be better than your gift combined with modern medical knowledge?"

Now Agnes paced. "I can't believe your destiny is to be less than the total sum of all you can be. I just can't." She stood still. "Did you ever ask the *kumu*? Damnation, I wish there were a way to thank her for stepping in. Those thugs might have hurt George."

"Tell me the truth: Did you have your pistol on you?"

"Of course I did! And for goodness sake, do not tell your father!"

"I won't." Letty put fixative on her final slide. "Anyway, the *kumu* already gave me her guidance. She said my gut, my *na'au*, would tell me, if I would only listen. You know how well I listen. Not very."

At this, Agnes chuckled.

"At one point I believed I could choose between science and this gift. Now I see there is no choice. No matter how I might wish to go back to how it was before, I can't. This fire has always been a part of me; I was fooling myself to think it wasn't."

"What if the science is just as much a part of you as the fire? Why can't the two come together?"

Letty stood and stretched. She came over to give Agnes a kiss on the cheek. "Thank you, I will think about it. Besides, I can't leave now, the business needs me."

"Is that true? Lang's Livery has survived for many years. Our debt worries may be behind us. Certainly your father and grandfather can figure something out."

"Maybe."

"If you will not listen to your *na'au*, please listen to me. You must go."

"Well, if you put it that way, I will take that loan."

Two hours later, Letty and Agnes sat on the lānai, shelling beans. Hannah sat at Agnes's feet, crooning to her dolly, while Rosebud poked about for crumbs. And the occasional bean. The other three dogs lay in the yard rather like hot stones in the sun.

"Your father should have been back by now with the news." For the first time, Letty noticed lines of worry on her step-mother's face.

"I know." With that, Letty exerted a bit too much force on the pod currently under her ministrations. Beans flew everywhere.

Hoofbeats heralded the long-awaited arrival. Not just George but the Princess too, and a gentleman who must certainly be the lawyer, Artemus Chang. Letty called into the kitchen for a tea tray and a broom. Hopefully she did not squish too many beans into the floorboards along the way. Wu appeared and took the horses. The three came up the lānai steps but remained standing.

"Artie, can you explain what just happened?" George asked. For once Letty could not read her father's expression. The Princess stood silent, fanning herself.

"You are not going to believe this." Chang himself looked a bit flummoxed. "Gannon woke up in his jail cell this morning missing a hunk of his hair. He has lived here long enough to know what that means. It's the *pule 'anā'anā*. How they say the old *kāhuna* pray you to death? With a lock of hair?"

Letty watched everyone's face register the same shock she felt.

"Yes," Artie went on. "It seems he told his lawyer it was a sign. He chose to plead guilty and do his time in jail. Where he will be under guard."

"What does this mean for us?" George had his hands in his pockets but did not look relaxed. Yet the edges of a smile danced on his cheeks.

Artie smiled. "It's over. Done. *Pau.* You owe him nothing. Not even a fight in court."

A celebration was in order. The Princess was a bit plaintive. "Might we have a spot of tea? And a chair? I am parched by all this."

"I think this calls for a spot of sherry too!"

The tea tray now decimated, Agnes, Letty, and the Princess remained comfortably settled into the deep lānai chairs. The men begged off to head back to the smithy to view some new engine. Most but not all of the escaped beans had been captured. Each woman sat lost in her own thoughts until Agnes broke the silence.

"I can scarcely believe the resolution of this mess is so simple."

K's frown surprised Letty.

"It's not simple. We have a new worry now. What does this business of the lock of hair mean? A *pule 'anā'anā*? In this day and age? And the rumor of dark *kāhuna*? There are few such dark ones left. This is all very strange."

"How is this different from the power of a Gate? Of my power? Or yours?" Letty reached for Agnes's hand to cover her own concern. Agnes became very quiet.

"This is what I must believe, that we are Gates of light only. Of the goodness of the *'āina*. The dark ones? They can cause harm—destruction or diminishment. We Gates cannot do that."

"Can't or won't?" Letty's voice emerged more sharply than intended. "How can you be sure?"

"I am sure of nothing. We have lost so much of the knowledge. But this is what my heart tells me."

"I have so many questions, and now the *kumu* is gone. Again."

"That is her way, Letty. She will pop up at the time you least expect. Goodness, I would have liked to see her giving those thugs what for. I'll wager she was magnificent."

"Of course, she conveniently disappeared. As she always manages to do." Agnes seemed relieved to grasp another thread of conversation. "We've come up with a plan for Letty to enter the veterinary program. She can leave for San Francisco shortly after the Gentleman's Cup. With her friends the Stansfields." Letty turned to Kahōkūlani expectantly.

"Yes, Letty, perhaps you might leave the *'āina* now. At least for a time. Although you may find you gradually weaken while you are gone." Kahōkūlani sat back a moment. "There is more for you to learn. I think it wise if you come back to 'Iolani with me and spend more time with Esther. You know Esther was my bodyguard when I was a child, do you not? I believe you do. She was also the first of my *kahu*."

Now Kahōkūlani leaned forward. "I know she was hard on you before, but only because she cares so much about the Gates."

Agnes leaned in too. "You must go."

"Of course I will go."

"Can you be ready tonight? We take the night steamer," the Princess said.

Once again, Letty would be on the same island as Timothy. Her flames danced a little jig up her spine.

CHAPTER TWENTY-TWO

Maka ʻIke

SEE CLEARLY

The steamer sailed into Hilo Harbor in the predawn light. Something about this time of day kept everyone's voices low. Unlike the merry greetings that were exchanged upon the afternoon arrival in Honolulu, this docking was more restrained.

Kahōkūlani and Letty were among the first down the gangplank. Tako greeted them with the wagon for luggage and supplies. Their horses drowsed, saddled and waiting.

"Thank you, Tako. Letty and I will head right out," Kahōkūlani said.

The rising sun was deliciously warm on her back. They had a long ride ahead. Tired after the all-night steamship journey, but in a strange way exhilarated, Letty hoped her energy would last.

"So, now that I have you alone . . ." The Princess kept her voice confidentially low. "I have been meaning to ask . . . is there anything romantic going on between you and Timothy?"

"No. Honestly. You and Agnes think so much alike. Really, it is nothing. He is just a good friend. Someone I enjoy talking to. We both lost our mothers young. He feels beholden to me for the horses. Besides, he says he must marry a rich heiress to get back in his father's good graces." She babbled and she knew it. Perhaps Kahōkūlani would read nothing into it. If Letty was lucky.

"How much does he know about your gift?"

"Well, he figured much of it out on his own, then asked me to explain the rest. He promised never to tell anyone." She gave the Princess a worried glance. "I mean, he saw the *kumu* on the day she came to tell me she was done with me, so he had a pretty big head start . . ."

"He saw the *kumu*? No one sees the *kumu* unless she wants them to. Why would that be?"

"And he sees my aura anytime something happens, so . . ."

"He sees your aura?" Kahōkūlani's voice came out in a squeak.

"Well, yes. That is acceptable, isn't it?"

"Let me just say it is unusual for people other than your *'ohana* and the Gates to see your aura, let alone a *haole* like Timothy. I don't know what this might mean. Perhaps Esther will know."

They rode on in silence.

She had forgotten what it was like to be at the center of Kahōkūlani's attention. Uncomfortable, as if under a microscope. Esther had not yet arrived, so yesterday Kahōkūlani had seized the opportunity to interrogate her about her sessions with the *kumu*. Even going so far as demanding demonstrations of each breathing technique. Then probing for when and how Letty had put them to use. Taking massive and copious notes. Absolutely as if she had Letty under her own microscope.

When Letty asked the Princess if she was perhaps writing a book, she did not even get the laugh she was expecting. Just a cryptic look. Anything was possible with K; she carried her old writing satchel with her the entire day.

Letty could only hope today would be different.

Thankfully, shortly after Letty downed her first cup of Isaac's coffee and possibly her third biscuit, Kahōkūlani announced she had pressing business matters at hand. Esther would not arrive until this afternoon. Might Letty amuse herself until lunch? That would be yes.

With a second cup of coffee in hand and a few biscuits wrapped in a napkin to take back to her room, the best use of her free morning hit her. Hapuna. The long curve of soft sand beckoned. She would take Malolo down for a splash and a run on the beach.

Letty threw on a worn *holokū*, something that she'd not feel bad about getting wet. Although if she was lucky, the beach might be deserted. Then she'd just strip down. She'd not even bother to braid her hair.

At the stable she bridled Malolo but did not saddle her. Why risk the leather? Grabbing a threadbare towel from the extras in the tack room, she went to the mounting block. This *holokū* was so loose it easily wrapped around her legs for riding.

They were off.

Coming down the steep hill from 'Iolani, she could see the south end of the half-mile-long crescent of sand. Empty. Her lungs filled with the heady scent of the sea. Still not a soul in sight. Could she be in luck?

She urged Malolo into a trot right down to the water's edge. The mare stepped into the shallows as a wave rolled in and began splashing with one leg.

Letty looked north. Maybe not so lucky; a horse and rider appeared around one end of the lava outcropping at the far end of the beach. The pair walked into the water belly deep, and the horse began methodically wading back and forth. Letty started in recognition. She would know that horse anywhere. And those broad shoulders.

She kicked Malolo into a canter to catch up. Whooping as she rode.

Timothy turned to look. Beneath his wide-brimmed hat flashed the white slash of his teeth. He wheeled Diablo around to meet her.

"Hail, fellow! Well met!" She hauled Malolo to a stop, wet sand flying.

"Now, don't flaunt your classical education to this poor farmer! What brings you back to this island?"

Her smile must have been nearly as wide. She could not exactly be forthright about the reason for this visit, could she? Kahōkūlani warned she must be careful what she said. "I am here to work with K's horses." She pulled back to take a look at Diablo. The stallion was wet over the knees. "Better question is what are you two doing at the beach?"

"Training. You know, conditioning. For the Cup. Don't forget if I win, I will have the last of the monies I need to buy that old sugar mill! Grandmama will be green I bought it out from under her. It is all part of my grand plan to return to England in triumph."

Letty always found it odd that he talked about returning to England and marrying well, all the while sinking deeper roots in Hawaii. Did he really think he could do both? Well, that was not her puzzle to solve. "Tell me about this training. You know I fancy myself an expert."

"The real Hank Smith has regaled us with tales of English thoroughbreds strengthened by wading in the Irish sea, so here we are. Wading. Excellent for the pasterns."

Her flames whipped up her spine. Whether it was the chance for mischief or just that something about this fellow brought out the worst in her, she could not tell.

"You know, we Hawaiians have our own ways of this."

"You do?"

"Oh yes, I would be happy to demonstrate. May I have Diablo for a moment?"

She slipped off as the wind whipped the old *holokū* around; a bit of hair flew into her mouth and she pushed it back. She'd best act nonchalant, all business, so as not to tip him off to her plans.

He did not hesitate as they exchanged reins, rubbing Malolo's nose with practiced familiarity. "I've ridden this lady a bit, you know. There are no better jumpers back in Britain."

While he was distracted, she struck. Yanking off Diablo's saddle and tossing it aside, she sprang up on the stallion's bare back, kicking him forward, straight into the surf and deep water.

Timothy hesitated mere moments before leaping onto Malolo, kicking her into a gallop straight toward the water in pursuit.

What he did not know was this: however much Malolo loved to jump, the mare hated swimming in equal measure. She skidded to a stop in the shallows, sending Timothy flying over her head into the surf. Letty squealed in laughter, wheeling Diablo around to help him up.

Somehow he'd kept his hat in place. Timothy emerged from the ocean with seawater running in torrents from the hat's brim. Still smiling, thank goodness. "Give me my horse back, you minx!"

"Not on your life!" Her flames sparked in giddy joy. Diablo coiled under her and took off at an all-out gallop. She leaned in to urge him faster, her hair flying behind. Blessed be, this horse could run. At the end of the beach, she reluctantly turned back.

Rowley stood forlornly holding Malolo almost half a mile away. Damnation, she would just have to run Diablo back.

The stallion stretched long and low beneath her. His speed beyond expectation, his joy in the run palpable. Timothy grew larger by the moment. She pulled up next to him.

"Now, that's how it's done." She knew she sounded a bit smug but did not care. "Would you like another demonstration?"

"Oh really? That's how this is done?" He'd dropped Malolo's reins and gazed up as if this were an entirely serious consideration. Until he sprang like a cobra, wrapping his arms around her and yanking her down. They fell together, his back on the sand. She found herself sprawled on top of him, suddenly flooded with awareness, feeling every point of connection through the thin, wet *holokū*. His hard frame beneath her gone harder. His gray eyes alight with silver fire. His fingers clenched on her waist. Her treacherous flames running rampant up and down her spine.

His eyes dropped to her lips. She licked the salt off as her flames exploded, shooting heat through her whole body. Her nipples hardened and the fire centered deep in her belly. His eyes widened. He must feel it.

In that moment she knew the truth of it. She could hurt him. Just as the *kumu* said. She rolled off, her flames chiding her in disappointment. Freeing herself from his touch brought another wave, one of regret. She stared at the sky and listened to his ragged breath by her side. Hers was no better.

"Well, that was instructive." His voice came out a bit strangled.

She was saved from the necessity of a response by a squeal from Malolo. She sat up to see Diablo giving the mare a flirtatious little nip.

"Oh no. Not that." She scrambled to her feet to separate the two horses.

Timothy remained silent, turning instead to grab Diablo's saddle.

Clearly it might be best if they stuck to discussing the weather on the ride back up the hill.

Three days later, Letty found herself doubled over to breathe in great gulps, wiping the sweat out of her eyes with the arm of her work shirt. Esther Ka'ahumanu Jefferson Flores bounced lightly on the balls of her feet as she swung the staff above her head. "Not *pau*, are you?" How could Letty have thought this ball of energy to be old? Who knew a woman that big could move so fast? Letty straightened, moving into a defensive posture. Esther came at her, cudgel whirling above her head.

The blow, when it came, rocked her. So Letty did the only sensible thing. She fell on her ass.

Esther performed a little victory shimmy. "Never underestimate the mother of five children."

Behind her, Kahōkūlani's voice. "Don't gloat, Esther." And then, "Who needs food?"

Thank the *'āina*. "Forever and always." Letty hoisted herself up to see Kahōkūlani holding a basket of sandwiches. She grabbed two.

The last few days had been a whirlwind. Or a typhoon. Or maybe a hurricane. First Esther stuffed Letty full of arcane Hawaiian lore. (She would never remember it all.) Then Esther introduced her to *ku'ialua*, the bone-breaking martial art of Kamehameha's warriors. (She still preferred her bullwhip.) Not to be left out, Kahōkūlani schooled her in *hula* and legal principles. (Because you never know when you will need to dance in the courtroom?) Then there was the singing. (Who knew the Gates had their own *mele*?) Perhaps it was time for a revolt.

"Honestly, ladies, I just need a bit of time to absorb what I have learned. This is all very overwhelming." Not to mention Letty was sore. If Esther tried to instigate another session of two-handed whip cracking, she might not be able to move her arms. For years.

And she'd heard nothing more from Timothy. When they parted—quite awkwardly after the little episode on the beach—he'd reiterated she must come visit the ranch. She had demurred, thinking then that it might be best, but if he asked again? She had expected that invitation, actually. Hoped for it. Dreamed of it. Conjured the mental excuses needed to accept it. She really did want to see the colt, and the new ranch house too, didn't she? But not a word. Perhaps his judgment was better than hers.

"Yes, yes, we understand." Esther nodded, breaking Letty out of her reverie. "A bit of a break is clearly in order. Would you like to ride tomorrow? Perhaps visit your friends at 'Iole? Just be back by teatime. Then we can cover a bit more ground before we put you on the boat home."

"Mahalo!" She did not know what she might have done had Esther not agreed; she truly did need a break.

"K, I might stop by Timothy's ranch too. It's not out of the way. I'd like to see Sunflower's colt and what he has accomplished on his new house." The flames only tickled a little bit at this announcement. She would be fine. Surely it would be best to see him and get any awkwardness over with. Hawaii was too small a place to avoid people.

"He will most likely be at the plantation. You might miss him."

"That's all right—I just want to take a quick look at the place."

Liar. She'd be devastated if he wasn't there. Although it might be best if he wasn't.

"I have the dinner invitation for you to give him. You can leave it with his cook if he is not there."

"I am happy to deliver it."

"Whatever you do, if you do see him, don't let on that you know who is coming! This will be quite the surprise." Kahōkūlani pulled a piece of heavy cream stationery out of her satchel and handed it to Letty. "Did I show you her letter? I so wish you could stay for another couple of days. At least you will meet Philomena at the Cup. I think you will adore her." Letty wiped her hand on her trousers and took the letter.

My dearest K,

I am beyond grateful for all you have done to get Timothy off to such a smashing start. Perhaps he does not share details with you, but each of his business ventures have borne fruit.

I must say he is reminding me of his great-grandfather, my own dear Papa, who had the Midas touch. It is as if Hawaii is a tropical hothouse for his talents! He's even hinted he'll buy the plantation next to mine all on his own! With his own sugar mill!! To become a full partner in Moran Sugar!!!!

A visit seems in order. Therefore I am planning a journey to see Timothy and to check on my Hawaiian investments. Clarissa will accompany me. Timothy has always styled her his favorite aunt! She is quite languishing to see you again. As am I!!

Naturally, I am keeping all this a secret from Timothy, so might we prevail upon your hospitality for a time? I have always found that the most delightful things arise when you surprise someone.

Oh, and I should love to bring you more pigs! Perhaps the Plum Pudding breed? Very old English and

*quite sun resistant! And perhaps a few chickens . . . Buff
Orpingtons might be good . . . or a Jersey cow or two . . .
or dairy goats? When our ship arrives in Hilo they will
christen it the Ark!*

All the best,
Philomena Moran Rowley

Letty laughed aloud. "My, what a bundle of energy. I will
be most disappointed to miss the promised parade of animals!
Through the streets of Hilo no less! If only I did not need to get
home for my own visitors. You can count on me not to betray
the surprise."

She pried her sweat-soaked shirt away from her chest. "And
now, ladies, I think I must bathe. Otherwise you will not want
me at the dinner table tonight!"

Esther watched Letty stride away. Kahōkūlani moved to stand
next to the big woman now leaning more conspicuously on her
staff than she had only moments before. "Trying to keep up
with the young one, I see?"

"I can't help myself."

"Did you tell her once again the price we Gates must pay
for our power, *kupuna*?" Kahōkūlani knew her tone was bitter.
"I worry about this thing with Rowley."

Esther took K's arm. "Walk with me. These old bones can
use the support." Leaning in, she spoke quietly. "I did. She told
me you already warned her. The *kumu* did too. Several times,
apparently. She was almost flippant. I am not sure she fully
comprehends what it means, that her affections might harm
the one she most loves."

"Call it what it is, *kupuna*. A sentence to a lifetime alone. That's what it means when your kisses can kill. A lifetime alone."

Letty shoved her bouncing braid back over her shoulder as Malolo trotted along the road to Hawi. She loved this particular ride. It took her from the austere, open, grassy landscape of the Kohala ranches into the lushness of the sugarcane fields. As she rode down the ʻIole school lane, the cane was so high that she was fenced in on both sides. Blue sky above.

Moran Sugar was close. She might go try to find Timothy at the plantation. Best not.

Turning in to the gate of the school, she waved at the girls out back of the old building, hanging laundry. The clotheslines were loaded with sparkling white sheets gently billowing in the light breeze.

One of the girls saw her and waved in return. Cries of "Letty!" and *"E komo mai!"* rang out. Letty jogged forward, grinning, pleased to see so many faces she knew. This visit would be the perfect antidote to entirely too many things in her brain.

Letty excused herself after lunch. If she was to be at her lessons by teatime and she wished to stop by Timothy's, she must get going.

As Letty neared Timothy's ranch, memories of the old cowboy who used to own the place came flooding back. Rawhide John, was it? Back then his cabin was a simple two-room affair, beautiful in its own way, with *koa* wood walls, comfortable chairs, and a big fireplace to ward off the winter cold of upland Waimea. She'd come to visit with the Princess, to hear stories of the old, old days.

But that time was gone. As the cabin was gone. Things were changing. Timothy was certainly seeing to that.

The new ranch house stretched long and low, angled to capture views of the ocean thousands of feet below. Unfinished doors gaped open, with windows not yet in, and it appeared the workmen were on a break. A perfect time for a curious person to take a look.

Letty entered through what she could only imagine would be the front door. Large, airy rooms opened before her, with high ceilings and lots of natural light. As she walked, she could see the resemblance to Princess K's home . . . big rooms for gathering and small rooms for intimacy. The kitchen set off to the back for fire safety but still big enough for family meals. Every detail was well thought out. Just like Timothy to be so orderly.

As she rounded one corner, she gasped.

The cowboy's cabin was not demolished after all! Rather, Timothy chose to build his home around it. As if the old cabin gave the great new house its heart. The stone fireplace remained, and the gleaming *koa* wood walls too. The only changes seemed to be wide doorways on either side of the fireplace leading out to the verandah.

Letty walked over to touch the fireplace, the stones almost alive in the afternoon's heat. Then she turned her gaze out through the opening in the wall surely meant to be doors. She could stand here forever, held captive by the vista over the windswept fields out to the rolling sea.

Perhaps she should tell Timothy these doors had best be glass . . . but then this was none of her business.

Letty's heart clenched. She'd be jealous of whomever became mistress of this house. It could never be hers. What the *kumu* and Kahōkūlani and Esther had all tried to tell her, she knew to be true. She was a danger to the one she loved the most. She'd never be mistress of any house, except her own lonely one.

It was the price to be paid.

Timothy entered the house through the new kitchen breeze-way; one of the laborers alerted him to his visitor. "Hey boss, some big *kine wahine* on roan horse, she inside new house!" the man said. His breath caught. It could only be Letty. He'd not expected to see her again so soon after the awkwardness on the beach. He'd asked her to visit, of course, but she had resisted. He had thought her wise at the time, but now his heart soared.

She'd want to see Diablo again, and the colt, he was sure. The house too. After all, whenever he invited her here the lure was always to see the house and the horses. It was unlikely she'd come merely to see him. She'd sent no message to let him know she would visit. He had no right to expect even that.

Moving quietly through the house to find her, he slipped through the doorway of the old cabin room. Pausing to watch as she ran her hands over the fireplace stones, as if they were old friends with stories to share. Perhaps they were. With one hand still on the mantel, she turned to gaze out the door open-ing to the ocean. Unruly hair escaped from her braid. The light coming through the open doorway made a rosy nimbus around her head. And her curves.

Timothy's mouth went dry. The most beautiful, intelligent, courageous, radiant woman he had ever met was standing here, in his house, as if she belonged . . . because maybe she did. What if what happened on the beach was no accident? How had he not seen this?

Suddenly uncomfortable, he coughed. She spun around. "Timothy, how wonderful! You have kept John's cabin and built around it! What a centerpiece for this lovely house! Will this be your library or your office? I can only hope that I will have the opportunity to visit you here to tell stories around this hearth again."

She babbled, betraying her discomfort at being caught poking about. He'd seen her like this before; it always amused him.

Timothy paused, then mischief overtook good judgment. "Actually, this will be my bedroom." He grinned as the color rose in her cheeks. "I will look forward to visiting with you here . . ."

Her eyes widened in disbelief. Pulling up to her full height, she crossed her arms to contain herself. "Timothy, I know that I am not the sort of lovely English rose you are accustomed to . . . or the kind of heiress you say you're so desperate to marry, but I still deserve a modicum of respect. If not for myself, then for the Princess. I am one of her own and should be treated as such."

She turned and slipped out the door opening, head held high. Timothy moved swiftly to catch up with her and grabbed her arm. "Letty, wait, that came out all wrong! I was making a joke! I did not mean that the way it sounded . . ."

"Oh yes, you did." She looked at the sky. "Our little episode on the beach was a mistake, not to be repeated." A knife turned in his stomach at her next words.

"Here is the thing, Timothy. You are white, and I am brown. In my world, that matters very little. I have learned that in your world, it matters quite a lot. Someone like me? Oh, I am good enough to flirt with out here in the country, maybe save your horse's life, anywhere you know none of your fancy friends will be watching . . . but it appears I am not good enough to be treated with respect." She tried to pull away. "I hoped you were different, that we could be friends, Timothy. I really did. But maybe that is not possible."

He felt as though he'd slipped off a cliff. He clung to her arm as if to save himself.

"Let go of me, Timothy." He dropped her arm like a hot rock. Tinges of red light rose off her hair. "Let me ask you this: Would you make a comment like that to your precious heiress, Adele? Or any white woman? I think not."

She turned away so he could not see her face. "This happened to me before, you know. One of the polo players at Stanford. I thought he was my friend. He offered me money."

"Letty! That is not what I meant!"

She glided to Malolo. He followed, tongue-tied. Once mounted, Letty pulled a white envelope out of her saddlebag. "Here. This is a message from the Princess. She wants you to join her for dinner soon—visitors from England, bring your fancy dress. I won't be there. That will save us both the trouble of pretending to be cordial. *Aloha*."

Timothy stood watching her gallop away, his heart sinking deep into his boots. Had any man ever been so foolish?

Letty rode Malolo hard, tears running down her face. What had she been thinking? Why had she gone to see him? How had she let one stiff-upper-lipped Englishman get under her skin? And her flames provided no help, as they clearly had other ideas. Like turning around and galloping right back to Timothy.

It was for the best. She was a *mākāhā*, a Gate, an opening to the power of the *'āina*. A woman who might never take a lover. That her kisses could kill? She did not doubt it. The flames now raging up her spine were proof. Her desire brought only danger.

Going home to Honolulu would be a relief. Irene and her family arrived soon; they'd be orchestrating Letty's return to

San Francisco. To the life she had planned for so long. Dr. Letty Lang. If only she thought that might be enough to fill her heart again.

She was sorry to miss the moment Timothy discovered who the Princess's English dinner guests were. He would be gobsmacked. She'd love to be a guest at that table. But even this was no longer Letty's place. Perhaps it never was. She rode on.

Tomorrow she'd ride to Kawaihae to board the steamer home. Honolulu beckoned.

Hilo Harbor, Hawaii Island, two days later

Standing on the Hilo dock madly waving, Kahōkūlani felt like a girl again. How could she not? Clarissa Rowley had been her best friend at Harrowden Hall, one of the few not put off by the color of her skin. K had never known such prejudice until her time in England. Clarissa had been her savior.

Then there was the dowager. Philomena Moran Rowley. Dowager Countess of Colborne.

Those many years ago, Kahōkūlani arrived in England a motherless girl alone in a strange land. On a school visit to Clarissa at Harrowden, Philomena somehow discerned Kahōkūlani was in dire need of a spot of mothering. Within moments Kahōkūlani found herself bundled into the Colborne carriage and off to Moran Manor for a holiday. The first of many. Philomena taught her to shoot, for heaven's sake!

From the day she left England on, rarely a week went by that she did not receive a long and newsy letter from Philomena. She always replied in kind. Timothy would be embarrassed to discover how much she knew about his foibles before he ever set foot on the Big Island.

And now this business between Letty and Timothy. Something clearly happened when Letty delivered the dinner invitation. But neither she nor Esther could get to the bottom of it. If anything, the girl became more adamant that she return to Honolulu as originally planned. The Stansfields were set to arrive, she said. And no, she couldn't stay an extra day or two to meet Kahōkūlani's beloved Philomena. Odd, frankly.

As the freighter approached, two fashionably dressed ladies at the prow returned her frantic waving. Captain Kalama, the rogue, stood with them, pointing her out in the crowd.

Thank goodness Hilo had a real harbor, with docks where ships could land and off-load on gangplanks. Kahōkūlani had insisted this was the place where Philomena and Clarissa should arrive. She did not think cages of chickens and goats in crates winched over the side of the boat in Kawaihae to be a very good idea. And especially she did not want to put Philomena at risk. It had been over twelve years since she had last seen her. Heavens, the dowager's hair was already silver then!

Bull pulled up next to her. "I have everything ready," he announced. "Tako will get the wagons with the livestock over the saddle before dark. He had some choice words about duck wrangling, but good humor prevailed. Your house here is prepared; Miyako is there with flowers arranged. You and the ladies will spend the night, and then I will attend you on the ride home."

"What if the countess cannot ride?"

Bull gazed up at the stick-straight woman with the silver hair now very clearly visible on the ship's deck. "I am betting she can ride, but just in case, I brought the wagon with the heavy springs. Stop worrying." He reached over to squeeze her hand. "I know how much she means to you. She will not find you a disappointment." She squeezed back. How did he always know? Her friend, her dear *kahu*.

Two gangplanks had been put onto the ship: one to the upper passenger levels, the other to the cargo hold. As the engines cut, the noise coming out of the hold crescendoed. Quacks, moos, bleats, and clucks gave counterpoint to the cursing of the stevedores. The stench carried downwind. The meticulous Tom Kalama was likely beside himself.

The dowager's animal parade began. First off, three golden Jersey cows, one trailed by a little bull calf. Four Nubian goats, crates of Buff chickens, and a line of white-and-black ducks that came marching down the gangplank. Then the pigs, all spotty—those had to be the Plum Puddings. Finally, the jaw-dropper: the biggest bull that Kahōkūlani had ever seen. Golden brown with a huge hump.

Arms encircled her as a dear voice said, "He is a Brahma. They are from India, and very good in the tropics. His name is Romeo. I expect he will live up to it."

Kahōkūlani whirled to embrace the dowager, extending her other arm to Clarissa. "I am so glad you have come!" She feared if she said more, words would fail her, and she might cry.

"And aren't you impressed with our little Noah's Ark? I was able to find most of the animals from my correspondents in California, but we have traveled with the pigs the entire way. As you can imagine, this made us enormously popular wherever we went."

The dowager hooked arms with Kahōkūlani on one side and Clarissa on the other. "Are we heading to your delightful demesne right away? Or staying here for the night?"

"We are going to rest here and clean up; the animals will be sent ahead."

"And do you think my grandson will be completely surprised?"

"Completely. He hasn't a clue."

Bull came forward with his hat in his hands. "I am honored to meet you, my lady."

"You must be the redoubtable Bull whom I have heard so much about. She certainly did not overstate your size. And don't you dare try to call me 'my lady.' I am here to rusticate!"

"We can walk or drive to the house here. I keep it as a place to overnight when I have business in Hilo," Kahōkūlani said.

"Let's walk, shall we, Mama? A little leg stretch will do us good."

"Agreed." The dowager waved her hand. "Oh, Bull, my good man, I am afraid we have a terrible amount of luggage! We even brought our own sidesaddles, since our dear Princess does not believe in them! Will you be orchestrating its delivery?"

"I will."

Kahōkūlani felt she ought to exert some control. She had forgotten how things would just be swept along by the force of the dowager's personality. "Let's be off, then."

"Yes, let's. We've so much to talk about." The dowager marched forward with a vigor that belied her age. "Now, about that delicious Captain Kalama . . ."

Chapter Twenty-Three

Hoaloha

FRIEND

Honolulu Harbor, Oahu, several days later

Letty stood on the dock, elbow to elbow with the seething crowd that greeted every trans-Pacific ship, her arms laden with the flowers of welcome. Trying her best not to think of Timothy Rowley and failing miserably. She desperately needed a cure for the hole in her heart where Timothy used to be. With any luck, the perfect antidote was about the sail into Honolulu Harbor. Her dear friend Irene and the entire Stansfield clan. Letty found Irene's four little sisters to be quite charming. Yes, just the distraction she needed.

They could not arrive soon enough, as her thoughts careened back to Hawaii Island. By now Timothy must know his beloved grandmama was there to visit. Letty was sorry not to witness that reunion moment. Ugh, that line of thought must be avoided. Now she'd best turn her attention to the reunion here at hand.

The steamship rounded the harbor lighthouse into view. Like one giant organism, the crowd on the dock surged forward, waving madly. Letty, laughing out loud, was swept along like a floating coconut on an incoming tide. This happened every time. She had always wondered why no one fell off the dock, but no one ever did . . . at least so far.

The ship neared enough that she could now discern the clump of energetic femininity that was the Stansfield 'ohana. Dear Mr. Stansfield stood sentinel at the rail with his six females surrounding him, his hand on young Glorietta's shoulder.

Letty's arms encircled a veritable mountain of leis to greet her friends. Still, she managed to wave madly and put her fingers to her lips for a wolf whistle. Glorietta was the first to spot her. The seven-year-old bounced up and down, pointing to where Letty stood on the dock.

The captain somehow always miraculously turned the ship at the very last moment, so that it slipped neatly into its berth. This time was no exception. The sailors began the tie-down. Two gangplanks were put into place, and the eager passengers began to disembark.

Glorietta, ducking and dodging through the crowd, was the first to reach her, wrapping herself around Letty's waist with a fierce hug. "Letty, Letty, I saw fish that fly!"

"Yes, you did, love. Yes, you did." She slipped a lei over Glory's head. "This is how we welcome people in Hawaii." She knelt and kissed the girl on both cheeks. Glory gave her kisses back and then began looking around. "Where is the pony? Irene says there is a pony."

"We will see him soon." The rest of the family were just now winding their way to where Letty stood. She repeated the welcome with each family member, even convincing the reserved Mr. Stansfield that his hat would benefit from flowers on it.

The Princess had graciously offered 'Āinahau as the Stansfields' residence on this trip. Kahōkūlani's coachman, Kaliko, and her houseman, Matteo, waited with the big, old-fashioned carriage. Both wore the royal livery, a tradition that Kahōkūlani clung to despite her otherwise modern ways.

"Mr. Stansfield, sir, do you know when your luggage is to come off? I can go assist the porter." Matteo dipped his head in greeting.

"Well, thank you. Actually, it will likely be two porters. As we have six females here with many festivities to attend, there are at least that many trunks."

Letty grinned. "Of course there are! That is why we brought a second wagon along, to carry the finery." She gathered the ladies and they set off for the carriage.

Glory climbed up into the coachman's seat and looked down at Kaliko as he helped the others load into the body of the carriage. "Please, sir, may I ride up here with you?"

Imogene, standing next to Letty, said in a low voice, "Astonishing how that child's manners appear when it will serve to get her way. You will have your hands full with her when you join us in San Francisco!" Letty chuckled in agreement. Even with the challenges of tutoring Glory, she would be glad to be gone. Despite being an island away, Timothy's presence was too close. She was no longer angry at him; perhaps she had never been angry in the first place. Heartbroken was more like it. Or disheartened. Downhearted. Something to do with her heart.

At least she was unlikely to see him until the Cup. And that was blessedly weeks away.

Kaliko gave Glory a wide smile. "Of course, miss, of course, but only if your mother agrees." Imogene made that dismissive hand gesture that is the universal mother's signal for "whatever she wants." Onward.

The crowd thinned. Kaliko brought the carriage up next to the wagons. Imogene motioned to her husband.

"Will you join us, Gaylord?"

"No, Imogene, we've still one more trunk to come off. I will wait here with Matteo and then follow you to 'Āinahau."

People on the street waved at Kahōkūlani's carriage as they passed by, with the occasional cry of "Princess! Princess!" Glory was in her element, waving vigorously at everyone whether they returned the salute or not.

Riding in the old carriage brought Letty face to face with all that had changed. Yes, many people still rode horseback. A few other horse-drawn vehicles passed. Chinese rickshaws and Portuguese women carrying bundles on their heads too. But the number of motorcars surprised her. How long might it be before no one wanted the Langs' horses at all?

As the carriage pulled through the gates to the great house, Kahōkūlani's staff came out to greet their guests. Not every visitor was invited to stay at 'Āinahau, but Kahōkūlani had taken a particular shine to Imogene and Irene. The Stansfields would have the honor.

Scheherazade was saddled and waiting for Letty. "I leave you in good hands here. We will see you for dinner tonight. Our house."

Letty would be the first to admit it, Agnes did know how to throw a party. From the moment the Stansfields arrived at the Langs' home, everyone proceeded to have a gay time. Dinner was a marvel. Conversation was lively. Irene remained immune to Liam's attempts at charm. Rosebud was doted on by all the girls—except, of course, tomboy Glory, who had her head together with Johnny's, talking about training the goat.

"George, might we take a tour of the place?" Mr. Stansfield asked.

"Why of course, Gaylord, though there is not much to see."

"Liam, would you care to join us?"

Wasn't this interesting? The men were repairing to the stable as if they sought a masculine retreat. And not a cigar in sight. Letty looked at Irene, and in wordless communication, they agreed. "We'll come too, Papa, as I want to check on one of the horses."

In the stable, Mr. Stansfield peppered her father with questions. All kinds of things about how the business worked and the land and buildings. About Papa's blacksmith business too. And his machinery inventions. "The shop is farther out of town," her father said. "I would be honored to take you there too."

"I would like to see it—perhaps this week. Tell me, how badly has the motorcar hurt your business?"

Her father paused. Letty knew he weighed his answer.

"It is hurting us, no doubt about it. But Letty has launched us into a new line of the business with her skill at training polo ponies. Polo is becoming very popular."

"Yes, yes. Polo. Very good. Letty is quite the talent with animals. We are all looking forward to her staying with us during her studies." Gaylord paused. "By the way, George, as you know, I am planning to sell motorcars in Hawaii. I've a few ideas I'd like to run by you. Perhaps over lunch tomorrow?"

She heard her father's murmured assent as he and Gaylord moved farther into the barn. Of course, Papa merely made conversation. He could not possibly think the market for polo ponies would fill the need, could he? Even with Gannon's debt gone, things were slow.

Still she was committed to San Francisco; the deposit made for her first tuition was not refundable. Thanks to Agnes and her hidden bank accounts.

She chose to think the distance from Timothy would be welcome. She wished she could tell Irene all about it. Timothy, the flames, everything. Maybe she would.

Letty entered Sinbad's stall to check a cut on his leg. She passed her hand over the wound, breathing slowly, letting her intention sink in. The big bay was one of her best polo prospects. He'd cut himself two days before on a bamboo stump while cavorting in the pasture. She wanted him fully healed before they shipped him to the Big Island for the Cup. Sinbad would not race, but he might possibly be sold. His sister Scheherazade too. It was business.

As she stood up, she was struck by how casually she now used her gift. When did it become second nature?

Mr. Stansfield continued his inquisition of her father. Irene leaned over the stall door, discreetly listening. She shrugged, giving Letty a look that clearly said, "I have no idea what is going on."

The girls moved on to the next stall. Inside was not one pony, but two. Standing next to fat brown Lau Lau was an equally rotund, mostly white pony.

"Letty, when did you get the second pony!"

"We borrowed her for your visit. I knew that Glory and Johnny might struggle with sharing Lau Lau, so this is Egg. She is Lau Lau's sister. The children of the family that own her have all outgrown her. They were happy to let us feed Egg for a while. She is just as sweet as she is fat."

"Glory will be over the moon."

"And we will all be spared some bickering."

Late the next afternoon, George arrived home from his lunch with Gaylord Stansfield, brow furrowed and strangely quiet. He called for the Lang 'ohana to gather in his office. Letty prayed it had nothing to do with her plans to return to San Francisco in a month. She lounged back against a wall for support just in case.

This must be about something else. Anything else.

Since there was only one extra chair, Agnes was designated to sit while the others stood. Liam came to join Letty against the wall. George held a fistful of papers. Lot paced.

Agnes settled in and looked pointedly at George. "All right, dear, what is this fuss all about? I have plans to go sunset sea bathing with Imogene, and I don't wish to be late."

"I had lunch with Gaylord Stansfield."

Lot was the first to speak. "We know that. At the Ocean Club. I assume you were the only Hawaiian in the establishment not wearing a footman's livery. Did the *haoles* try to throw you out?"

"No, not that, at least not this time." George swallowed. "Gaylord made me an offer. All of us an offer. A business deal. Quite out of the blue." The rest of the words rushed out. "Stansfield wants us, Lang's Livcry, to be his partners in a new automobile dealership here in Hawaii. He says it's a natural, that horse traders on the mainland are turning to selling cars to save their businesses."

This time George gulped. "How can we say no?"

Agnes worriedly bit her lower lip. "This seems almost too good to be true. Where is the catch? Why would he do this?"

Liam squeezed Letty's hand. For once he stayed quiet.

"I honestly don't think there is a catch. He sincerely believes he will make more money in partnership with us. People know us here, they trust us. We've done business with everyone in the territory, and we've done right by them. With our reputation on the line, he is confident he'll sell more cars."

"My my. If we can't sell horses, we sell horseless." Lot chuckled at his own witticism.

"The first car arrives next week. Stansfield plans to sell cars in Hawaii with or without us, so he already procured the cars. With us, he gets in business very quickly, beating the competition. Without us, he'll wait months."

George shuffled the papers in his hands. "I have the proposed deal right here. It is a full partnership. Stansfield has five sales offices in California; all are successful. He has invited me to visit with any of them."

"Here is my thought, then." Agnes laid a protective hand on her belly. "My vote is you tell Gaylord yes, but subject to working with the lawyer. Then my fears will be eased."

"Here, here to that!" Lot nodded emphatically. Liam began a knee-popping *hula*. Letty sagged against the wall in relief.

George already jumped ahead. "You know the Gentleman's Cup is coming up. I told Gaylord it is the perfect opportunity to whip up interest . . ."

Letty watched her *'ohana* embrace the future. A dark cloud lifted. She could leave for San Francisco with no guilt. If only she could share the news with Timothy. Except she couldn't. She'd certainly seen to that.

Timothy was in Honolulu for a bit of business. Or so he told himself . . . and his grandmama . . . and anyone who might inquire. Otherwise, he'd have to admit he'd come to beg Letty's forgiveness. Well, that was important business in and of itself.

The moment Timothy arrived at 'Āinahau, Liam commandeered him. Hadn't he heard the Langs were to join the Stansfields in a motorcar venture? Didn't Timothy admire motorcars? Mightn't Timothy care to join Liam and Gaylord in meeting the *Theodora*? Kalama's freighter carried the first vehicle for the new enterprise.

Oh, and one little thing. All Timothy must do is drive the wagon back to the livery once it was done. Of course he'd said yes. He could not have engineered a more perfect cover to go see Letty.

So now Timothy stood next to Liam and Gaylord on the Honolulu docks. Gaylord was already at the gangplank, pacing like a proud papa. Liam stood back, his arms wrapped tight around his chest, hands in his armpits as if to keep them still. It was impossible to say who was most excited about this arrival.

Captain Kalama leaned over the rail. "Stansfield! The car is in a crate! I am bringing it shoreside with a winch. STAND BACK!"

The stevedores set to work immediately, using crowbars to unpack the big vehicle. Not surprisingly, a small crowd gathered. In the week since the Stansfields arrived in Honolulu and the deal was struck, the Langs had taken every opportunity to broadcast the news. Honolulu was abuzz with anticipation.

Gaylord rubbed his hands together. "Well, Liam, my boy. You are about to see the finest car ever made."

"I am beyond excited, sir."

Timothy thought it best to leave them to their motorcar love affair. He went back to the wagon to retrieve the can of gasoline. The very one Liam had nearly forgotten. Percy stood peacefully tethered to the wagon, despite the hustle and bustle of dockside. Timothy gave him an ear rub, then grabbed the gas can. It was a good thing someone was thinking clearly. Left to themselves, Liam and Gaylord might have unloaded a car that was going exactly nowhere. That would not have been a boon for the sales campaign.

The last of the crate walls fell away, revealing a huge shape swathed in blankets and cotton wool. With a reverence verging on ridiculousness, Liam and Gaylord unwrapped the big car. The crowd murmured its appreciation.

Timothy went back to the wagon. His work here was done. Now on to the day's real challenge. Letty.

As he drove back up Beretania, a roar erupted behind him. Not just the noise of a motorcar; cheering too! The wagon team tossed their heads but otherwise remained unruffled. He looked back. Percy trotted along behind, cool as a cucumber. That might change when the car passed by.

He did not have long to wait.

Sounding quite like a big ship churning into the harbor, the car flashed by, horn blaring. Liam hung out of the passenger side, waving like a madman. The wagon team shied a bit, but Timothy had them back under control in an instant.

The car made a U-turn and circled back. As it came even, Liam yelled, "I am taking him the long way to ʻĀinahau. We want to show this beast off! See you there after you drop off the wagon! We'll give you a ride then!"

Timothy could not even nod before the Oldsmobile roared off, a cloud of exhaust billowing out behind. He headed on to Lang's. And to the business that mattered most.

He pulled the wagon into the livery yard. Letty emerged from the stable with an unreadable look and stepped up to lead the team inside. She already had her hand on the reins to guide the horses into the unhitching area. He hopped down and stood next to her, his hands behind his back.

"I am an ass and a moron; please forgive me. Who else can I discuss the Pimpernel with?"

"How about just saying hello?"

"Hello. Let me repeat, I am an ass and a moron . . ."

"I fully understand that. You are forgiven."

That was simple. Maybe too simple.

She began to move the team and wagon in and then stopped, her hand on one of the horse's necks as if to steady herself. "You understand, don't you, Timothy, how much we have shared over the past few months? You know things about me that almost no one else knows. I know a few things about you too. I trust you. I still do. Your friendship means the world to me, and I hope mine does to you."

"And?"

"Just that. We are friends and I am glad to keep it that way."

He was a fool to hope for more than this.

As she moved the team on into the barn she called back, "So if you are truly sorry, why didn't you write me a poem? That is what the Pimpernel would do . . ."

"Then I must take it upon myself to try to find the perfect rhyme for 'moron.' Perhaps 'Moran'?" Her laughter belled out from within the barn as his own smile of relief spread across his face. He needed Letty in his life. In any way possible. Even if they must be only friends.

She emerged from the barn, removing her gloves. "The real trick will be finding a rhyme for 'ass.' But I am sure you are just the man to do it."

Sink me.

CHAPTER TWENTY-FOUR

Hoʻokoa

BE BRAVE

Letty pulled her braids up on the top of her head. Anything to get them off her neck in the humid late summer air. The heat of her flames only added to the discomfort. The coolness of San Francisco would be welcome once she returned.

These last few languid days had slipped into a comfortable pattern. George and Gaylord met to discuss business. Liam propped open the hood of the Oldsmobile and lost himself in tinkering, only taking time out to exercise Captain for the race ahead. Imogene and the older girls went sea bathing with a picnic lunch, Agnes and Hannah joining them most days. Letty participated when she could between bouts of horse training. And hoping that Timothy might again visit. Like today, in fact. A friendly visit, of course. He had even made an appointment. To see a horse.

Perhaps she and Timothy were succeeding at this friendship thing. If only she weren't left with a dull ache deep in her chest. And occasionally lower.

Glory confidently rode Egg through the livery gates, followed by one of Kahōkūlani's grooms. She'd spend her day with Johnny under Wu's watchful eye.

Johnny hopped off the porch to greet Glory, the three musketeers dancing around his feet in expectation. Yesterday had been devoted to toad hunting. The day before to building a fort in the bamboo grove. At least the children knew how to be friends. Perhaps she should ask Timothy to join her in a good toad hunt.

Agnes settled Hannah into the pony cart for the day's outing. She thanked Kahōkūlani's groom for escorting Glory. "Don't worry about coming to get Miss Glory this afternoon. One of us will bring her back." The man nodded and rode out.

Wu stood next to the cart, holding the pony's cheek piece. "We have more good fun today, Missy Agnes, so no need come home early. Children help me get ready for big race."

"Thank you, Wu."

Agnes pulled away, waving to Letty and driving the pony cart like it was second nature. Would they all ever be as comfortable driving the new motorcars?

Johnny and Glory badgered Wu. "How do we help? Do we get to ride the big horses?" That from Johnny.

"I am just the right size to be a jockey." Where did Glory get these ideas? She would be a handful for Letty to tutor once they returned to San Francisco.

"No. Mo bettah yet. We make saddles pretty." Letty suppressed a smile. This was Wu's wiliest trick, making you think whatever work he needed you to do was special and fun. Well, perhaps at that age, everything was fun.

"Glory, what is that poking out of your saddlebag? Is it a walking stick?" Glory pulled the item out of the bag and presented it to Letty as if it were a queen's scepter.

"This is my baseball bat. I promised Johnny I would show him how to play."

"But I thought only boys played . . ." The instant the words slipped out of her mouth, Letty realized her folly.

Glory pulled herself up to the maximum of her seven-year-old height. "Mama says I can do anything boys can do. I like baseball. I hit things. Hard."

"I am sure you do." Letty handed the bat back, then mounted Sheba. Captain would need all his energy for the big race, so she rarely rode him these days. Liam handled his training. "Wu, I should be home before lunch. Timothy Rowley is expected later." She patted the sweet mare on the neck. "And keep those two out of trouble."

"You betcha, no worry." Wu held up a saddle brush. "We see who make da best shiny leather. Then ride ponies in pasture, eh?"

At noon Letty trotted into a quiet stable yard. She dismounted to walk Sheba through the open stable door. Snores emanated from the tack room.

"Wu, where are Johnny and Glory? I think Cook has lunch ready."

Wu started awake and then blinked. "Lunch a'ready? They are riding in pasture."

"I will get them."

She jogged Sheba around the big pasture. Because of the clumps of trees, it was hard to see where the children might be. She'd called out to them, but they must be ignoring her. Johnny would get a talking-to once she found them.

Odd . . . at the very back edge of the pasture, the fence was down. And not like it had fallen down, more like it was taken down on purpose. The grass was flattened as if someone had gone through it. *Lovely.* The little demons had let themselves out. There was nothing to do but follow them.

Timothy was back in Honolulu for another few days of business—at least that is what he'd told Grandmama. Again. She'd cocked an eyebrow but not pressed for further explanation. Except to comment that he might want to buy a sailboat instead of a sugar mill.

There was no way he could explain to Philomena about Letty. Hell's fire, he could not explain it to himself. The bone-deep attraction to someone completely unsuitable, who claimed she had no interest in him. If only he could forget the feel of her body that day on Hapuna. The flash of heat . . . or the sight of her standing in his ranch house . . . or her rising out of the ocean the day she saved Diablo . . .

This afternoon he had an appointment at Lang's; he needed more polo ponies, didn't he? What a farce. What he needed was to be back at the ranch schooling Diablo for the race. The race he must win to finally buy his own plantation. The one with the sugar mill. But here he was instead. Pitiful that he was reduced to this subterfuge, but he was longing to see Letty, and any excuse might do.

As Timothy rode into the stable yard, a very agitated Wu came bursting through the pasture gate. "Wu, what's wrong?"

"All gone and fence down."

"The horses are gone?"

"Miss Letty and children too. Maybe half an hour ago."

"Well, I am sure they will turn up in a moment."

"Very worried. Miss Letty never late for lunch."

"That's true." Timothy walked through the stable, giving everything a close look. It would be just like Johnny to be hiding close at hand.

"Wu, why are Johnny's dogs locked up?"

"To keep out of way while *keiki* ride."

Timothy grasped the latch of the stall door holding the three dogs prisoner. They bounced in anticipation of escape. "Give me half an hour—I will be back with them. If not, send a message to George."

He opened the door to an explosion of dogs. These little fellows might not be bloodhounds, but they would find their man. He was sure of it. The dogs' hullabaloo deafened. He and Percy best get going or they'd lose them.

The three dogs made several circles around the field, then a beeline toward the farthest reaches of the pasture. Ahead, Timothy watched the pack go right through a break in the fence. *Strange.* The Langs always kept their fences in such good repair.

The dogs ran like they knew what scent they followed. He bet they did. Timothy put his heels to Percy.

The going got rough quickly. He ducked to avoid being hit by branches. The little pack slowed down, tongues hanging out, but kept moving. The trail now led almost entirely straight uphill.

Percy whickered and got an answering response from another horse. Ahead through the trees he glimpsed a flash of white, Egg's spotted rump. There, in a sort of clearing, stood Lau Lau, Egg, and Sheba, all with their reins trailing on the ground.

"Letty! Johnny! Glory! Where are you?" No answer. The hair went up on the back of his neck. The dogs chose a path too narrow for horses. He grabbed Letty's bullwhip from her saddle, then noticed something sticking out of Egg's saddlebag. Some sort of a long club. That might be useful too. If they had fallen down a cliff, he would need something to pull them up.

The dogs barked in the distance.

Letty huffed up the trail. She would personally administer the punishment for this. Not only had the children led her on this wild chase, they made her miss lunch.

"All right, you two! Come out now! I know you are hiding!"

She stumbled. Hands gripped her on either side, pulling her upright. She found herself gazing into a pair of dark pools that passed for eyes. Three skeletal men in tattered clothing held her. "Welcome, *mākāhā*."

The men dragged a struggling Letty into a clearing at the edge of a steep cliff. Both children appeared in the mouth of a lava cave; a bamboo grating held them in. Johnny called out. One of the men gave a low hiss and the boy fell back, holding his ears and whimpering.

"You see, *mākāhā*, we have the children. Just do what we say, and all will go well." This from the man with the dead eyes.

"What do you want?" The fingers of her captors dug into her arms. The men smelled of rotten things. She struggled not to gag. "And my name is not *mākāhā*, it is Letty. You have the wrong person. Let us go."

"Oh no, you are the one. The heat of the living land fairly rises off your skin. You have the gift of the *'āina*." His nostrils widened. "I can almost smell the sulfur. Yes, you will prove most useful."

If she were by herself, she might try to shake them off and run. But with Johnny and Glory in that cave . . .

To make matters worse, the three musketeers burst out from the bushes. Barking at full cry, they headed straight for Johnny behind the bamboo grate.

"Go, lock them in with the children."

One of the men swept the wriggling mass of dogs into the cave. This might be her only chance to pull away.

Instead her arms were wrenched back harder. "I know you think to flee. Do not bother. You will help us and then we shall see."

"What do you think I can do?"

"Such modesty. You are a Gate, a *mākāhā* of the power of the *'āina*. You make intentions real. We have an intention we need a bit of help with, that is all." He lifted her chin to look right into her eyes. "We have been watching you. We know you are . . . helpful." The men dragged her to a square block of lava with objects on it.

"That's hair."

"Why, so it is."

Acid rose in her throat. "What are you doing with that?"

"You know what we do with that: we make someone pay the price."

"No!" Her voice came out in a howl. "I cannot help! Not that!"

"Oh, but you can, and you will. It is Gannon, you know. The money lender. Surely your *'ohana* wants vengeance?"

"No!"

As he rounded the edge of a large lava rock, Timothy heard a man's voice. "You will do as I say, woman! You are nothing! Worthless!"

Three ragged men surrounded Letty. She knelt next to a large black stone with her arms held behind her.

"You don't understand. My gift doesn't work that way. I am a Gate for healing only."

"Is that what she told you? The witch with the white wave in her hair?" He leaned forward to hiss in her ear. "She lied. Enough of this. Lio, throw the girl child off the cliff."

The dogs began to bark again as the man called Lio pulled a kicking and struggling Glory out of the cave. The man interrogating Letty chuckled. "You can spare the child if you do what we ask."

Glory screamed. Letty crumpled to the ground. "Stop! I will do what you say."

"It is very simple. All you must do is breathe . . ."

Timothy saw his chance. All eyes were on the objects on the stone. The two men with Letty placed their hands flat on her back. If he could free Letty, between the two of them, they could make short work of this trio. Maybe.

He edged around the cliff, Glory's club in hand, ready to strike. Johnny saw him. Timothy held his finger to his lips. Johnny nodded. The man holding Glory freed her to turn his attention back to Letty and the stone. Glory surreptitiously began to pick up rocks, all good until the three musketeers started barking again.

It had to be now. Timothy ran forward with a howl, club swinging. Startled, the men jumped back and lost their hold on Letty. She threw punches. Glory threw rocks. Johnny yelled. One man fell to the ground with a grunt while the other two fled. Timothy tossed Letty her bullwhip, then gave the club a whirling throw. Thunk. A second man went down as the third escaped over the cliff.

Letty flew past Timothy to peer over the steep edge. "Gone, and he was the leader too. These cliffs are riddled with caves. He could be hiding in any one of them. We'll never find him."

Timothy herded the two sorry specimens back from the cliff, club in hand.

"Let me out! It's creepy! There are bones in here!"

"Hold on, Johnny." First Letty walked to the stone. Pulling out a handkerchief, she carefully wrapped the hair and other objects in it. Then she helped Glory pull aside the grate to open the cave. Letty stuck her head in. "No wonder you were frightened. This is a burial cave, and quite ancient from the looks of it." Johnny came racing out, dogs jumping between his legs.

Timothy stood over the two men. Up close they looked even more pitiful. Glory grabbed his arm. "Mr. Rowley! Don't hurt my baseball bat! It will be ruined if you hit that stinky man with it."

"If he stays still, I won't have to."

Letty unfurled her bullwhip and snapped it. Red lights flickered around her. "Timothy, I must talk to these men."

"Be careful."

He stood aside, ready to jump in if needed. Poor bastards. He would not want to be facing an angry Letty with a whip in her hand. Ever.

"Your names." The men were silent. Letty flicked the air above each one delicately with her whip. "Your names . . . *now.*"

"Keolo."

"Lio."

"And the name of your leader."

Again, silence. Letty made her whip dance around them once more, still without contact. It sang like the crackle of flames on dry tinder. She was magnificent. And scary.

"He has no name."

Her whip kissed the man's hand.

"Kalai."

She shook her head. "I doubt very much he shares a name with a god, especially the god of poisons."

Her whip sang out over their heads.

"Hewahewa."

She moved closer to the men. "Hear me. I let you go to carry this message to the one who dares call himself Hewahewa. I am guided by she who rides the white mule . . . the old one. She protects me and my *'ohana.* Understand this: If you make trouble for me, you make trouble for her. Then she makes trouble for you. Go now."

She stepped back as the men scuttled like crabs over the edge of the cliff. The red lights around her faded.

Timothy waited behind. "Why did you let them go?"

"Did you see them? They are the last of their kind. They are starving. If I had turned them over to the police, they would have gone to jail and perished."

"What's this about Hewahewa? And was that a lock of hair?"

"Later. Now we want the children to see this simply as a gay adventure." She pasted on a smile. "How is everyone? I am hungry. Anyone else?"

"Me!" Johnny and Glory spoke as one. Glory reached out to take her baseball bat from Timothy. She fingered the nick in it from Timothy's throw, sighing as if the weight of the world were on her shoulders. "I knew I should have left it at home."

The two began running down the trail back to the horses, the dogs dancing behind them.

Letty stood stock-still for a moment, eyes down, breathing deeply. Then lifted her face to his, lower lip trembling slightly. Good god, all he wanted to do was kiss her. Until she broke the moment.

"Last one home gets the smallest piece of pineapple cake!"

After lunch—where large slices of pineapple cake were had by all—Timothy and Letty rode back to ʻĀinahau with the children. Kahōkūlani stood on the big porch steps feeding tidbits to her peacocks. Letty had never been so glad to see her.

Agnes's pony cart was under the banyan. Sounds of the girls playing emanated from inside the house. Timothy ushered the children in to join their siblings. Following Johnny through the door, holding Glory's hand, he turned to give Letty a nod. She mouthed a silent "thank you" in return, wishing she was the one whose hand he grasped. Silliness.

Letty pulled the handkerchief out of her pocket and dropped it into Kahōkūlani's lap.

"What's this?"

"I was told it is Gannon's hair. You know, the hunk he woke up missing in the jail."

"Thank goodness you retrieved it. How did you get it?"

"Well, that is the interesting part. Three emaciated old men trapped me in the belief that I could be a *mākāhā* for them to complete the *pule ʻanāʻanā* on Gannon." She suddenly needed to sit down. "The leader called himself Hewahewa."

"Hewahewa? Like Kamehameha's high priest? That was a hundred years ago! I have not heard that name since I was a child!" Kahōkūlani grasped Letty's hand. "Where are these men now?"

"Well, something told me I had to let them go . . . to be merciful . . . so I did. But I made threats."

"Threats?"

"Yes, that a tiny woman on a white mule would haunt them . . ."

Kahōkūlani gave a rare laugh. "Well done. It does not get much more frightful than that." She poked the handkerchief. "I suspect Mr. Gannon will be very glad to see this little bundle of hair. I don't wish the *puleʻanāʻanā* on anyone.

"I should tell you I was worried enough to call in *kāhuna* to protect Gannon in the jail, some friends of Esther's from over the Pali. Chen Zhou very graciously chose to look the other way. Gannon had actually begun to waste away. I had reason to fear the *puleʻanāʻanā* was working."

"Could they have used me as a Gate for their evil? They put their hands on my back like they could."

"I don't know, child, I just don't know. So much knowledge has been lost. How are you explaining this all to Agnes and Imogene?"

"The children will tell them the truth. As they see it. They babbled about it all the way home. That some crazy old men lured them away from their ponies. But they saved me. By yelling and throwing rocks. Or something like that."

"Quite. And Timothy?"

"I never need to explain. He always seems to know what I am thinking."

Kahōkūlani raised one eyebrow.

"Anyway, he heads back to his ranch tonight. His grandmama is waiting. And that Adele Simmons." Letty was attempting to be grateful Timothy had a more suitable object of his affections. It was not easy.

"Quite."

'Iolani Ranch, Hawaii Island, the 25th of August, 1909

Adele's fingers dug into Timothy's right shoulder like talons. This was perhaps not the best of his ideas, giving Adele a riding lesson. But she was trying so hard to please. She always did.

Heading to Kahōkūlani's to borrow sweet old Fairy seemed just the trick. Or so he had hoped. Yet here he was walking the elderly pony ever so slowly around Kahōkūlani's paddock. As the terrified Adele mangled his shoulder with one hand and clung fiercely to the pommel of the saddle with the other.

He'd owe Fairy a lump of sugar for this. Bull lounged on the paddock fence, grinning like a man contemplating how best to torture him about it all. Timothy had been the target of Bull's mirth before. He avoided it when possible. Unfortunately, it was abundantly clear today's activities provided too fertile a field to be ignored.

Grandmama, the Princess, and Adele's mother stood in the shade of the big stable door bearing witness. Mrs. Simmons's indistinct voice ran on, punctuated by Grandmama's occasional "mm-hm" and, rarer, "quite." Kahōkūlani said nothing.

Timothy led the pony and the frightened woman around the perimeter of the paddock once again.

In a low voice he said, "Adele, please breathe."

Her breath came out in a whoosh. "I am so sorry."

"You don't need to be sorry, I just don't want you fainting. You might scare dear old Fairy." Really, Adele tried so hard. Almost too hard. He could become fond of her.

Unfortunately he craved more than fondness. All he dreamed of now was flame.

He might have predicted Grandmama would have an opinion about this. But she held on to it until that evening. With her after-supper brandy in hand, out on the plantation lānai.

"Very thoughtful of you to give the young woman a riding lesson, my dear."

That tone was familiar, as was the sort of sentence that has a hidden "but" at the end of it. He decided to jump right in. "But what?"

"Her mama seems to believe you have intentions. Do you?"

His chest constricted for a moment. "I don't know." Then a breath. "I might." He needed to get over Letty. She had made it plain that there was no future between them. She was right. But Adele? An American oil heiress would be quite acceptable in London. If he could only figure out how to leave her mother in San Francisco. Or on some remote desert island.

"And why is that?"

"She is a lovely lady. Very kind. She told me she longs for her own household."

Philomena pursed her lips. "I can hardly blame her for that. Anything to get out from under her mother's thumb, I'll wager."

"Adele is exactly the sort of wife who can help further my business ambitions."

"And what exactly are those?"

His grandmother knew he'd found another plantation to buy, and a sugar mill. This one in his own name, with the money he'd already squirreled away. He almost had enough. The Gentleman's Cup purse would put him over the top.

But his other motivation? He'd not admit to his grandmother that he was driven to show his father how wrong he had been. To show that the worthless fourth son could marry well and make his own fortune to boot. He rarely confessed that motive to himself.

"Timothy, we are in a new world. When I married your grandfather fifty years ago, marrying for money was what one did; no one thought twice about it. It is different now. You can make your own money; we already know you have the gift. Why would you spend your life saddled with someone who did not amuse you? Who was not your good friend?"

"It's not like that, Grandmama. I like her very much."

"Pah! Don't be so old-fashioned! That milquetoast will bore you thrice over. Understand this: I cared for your grandfather. But love? Not really.

"You have a choice, you know. Your generation. You can choose love. If I had it to do over, I might have made that choice."

He sat down on the floor next to her chair just as he'd done as a small boy, a whiff of her rose perfume taking him back. She ruffled his hair as she spoke. "My life was full but very lonely. Yes, to do it again, I would choose love."

"I will think about it, Grandmama."

Except that he had no choice. There was no love to choose. The one person he could love, he could never have. Never. Or so she said. She had other plans.

CHAPTER TWENTY-FIVE

Anaina

CROWD

MacHenry Ranch, Hawaii Island, the 3rd of September, 1909

Letty paused in her brushing of Scheherazade, resting her arm comfortably on the mare's back, to take it all in. Swirls of bright color. Flower-bedecked horses. Smiling people. Was there any more glorious affair than a gathering of Hawaiian horse lovers?

MacHenry Ranch had played host to the famous Gentleman's Cup for over two decades now. She'd attended the festivities every year since she could remember. The Cup began with a few days of social whirl before the races: rodeo, dancing, and of course, *lū'au*. Then the main event: a brutal three-mile race to decide who would take the cup home. Today was the opening day.

She wondered that she had not yet seen Timothy, though he must certainly be here. If he still intended to race, that is.

In the distance, Letty watched her grandfather walk from tent to tent, shaking hands and slapping backs. Tall and silver haired, he still cut quite a figure in any crowd. Here he was a bit of a celebrity, having won the very first Gentleman's Cup on his now-long-dead stallion Windjammer, Captain's grandsire.

Timothy rode around the corner of one of the far tents. Letty held the brush up to wave but thought better of it.

The man trotted toward her anyway and dismounted, smiling broadly. "Letty! I am so very glad to see you!" His hand was extended, eyes warm. "No more crazy old men to chastise?"

"Only you," she teased. She shook his hand, stifling the urge to fly into his arms. She stared up as if to drink him in. This had to stop.

"Have you met my grandmother yet?" he asked. "She was here yesterday to set up."

"We just barely arrived, so no."

"Grandmama and Aunt Clarissa are staying out at the plantation house in Hawi, since the ranch house is not ready." He grimaced. "They are 'beautifying' the place. Thank goodness I will not be living there anytime soon!" His voice dropped a dramatic octave. "There is discussion of eggplant drapes."

Letty snorted with laughter. "And how is the new ranch house coming along? Any thought of eggplant drapes there?"

"I can't wait for you to see the progress; the house should be completed by Christmas. But you really must come see Lohiʻau! Perhaps after the race? He is magnificent." Timothy arched one eyebrow. "He glows red in the sun—just like you. Can you imagine?"

She'd not rise to that bait. "Perhaps before we head home? We brought over some horses to sell, and Captain to race, of course." She reached over to scratch Champagne behind his left ear. "By the way, thank you for persuading A. J. to add a jumping exhibition. The Princess is loaning me Malolo."

"Yes, I know. Much to my chagrin, I asked to borrow her too late. You and I have yet to see who is the superior jumper."

"I am."

"Of course you are. Best at everything, that's you."

"I only do it to keep you humble."

"Quite."

He grasped her hand again. A tendril of flame shot up her arm, straight to her heart. "All is well? Your plans for school are still afoot?"

"Truly." She squeezed his hand in return, absurdly grateful that he asked, relishing the steady strength of his clasp. Then dropped his hand. She mustn't ever forget that her love might kill him.

"Have you seen the Letwins? They always aim to take the Gentleman's Cup back to Maui. The talk is all about their new thoroughbred stallion—he looks to be the favorite."

"I saw him, a big chestnut with long legs. Archangel. Diablo can best him. Such an appropriate choice of names, don't you think?" Timothy arched an eyebrow in an attempt to look devilish. He did not quite pull it off. "That angel is going to eat my devil's dust."

Timothy might talk cocky, but Letty knew he was savvy enough to warrant the Letwins' horse a serious threat. "Besides, I have no choice but to win. Grandmama will shoot me if her horse does not carry the day."

"I can't wait to meet her. She sounds like my kind of lady."

"Hah! I can only imagine the two of you together. Fire personified."

He spoke more quietly. "And I am serious about winning. This purse would give me the last of what I need to buy my plantation. I need to complete that deal soon so no one else will buy the property out from under me."

"Ah, I wondered."

Liam trotted up on Sinbad. He did not dismount so much as throw himself off the horse. "Rowley, old man! I have not seen you since the magnificent driving machine arrived! Have you heard the news? We sold our first car! Not only are we going into the motorcar business, but I will be the head mechanic!"

"After you finish school, that is." Letty was a stickler for the full story.

"Details, details, sister mine. Details are the province of lesser mortals."

Timothy turned back to Letty. "Will I see you at the *paniolo* dance tonight?"

Letty nodded as something across the way caught her eye. "Timothy, is that Mrs. Simmons I see?"

"Um, yes. And Adele is here too. They were visiting the Letwins . . . again . . . and jumped at the chance to come meet a real dowager countess. That would be my grandmother." He turned to look disconsolately at the woman moving through the throng, Adele now visible in her wake. "I gave her a riding lesson a few days ago." He looked back at Letty with a challenge. "I just keep saying to myself, *Her fortune is large . . . her fortune is large . . .*"

"You poor thing." She patted his arm. "You'll figure it out. Besides, Timothy, Adele is not the only heiress here. What about Lokelani? Or even Irene?"

"Adele is actually very nice and loves horses. Tame ones. Kahōkūlani even let her ride Fairy."

Timothy moved off, pulling Champagne behind him.

"Can it be that important that he marry money?" Liam fingered Sinbad's reins. "This is not about you in some roundabout way, is it? Is it?"

"Of course not. It's complicated."

"Hmmmm. It's always complicated."

"Oh for heaven's sake. Timothy is estranged from his father. He has convinced himself that if he marries an heiress and takes her home to England, all will be forgiven." Hopefully she did not sound too waspish about this. "I wish I thought life was that simple."

"Whatever you say, sister mine. Anyway, Papa sent me to fetch you. The Letwins want more polo ponies, and they want to speak to you."

At teatime, back at 'Iolani, Miyako helped Letty slip on a simple white sprigged cotton *holokū* with just the perfect touch of ruffles.

"*Mahalo*, Miyako!"

"This fit just right unless you grow over summer." Miyako raised one expressive eyebrow as she looked Letty up and down. "You no more grow, yes? You already plenty big."

"Oh, I am done, for sure!" At least she hoped so.

Letty was saving her blue silk *holokū* for the gala celebration after the big race. Amazingly, Miyako had cleaned and repaired the dress, adding more embroidery to cover the torn places. If anything, the dress was even more beautiful. Letty would wear it as a badge of honor. . . of how grateful she was to be a survivor . . . thanks to Diablo. If Diablo raced well, so much the better.

Agnes walked into the kitchen wrapped in one of Kahōkūlani's Japanese robes, her baby belly just barely visible. "Miyako! That is lovely. Letty looks perfect."

"Letty one big *kine wahine*, joy to make dress."

"Agnes, did you get a good nap?" Letty asked.

"Delicious. I am ready to be the belle of the ball tonight."

"I talked to Timothy today."

"How is he?"

"Bound and determined to marry himself an heiress! Adele Simmons and her mother are here on the hunt again, after another visit on Maui. I gather that our Timothy is once again the prime target. Mrs. Simmons seems positively transfixed by the prospect of a dowager countess as a grandmother-in-law."

"The poor man." Agnes came closer. "And how do you feel about that?"

"Fine. Of course. That's what he wants."

If only she believed that. Her flames most certainly did not.

Chapter Twenty-Six

Hula

DANCING

Strings of colored lanterns crisscrossed the big MacHenry Ranch lawn. Racing mobs of children swirled like schools of yellow tang on the reef. Ti leaf–bedecked tables groaned under the weight of platters of food: roast pork, sweet potatoes, *lau lau*, poi, spiced pineapple, and of course *haupia*—the traditional coconut pudding. Letty loved a good *haupia*. The MacHenry Ranch cook was famous for it. Over an open fire pit, a bullock turned on a spit.

Letty and her *'ohana* plunged into the throng. Horsemen from every island knew the Langs. And now the family was to be in the motorcar business? Such news! She found herself quite enjoying the moment.

"Letty! Letty!" Lokelani Letwin muscled her way through the crowd to take her hand. "Are you well? Last time I saw you, it was a sad day on the polo field!"

"Today I could not be better. When did you get here?"

"Just this afternoon. Would you believe Papa chartered one of Captain Kalama's steamers to bring his prize stallion here a week ago? But not me. Oh no! I, as merely the one and only daughter, must wait to take the scheduled boat. If I only had hooves and whiskers, I might be loved!" She flipped her blond curls to the opposite shoulder like a nice flip of a mane.

"It is the same in our family; the horses always come first. It's business."

"I hear now it will be motorcars! Come greet Mama when you are settled. I know she would love to see you."

At that, Letty recalled her manners. "Have you met my stepmother? Lokelani Letwin, this is Mrs. Lang."

"Agnes to you, my dear. Letty has told me so much about you."

Lokelani dimpled prettily. *Honestly, sometimes things are just not fair,* Letty thought. "My pleasure." Lokelani waved as she whirled away.

Agnes patted her arm. "Of course you've never even mentioned her. But I promise to protect your secret. Now go— no need for you and Liam to stay with us. I am going to find Imogene and introduce her to more of our world. I am sure all and sundry need motorcars!"

Agnes glided away as Letty turned to take in the scene. Timothy stood across the way at the center of a cluster of women, including Mrs. Simmons. She may as well get this over with.

"Letty!" Timothy yelled, his relief at a possible distraction visible. "Please come meet my family." As he moved to her side, she glimpsed two of the most elegant women imaginable. The older one stood ramrod straight, silver hair piled high, dressed in a simple dove-gray gown that set off the richness of her diamond earrings and lavaliere to perfection. Beside her was a younger version of herself, all in black, talking animatedly to the Princess.

In contrast, Mrs. Simmons, in something mauve and beaded, more suitable for teatime than a *paniolo* party, sat fanning herself furiously in the heat, all the while attempting conversation with the dowager. Adele stood a bit away from her mother and chatted with Hugh Letwin. Count on Hugh to play the gentleman; he gave Adele his undivided attention.

"Timothy, I am very much looking forward to meeting your family." She took his proffered hand as he drew her toward the silver-haired woman. A trail of fire danced up her arm. Damn her traitorous flames.

"Grandmama, might I introduce my friend Letty Lang, whom I have told you so much about . . ."

Letty gave in to the temptation to drop a full-on curtsey, the sort more proper for a royal audience or a debutante ball. Decidedly over the top for a country dance. The grand curtsey—another skill acquired at the Redwood School. "Charmed, my lady."

The dowager countess gave out a melodious laugh as she reached for Letty's hand. "Timothy did not tell me you were cheeky in his descriptions of your many competencies." Letty found herself captured in the woman's direct gaze. Eyes twinkling, the dowager countess went on. "Let's see, if I have this right, you are the one who saved the stallion, delivered the colt, trained the polo ponies, owns a beastly little dog, and has read *The Scarlet Pimpernel* four times. Or perhaps five. Does that cover it?"

Letty's cheeks warmed. "Yes, madam." Goodness, she hoped that Timothy had neglected to share that she also was known to glow red!

"Quite. Well, I am most delighted to meet you, my dear. Timothy has need of good friends on his adventures here. He is fortunate to have made your acquaintance."

"And this is my favorite aunt, Clarissa Rowley Jones," Timothy said. "Miss Letty Lang."

Clarissa also took her hand in greeting. "He calls me the favorite aunt because I am his *only* aunt. K has told me so much about you. I do hope that after this charming event we can find time for a quiet cup of tea. I am eager to learn more about your islands."

"I am pleased to meet you too. I hope to stay with K for a couple of days after the race. I am sure we shall see each other."

Simple good manners suggested to Letty that she greet Mrs. Simmons. "Mrs. Simmons, how nice that you and Adele are able to visit the Big Island again. I hope you will enjoy all the festivities."

"I have no doubt we will." The chill with which Mrs. Simmons replied brooked no further comment.

Letty refused to let the woman fluster her. She turned, waving to Timothy as she moved away.

Mrs. Simmons's voice behind her was unmistakable. "So very gracious of you, Countess, to greet a member of the working class that way."

Letty also heard the dowager's clipped reply. "As I see it, at the end of the day we are all working class. And we'd best not forget it. That's why people lost their heads in France."

Indeed.

The *paniolo* affair had something for everyone. No dance cards, just dancing and plenty of it. Everything from polkas to waltzes. All Letty's 'ohana were notoriously good dancers, those long Lang legs offering a clear advantage. Her grandfather, always a particular favorite of the ladies since his days in the royal Hawaiian court, tonight struck Letty as the most dashing figure in the melee. Well, except Timothy, of course.

At a break in the music, Lot sidled up to her. "I think I would like to dance with that lovely silver-haired woman standing with Timothy. She's swaying to the music and no one is asking her to dance. What must she think of our lack of hospitality? I am just the man for the task."

"*Tūtū kāne*, you know that woman is Timothy's grandmama? The dowager countess? Are you sure? What if she says no?"

"Pish, I know a woman who'd like to dance when I see one. Take me to meet her."

If she refused to do it, he would just head over there anyway. Letty began wending her way through the crowd with Lot right behind her.

"My lady? May I present my grandfather, Lot Liholiho Lang? He has a request of you."

Her *tūtū kāne* rendered a deep and courtly bow. Letty sometimes forgot he'd been one of the queen's favorites too. Clearly he had not forgotten.

"Shall we dance, my lady?" For some few seconds that seemed like an eternity, the dowager said nothing. Letty began to pray for the earth to swallow her up.

Then: "That would be divine. Please call me Philomena. Shall I call you Lot?" The vision in dove gray sailed off on the arm of her grandfather, right into a *paniolo* polka. Letty turned to watch in amazement. That woman could dance!

"Now it's my turn."

Brushing sandy curls out of his eyes, Timothy delivered a smile that would make any heart melt. In hers, it kindled a blaze. "No, what I meant was, it is my turn to ask you to dance. A waltz is next, I think I can manage that. Shall we?"

A waltz. He would put his hands on her. Tiny tendrils of flame jigged up and down her spine. She must say no.

"Yes, of course." Her skin went straight to flame where he placed his hand, pulling her out into the swirl of dancers as the music changed to the swooping cadence of a waltz.

Why didn't she say no?

She would seize this moment to last a lifetime. She'd sur-render to the night, the man, and the music. Just this once. Only this once. The cooler night air caressed her legs as her dress belled out when they dipped. Her hair came loose from its pins to fly with the dance's pulse. Laughter and fire bubbled up.

And she'd be gone away to San Francisco soon enough.

CHAPTER TWENTY-SEVEN

Heihei Lio

HORSE RACE

Kohala, Hawaii Island, the 5th of September, 1909

Even in the early morning, you knew the day would be hot. The heat already shimmered over the blue Pacific. Timothy rode Champagne toward Kauluwehi with Diablo trotting along on a lead rope behind, docile as a lamb. Or not. The stallion had a slow burn, but when he caught fire, best get out of the way. If the horse raced the same way, this could be a very good day indeed.

Behind, at enough distance to avoid eating his dust, rode his grandmother and aunt. Hank Smith brought up the rear with the equipment wagon, also loaded with clothing changes for the ladies and two precious blocks of ice.

Hank's reunion with Grandmama had been touching. Timothy would not forget it: "Dear Hank, you are looking well." Then Hank falling on his knees to say, "Can you forgive me, my lady? I failed you," in a voice that was almost sobbing. Her reply was pure Philomena, crisp yet kind. "Stand up, my man. All is well that ends well, and this appears to be ending very well."

Timothy reached down to pat Champagne's neck. Grandmama's visit had him questioning all his assumptions. What if he chose not to go back to England? Some days he just wasn't sure of anything. Life in Hawaii was more than he could ever have imagined, yet something called him home. But to what? Surely there was nothing for him there? Unless, of course, he appeared with an heiress as his bride. Perhaps then reconciliation with his father was possible. Or not.

He had a proper heiress staring him right in the face. Adele. She fit his every logical wifely requirement except one: he was not in love with her. Grandmama had cornered him once again this morning to press her point. Her take on the situation still surprised him. That he marry for love? If only it were that simple.

"I will think about it, Grandmama." That's what he'd told Philomena.

He was thinking about it. He couldn't stop thinking about it. Every tall, bronzed, fiery, fearless, and unforgettable bit of it.

Damnation.

Timothy stood in front of the big white tent, wearing his ranch colors—buff breeches and a white shirt with a wide, fire-red stripe across the back. The simplicity of the design pleased him. But no jockey cap. Rather, like the other gentlemen, he sported a Panama hat. This was Hawaii, after all.

Today he would race not only for the purse that might give him full partnership in Moran Sugar, but also to prove to himself, once and for all, that he belonged.

Letty appeared at his side wearing her working uniform: a divided skirt and a Lang calico work shirt, hair in two practical braids, her *paniolo* hat firmly down around her ears. She looked beautiful.

"I brought you something. Give me your hat."

He handed it over without comment.

"This is a hatband for the Big Island. It is *lehua* flowers, the red of your colors. Like fire." She deftly arranged it on the hat. "*Lehua* is a sign of Pele's favor. And mine." Handing him the hat, she stood back, unsmiling. "Put this on so I can see if I got it right."

She gave him a critical look. "That will do. May I give Diablo a kiss for luck?"

He nearly quipped, "What about me?" but thought better of it.

Letty stood in front of the big stallion. As before, Diablo leaned his whole head against her chest and breathed. Bloody hell, had she just flashed red? Timothy gulped as he watched Letty kiss the horse on the end of his nose.

"Here are the facts, Timothy. Our Captain won't win; he never has. He just shows well every time. It's good for business that he runs. Helps us sell horses." Her hand returned to stroking Diablo's neck. "But this one? He is precisely the gentleman to win the Gentleman's Cup. He just told me he is ready. Trust him, Timothy. He has a great heart."

Then she simply turned and walked away. He'd not said a word during the entire encounter. He didn't need to.

Diablo turned his great head to give Timothy a nose. "Right, old man. We'd best not disappoint her."

Grandmama emerged from the tent, fanning herself. Clarissa followed.

"Was that Letty?"

"Yes, I think she just bewitched our horse so he can win."

"Well, I keep wondering if she hasn't bewitched *you*."

He snorted. "Honestly, Grandmama, we are just friends. That's all it can be. Why can't I have a friend of the opposite sex? Why must it always be a romance?" How could he explain what he felt about Letty to his family when he did not understand it himself?

"Because it looks like a romance." This from Clarissa. "You need to get your thoughts together on this, nephew. Because some people might say you are leading her on. And what of harming her reputation?"

"Women in Hawaii don't have 'reputations.'"

The women gave simultaneous guffaws. "We must pull you out from under your rock before you turn into a complete lizard. *Of course* they have reputations." Clarissa shook her head. "Reputations are the prisons we women have been held in for millennia. They should not matter, but they do."

"You could hurt her, Timothy. People are already talking."

"I'll be careful. Now I have a race to ride."

He headed off to the paddock, where all the riders gathered to shake hands and mount up before the parade to the track. Letty worked at the other end of the paddock, helping Liam mount up.

Timothy maintained a firm hold on Diablo, although he did not need to; the stallion stood stone-cold calm. Perhaps the competition would mistake this cool demeanor for lack of fire. The element of surprise might work in their favor. Timothy could only hope.

Timothy had his hand out to wish Hugh Letwin luck on Archangel, when his bum knee buckled with searing pain. He'd been kicked.

Hank Smith grabbed Diablo's reins. The rider whose horse delivered the blow babbled his apologies as Timothy fought to get up.

"You want to ride in this race?" This was Letty. Magically beside him, her voice already altered by her breathing.

"Yes, I do."

"Pull yourself up by the stirrup leathers and let your leg dangle. When you feel the warmth from my hands, I want you to say out loud, 'I will ride . . . I will ride . . .' Understand?"

He did as he was told, while Hank made every attempt to look as if this was an everyday occurrence. Thankfully others had their own horses to get ready. Letty knelt to grab Timothy's knee, cupping it with both hands. She breathed in earnest now. The warmth from her hands damn near burned. "Chant your intention," she gasped.

"I will ride . . . I will ride . . . I . . ." *Oh my god.* The pain . . . receded.

"Mount up." She glared at him, flinging her braids back. "And you take him out to win." Diablo turned his head to nudge her. "Yes, you win."

Timothy could not look her in the eye, or he might lose his composure. "We will see you at the end."

Watching Timothy ride away, Letty realized people were staring and whispering. Lovely. Well, if people were going to talk, she might as well give them something to talk about.

"Hank, at the end of the race, he will need ice on that knee."

The little man nodded. "Never you fear, ma'am. I already have ice pails ready for all our brave beasts. Mr. Tim can have his right along with Diablo."

Letty went to join her family along the rail at what would be the final turn, rubbing her neck to ease the tension. The parade to the post began.

For the Gentleman's Cup, every racer must ride his own—or his family's—horse. No hired jockeys. Chartwell no longer rode, but two of his horses, Windsor and Levitation, were racing, with family members doing the honors. Hugh Letwin rode

Archangel. Liam had Captain well in hand. The other horses in the race were not familiar to her. Letty counted a smaller field than in previous years, but still a tough one. A race this long required almost four turns around the oval, a test of both speed and stamina.

In theory, a starting line is simple. Horses line up and a pistol is fired. But in practice, that theory crumbles. Today was no exception. Horses reared, jostled, and turned tail. Except Diablo. He stood as if nothing in the world could be more tedious.

Lot leaned over. "Letty, is something wrong with Timothy's horse?"

"No, that is just his way."

After an eternity, the pistol shot cracked. And they were off.

Liam broke in the middle of the pack with surprisingly good field position.

But not Diablo. The stallion ran next to last. He hardly looked to be galloping, his gait more like a canter in the park. To her left she heard, "Get a load of that big bay. He must be a dog. Hope Rowley did not pay too much for him."

The pace of the leaders was blisteringly fast. By the end of the second turn around the track, some of the horses seemed to be tiring.

Liam had Captain in fifth place, and the eight-year-old looked steady. If he could keep up the pace, it might be his best finish yet. The field held solid with little change through the third round. Archangel kept the lead at a blistering pace.

And then there was Diablo. When would Timothy make his move? She'd seen the horse run. Was Timothy in pain? If she knew anything about him, it was that he'd ride right through pain. And he needed the purse; only a win would do to buy his sugar mill.

The horses came back around to start the final circuit with still a good distance to go, almost three-quarters of a mile. *Wait, was Diablo moving up?* George began pounding her on the back. "Look at that damn Rowley! He was acting the ringer!"

Diablo now ran full out, long and low, his legs stretching in a ground-eating stride. Timothy, hat long gone, stayed glued to his back. Diablo gained on the leaders, but would it be enough this late in the race? She squeezed the rail so hard she got a splinter. Irene had an arm around her. The roar of the crowd faded. Letty held her breath . . .

Chapter Twenty-Eight

Lanakila

VICTORY

In the MacHenry box, Kahōkūlani had one arm linked with Captain Kalama's and the other waving madly in the air.

The dowager was on her feet, screaming, already hoarse. "That's my boy! Ride him!" Clarissa jumped up and down like a young girl.

Mrs. Simmons stared fixedly through field glasses. The nearsighted Adele kept asking what was happening. And how Hugh Letwin fared.

"Diablo is moving up now, moving up fast," the dowager announced with much satisfaction. "That is how we Rowleys carry the day. Slow and steady, and surprise them at the end."

As the horses pounded into the final turn, Letty crossed her arms to hold herself together. Her mouth went dry. Diablo gained ground relentlessly, fast and steady like a freight train coming downhill. A runaway freight train. But Archangel still had a commanding lead. Until—could it be?—the big chestnut visibly began to tire.

Diablo swept past Archangel just as the field rolled by the Langs' position on the rail, heading to the finish line in front of the MacHenry box. Wild cheers exploded. Diablo won it! Going away! Timothy struggled to slow the stallion and turn him. Diablo gave a victory hop before heading to the winner's circle.

Letty broke away from her family to weave through the crowd. What if Timothy could not walk? Would he need help? Ahead, A. J. Chartwell pulled the big silver bowl that was the Cup out of its protective traveling case. He held it aloft on his way from the box to the dusty track.

Thank goodness, Hank was right there to take the reins. Diablo stood quietly, glistening with sweat but scarcely even blowing. Timothy dismounted, grasping the stirrup for stability. Letty slipped under the fence but hung back. She did not want to cause another scene, yet she would be close if he needed her.

A. J. Chartwell delivered the traditional salute. "The gentleman triumphs!" The crowd roared. One of the MacHenry housemen popped a huge bottle of champagne and poured it into the winner's big silver bowl. With no further ado, A. J. dumped the entire contents over Timothy, to everyone's amusement.

Now for the flowers. The race judges came forward to place a horse-sized lei on Diablo, woven with every Hawaiian flower imaginable. Letty smelled it from where she stood. At this, Diablo began to get a bit restive.

Then A. J. presented Timothy with a magnificent lei of ferns and maile leaves, fit for a prince. In the Cup tradition, the winning gentleman asked one of the ladies in attendance to place the lei around his neck with a kiss on each cheek. Adele's mother pushed her forward. Letty hoped that Timothy would give it to his grandmother instead. After all, she'd bought the horse.

"Letty?"

She started and stood upright as Timothy limped toward her.

"This could never have happened without you." He held out the lei to her, continuing in a low voice, "Please don't make a fuss. It will make me most happy to share this victory with you."

"I am honored, Mr. Rowley." She swallowed as she put the fragrant lei over his head, then kissed him on each cheek. The stares of the onlookers burned into her. For the second time today.

Behind her, she saw that the face of Mrs. Simmons had turned a rather violent shade of purple. Roughly, the woman grabbed Adele and headed back up to the box.

Kahōkūlani mingled with the crowd. "Yes, she assisted in training . . . They are great friends, nothing more." Then, turning to another group, "Actually, she saved the horse's life in an accident at sea. Of course he is grateful. It is nothing more . . ."

Timothy and Letty were surrounded by a throng of people, but it felt like they were standing in a bubble.

"How is your knee?"

"Damnable, but I felt good enough to ride."

"I am not a miracle worker."

"Yes, you are." He leaned in. "I am sorry to be playing havoc with your reputation, but this just seemed right."

"Hawaiian women don't care about silly things like reputations."

"What do you care about?"

"Not doing anything foolish. You."

For once, she'd rendered him speechless.

She rolled her eyes and turned to yell, "Hank! Don't forget what I told you about the ice!"

"I have it taken care of, ma'am."

"Well then, I will see you tonight, Timothy. Prepare to be the belle of the ball."

Letty walked to where her family waited for Liam and Captain. It was all she could do not to turn around and run back to throw her arms around Timothy.

Liam threw himself off Captain, exercising even more than his usual swagger as he accepted congratulations all around. "Best finish yet, father mine! You should have let me ride him sooner!" George gave him an enormous hug that almost lifted Liam into the air. "Third place in this field is a big achievement." George gave a wicked grin as Lot began to pound Liam on the back. "But don't forget I can still arm-wrestle you to the ground!"

"Boys, boys, can we settle down a bit?" Agnes had Johnny tightly by the hand. Little Hannah was at least up out of the fray, safe in Mālama's arms, although she cried and reached for her father.

Letty gave Liam a kiss on the cheek. He put his arm around her for a hug. "There you are, sister mine! Were you congratulating the winner? And what did you do to Timothy's knee in the paddock before the race?"

"Yes, I would like to know that too." Agnes leveled a stern eye on her.

George took command of the situation. "Let's get this horse cooled down. I know you ladies need to return to 'Iolani to dress for the evening. Agnes, can you drive the wagon?"

Letty perched at one end of Kahōkūlani's long front verandah, keeping her head down in a book. Letting the late-afternoon breeze dry her wet hair. Agnes sat at the opposite end, fanning herself against the heat. With luck, Letty could avoid the interrogation that Agnes likely longed to give her. Or not.

Agnes mused aloud. Very loud in fact, clearly intending to be overheard. "'We are just friends.' Utter nonsense. If Mr. Timothy Rowley thinks he can casually break our Letty's heart and then move on to marry an heiress, *he is mistaken*." The tempo of her fanning increased, as did her voice. "I am now thinking fondly of my pistol."

Letty snapped her book shut and stood, only to see her father ride into the yard. George handed his horse over to the stable lad, brushed the dust off himself, and came up on the verandah, looking a bit defeated. "I won't deny it, Agnes; it is just as you said. The gossip about Letty and Timothy is deafening." He leaned against one of the pillars, watching Letty's approach. "Perhaps you should stay home tonight, Letty."

Agnes leveled a skeptical eye on Letty, one eyebrow lifted. "And what have you to say to that, dear?"

Before Letty could respond, George surprised her. "Or perhaps we must come to accept you are not a child anymore, but a young woman grown. Who are we to tell you how to live your life?"

Agnes ignored him. "Letty, your father and I hoped to speak with you about Timothy."

"Well, we can make that conversation short and sweet." Letty put her hands on her hips. "Timothy and I are just friends, that is all it can ever be. Heaven knows *my* life is too complicated for anything else. In a few weeks I go back to San Francisco to attend veterinary school. Thanks to you, Agnes. Until then, I promise not to do anything rash." She smiled. "Well, anything rash about Timothy, that is!"

Letty hoped that sounded convincing. It was certainly what her head told her; unfortunately, her heart had yet to come around. And her flames? They might never capitulate.

"We could not ask for more, dear. People will always talk." George began walking to the front door, clearly believing the conversation at its end.

Agnes tilted her head back to look at Letty through hooded eyes. "Yes. Of course. That all sounds very logical. Unfortunately, 'logic does not always carry the day once the heart is in play.' That charming poem was in a letter your father wrote me during our courtship."

George turned slightly green but stayed silent.

"Papa! You did not!"

"He did. Quite the romantic, your father. Honey, I just don't want your heart broken. Please be careful."

"I'll try." Too late for that.

CHAPTER TWENTY-NINE

'Oli'oli

GLADNESS

Hidden in the shadow of one of the great trees, Letty watched the celebration unfold. She'd not thought it would be so difficult to turn away from what was in her heart. Especially here, especially now, at the moment of Timothy's victory. But she must if she was to protect him. From her own dangerous self.

Kauluwehi, the MacHenry house, glowed with light as people spilled out onto the lawns.

Princess K, radiant on the arm of Captain Kalama, unabashedly wore her tiara. George and Agnes drew Gaylord and Imogene along, eagerly introducing their new business partners to Hawaiian society. And wonder of wonders, Adele twirled on the arm of Hugh Letwin. She looked almost pretty.

Across the lawn a flower-draped Timothy held court, his proud grandmama on one side and his auntie on the other. Undoubtedly they relived the race with every congratulation. She longed to join them, but hesitated.

"Shall we dance, my child?" Her grandfather, Lot, extended his hand. He wore his court livery from his days with Queen Lili'uokalani and looked particularly dashing.

"That would be lovely, *Tūtū kāne*."

As they circled and dipped to the old-fashioned waltz, he said quietly, "The gossips are ablaze about you and Timothy. Once we are through with this dance, I will lead you over to Timothy's *'ohana*. That way, everyone will know that you have my approval."

They dipped again in perfect time to the music, the train of her *holokū* swishing behind her. "For my part, I will ask the lively dowager to dance again. Then you will have a moment to congratulate Timothy without appearing forward. Use your best judgment after that."

"Don't worry, *Tūtū kāne*. Papa and Agnes already had 'the talk' with me. I will do nothing foolish."

"I know you won't be foolish, child, you never are. I merely pray that you will not be hurt."

She was not the one in danger; no one understood that. Rather Timothy was the one likely to be hurt if she made a mistake. And she wasn't even certain how her flames might harm him. She just nodded as they swirled ever closer to where the victorious Rowleys stood.

"My lady, might I have this dance?" Lot inclined his head to Philomena.

"Delighted."

Letty slipped into the vacancy left behind. "Timothy, how are you enjoying the spoils of victory?"

"Very much." His smile nearly split his tanned face in two. "I like winning."

"Well, don't let it go to your head. I know for a fact that one of your nicknames is Piggy. K told me."

Clarissa laughed. "I had forgotten about that, nephew! You and your pigs."

Letty turned to her with a conspiratorial grin. "I consider it an important part of our friendship that I keep him humble."

"Quite."

"Timothy, again, congratulations. You were mounted on the best horse, but your riding wasn't too shabby either." She looked out at the dancers. "And if your grandmother survives her dance with my grandfather, please extend my respects regarding her excellent choice of Diablo. As a horse trader's daughter, I know what I speak of. He is a rare one."

"May I have a dance later, Letty?" Timothy asked.

"As long as we are careful of your knee." If only his knee was all they need be careful of! She might have said no. But people would talk whether they danced or not. And she craved another memory or two to carry to San Francisco, even if they were memories of the things she could not have. Ever.

Guests found places around the perimeter of the great lawn. No one wanted to miss the final tradition of the Cup: a men's *hula* in honor of the victor. Letty stationed herself with one hand on the trunk of a palm, the other on the back of Agnes's chair, ready to take it all in. Timothy stood across the lawn with a look of sheepish expectancy. He'd been to the Cup before; he must know what was coming.

As a more strident drumbeat rang out, men appeared from all sides. This was to be *kāne hula*, the ancient bent-kneed, hip-thrusting warrior dances, exactly what the missionaries had hoped to erase. They failed. Each year, more men joined the throng. A wild dance celebrating the victory erupted.

The men ran to hoist Timothy on their shoulders, carrying him around. Everyone clapped as the drumbeat spiraled upward. Letty sought Philomena's face to see if she was completely appalled. On the contrary, she clapped as if her very life depended on it, her face shining with pride. Lot stood next to her, leaning in for a private word, Philomena laughing in response. Hmmmm . . . was her *tūtū kāne* using his own best judgment?

"I am sorry, but I don't think this knee has a dance in it. Will you walk with me?" He grasped Letty's hand and began to guide her toward the gardens behind the house. Somehow not surprised to find her hand hot to his touch.

"Timothy, people are already talking—not that I care, but Agnes does."

"I know; I am sorry for that too. But I just need a private word."

They stepped through a poinciana hedge into a quieter world. She stopped, pulling her hand away.

"All right, what have you got to say? I don't want to be away too long."

"I need to talk to you. I spoke with Adele after the race. I told her the truth; she and I just don't suit. As it happens, she is carrying a huge torch for Hugh. She was relieved to be rid of me. Her mother has been pressing her hard."

"My, you got out of that neatly. Who is your next targeted heiress? Lokelani?"

"Well, you see, that's the thing—try as I might to avoid it, I keep finding my target is you." There, he had said it.

"Well, that's flattering. You would rather avoid it? You certainly know how to make a lady feel swell." She stood with her arms crossed. He could see the laughter bubbling. Then her face turned serious.

"Timothy, I am no heiress. And this is not a joking matter. You know my life is not my own, that I must pay a price for who I am. Besides, there is too much distance between us."

As if he cared.

"What about this distance?" He pulled her close and kissed her. Gently. Her warmth felt so right in his arms. She pulled back, but not away, her face pensive, her eyes searching. Her lips formed a barely whispered yes as she softened against him. Fire laced him as he kissed her again, harder. Her mouth melted open, and the tips of their tongues touched. The wave of heat off her body stunned him. His heart now so full it felt like bursting, almost too much to bear. Then suddenly gone as she pushed away. He found himself panting, scarcely able to breathe.

"I told you. I can harm people with my affections. I almost hurt you, just now."

"I can take it." Wasn't it natural that she leave him breathless? He reached out to pull her close again. "Can we get back to our discussion?"

"What is to discuss?" That having been said, she relaxed into his arms again as if she belonged there. As if her body gave a lie to her words. "We have a deal, just friends."

"Are you joking? What did that kiss just prove?"

"Nothing."

"Be serious. I think we are meant to be together."

Now she did pull away. "It doesn't matter how we feel. The gulf between us is too wide. It is what I told you before. I cannot forget that you are *haole* and an English aristocrat to boot. Me, I am a *hapa* horse trader's daughter who has just barely scraped together enough money to go back to school." She placed a hand on his chest as if to push him away. "And, you could die."

"We can find a way."

She shook her head. "No, we can't. We are both too bound up in things we don't fully understand. For me, it is my power; for you, it is your father."

She leaned forward and gave him a quick peck on the cheek. "Your friendship is a great gift, Timothy. I trust you know how much I cherish it. But that is all there ever can be." She turned away, gliding off like the princess she was, the train of her dress gently accentuating her every movement.

His heart, which only moments before felt full to bursting, contracted to nothingness.

The kiss had completely undone her. If only they were wrong, Esther, Kahōkūlani, and the *kumu* too, but they weren't. She might hurt those she loved with her power. She knew it again with certainty as they kissed, the flames arcing with desire, the entwining of pain and pleasure. The feel of his heartbeat racing beyond sense. Dearest Timothy. He would never understand. Now she needed to get away, far away, so she could watch her own heart fall to pieces. It was over.

CHAPTER THIRTY

Lu'ulu'u

SADNESS

"I told him to watch himself." Philomena bit her lip as she saw Letty emerge from the garden, the girl's face a mask of stone. Timothy followed, his own expression looking like he had lost, not won, the race.

"I fear it might be too late for that. I rather like the girl," Clarissa said.

"I must say, when I urged him to seek love, I was not expecting this result. I just wanted him to rid himself of the Simmons girl. I should have known it could not be that simple."

"Truly, Mama, of all our family, Timothy has always been the most decisive. Of course he jumped in. I should like to think this will all turn out well for him. And that girl too. I just don't see how. Have you given him the letter yet?"

"Once we are settled back at the plantation, I'll pass it along. It seemed a distraction from the Cup."

The Gentleman's Cup now two days past, Timothy found him-self ensconced at the plantation house with Grandmama and Aunt Clarissa. He'd not spoken to Letty in the aftermath of the kiss; in fact, she'd left for Honolulu abruptly with no good-bye. The story was she decided to go back with the Stansfields to see the family off on their return voyage to California. Not a surprise, really. Now here he sat, surrounded by samples of possible eggplant drapes. *Ugh.*

The plantation house was at a lower elevation than the ranch, toward the village of Hawi, so the clime was both warmer and wetter. The ladies opined that they much pre-ferred it "uphill." Could he please complete his ranch house forthwith? Grandmama was offering to oversee the workmen. That must be avoided at all costs, or there might be a walkout.

His thoughts kept circling back to Letty . . . and the kiss. Letty insisted there was danger. Yet all he had felt was heat. And desire. Desire beyond all expectation.

Timothy headed in for the morning tea that his grand-mother held sacred. He'd not yet converted her to Kona coffee.

After drinking her second cup of tea, Philomena handed him a letter and said, "I shall be out on the lānai fanning myself should you care to discuss it." Clarissa disappeared to the sta-bles as soon as she saw the white envelope.

Dear Timothy,

You may be shocked to receive this from me at such a remove. Papa forbade all of us from speaking to you, but now he is unlikely to discover my transgression. You see, he is failing, both mentally and physically. His hab-its have begun to take their toll. That is why I reach out to you.

First, you must know that all your letters to Papa were not in vain. As you might expect, he did not read them. But I did and chose to share them with our siblings. We are all amazed and heartened by everything you have seen and accomplished. I can only hope that someday you might choose to welcome us in your tropical home.

But back to immediate matters. As Papa's mind has begun to wander, he has been asking for you. I thought you might care to know. The doctors tell us that he may live for some time yet, but that his intellect will continue to fade. Perhaps you will want to see him while he can still remember who you are.

I have reached an arrangement with our man of business where I have taken charge of the estates and other matters, so Papa is freed of that burden . . . although I am not sure he sees it that way. It is quite overwhelming, which leads me to the selfish purpose of this letter. Might you consider returning to England? Your family is in dire need of your energy and acumen.

You don't need to commit now to staying, but if you come home to see Papa we can discuss what might be best. Again, we are all so very proud of you.

Your brother,
Royce Parkhurst Rowley

He folded the letter and headed to the lānai. "I note Clarissa retreated to the stable the moment you pulled this letter out." He slumped down next to his grandmother in the rattan love seat. "May I assume you both know its contents?"

She grasped his hand. "Yes, we do. Once Royce told me what was going on, I went to see your father. It is as he described. The mental decline is particularly marked. He had difficulty recognizing me."

"Well, that is not overly surprising, since by my best guess Father has not seen you for ten years, perhaps? Since right after the accident?"

"Thereabout."

"Letty told me I needed to make peace with my father."

"She did?"

"Yes, it is a very Hawaiian thing, *hoʻoponopono*, clearing the air." He looked up at the ceiling, then off to the horizon. Anything to avoid looking at his grandmother. "What was the term she used? That I am 'bound up' because of my father. And she doesn't know about the accident. She's never asked."

"She doesn't know that your own father ran you down with his carriage? While stinking drunk? And blamed you?"

"Grandmama, it was an accident."

"Timothy, I was there. You know what I think. Quite perceptive of Letty to figure out you have issues with your father. 'Bound up' indeed."

He squeezed her hand. "You'd best not have been joking about marrying for love. Because Letty is the one. She just doesn't believe it yet."

"I surmised that. She will never be accepted in England, you know. The skin is a barrier, never mind the lack of family or fortune."

"It is a bit of a problem here too." Timothy rubbed the back of his neck. "I will certainly return. Shall I go with you?"

"I was going to propose that I stay here until you return. You have good management, but it is always sensible to have an owner in residence. And, to be perfectly forthright, this climate is agreeing with me. My rheumatism has never felt better. Why stand for another cold English winter? I can leave here next spring."

"Does the family really need me?"

"I am afraid they do. Royce, thank goodness, does not have your father's vices. But he was raised to be a man of leisure. As have all your siblings. None of them is prepared for these responsibilities. You reinserting yourself into the family would be a godsend."

She put her arm around him. "Promise me you will think about this carefully. Just because they need you doesn't require you to sacrifice your life for them. I mean, where have they all been the last few years? Other than toadying up to me for an increased inheritance."

"Really, Grandmama, is it that bad?"

"I don't know, but let me tell you this. I come here, and I see the life you have created for yourself and meet the people who value and respect you . . . then I cannot imagine you once again mired in the family cesspool." She shook her head. "Forgive me for speaking so plainly."

"Well, let me think about it. Clarissa heads home in a week or so, does she?"

"Yes. She must be sure to be there for the boys' school holidays in October."

"I can be prepared by then." He gave her his most wicked grin. "And just to confirm that I am still in charge, you are forbidden to ride Diablo in my absence. I know that is what you were planning!"

She dished it right back. "Oh, no worries about that, my dear! I have a better plan! The dashing Mr. Lot Lang will be bringing Letty's mare Scheherazade here later today for my perusal. I intend to buy her as my mount. The negotiations will be lively, I have no doubt."

Timothy leaned over to kiss her on the cheek. "Well, I shall wait with bated breath to hear the outcome of these dealings. I doubt the poor man knows what he is up against."

"That is quite the point, actually."

"I am heading to Honolulu for a couple of days. There is a young woman off to veterinary school, and I want to wave her goodbye."

His grandmother squeezed his hand.

"Of course."

CHAPTER THIRTY-ONE

Alaheo

GONE

Lang's Livery, Oahu, mid-September, 1909

The morning of Letty's departure dawned bright and beautiful. Since she did not have to be on the docks until nearly noon, she lazed in bed, dear little Rosebud in the crook of her arm.

Her sleepy mind wandered. *Timothy.* Timothy again, always Timothy. Thoughts of the man arrived unbidden. And with them, the fire. Not just up her spine but in her belly. And lower. She had revived her old counting tricks, but nothing worked. The sooner she got to San Francisco the better.

The little dog decided it was time to rise and shine. She moved in to lick Letty's ears. It tickled. "All right, sweetheart, I'm up. You are in for a big journey today." She'd packed a separate bag with everything Rosebud might need aboard ship. How ludicrous, a dog with baggage. Thank goodness Captain Kalama had offered her a private stateroom. Rosebud would travel with her and not in the hold.

She swung her legs out over the side of the bed, looking down at her toes.

"Yes, your toes matter. Don't forget what I taught you. You must be barefoot on the land so the *ʻāina* can give you strength."

Startled, she looked up to see the *kumu* sitting calmly in the chair across from her bed. "*Kumu!* Why are you here?"

"To bless you, child. You will be gone away where I cannot be. I wish to give you my blessing."

She came to where Letty sat open-mouthed on the bed, placed one hand on each side of Letty's face, and leaned in to breathe. Letty flooded with profound feelings of goodness.

"Yes. Very good." The *kumu* removed her hands and glided back across the room. "Remember to breathe when you wish to find this place again. It will come to you." The *kumu* placed her hat back on her head.

"Now, shall we head to the breakfast room? I must greet your friend and fierce stepmother before I go." Rosebud followed the *kumu* as closely as if she were dangling a ham from her wrist.

Letty hurriedly threw on a robe. She heard Agnes gasp in the kitchen. And then scraping as a chair was shoved back from the table. She peeked through the door over the *kumu*'s shoulder. What was Timothy doing here?

First the tiny woman headed to Agnes, backed up against the sideboard for support, eyes wide with surprise. The *kumu* was so small she made Agnes look big. Almost. "Thank you for your care of the Gate. May I touch you?" Agnes nodded as the *kumu* delicately placed a hand on her abdomen. "Ah, he will be another strong one such as she. The *ʻāina* will be glad of him. Be well."

The *kumu* turned to Timothy. He burst up from the chair, his face ashen as though he saw a ghost, eyes wide and slack-jawed. "May I touch you?" She rested her hand on his arm for only a moment, then reached up, motioning him to lower his head. He leaned down to her slowly, still bemused. She put her hands on each side of his face to stare deeply into his eyes. "Ah, very good. *Kahu*, you will do what is needed. You will find the path and walk it."

Then out the door she went, leaving the three of them frozen and speechless. A moment later she could be seen riding through the gate on her mule, her dog trotting behind.

Timothy was the first to find his voice. "Who *is* she?"

Agnes threw up her hands. "We don't know—she just shows up from time to time. And says things we don't understand!"

Letty dropped into a chair, and Rosebud jumped into her lap. "She came to bless me for my journey." She sat silent for a moment, her fingertips tracing the little dog's velvety ears, then turned to Timothy. "What are you doing here?"

"I was hoping to see you before you left, maybe even drive you to the docks. Perhaps to save Agnes the trouble . . ."

"Oh yes, this is all about Agnes . . ." She immediately regretted the waspishness in her tone.

"Letty, I would like to drive you, if I may."

"All right."

The wagon was loaded. Rosebud was inside her fancy new traveling cage, complete with her name on it. Letty's trunk was in its usual weighty, book-laden state. She'd made her farewells to her father and Liam last night, since they left early this morning on business. Apparently, someone wanted a motorcar on Kauai. Hugs were given to Johnny and Hannah, and a note had been penned to the Princess. And another letter sent as well.

"You will write every week, you promise?" Agnes's voice sounded strained.

"I promise."

"And say thank you again to Imogene for letting you stay with them."

"I will."

Letty pulled her stepmother into a fierce hug. "I love you. Thank you for all you have done for me." Agnes's eyes pooled. Her own tears bubbled just below the surface.

"I love you too. Come home safe."

"You can count on it. *Aloha*."

The wagon rolled out into the fragrant sunlit morning.

They rode in silence, Timothy's hands clenching and unclenching on the reins. Letty could not keep her eyes off him, though she kept her gaze a sideways glance. She would drink in the sight of him if she could. Then he spoke.

"Letty, what did it mean when she called me '*kahu*'? That's what the *kumu* called me, right?"

"Heavens if I know. It means 'guardian.' She is always speaking in riddles. I think you should ask Esther."

"You know I'm a bit scared of Esther."

"That's wise. She is a mean one with a bullwhip."

"I'm not kidding."

"Then ask Bull. He is a *kahu*."

More silence as they rode along. She fought the urge to lay a hand on his arm.

"I am going to England to see my father; he is not well."

"I am glad you are going, but sorry to hear he is not well."

More silence. Then, "Letty, about that kiss." He paused, chewing his lip, before his words tumbled out like a tidal wave. "I refuse to regret that I kissed you. I don't know what it means about the future for us, but I do know this. What is between us is something special. It's like electricity. I know you feel it too."

"What am I supposed to say to that?"

"Well, what do you feel?"

Her flames sprinted up and down her spine like chittering monkeys on a tree trunk. What her heart wanted to say she could not say. Ever. Instead the harsh truth must suffice.

"I won't deny that I feel the same spark. But it doesn't matter. You know I can hurt you, you must have felt it when we kissed. There is the price to my gift. It is a price I will not let you or anyone else pay."

"But what if I don't care? What if I don't believe the legend?"

"Timothy, be reasonable. The danger is real and you know it."

She plunged ahead. "And now, it is more than that. We both must figure out who we are. I need to discover if it is even possible to be both a modern woman and an ancient Gate. I might fail at both. You? You need to go home to England to deal with your father and your family. Will you live to appease them? Or be your own man?"

"That's a touch harsh."

"But it is true and you know it."

She rested her hand next to one of his, conquering the urge to grasp it. "Even then, you know there is little chance for us. The world won't have it. Look at the difference in the color of our skin."

"I will be waiting here for you when you return."

"Don't make idle promises, Timothy. What if you decide to stay in England?"

"Then I will come back to get you."

"We will see." She was such a coward, she could not say never, even when she should. Because it was never. Never ever. Her heart clenched.

He stopped the wagon in the shade of a tree and pulled her toward him. "I need both hands to do this properly." With his palms on either side of her face, he delivered a sweet kiss, deep and lingering.

She could not stop herself—she leaned into the kiss, eyes wide open. As her flames pirouetted in response, Letty watched the wonder bloom in his eyes. She pulled away, unwilling to mar the moment. "Yes, we shall see. Now I have a boat to catch, my fine sir."

"At your service, my lady."

The wagon rolled on.

She stood at the rail of the ship, waving at the sandy-haired man standing tall over much of the crowd at the pier. In a different life, Timothy might be just the sort of man she'd choose: strong, decent, caring, and with a dash of stubbornness thrown in to make life interesting. But not in this lifetime. Not anymore. The depth of what the ʻāina would take from her only now began to sink in.

How typically thoughtful of him to come send her off. How thankful she was that she'd written and posted the letter yesterday, while her head was clear. While it was easy to say the words. On paper. With a pen. There she could say it with finality, say what must be said. That she must never see him again. She couldn't have managed to say it aloud, not while her lip quivered as the ship pulled away.

Most likely he'd not forgive her. That must be for the best. That's why she wrote the letter, wasn't it?

Timothy sat in one of the chairs in Kahōkūlani's office at ʻIolani Ranch. He leaned forward, turning his hat in his hand. Perhaps with a bit of nerves. It did not help that the chair was too small and creaked a bit if he moved even a whit. Kahōkūlani peered at him over the top of her glasses.

"Really? That is what the *kumu* said? You are certain."

"Absolutely certain."

"Tell me again."

This meeting was not going the way he had expected. Kahōkūlani seemed alternately annoyed and dismissive. Perhaps incredulous. But he would not leave without an answer.

"What she said was '*Kahu*, you will do what is needed. You will find the path and walk it.'"

"Now describe her."

"K, for heaven's sake, I know what the *kumu* looks like. And so do you. A miniscule woman on a gigantic white mule. This really happened. This is what was said."

Kahōkūlani sat back. "Well, this certainly complicates matters. Do you even know what a *kahu* is?"

"I thought I did, but now I am not so sure. Some kind of guardian."

"A *kahu* is that and so very much more."

This time he let his frustration spill out. "So explain it all, please, and I will leave you alone."

"Well, there's the rub. I can't. So much of the knowledge has been lost."

"K, help me. I am in love with her."

"Does she know?"

"Not exactly . . ."

Kahōkūlani's demeanor gentled, for the moment, at least. "That is not going to help, you know. The love. In fact, it makes it worse."

"How could this *kahu* be me? I am not even Hawaiian."

"All I can think is that the *'āina* has claimed you, chosen you for its own. You love the land."

"I still don't understand."

"You are bound to the *'āina* now, whether you like it or not. What the *kumu* would say is, 'Once the land has chosen, it will not be undone.' That is how it is."

"So I have no choice?"

Kahōkūlani rolled her eyes. "Do you think I had a choice? Or Letty? Now you should talk to Bull. Perhaps Tom Kalama too."

"Tom?"

"Yes, there is another story there." Kahōkūlani looked away. "One it may help you to know." Her voice diminished. "Tom is my intended *kahu*. It has not gone well. We have had . . . difficulties." She turned back, brisk once more. "I wish you good luck, Timothy, for you and our Letty. Perhaps you will find a new path."

He must.

Transcontinental Railway, Great Basin Desert, western Utah

The vultures made lazy circles in the sun-scorched sky where the rail lines ran straight and true into the horizon. Who could survive a fall off a train at full throttle? No one. The vultures confirmed it.

The two guards sweltered in the afternoon heat as they rode along the tracks back to where the accident must have happened. Strangely, there was only one body. The dead man's face was already unrecognizable. And the birds had even begun to tear at the purple plaid suit. Waving them away, the guards began searching pockets to see what they could find. No money or papers; there was nothing left except an empty pair of handcuffs.

"Should we start tracking him?"

"He won't make it. The critters will get him. Besides, I have a better idea." The guard turned to pull a rope off his saddle, then a blanket. "We take this hunk of meat to Chicago to collect the reward." He toed the body onto its side. "Hell, he looks just like Frank Allerton to me."

"He sure does."

In a dry creek bed, not one hundred feet away, the man lay hidden. *Fools.* Too bad they would not be able to collect the reward, as it would end the search forever. But he did need their horses to get back to San Francisco. He stood up and started shooting.

The vultures were back only minutes later. What a rare feast.

PART THREE

Holapu ke ahi, koe iho ka lehu

THE FIRE BLAZED UP, THEN ONLY THE ASHES WERE LEFT

CHAPTER THIRTY-TWO

Puhi

BURN

Stansfield Mansion, Pacific Heights, San Francisco, California, early October, 1909

"MISS. LETICIA. YOU. HAVE. A. CALLER."

Franklin, the Stansfields' butler, stood at stiff attention in the doorway of the upstairs study. The man always seemed to speak in capital letters. Somehow she knew he disapproved of her modern ways. Doctor of veterinary medicine? A woman? How outlandish!

But that sort of attitude made no sense in the service of this family, a family with five women in it—one of whom was San Francisco's leading suffragist. Fortunately, Mr. Stansfield, as the lone male of this 'ohana, possessed both a keen sense of humor and the patience of Job.

She could pinch herself at her good fortune. To be living here, with Irene's family, while she trained with Dr. Feeney was the perfect situation. She was treated almost like a daughter. Rosebud too. Well, sort of.

Letty peered over the top of the anatomy books piled like a fortress around her. The first two weeks of school had been daunting. She'd believed she was ready. Miss Fred at the Redwood School had believed she was ready. Most importantly, Dr. Feeney still believed she was ready, even without any real college. Her internship in his clinic had been the preparation.

But still she was behind. The result was a need to study almost around the clock. Not to mention keen resentment from her better-prepared—and male—colleagues.

Undoubtedly, this "caller" was one of her fellow students on a prank visit. She had been the butt of numerous jokes since the term began.

"Who is calling, Franklin? Where are they now?"

"The caller prefers to introduce himself. He awaits in the library." Franklin could almost be described as smirking, if such a serious man ever did such a thing. This was undoubtedly another of the pranks, probably that idiot, the odious Mr. Ogilvie.

"Thank you. I will come right down." She considered taking off her apron and straightening up her hair. But what better way to show disdain for the pranksters than to appear in disrepair? She would even leave her glasses on. As she walked down the hall, Franklin's dismayed stare burned into her back.

At the bottom of the mahogany staircase, the double doors to Gaylord Stansfield's beloved library were closed. She used more force than intended, and the doors came open with twin thwacks.

The tall man standing next to the fireplace turned to face her. For once his unruly curls were neatly trimmed. His clothes bespoke their expensive origins, framing his broad shoulders to perfection. Her heart soared and then plunged to the bottom of her chest. How was it possible that the one person in the world she most desired to see was also the one she most dreaded to see?

He heard the door open but stayed staring at the fireplace a moment longer. His mind roiled with doubts. Perhaps it was just the butler, Franklin, returning with a rejection. What was he thinking to have come here? The letter said it all. They could never be more than friends. It was too dangerous, she claimed. "Goodbye," she had written. "I hope you meet the woman of your dreams in England."

Unfortunately, it was far too late for that. Letty was that woman. And his heart was not willing to take no for an answer.

"Timothy. I was not expecting to see you."

She stood stiffly at the doorway. He had hoped she might be happy to see him. Apparently not.

"I thought you'd pass through San Francisco on your journey to England. That's why I sent the letter. So you would not stop to visit."

Letty pulled the double doors shut behind her.

"Letty, you should know by now that it takes more than a letter to stop me."

"How about 'I never want to see you again'? How about 'This is over'? Perhaps 'We have nothing to discuss'? Or, 'Don't kiss me, you could die'?" She slapped herself on the cheek in fake wonderment. "Oh wait, didn't I put all this in a letter?"

Red lights sparked around her like embers. Her hair had come loose from its braid, and curls framed her face. The reading glasses slipped down to perch precariously on her nose. Her laboratory apron displayed stains he did not care to know too much about. She took his breath away.

Leticia. His Letty. What must he do to convince her that dying from one of her kisses might just be preferable to living without them?

"Can we take a walk? I understand there is a tea shop on the other side of the park. Brundidge's Cozy Corner."

"Who told you that? Imogene or Gaylord? Did they know you were coming?"

"Does it matter? Anyway, K told me."

She shook her head, her shoulders drooping in what he could only hope might be resignation. If he was so lucky.

He employed his most wheedling voice. The one that had worked on endless rounds of governesses after his mother died. He recalled now that it had never worked on Cassandra. Or Philomena, for that matter. It had to work now.

"Come on, just a spot of tea . . ."

Letty flung open the double doors again, only to find Franklin with her wrap in hand. He most certainly had been listening at the door. She glared at the butler as she pulled off her apron. She seized the wrap, leaving Franklin holding the laboratory apron away from himself as if it were a dead thing. Timothy bit his lip to keep from laughing. How could he not adore this woman?

Off they went.

This was her fourth autumn in San Francisco. Letty always found it the most beautiful time. Less fog, more sun, and a sense of the change of seasons. A walk and a cup of tea might do her good. Anyway, she preferred to be out of the house for what must be said to Timothy. Belatedly remembering her manners, she thanked Franklin for her wrap, ignored Timothy's proffered arm, and marched out the door.

"I don't think that man approves of me in his household."

"The butler? Franklin? He is probably just unnerved by the fact that you are taller than he is. Or maybe it is the scowl you give him. That scowl scares me."

"Right, Timothy. That explains why you are here. You are so easily frightened."

"Now, now, why don't we catch up a bit with polite conversation as we cross the park?"

"Whatever you say."

"Shall we start with you telling me all about slicing up dead animals? I am perishing to hear all the details."

He always knew how to make her laugh.

Brundidge's was a delight. Real English tea properly served and a bonus of cucumber sandwiches. Just like Kahōkūlani preferred. No wonder the Princess favored this place. The owner, a transplanted Brit, fluttered about like an agitated sparrow at the realization that a genuine English aristocrat, and a friend of Princess Kahōkūlani, graced the premises. Other patrons turned to stare.

"Perhaps we need to walk if we are to speak in any meaningful way . . ."

Letty nodded. She'd been a bit short in her responses to his conversational gambits. There was no good outcome to this visit. She hoped to keep it as brief as she could. It would still be painful. Just like watching his strong hands holding a delicate teacup was now painful. She could not shake the desire to have those hands on her. But she must. To keep him safe.

Timothy gave a blazing smile to the proprietress as he settled the bill. Letty tried not to roll her eyes as the poor woman babbled her thanks to "his Lordship."

Then, predictably, the woman turned an appraising glance on Letty. As Timothy helped her back into her wrap, Letty watched the wheels turn in the woman's head. What could his Lordship be doing with a woman with such dark skin? One who was clearly not a servant? Yes, so predictable.

Just further evidence that nothing could ever be possible between them. They were too far apart, too different . . . the world was not ready to accept them. Maybe in Hawaii, but certainly not here. And only if you ignored the fact that her affections could kill him.

With his customary grace, Timothy swept the door open and offered Letty his arm. Her breath caught. She wished that the beauty of his movement did not stir her. That his touch on her arm made no flames tap a dance up her spine. But there you have it. Just as she could not help but take pleasure in the simple joy of accepting the arm of a man taller than herself. The proprietress watched stonily.

Apparently, the lady's silent stare had not gone unnoticed by Timothy. "Mrs. Brundidge, thank you for your hospitality today. I am pleased to have shared something so very English with my dear friend, Miss Lang. You know she is a princess of old Hawaii herself. Just like our Princess K." The woman's eyes snapped open. She began to babble her goodbyes to Letty just as Timothy swept the two of them out the door.

They made it across the street to the park before Timothy's outburst. "Promise me the next time you go to the Cozy Corner you will wear one of Imogene's tiaras. That should fix her!"

"Most likely her head would explode." Letty did have to laugh at the prospect. "But, Timothy, this is a perfect example of what I have been telling you. Even if we could find a way around my . . . powers, people will never accept us. It is better in Hawaii, but here? And what about England? I have been told there are places in London that I would never be allowed to enter the front door. I could not live with that."

"You won't have to." He grasped her arm, firmly drawing her farther into the park, then pushing through some shrubbery. "Because if I must, I will move to the wilds of Tasmania for us to be together."

She could read his intention in his eyes before he acted on it. "No, you won't."

"Yes, I will." He grabbed her close and began to kiss her neck, then moved abruptly upward to her mouth, raking her lower lip with his teeth. He smiled. "Yes, I will."

She reached one hand up to slow him. A tiny bit of stubble on his cheek sandpapered her fingertips. He smelled of sandalwood and warm winds. Where was her self-control in all this? Where now was never?

"Timothy, are you sure?"

"I have never been more certain."

His next kiss began softly enough. She leaned in to catch the feel of his taut strength up and down her frame. Surely she could stop before anything bad happened? His tongue slipped into her mouth, gently exploring, then probing with more insistence. She responded in kind, grasping him nearer and panting into the fire he had ignited. She could kiss this man forever.

And then he fell.

He could not breathe. A fist of fire squeezed his chest, and nothing could dislodge it. He could see Letty, but as if she were on the other side of a thick pane of glass. Her lips moved. She must be speaking, but there was only a roaring in his ears. He lost consciousness.

Crack! He heard the blow as much as felt it. Blinking his eyes open, he found Letty peering at him intently. Her arm was raised to slap him again, then it dropped back once she saw his eyes flutter.

"Damn you, you are not dying here in this park! I will not have it."

She shook him, then pounded on his chest. He tried to speak, but his words came out as a wheeze. She was crying. Her aura flashed erratically around her; her breathing was erratic too. Then suddenly, she steadied. His pain ceased as he felt the flow of power through her hands. She breathed slowly, intently, just as he knew her *kumu* taught.

She pulled him to his feet. He stood, barely.

"Do you believe me now?"

He looked down, silent as she leaned over to brush the dust and twigs from his clothes. And perhaps to hide the next round of tears.

"I cannot live with myself if I have hurt you." Her voice seemed diminished.

"I am all right. Just frightened. And perhaps a bit ashamed of myself."

She met his eyes again.

"As I said, do you believe me now?"

His own eyes were wet. He pulled her close and held her tightly, resting his chin on the top of her head. Her careful, measured breathing told the tale. All was lost.

"Yes, I believe you now. I just don't know how I will find a way to live with this truth."

"Neither do I."

Chapter Thirty-Three

'Ona

INTOXICATION

Russell Square, London, England, early November, 1909

All of society decreed this very party to be a most grand affair. But weren't all the parties he attended? Since returning to London he'd been identified as something of a catch. Albeit a bit rusticated, but still a catch. It clearly did not hurt to be one of the heirs to the Moran fortune. No one cared a fig what he'd been up to in Hawaii.

Most of the guests undoubtedly found this house magnificent. Marble floors, crystal chandeliers, carved oak. And gilt, fake gold everywhere. Not to mention eggplant damask drapes. Just as Grandmama threatened for the plantation house. Ugh. All the houses now seemed the same.

What he would give to see a bit of koa wood . . . or the sunlit sea.

Waves of celebrants ebbed and flowed from the drawing room down the corridors and then back into the ballroom. Timothy bobbed along with the tide until coming to rest up against a pillar. With this gallant pillar at his back, he could remain upright: no one need know how very foxed he was. Tally ho!

He was learning to appreciate drunkenness, what his father might have seen in it. When he was drunk, the despair over Letty slipped away. Unfortunately, it reappeared each morning, along with a vicious headache.

"Timothy?" A too-small blond woman appeared at his left. Well, perhaps not too small.

His standards had changed; now he compared all women to Letty's perfect size. Her perfect everything . . .

"Timothy! Look at me!"

He looked. Nice blue eyes, smile lines. "Cassandra?"

"Yes, Cassandra. As you well know. Perhaps Mrs. Cannondale to you, in this condition. Put your arm around my shoulder, I am getting you out of here."

"Oh no, I really like my pillar. I am thinking of naming it . . . something like Percy . . ."

Now her face swam before him. "What d'ya think? Percy the Pillar?"

"What I think is that I am taking you home with me. Now."

On his right, the face of a stranger floated into view, a man with a beard of tiny braids and a turban. Laughing eyes. Perhaps he would be joining the circus. "Hallo, are you one of Cassie's friends?"

The man merely smiled, grasping Timothy's other arm. "Ah, Cassandra, my dove, you are correct as always. This one needs our help. He has been chosen. He must find his path. We will teach him to breathe." That was the last he remembered.

🔥

Timothy woke in a strange room with stripes of daylight seeping in around the heavy drapes. The stench was noxious. He had clearly evacuated everything and sundry from his stomach at some point during the night. Thankfully, his aim on the chamber pot had been spot-on, or the whole affair might have been even more distressing.

A knock on the door announced a tiny man dressed in white robes, who entered with a tea tray. Oh, yes, he remembered now. He must be at Cassandra's. She brought her servants back with her from India. Rumor had it that was not all that sailed with her . . .

"Sir, Madame has requested your presence in the ashram. I have brought you clothes for the lesson." Ashram? Lesson?

Well, it was not as if he had anything better to do.

Once dressed in the oddly loose-fitting clothing, he trailed the man into what, in most English townhouses, might be called the conservatory. Cassandra had taken it to an extreme. Giant potted palms filtered what bit of winter sunlight came through the glass ceiling. His stomach gave a lurch at the smell of something burnt and herbal. Rather like a burning cane field. Cassandra appeared from between the palms afloat in something blue and gauzy. Behind her came the man he vaguely remembered from the night before. Who could forget a beard of braids like snakes?

"Ah, my dear Timothy. I am so glad to see you've awakened." She glided forward to gaze up at him. "Lean down." Her nose wrinkled, then she fanned her face. "My, what an incredibly fine set of bloodshot eyes you have, my boy. And your stench is beyond description."

From the back of the room came the low rumble of the bearded man's laugh. "Please, Cassandra, let us feed the poor man before we take him to task. He has much to learn."

The man emerged from the shadows. Bright blue eyes twinkled in a deeply lined face. "Sir John Woodruffe, master of esoterica, at your service." The man came closer. "And I know who you are, sir. Or perhaps better, what you are. One who has been to a place where the heart of the earth comes near. One who has been called. How to say this? You will find the path and you will walk it."

Timothy started. "How do you know what she said?"

"Ah. So, there is a she, perhaps more than one. Tell me who said this to you."

His stomach lurched. Cassandra grabbed his arm to support him. "John, as you said, we must feed him first." She drew Timothy toward a table with silver trays of food. The servant pulled the covers off to show the contents.

Timothy bit his lip, hard. "Please, no kippers."

Woodruffe's gruff laugh rang out again. "No, my boy, no kippers for you. At least not today."

Three days later, Timothy found himself entirely sober and perched on a cushion in what he now understood to be the lotus position. The first time he'd made the attempt, his body had revolted. Woodruffe made a joke about his stork legs. Today he settled right in.

"This may surprise you," Woodruffe said, "but what you seek will be found in the warrior's breath. The line between love and war is razor thin."

Indeed. Perhaps this was war. The war to win his love, his Letty. He would find the path and walk it. And he would win. And breathe.

Timothy's brother emerged from the earl's bedroom, shutting the great oaken door after him. Not even teatime, yet darkness gathered in the late November afternoon. Timothy stood waiting in the vast upstairs hall of Colborne House, knowing full well a challenging conversation lay ahead. Royce Parkhurst Rowley, soon to be the twenty-third Earl of Colborne, had clearly decided to swallow his pride.

"I wish you would not leave us, Timothy." Royce grabbed his hand, then awkwardly dropped it. "Can't you see we desperately need you here?"

"We have been through this time and again, Royce."

Timothy stood resolute, sweeping back his overlong hair. By London standards he never found the time to be properly groomed. Thankfully no one in Hawaii cared. He could return soon enough.

"I am highly confident in Mr. Boylston. He has put forth a conservative plan to manage the estates. There is really nothing more I can do here."

"Tim, I am begging you. Please stay."

"I can't. Grandmama awaits my return. I have my own businesses to tend."

"You will break Cassandra's heart if you go."

At that Timothy laughed. Of course Royce would misinterpret his time at Cassandra's. Timothy would not even dare explain Sir John to his brother. "I doubt that. I have been her latest amusement, that is all. She is double my age; anyway, it is completely platonic. Cassandra and I have corresponded for years. I'm a novelty. She has enjoyed having someone society deems to be an exotic as her occasional escort. Now that everyone in London knows just what a dreadful bore I am, I doubt I shall even be missed."

He watched Royce bite his tongue, his brother's thoughts painfully transparent. With good reason. Timothy's first few weeks in London had been a glittering parade of lovely women and late nights. He'd come home extravagantly drunk on more than one occasion. Then suddenly it had all stopped. Thanks

to Cassandra. And her friend, the master of esoterica. Now he
had hope.

"Well then, travel safely. And give Grandmama my regards.
Tell her that I intend to do my very best with what lies ahead."
Royce looked back at the door. "It won't be long now."

Timothy reached out and took his brother in an awkward
embrace. "This is what we do in Hawaii, Royce. It is called
pūliki." Timothy released him. "If we were in the islands,
I would also kiss you on both cheeks, or touch foreheads to
share breath, but I suspect you are not yet ready for that."

Royce shook his head. "You are right about that, old man."

"Don't be a stranger. When the dust settles, bring Belinda
and the children. The islands heal, and you may need that."

Timothy descended the grand curving stairway of Colborne
House, his knee barking in the cold. The steamer to New York
sailed at midnight. Sadness enveloped him. The reconciliation
with his father he had longed for would now never come to
pass.

The doctors said the earl's liver was failing, quickly now.
Not surprising, given his father's years of drunkenness.
Timothy recalled often seeing his father with a glass of brandy
at breakfast. He shuddered to think that as a boy he'd thought
it normal. Didn't everyone's father drink in the morning? No
child of his would ever have that thought. That is, if he had any
children.

Breathe, Timothy. That's what Sir John said. "The breath
will be your salvation." And perhaps his only hope for children.

Grandmama's solicitor waited in the downstairs library.
Something more to be taken to Hawaii at the dowager countess's request. Timothy prayed it was not another head of

livestock. He was traveling with a small menagerie already. The woman must be stopped.

The elderly man rose as Timothy entered the room. "No need for that, Carstairs. No formality here. What does Grandmama require of me?"

"Greetings, your Lordship. Madam has requested that some of her jewels be transported to Hawaii."

"Do you have the jewel box?"

"Well, you see, sir, it is more complicated than that. She has specifically requested that you wear them on your person for security." The man held out what looked to be a very old padded leather bag with a long strap and a shoulder loop.

Timothy reached for the bag. Goatskin, by the feel of it. Finely tanned and carefully layered. He looked at Carstairs, bemused.

"Seriously?"

"Yes, she was quite adamant about it. Some of the pieces are very old and have been in the vault for a generation. The bag itself is easily several hundred years old."

"Well, I suppose I can obtain a jewel chest for it. That would assuredly be safer."

The solicitor shook his head. "No, my lord, Madam was most specific. If you will not promise to wear the pouch, I am to take it back to the vault."

Timothy smoothed his expression and pulled the strap over his shoulder. If he was not mistaken, the solicitor was a bit uncomfortable.

"And you see, sir, I am to tell you that the bag is to be worn under your shirt and on the left side, over your heart. She said I was to impress this upon you."

"Quite right. Of course. I am sure this is the proper thing."

Poor Mr. Carstairs looked much relieved. He thrust a white envelope forward. "You are to carry this with the bag and open it once you are on the final ship back to Hawaii."

"Of course, I shall do just that."

"Thank you, sir. I know you sail tonight. Please give your esteemed grandmother my sincerest regards." The old man looked up at him and winked. "You might also tell her it would be most gracious of her to return to London while I am still alive."

Now Timothy did chuckle. "You can count on that message being delivered, sir. She has quite taken over my house!"

Stansfield Mansion, Pacific Heights, San Francisco, California, early December, 1909

Letty walked down the hall from her own room to Irene's big bedroom, enjoying the silky feel of the Oriental rug on her bare feet. Rosebud bounced along beside her.

Irene was home for the weekend. Mills College seemed to be agreeing with her. Still, Letty knew her friend liked a dose of the city whenever she could get it. Last night two old friends from Redwood had visited, giving the young ladies a full complement to play poker. And play they did, until well past midnight. Money changed hands. And a cameo brooch. Perhaps some sherry had been imbibed. The butler would never tell.

This morning, their political duties awaited.

"Get up, sleepyhead! We have a march to attend today!" The ladies intended to storm city hall and demand the right to vote.

"Your mama, Imogene the Warrior Queen, will expect you to be ready for battle by the time we sit down at the breakfast table. You must not disappoint!"

No one called Imogene "the Warrior Queen" to her face, of course, but all the girls referred to her that way in private. Just as Letty's own stepmother had become Agnes the Lioness.

Rosebud made a flying leap to the top of Irene's mound of covers. Leonardo the cat hissed and whacked her on the nose. Rosebud tumbled down, whimpering.

Irene sat up. "Is she okay?"

"The little beast isn't hurt, just practicing her drama skills. This happens almost every day in some fashion. I keep thinking that Rosebud will learn to leave Leonardo alone, but not so far."

"I think Leonardo outweighs her."

"Without doubt." Letty scooped Rosebud up in her arms and tapped her on the nose. "You, young lady, better hope that cat never decides to show you who is boss. He has sharp claws and you don't."

Irene lay back down. "I am sooooo tired . . ."

"Me too, but your mother, and the future of womanhood, awaits."

Irene eased herself carefully out of bed so as to not disturb the cat.

"College is still good?"

"Yes. It is not that much more rigorous than what we got from Miss Fred at Redwood. What it lacks is the vigorous part. I am pining for more sports. Who knew that I would miss field hockey?" Irene hurriedly began to dress.

"Well, you will get some walking in today. That is certain."

Irene poked her head out of the top of her camisole. "Are your colleagues at Feeney's still being vile?"

"I do my best to ignore them, but yes. The latest gambit is to insinuate I am actually a man in women's clothing. And whenever we are working with—shall we say—any male animal's body parts, they want to know how big mine are."

"You must be joking."

"I wish I were. I am taller than every one of them, and that does not help." She set Rosebud down with a pat. "My greatest veterinary triumph to date is this little beast here. She's finally minding her manners. No more messes in the house. Your mother has been most forbearing."

Irene sat down to pull on her boots. "Don't change the subject. How can Dr. Feeney allow them to do this?"

"Oh, he doesn't know. They are nothing if not sneaky. And I am not about to tell him. I can deal with it."

"Yes, but you shouldn't have to."

Letty had no response. "I will see you downstairs."

"Letty, wait—you really do look haggard. Are you getting any time to walk barefoot? Like the *kumu* told you?" Sometimes she wished she had not told Irene so much about her fire. Irene had always been bossy.

"It's been too cold. On top of that, I am at Feeney's ten hours a day. And the operatory is in a part of town where you do *not* want to take your shoes off."

"I am glad you are going home for the holidays, then."

"I won't lie. I can't wait to get on that ship."

The Stansfields' breakfast room was brightly lit to offset the December morning gloom. Mr. Stansfield sat reading the newspaper with his customary steaming cup of coffee. Irene's sisters were arranged around the table in various attitudes. Matilda, reading the business portions of the paper her father had previously perused, poked at her coddled egg. The twins, Anna and Jeanine, whispered secrets back and forth. At least there was no giggling.

The irrepressible Glory had a book about cowboys propped up in front of her plate. Once she learned that the *paniolos* in Hawaii—like her beloved Wu—were the original cowboys, she had jumped into research on anything to do with ranching.

A few days prior, Letty discovered Glory reading one of her anatomy books on cattle—bulls, to be precise. "What is a scrotum?" was not exactly the sort of question Letty wanted to answer for a just-turned-eight-year-old. Funny, that was the same topic her tormenters at Feeney's were so obsessed with.

Letty filled her plate. Her appetite had been on the wane, but she knew enough to eat.

Imogene breezed in, the very picture of a glamorous crusader for women's rights. If there could be such a thing. Somehow Imogene, with her raven hair piled high on her head, made a simple shirtwaist and porkpie hat look like the most elegant of garb.

Letty felt particularly gawky and outsized today.

"Ladies, are we ready? Where is Irene?"

"She will be down in a moment. I just left her."

"Gaylord, are you driving us?"

Mr. Stansfield did not even appear from behind the newspaper. "Of course, my dear."

Irene trooped through the door.

"Irene, eat quickly—we must be off."

"Just as soon as I have coffee . . ."

He could not believe his luck. Here he was stymied by crazed women waving signs in Union Square, annoyed that they blocked his way back to Chinatown. He had a high-stakes game waiting in a private home on Stockton Street. Perhaps if he tripped someone, that might scatter the crowd. Then a very tall woman caught his eye. It could not be her, or could it? She turned around. Unbelievable. Her dark skin set off by that hair was unmistakable. The hair was even redder than he remembered.

Well, well, well. That bitch, Letty Lang, right here in San Francisco. What could be better than this? Revenge was always sweet, no matter how—or when—it was served. No need to go to Hawaii now. All he had to do was follow her. Opportunity would come his way. It always did.

Chapter Thirty-Four

He ʻīlio kawaū

A DAMP, COLD DOG

San Francisco, California, mid-December, 1909

At nearly 9:00 p.m. Timothy stepped wearily off the Southern Pacific Pullman car into the harshly lit San Francisco railroad station. The twelve days since he'd left London seemed an eternity. First, six days on the ship across the Atlantic, and then this seemingly endless train ride. He'd taken the southern route to avoid the worst of the December weather.

Royce had been appalled that Timothy traveled without a valet. Quite frankly, at this very moment he would not mind having a manservant. But he would never admit that to his brother.

Now Timothy was beyond grateful that Gaylord had offered a car and driver to meet him at the station. Perhaps he should be even more grateful that all the animals were sent ahead on another train directly to the Oakland docks. The last thing he needed at this late hour was to be dealing with a herd of Hereford cattle.

His heap of luggage remained an embarrassment. Quite likely the porters had gossiped all the way across the continent about why any man traveled with so many trunks. If only they knew his grandmother, they would surely understand.

It wasn't just the animals. Grandmama had him bringing back any number of things for the holidays. Champagne for the Princess, a packet of dried fruits for a Christmas pudding, and her own Moran Manor hams. A crate of delicacies from Fortnum and Mason. And gifts, already in fancy wrapping, from Harrods.

She even demanded he bring her more jewelry. To his eye, she already had more than she needed for the simpler life of Hawaii. But whatever Grandmama wanted, he would always do. Just as she instructed, the pouch with the baubles was safely strapped inside his shirt. Over his heart. He found it oddly comforting.

Light blazed from the mansion in welcome as the car pulled into the circular drive. Still, no amount of light would ever be enough to push back the foggy gloom of San Francisco on a night in December. It was as bad as London. This city, surrounded by the sea, just smelled better.

"Timothy!" Gaylord came out the front door and embraced him. "We are delighted you are able to join us for a few nights."

"Thanks for such a brightly lit welcome. Is everyone up?"

"Hello, Mr. Rowley." The little girl stood straight and proud on the upper step.

"Why, Glorietta, you have grown! Thank you for waiting up for me."

"Truthfully, I am waiting up for Letty. She promised to explain a picture in one of her books to me."

"Ah. Well. I appreciate the honesty. Where is Letty?"

"She is due home any moment. I sent Franklin to meet her at the streetcar." Gaylord ushered Timothy inside.

"It seems a bit late."

"Dr. Feeney insists that his students take turns cleaning the operatory. Tonight is Letty's night to clean. When she is finished, one of the other students walks her to the streetcar, and then we meet her at this end. I am not entirely happy with the arrangement, but there you are. She won't let me send a car for her. She does not want the other students to think she is putting on airs."

"Well, that sounds like our Letty."

"Jackson will move your luggage to the guesthouse. Might I offer you a glass of brandy?"

Before he could accept, Timothy's breath caught. Hard and sharp, like a kick in the stomach. Panting and suddenly clammy, he looked around for the source of his discomfort.

At that moment Franklin came rushing up the drive.

"Mr. Gaylord, Miss Letty was not on either of the last two streetcars. There is only one more coming in. We should send the car just in case."

Now Timothy had chest pains. And the overwhelming sense that he must find Letty. Immediately. Now.

"Let me go with the car. I assume the driver knows where Feeney's establishment is?"

"Right. Rowley, I would go, but I must retrieve Imogene. She attended a suffragist meeting tonight."

Franklin appeared relieved to see immediate action taken.

"I will head back to the end of the streetcar line, sir."

Timothy was already out the door.

She must admit to it: she was tired to the bone. Always running to catch up, since all of her fellow students had more preparation than she, but never quite succeeding. And no contact with the 'āina.

The four men had been even messier than usual. The results of the dissection of the dead carriage horse lay scattered everywhere. *Ugh.* She longed for the smells of gardenia and ginger. Anything to get the odor of carbolic acid out of her nose.

"Miss Lang, do hurry. It seems tonight I have drawn the short straw for the task of escorting you to the streetcar. I will be waiting at the Glass Orb down the street." This from James Ogilvie, the leader of the oppression. "Come, gentlemen, our pints await. Let us leave the wench to her rightful duties." The four of them streamed out, backslapping.

How had she not bitten off her tongue in the last three months? It was apparent from the outset that any attempt to engage these fellows would meet with hostility and derision. So she had just stopped trying.

There was a knock at the door. A ragged, bent-over old man entered carrying a whimpering black-and-white-spotted dog. "You be the nurse? This here fella's leg be broken."

"I can see that. Put him right up here on the table."

"I can't pay nothing."

"That's fine."

The man hovered around the end of the examining table. She could see him looking at all the surgical instruments that lined the walls. Then he sniffed at the half-dissected horse and moved to the other side of the room.

"Don't worry. This is a simple break. I can set it easily."

The man shuffled to a chair and sat down.

"Ain't you done for the day?"

"Just cleaning up for tomorrow."

Ogilvie's snarling face appeared at the doorway. "What is holding you up?"

"We have a patient; this dog has a broken leg. I am going to set it."

"Where is the owner?"

Letty nodded toward the chair as she worked to calm the dog. She had to be very careful about using her breathing, since it had become one of the targets of the teasing. Perhaps she would use a bit of ether.

"Is this your dog, sir? Can you pay for his care?" Ogilvie's tone was belligerent.

The man slumped farther into the chair as he shook his head no.

"For Pete's sake, Letty, throw him out and finish cleaning up. I will wait another five minutes for you, but that is all. After that you are on your own."

"Right, as if that were anything new. I'll be fine—you just go. I refuse to turn away this animal."

"You will never survive as a veterinarian if people don't pay you."

"Thank you for that brilliant insight. I will be fine. See you tomorrow."

Ogilvie stomped out. She could hear him hallooing to the other three that he was done nurse-maiding the crazy woman. Hah! If they only knew just how crazy this woman was, maybe they would think twice. Wishful thinking.

The man got up and began shuffling around again.

"It will just be a few minutes, sir, while the dressing sets." She slipped into her practiced breathing. She had given the dog a bit of ether to settle him down, but not much. She set the ether cup aside. Now she could feel the dog's pain and fear recede as warmth flowed through her fingers. This was why she was here. This was what was meant to be.

"Put your hands behind you."

She started out of her trance.

"Sir, no need for a robbery, I will give you what I have . . ."

Her right arm was wrenched behind her as something hard pressed into her back.

"Yes, you will give me *everything* you have."

His voice . . . but Allerton was dead . . . gone to Chicago to be hanged . . .

"Lean forward and breathe into the ether cup you had for the dog."

She struggled.

"Now."

He yanked her arm harder and hit the back of her head. Her last thought was that she had not meant to put so much ether in the cup.

Letty's head hurt murderously. Nausea. Oh god, she needed to roll over so she could vomit. Only she could not move. She turned her head quickly to at least spit the bile out of her mouth but choked. Things began to swim into view. The wall of surgical saws. The overhead lights illuminating the operating tables. The dead horse. The man rifling through the trays of scalpels she had just cleaned. Allerton.

Still confused by the ether, she tried to speak, but found she'd been gagged with what must be yards of gauze. She struggled to rise.

"Don't bother trying to get up. These tables are obviously designed for large animals. They will work admirably for what I intend for you."

Leather straps secured her, arms and legs spread-eagled, and there was even a webbing across her chest. She tried pulling her legs and her calves cramped. *Think, Letty. There must be a way to get free.* But only a cold wave of terror emerged.

"Ah, just what I was looking for." He walked to the table, holding one of the longest scalpels. She had used it just today, the specialized one for big, initial cuts. Now she would throw up. At least that way she might suffocate.

"There's no horse to save you now, is there?" His little chuckle chilled her further.

In the car, Timothy's agitation only intensified. His breath uneven. Sweat pouring down his back despite the cold night. His wrists itched and ached. The muscles in his calves cramped. Then suddenly he wrenched forward with nausea. "Are we close? I could get out and run."

"Not yet, sir. I can get you much closer. Just a moment. And not in this neighborhood, sir. Mr. Gaylord would have my hide if I let you out of the car here."

Timothy grabbed the car door, his instincts urging him to jump out. It seemed an eternity until the vehicle pulled up in front of a dilapidated warehouse. One of a handful left standing since the earthquake. Lights glowed from greasy windows on the upper floor.

"This is where the school is, sir. I've not driven this close, as Miss Letty never wished her colleagues to see the car. She will not want us to cause a scene."

Timothy jumped out. "If you do not see me in five minutes, start honking the horn and get help. We will make a scene if we must."

She was here, though he could not explain how he knew it. And in danger. He headed for the entrance, then fell to his knees as a searing pain lanced his right foot.

"Are you all right, sir?" the chauffeur yelled out the car window.

He did not respond. He just kept going.

She went awash in icy sweat. Her flesh was on fire. The scientist in her wondered, Was this her power? Or just fear? Allerton pulled on her right boot. It came off with a pop. He grasped her foot so hard she thought bones might break, then—searing pain. She screamed, but the cry came out garbled through the bandage in her mouth. The bastard had pierced the sole of her foot.

"I like starting with feet. You see, the pain there is some of the most exquisite. It rather sets the stage for what comes next."

As she stared straight up at the ceiling, the tears ran out her eyes and pooled in her ears. She panted with the pain.

"Actually, I think I would prefer to hear you scream." Without warning, he stood poised at her side. She flinched as he made a sudden thrust at her left eye. "Fooled you, didn't I?"

The scalpel sliced neatly though the gauze. She spit the wet lump out while he pulled the wrappings away. She had to know. "Why?"

"You know why, you little bitch. You think you are smarter than me. You ruined my game with your stupid Englishman. He smelled of an easy swindle until he got suspicious. All because you talk too much."

She was too frightened to scream. "Oh, I never liked your nose—let me fix it." He nicked her before she could think to move. Blood seeped into her mouth, its taste metallic. She lifted her head to try to keep breathing. The dog awoke from its ether-induced stupor and began to whine.

"Shut up, you stupid mutt. You are affecting my concentration." He grabbed the bigger scalpel and turned toward the poor dog. "Perhaps it's time to get rid of you."

🔥

Timothy saw blood dripping from one of Letty's feet. What had the bastard done to her?

Edging along the wall, he eased one of the surgical saws off its hooks to grasp behind his back. A distraction. He needed a distraction. Perhaps he could throw something. He steadied his breathing. The whimpering from the dog in the far corner turned into a howl of pain. Allerton moved away from Letty to yell at the animal.

God knew where his own howl came from. Allerton spun to face him, scalpel in hand. Timothy moved in on pure instinct, launching a ferocious barrage of hits with the surgical saw. He rejoiced to feel them connect. Rejoiced to see his opponent's blood on the floor. On himself.

Until Allerton lunged and connected a blow to his chest. Like a scrape of fire. Timothy froze as Allerton leaned in to twist the scalpel and then jumped back, pulling the blade out of a tear in his shirt.

"You won't be recovering from that anytime soon."

Letty watched Timothy stagger. Maybe Allerton hadn't hit his heart, but it was close. Maybe a lung. Allerton stood back, seeming to savor the moment. A cry of anguish escaped her lips.

"I will be back to you shortly, my dear. Let me just finish up with his Lordship here."

Timothy staggered again. He dropped to one knee, eyes glassy. Allerton stepped in to finish him off, lifting the scalpel for the final blow.

But Timothy reared up like an avenging angel, thrusting the saw upward into Allerton's chest, lifting the man completely off the ground with his force. The tip of the surgical saw protruded from Allerton's collar as he fell backward.

Unmoving. Timothy stood over him, breathing like a man who'd just climbed a mountain. Then he went to the corner and threw up.

"Timothy! If you have breath left, get to me! Maybe I can help."

He limped to her side. "Yes, I am sure you can help."

"You have a chest wound. You don't have much time. Set me free."

"I think I only have time for one thing."

His mouth covered hers with all the force of his need. He kissed her greedily. And she kissed back.

Her fire arced in a nimbus around his head. "Damn you! Stop this and help me up."

He pulled back with a crazed grin. "See, I am not dead."

"But you will be if you do not SET ME FREE."

He gently unbuckled all the straps, cradling her savaged foot in his hands. "I should have made him hurt more."

"Timothy, for heaven's sake, you skewered him! He's dead! You must be in shock, otherwise you would be on the floor. Take off your coat and shirt."

"Only if you kiss me again."

He was clearly delirious. He breathed strangely too. She fought down a rising panic. Sliding off the table onto one leg, she pulled away the reddened cloth from his chest.

What?

He looked down and began to laugh.

She found herself babbling. "You were staggering . . . you were hurt. I saw it. This . . . this is barely even a scratch. He cut . . . this . . . this . . . leather pouch, not you."

"I said to myself, what would Sir Percy Blakeney do if his lady love was in the hands of a knife-wielding madman? Play along with the bastard! So, I did." He grinned like a madman himself. "Sink me!"

She started to laugh herself, only at the edge of hysteria. He leaned down and kissed her again, soft this time. His arms encircled her, lifting her up. She felt boneless. "Now we must take care of you. But please note I have been kissing you and no one, I say no one, is dying here."

She cocked her head toward the whimpering at the other side of the room. "Timothy, we cannot leave this dog. I won't have it."

Franklin and Gaylord burst into the room, pistols drawn. Imogene was right behind, her pearl-handled derringer at the ready.

Gaylord quickly surveyed the situation, poking Allerton's body with his toe. "Well, well, well. You seem to have carried the day, Rowley. Quite an expedient dispatch. Right through the solar plexus. Or did our Letty do this?"

"She is bleeding, Gaylord. I don't think it is serious, but we need to get her home."

"Right. Imogene, can you take charge? I will wait here for the police."

"The dog—we must take care of the dog." Letty was adamant. The whimpering from the corner became a low whine.

Gaylord patted her on the arm. "We have already sent for Feeney. I will make sure he fixes the dog right up. That is, immediately after he delivers to me the young man who failed to get you safely home tonight."

The room began to spin, and that was the last thing she remembered.

Chapter Thirty-Five

Mea Ola

SURVIVOR

Stansfield Mansion, Pacific Heights, San Francisco, California, the morning after

Her foot throbbed. Her nose stung. Her eyes popped open to the realization of the night's horror. Reflexively she rolled into a ball, hugging her knees close, pulling her head under the covers. The enormity of what had happened—or almost happened—was too big to grasp.

A large and familiar hand reached under the covers to stroke her cheek as tears cascaded over her nose to pool on her pillow. She turned to kiss his fingers. He was alive and so was she. Perhaps the day could be faced.

Timothy eased the covers back a bit and peered down at her. "You have slept a very long time." From the look of him, he had not.

"What happened to the poor dog? The one that bastard mangled? I have to know."

"Yes, you do." He cradled her shoulders as he pulled her up. "Take a look."

In a corner, a pile of blankets sheltered a black-and-white-spotted dog with a plaster cast on one leg. Curled up on top of the dog was Rosebud. Letty gave her own bark of laughter.

"I think your little beast has a new friend. She is quite protective. Glory came in at one point to declare the dog's name to be Pinto. Because, as she tells me, that is what black-and-white cowboy horses are called. You slept through the entire affair."

She leaned fully into his embrace. "I need to get home. Back to the 'āina."

"That is clear."

"But first I must see Dr. Feeney. I have two more days of my term to finish."

"The term is over. Continuing studies are impossible. Constables have been crawling all over the Feeney establishment. Dr. Feeney was here himself this morning with the execrable Mr. Ogilvie in tow. The roses over on the dresser are his atonement offering. Gaylord wisely did not advise me Ogilvie was in the house, else I might have committed my second murder in less than twenty-four hours."

"Are you all right?"

He paused, biting his lip. Goodness, how could she find him adorable at a time like this? But she did.

"I am haunted. Even though Allerton was intent on killing us both, I can't take ending any life lightly. You must think me a coward."

She sat up and turned to put her arms around him. "No, I think you are a true hero, a man with a soul . . . a man who acts with *pono*, as we say. Righteousness."

She could not say who rocked whom as they swayed in a tight embrace of mutual comfort. Until the doorknob turned.

Letty jumped away from Timothy as if she had received an electric shock. Imogene peered in.

"Greetings, you two sleepyheads. The physician is here to see if Letty's foot is safe for travel. If you want to be on that ship to Hawaii tomorrow, I suggest you let him in to clear you."

"Tomorrow?"

"I hadn't had a chance to tell her yet."

"So what have you two been doing in here?" Imogene's stare at Timothy was pointed. You slept on her floor all night."

Timothy looked sheepish. "She just woke up!"

Letty regained her composure. "How can we leave tomorrow? There is no ship scheduled."

"Kalama has a cargo ship leaving. Bound for Hilo. On the noon tide. I had previously arranged to put the livestock aboard. Tom offered me passage. He keeps a suite or two of cabins on all his ships for personal use. There will be plenty of room for you too."

She felt a black wave of despair crest over her. "I can never come back, can I? Feeney won't have it. I'm just trouble."

"We will cross that bridge as it comes. We will find a way. Let Imogene get you ready for the doctor."

"Yes, dear. I brought one of my robes for you to wear."

Timothy stood to leave the room. Somehow all the light went with him.

CHAPTER THIRTY-SIX

Holokai

SEA VOYAGE

**Aboard the Freighter *Theodora*,
on the Pacific, one day later**

Timothy stood at the ship's forward rail as the sun went down. Perhaps three hours out of San Francisco, he had already lost sight of land. The gray December ocean rolled the ship in the gathering gloom.

Letty slept, safely tucked in the shipowner's cabin. Since the attack she'd slept almost constantly, tossing and turning. He would be more worried if he could not see her color improving and her restlessness decreasing. She needed to be home. She needed to touch the *'āina*, to be nourished by the living land. What had Sir John called it? The place where the heart of the earth comes near. Now his home too. So much had changed.

He pulled the crumpled, bloodstained envelope from his pocket, amazed that his grandmother's superstitious insistence on his wearing the pouch had saved both his life and Letty's. This was not a coincidence.

My dearest Timothy,

Perhaps as you read this, you sit in a deck chair on a steamship heading back to your true home. That you are reading this letter at all means you chose not to accept the challenge of our English family. It is the choice I hoped you would make. I know in my heart that Hawaii holds your future.

By now you have worn that leather pouch for many days, wondering by what old lady's foolishness I required this of you. I can't say precisely; it was just my sense that you must carry it over your heart.

The contents are meant for your future bride. The jewels that you see within may not seem that impressive, but they are laden with your own family history. They might also be a bit magical.

The ruby ring belonged to your great-great-grandmother, Callista. Perhaps I told you that she claimed to be one of the notorious white witches of Wales? A very tall woman who spoke her mind, she captured the heart of a sea captain named Moran. This Spanish ruby was his betrothal gift. She wore it until her death. No one has worn it since. When I was a child, she told us she could see our every mischief in its depths. That kept us in line, I can assure you.

Now I believe the ring is destined to go to another woman of substance and magic. I think you might know one of those?

*You can examine the other pieces at your leisure.
Even the pouch was your great-great-grandfather's.
Remind me to tell you all the stories behind it.*

*All my love and pride,
Philomena*

Letty awoke to the rocking of a ship underway. She barely remembered embarking amid the fury of the day's activity. Somehow Timothy had been everywhere, handling everything. If they were at sea, it meant she'd slept through it all.

She propped herself up on her elbows, the bedcovers slipping from her shoulders in the wintry air. Night had fallen outside her cabin window. Really, she had been sleeping entirely too much.

She lay back, shrugging the heavy covers back up around her neck. Truly she did feel better. Although she might never feel quite like herself again.

The door to the adjoining cabin opened stealthily.

"Ah, I caught you awake!"

"Yes, and hungry!"

"Of course you are. Dinner is on the table. Let me help you."

She swung her legs off the wide berth and warily stood up before taking his arm. Her legs felt stronger, her foot less painful.

"This is by far the nicest ship's cabin I have ever inhabited. Usually I am much too tall for the berth. Not this one."

His wicked grin said too much. "I know better than to joke with you about bedrooms . . ."

She blushed and averted her eyes, remembering all too well the dressing-down she had given him in his soon-to-be ranch house. A lifetime ago.

Her mouth formed an involuntary "oh" as they entered the next room. A little table awaited, with white linens and flowers. Covered silver dishes exuded wonderful smells. Her stomach rumbled. She was starving.

"Shall we eat? Then I have news to share with you."

"A very good plan. I must admit to being famished."

"Yes, I believe I heard your stomach make that announcement."

Timothy delighted to see Letty eat. The woman was completely unaware of how sensual she was in her enjoyment. Now she poked about with one finger to get the last crumbs of lemon tart off her plate. His mouth went dry as she licked that same finger.

The goatskin pouch lay at the edge of the table. He wondered when he'd have the courage to present her with its contents. He grasped her other hand across the table, lightly caressing her wrist, marveling at the difference in the color of their skin. He could not imagine it now as anything other than beautiful. As she was beautiful, inside and out. How had he not seen it on the day she rose from the ocean like a goddess of deliverance bringing Diablo to safety? This woman was his destiny. Now he had only to get her to believe it. And himself to survive it.

Her breath caught at his caress. He raised his eyes. The collar of her *holokū* lay open in a deep vee, one that revealed the fluttering pulse in her neck and a bit more. Bloody hell, perhaps she had nothing on under that dress? He shook his head to clear it, feeling her eyes on him.

"Um, there were a few things I failed to tell you when I came to see you in September. We got a bit distracted after the kiss in the park."

"What things?" She pushed away the plate now cleansed of any trace of the lemon tart.

"Before I followed you to San Francisco, I went to visit K."

"Why?" Her face showed complete puzzlement.

"Do you remember what the *kumu* said to me on the day you left? She called me *kahu*."

"And?"

"It means we are bound together for the rest of our lives. Every Gate is to have a guardian, a *kahu*. I am yours. It is part of the prophecies . . ."

"But you are not Hawaiian . . ."

"The Princess believes the *'āina* has claimed me, chosen me for its own. Because I love the land."

"I still don't understand."

"Precisely what she said was, 'You are bound to the *'āina* now, whether you like it or not. Once the land has chosen, it will not be undone.' Then she rolled her eyes."

"She did not."

"I am afraid she did." He squeezed her hand as much to calm himself as reassure her. "Then she sent me off to see Bull. And Tom.

"Here is the thing. I was foolish and prideful when I came to see you in September. I thought being your *kahu* must mean we could be together, in spite of what Bull and Tom told me. I thought I was the one man to be stronger than any prophecy. Then you knocked me over in the park, and I realized that things are never that simple."

"Why did you think that? Bull and K have never been together, and she is not with Tom either."

"Bull told me he and K were never meant to be together. Tom may be the one for K. But there are difficulties . . ."

"And . . ."

"I think we may be different."

"That day in the park was the first time I accepted that the danger is real. I went off to London in a funk. But I could not stay away. I woke in the night longing for you. And for the *'āina*."

He moved from his chair to stand next to her. He'd force the next words out if he must.

"I felt it, Letty. When the attack happened, I *felt* it. I was standing in the entryway of the Stansfield house. Something punched me in the gut. I *knew* you were in danger. That something was terribly, terribly wrong. I almost stopped breathing. Then in the car, the closer we got to you the more I sensed your bonds, your panic. I even felt the pain when that bastard pierced your foot."

She grasped both his hands. "Timothy, there is no need to speak of this."

"There is every need." He drew her up, clutching her close, relishing the feel of her safe and whole against him. "Understand this. Whether we can be lovers or not, we will never be separated again. Never." He pulled her even closer, placing her arms around his neck, wrapping his own arms around her. His lips grazed her neck before he pulled back to search her face. "But I hope and pray we can be lovers."

Unsure of her answer, he paused. Until she pulled his head forward into a deep kiss. A whispered yes lifted his heart, her heat warming his soul.

He swept her up to carry her back to the big berth in the next room, nuzzling her neck as he did so.

"Shall we give this love thing a try again?" he suggested. She went still.

"I don't want to bury you at sea."

"You won't. My self-control is greatly improved since London. I learned how to breathe. Like the *kumu* taught you. That's what I want to show you."

"You learned to breathe?"

"Yes, from a man who calls himself a master of esoterica. It was . . . strange. He knew the exact words of what the *kumu* said, that I "must find the path and walk it." There is no way he could have known. He gave me hope."

"Where are the dogs?"

"In my cabin. Don't try to distract me." She wriggled in his arms as he began breathing into her ear. He loved the heft of her, every perfect inch. And yes, she was naked under that *holokū*.

"Timothy, we should be frightened." She shivered against him, her body cooling. Perhaps a distraction was in order.

"Is this your first time?"

She reared back to push away. Her aura arced between them where he held her fast.

"Bastard! What a question!"

"Letty, please. Hear me out! Anger is a much better place to start for what we must do. Not fear. That's part of what I learned. Please stay angry and breathe." He adjusted her weight against him. "I have an idea, a theory. Based on what I learned.

"And if it is any consolation," he said, "I must admit I don't have much experience at this either."

"As I said, bastard." But she breathed. "I am still afraid."

"So am I." He turned to look her directly in the face. "But I want to believe that as long as we are together, we can conquer anything."

Except the extremely painful arousal he was now experiencing. That might prove more difficult to resolve. But at least, now he had hope.

Chapter Thirty-Seven

Aumoe

NIGHTTIME

She lay quiet in his arms as he carried her, stifling the urge to ask if she wasn't too heavy to carry. Somehow, for that brief moment, everything seemed just as it ought, his warmth and strength enfolding her. Safe.

Or not safe. Not safe at all.

Timothy flopped down on the big berth, the force of their combined weights causing it to creak. They burst into nervous laughter, like guilty children off on a forbidden adventure.

Gently he turned her to sit on his lap facing away. His hands kept roving, his mounting urgency apparent in every caress, even as her own desire grew. Each brush of a fingertip kindled its own spark of flame. Now he stroked her back, his breath tickling the back of her neck. Shooting stars burst up her spine. Then down. So very far down.

"I just needed to touch you."

Just as she needed to be touched. "Yes."

She gasped as one hand moved to cup her breast, a slow finger circling her nipple. Her reaction was as swift as it was unexpected, the fire coalescing in her belly, her back arching of its own accord. This must stop before someone got hurt. If only she wanted to stop.

Timothy placed his other hand on her belly to pull her close, molding her backside against him. Flexing and rocking against her buttocks, his hard readiness gave testament to the fact that this was real. That he wanted her. As she wanted him.

He moved his hand down, fingers seeking the source of her need through the thin cotton of her *holokū*. She panted. She might lose control at any moment.

"Timothy, we have to stop."

"Is that a no?" His own breath was rapid.

"I just don't want you hurt. I could not live with myself."

He pulled her sideways on his lap, wrapping his arms around her as if to protect her. If only. His breath slowed but remained ragged. His chin rested on her shoulder. "I am willing to take the risk. Please?"

Speechless, she nodded. The hope in her heart betrayed her better sense.

"Stand up, sweetheart."

Rocking on quaking legs, she avoided putting weight on her injured foot as best she could. The rolling ocean did not help. Letty laid a hand on Timothy's shoulder to steady herself, only to have him incline his head to kiss that hand. Chicken skin. If you can call it that when accompanied by fire.

"All right, what is this theory of yours?" She could only be grateful her voice did not quaver. Think of this as a science experiment, that is what she must do. An experiment that might forever change her life. Or end his.

"When you are using your gifts, you breathe, right? That is what the *kumu* taught you?"

"Yes, so?"

"Did she teach you anything like warriors might use . . ."

"What are you suggesting?"

"That we breathe. Together. As if we are one being."

"That's it?"

"Yes." Timothy exhaled, his breath dropping into a pattern. "The man I met in London. The master of esoterica. From India. What they call a guru. Named Woodruffe." He exhaled again. "He taught me the line between war and love is razor thin." She started to speak, but he placed a finger on her lips as he sank deeper into the breath.

She knew this pattern, the warrior's breath. She flashed back to the day the *kumu* had taught it to her. The breath for war that gave her peace. She began it.

"Now, look at me. In the eyes."

She looked, seeing his gray eyes filled equally with longing and fear. Her own must mirror the same. Her gaze dropped.

"Please. Keep looking right at me. That's what Sir John told me. Otherwise this may fail."

"Well, we can't have that." She kept her tone light even though they both knew what was at stake.

"And no more touching. Not yet."

She pulled her hand from his shoulder, careful to keep her eyes on his.

"Now we breathe. One deep breath in, two shorter breaths out. Then hold."

Yes, the warrior's breath, just as she learned it.

"That's it?"

"I hope so." She watched the smile crinkle about his eyes. "It's all we've got."

But there must be more.

"We breathe until we find a rhythm, a rhythm together, where we breathe as one."

This she understood. The *kumu* had shown her this too. Breathing together shared the gift. Touching might make it more so. But no touching. Not yet.

Her lungs expanded with a spark of hope. One breath in, two out. The meter was familiar, comforting even. Her eyes dropped to Timothy's chest to see it rise and fall almost in unison.

"Don't look away!" His voice hoarse with concentration. "Think about what you want, your intention. What do you want?"

Him, that's all she wanted. Him. Always. Forever. Body and spirit. Him.

Then she felt it. A connection through the breath, deepening with each inhale and exhale. As if his breath caressed her, his desire rampant. Liquid flame pooled between her thighs. A frisson so hot it seemed to be ice raced up her spine.

"Do you feel it?"

She nodded.

"So do I." His eyes widened. "I can see your aura. Burning."

Never taking his eyes off hers, he drew up her *holokū* bit by bit. The cabin was cool with the winter on the Pacific, yet there must be steam rising off her body. She raised her arms and he pulled the dress over her head. Her aura flickered around her arms.

"I can't bear it if I hurt you."

"You won't." He pulled her to him, hands splayed across her back, every finger alive with heat. His lips came down on hers hard and she responded in kind. Joyous flames kindled, first hot then cold. She shivered. The breathing pattern broke.

Timothy dropped to his knees, face white. She grabbed his arms to yank him back up.

"Are you all right?" His breath shallow now, panting. He nodded. She resumed the warrior's pattern deep and strong. If he could be this fearless, so could she.

"I feel a bit winded, that's all." His own breath steadied, reclaiming the pattern. "Anyway, now it's my turn." He smiled with that bit of mischief she treasured. Then began to tear at his own clothes.

"Let me help. We've no need to hurry." This to give herself time to sink back deeply into the breath. To be sure he was with her.

Hands on his shoulders, she smoothed his collar, then undid the shirt buttons. One. By. One. Breath. By. Breath. The sweet excruciation of delay fanning the fires within. Heat in her hands made the task difficult. Pearl buttons slipping away from moist fingers. She pushed his shirt open, placing both hands on his chest. When she pulled away, red marks remained where they'd rested.

She lifted her eyes to find him staring at her. He swallowed. She spoke. "No fear. Keep breathing."

He shucked his shirt off as she reached to the waistband of his trousers. Her breath low and steady, the pattern so ingrained now it seemed the only way to breathe.

"Wait." He covered her hands with his own, shivering.

Her gaze flickered up to meet his, smoldering and vivid. "Why?"

"I need you to look at me again. Help me."

"Is this what you learned in London? What they told you to do?"

"Yes." A quaver in his voice. "Please."

She met his gaze as she breathed, deep, slow, and steady. He struggled to keep his own breath in line. She moved her hands back up to his chest. He shivered again. Could she pull him to her?

"Timothy, keep breathing."

She pressed on his chest as she breathed. Deep breath in, two breaths out. The rhythm grabbed him, carried him, his heartbeat steadied under her hands.

She went lower, fingertips tracing the hard planes of his chest, a palm on the ridges of muscle beneath his rib cage, exploring as she slipped his trousers down to a puddle about his ankles. She reached to grasp . . .

He seized her hands. "Letty, wait," he croaked.

"Are you all right?"

He nodded, licking his lips.

She smiled. She could wait. But not forever.

She straightened up slowly, their hands still joined, swaying with the rhythm of her own breath. She might swear she saw firelight reflected in his eyes, yet there was no fire in the cabin. Except her own.

The ache to be with him . . . part of him . . . one with him . . . engulfed her. The desire for him, to be together and never apart. This was the moment. The last chance to turn away. The path now open for them to walk. "We must name our intention. Aloud."

He licked his lips before he spoke, his breath steady and sure. "I will be one with you, always together and never apart." She marveled at his words. Almost as if he'd plucked them from her mind. "I am yours as you are mine."

Her swaying ceased as her senses deepened with the intensity of her flames. Her hands traveled up his arms to cup his face, thumbs gently stroking his lips.

"You have spoken it. Do not forget that intentions have power."

He nodded.

"I'll answer."

She began to sway again, moving ever closer, the soft skin of her belly brushing his erection. Taut nipples grazing his chest. She might either explode or faint. But she would not stop breathing. Each breath so deep and strong it bound him to her.

"And I am yours, Timothy, one with you, as you are mine. Never apart, always together."

There, now she'd said it, the truth of it dancing through her body along with the flames. Timothy pulled her into a deep and desperate kiss. Letty's hands raked though his curls, leveraging the kiss deeper. Her body melted against him as she opened herself completely. Their tongues touched with an arc of fire.

She could not name what happened next. Her leaping fires transformed to the banked coals of the hearth, the *imu*. Still strong. Still radiant. Still coursing with power. But bridled under her hand to wield as she would. As she chose. To wrap her lover in her care. To open to receive him. She reached a hand to cup his cheek, her aura no longer flickering, her hand now limned in steady firelight. The red glow embracing him as well.

They'd be safe now, she knew it. Her fear banked along with her fire. She kissed him with that surety, willing her warmth and love to surround him. He moved his hand between her legs again, even as he laid her down on the berth. A rhythm as old as the ocean swept over her.

Her back arched as her response shattered her. Still, her breathing held, the embers of her fire steadfast, unwavering.

"Beast," she breathed, pulling in his scent—sandalwood and warm winds and now something else.

"Ah yes, but remember I am *your* beast. And anyway, aren't you about to be a doctor of animals? That must make you very, very good with beasts."

Before she could retort, he moved to kneel between her thighs. She clenched.

"What are you doing?"

"Keep breathing, sweetheart. I just want to taste you."

He lowered his head to her most sacred place. She gasped, his mouth teasing her, exploring her, piercing her. His tongue thrust deep, then flicked up. Again and again, faster and faster. Her hips writhed. Her flames burning ever hotter.

The tables had been turned. Maybe he would kill her. And maybe she would like it.

Suddenly he stopped. He was panting, breath ragged again. He shivered.

"Nooooo . . ." The wail came from the pit of her being.

She pushed up to look him straight in the eyes, to draw him back into her warmth, to surround him again. Her breath steadied into the chosen pattern, and his followed. A slow smile of wonder spread across his face. Perhaps they might both survive this night after all.

His tongue returned, finding its rhythm once again, following the breath. *In once, out twice. In once, out twice.* She cried out, plunging over the edge into pure joy.

He lunged up over her, supporting himself on his elbows.

"There is more where that came from." He leaned in to kiss her, his mouth slippery. She ran her tongue over his lips, then grasped his lower lip in her teeth. He shuddered. "Be careful, or this will be over before it has begun."

She laughed to think she had that power. Because she did. "Quite right, my lord!"

Grinning wickedly, he settled between her legs and thrust. She gasped as he paused.

Her flames stepped in. She angled her body up, wrapping her legs around his hips, pulling him deep. He thrust again and the fire at her very core became liquid, molten. His eyes shot wide and he paused once more. Beads of sweat dripped from his brow; she licked the salt from her lips. Her center gripped and pulled.

"Keep your promise, Timothy. Be one with me."

With a moan Timothy fell onto her, kissing her with an open mouth as he thrust once more.

"Never, we will never be apart again."

And together always.

Chapter Thirty-Eight

Wana'ao

DAWN

Freighter *Theodora*, Pacific Ocean, the next day

Timothy opened one eye only to discover his nose mere inches from the cabin wall. He heard humming. No, singing. Then a little bark. He rolled over to see Letty sitting across from the berth, Rosebud on her lap, scratching under the dog's chin as she sang.

"Good morning, sleepyhead! I took care of our fellow travelers and now have returned to see if you need any more of my . . . shall we say . . . ministrations."

He flashed to the moment she had turned the tables on him, moving to straddle him . . . *No, don't think about it.* If he did, he would not be able to decently get out of bed.

"Rosebud! Go get him!" She dropped the little dog on Timothy's head and stood back laughing as Rosebud began furiously kissing and pawing him.

"Letty, make her stop! Who knows where that mouth has been!"

Letty leaned over to pick up the dog with one hand, putting one of her fingers on his lips as she did so. He could see the swell of her breasts in the loose collar of her *holokū*. "I know where *your* lips have been."

Bloody hell, he would surely not be able to get out of bed without embarrassment now.

She stood up with a self-satisfied smile. "I think breakfast is in order, sir. I shall return Rosebud to the dog's cabin—which, by the way, we must pay to have fumigated or Tom will be distraught. Then I'll join you in the next room to break our fast. You have the mystery of the pouch to explain. And the tattoo of the red flower on your hip."

He sat up on his elbows. All the while carefully keeping the sheet draped across his lap. "The tattoo is a simple story. Bull and Tom got me drunk. It's your flower, the *lehua*. Every Gate has a flower. Every *kahu* has a tattoo."

"Quite."

She swayed out the door, the dog tucked under her arm, the *holokū* accentuating her every movement. If the missionaries thought those dresses were hiding something, they were completely missing the point.

He groaned as he threw his legs over the side of the berth. Maybe if he kept his shirt untucked . . .

Letty sat at the table, having already started on a bowl of fruit. The leather pouch still sat between the place settings, tied together with string, showing rusty bloodstains. He slipped into the chair opposite her.

"Coffee?"

Suddenly he could smell it and the craving kicked in. Real Kona coffee. He'd recognize the scent anywhere. Once he'd tasted Kona coffee, his morning tea had gone by the wayside. Was this more evidence that the *'āina* had taken him?

The silence of serious eating reigned until the meal was finished.

Letty sat up very straight, wearing her unmistakable get-down-to-business face. Timothy had seen it enough times to know. She spoke.

"Last night you said you had many more things to tell me. Where should we start?"

Her eyes were glittering, even fevered. Was she nervous? The morning-after jitters? It was clear he should reply with care.

"How about we start with 'Good morning, I love you'?"

"You do?"

"Yes, what did you think last night was about? I love you. It's just that simple."

Her hands clenched together, rimmed by the faint but steady light of her aura. He could see it constantly now.

"I love you too. But I am not sure it is simple at all."

"You heard me state my intention. You know what that means."

"Yes, yes, I do."

"I told you, a friend of a friend in London taught me things. About breathing. And intentions. Woodruffe." He was already nervous given what he was about to do, and her seriousness caught him off guard. He'd best just get to it. "Someday I might take you to meet him."

She looked away. "I doubt that."

He reached for the pouch, untied the string, and pulled out the ruby ring. Even in the limited light of the cabin the stone flamed, the old mine-cut diamonds surrounding it reflecting its glory. Fancifully, he wondered if the ring recognized her power and greeted her.

Standing up, he went to her side of the table. Down on one knee, wasn't that how this was done? As he knelt, he wobbled on his game leg. All the while Letty sat like a cornered rabbit.

"Please do me the honor of becoming my wife."

"I will be no one's wife. I am a Gate."

"Fine, we will not marry. We can just be together day and night and let the whole world talk about us."

"Besides, I intend to be a doctor for animals. Wives don't do that sort of thing." She averted her gaze.

"You will. I promise you. Whether you are my wife or not." He moved to get his knee to stop aching. "I have already asked Gaylord to find us a house in San Francisco. So you can go back." He shifted the knee again. Nothing worked. She stayed silent, face turned away. He barreled on.

"Where did you get such medieval ideas about marriage? I thought you were a suffragist, a believer in equal partnership," he said, reaching out to turn her face back to his. "The Letty Lang I love thinks she can do anything." The knee spasmed, but he would be damned if he was getting up until she said yes. Assuming she ever said yes. "Please? Just say yes?" Impulsively, he thrust the ring forward. He searched her face, fearful that he'd overplayed his hand.

Slowly she leaned to touch his knee, her breath soft, the comfort immediate. She reached to take the ring into her cupped hands. The light of her aura surrounded her, setting the ring afire with an answering glow.

"This ring saved your life. And now your life is mine. As my life is yours. Yes, a thousand times, yes." Her smile bloomed, the edge of mischief. "Although we can wager how long it might be until you regret asking me. Not long, I expect."

He slipped the ring on her finger, somehow not surprised that it fit perfectly, his own grin so wide his face might crack. "Oh, I already regret it, and I look forward to regretting it for many years to come." He pushed himself up and pulled her to him for a kiss.

She melted against him, mouth soft and willing, her heat filling him with wonder. Then she tipped her head back.

"I do so love a spate of regrets." She breathed, the pattern an invitation. "But even more than that, I love you."

Sink me.

They sailed past Pepe'ekeo heading straight for Hilo Harbor. She stood on the deck, Timothy behind, wrapped around her like a morning-glory vine. His chin rested on her left shoulder, breath tickling her neck. She reached up to touch his cheek, the ruby ring smoldering as her flames now smoldered. Strong and centered, hers to command.

"I think we can expect a welcoming committee."

He responded with a nibble on her earlobe.

"You are certain your grandmother will not be shocked?"

He pulled her even closer, if that were possible. She could barely breathe. "You saw the letter she sent with the ring. Grandmama has always had a soft spot for equally ferocious women."

"Perhaps I am a bit browner than she remembered."

"Letty, why are you torturing yourself? You saw K's telegram. I think that 'PREPARING YOUR WEDDING—STOP—ALL JOYFUL—STOP' says it all."

"Does she know I will go back to school? What about your plantation?"

"I have a manager, for heaven's sake."

"And that you have to follow me everywhere like a faithful dog?"

His voice came out muffled through her hair. "It's a good thing you can't see my face at this moment because my eyes are rolled so far into my head I can see the back of my neck. Please! You have to stop this. You drive me insane." A big sigh loosened some hairpins. "I am your *kahu*. Following you around is my business now."

At this he lifted her hair to deliver a big sloppy kiss on her nape. Then he licked her.

"Well, that was a bit doglike."

His laughter rumbled comfortingly against her. Until an outburst.

"What the hell! Letty, look!"

The dock at Hilo had swung into view. Giant feathered standards, the *kāhili* of royalty, waved in the air. Surrounding a person with just as many feathers on her head. That could only be Kahōkūlani.

And music? Could that be a tuba? And drums? A tall man, quite possibly Liam, stood brandishing Hawaiian and British flags.

As the ship steamed closer, more figures could be discerned. Agnes hung on George's arm, frantically waving. Timothy's grandmother arm in arm with Letty's own *tūtū kāne*. Bull in the back with horses. A big banner saying "Welcome Home."

"Well, my love, I think you have your answer. Our families approve."

On the hill above the harbor, a tiny woman sat on a white mule watching the scene unfold. This Gate had found her path and walked it. Her *kahu* too. A brave and worthy man, thank the *'āina*.

Now, the woman could only pray more would be found. Until there were nine. Until all were bound. The *'āina* demanded it. Yes she had her own path to walk. Her own *kuleana*. Only then could she rest. And she did so long for a rest.

The mule snorted with impatience. The dog sat at her side, tongue lolling, gazing up with readiness. The path beckoned. They were off.

EPILOGUE

E lei kau, e lei ho'oilo i ke aloha

LOVE IS WORN LIKE A WREATH THROUGH THE SUMMERS AND THE WINTERS

Rowley Ranch, Hawaii Island, New Year's Eve, the 31st of December, 1909

Diablo turned his head and gave her a nudge. Letty laughed but kept a good hold on her *pā'ū* skirt as Kahōkūlani wrapped it. To protect her wedding *holokū*. On the ride to the church. For her own wedding. The mind boggled.

Agnes and Philomena stood to the side holding the flowers, lei after lei, for herself and the horse. Kahōkūlani gave a swift tug on the rope holding up the overskirt.

"*Oof!* K! I think that is tight enough! We wouldn't want to wrinkle the dress!"

"I just wanted to be sure you were paying attention. Don't forget I am expert in this. There will be nary a wrinkle when we unwrap you at the church."

Philomena nodded. "These *pā'ū* overskirts are ingenious. I may try one for my next hunt in Scotland. Not to mention that I've become very fond of dresses that need no corsets. Perhaps I shall flaunt one in London next season."

Kahōkūlani gave another fierce yank before responding. "Now, that will cause quite a stir, Philomena."

"Well, you know I do love a good stir."

If they were trying to distract Letty, it wasn't working. Her stomach did flip-flops. Her aura dimmed. Agnes touched her arm. "Letty, are you all right? You look a bit pale."

"I'm fine. Just nervous, as you might expect." Her stomach gave another lurch. Or perhaps more than nervous. She breathed a pattern to summon her flames, her aura steadied. How different it was now that the flames were hers to command. Not the other way around.

Kahōkūlani finished the wrapping and stood back to admire her handiwork. Soft cream calico draped like wings to cover the old ivory silk *holokū*. The gown had been Letty's mother's; no one but Letty seemed surprised that it fit her perfectly.

"Let's mount you up."

"Wait, Letty needs her *haku lei*." Letty inclined her head forward so Agnes could place a crown of ferns and flowers on her head. She kissed her stepdaughter on each cheek.

"You are such a miracle, my dear."

Kahōkūlani's voice was gruff. "She is more than a miracle; she is our future. Let us get you on this horse."

More leis and kisses as she stepped to the mounting block. Diablo turned his great head again with a welcome whicker. And a nudge.

"I swear that horse knows what's afoot." Philomena handed up the reins. "I am impressed that Timothy made a wedding gift of him to you."

Letty reached down to squeeze Philomena's hand. "And I am beyond grateful for my gift from you."

"Pish posh, every Moran woman has her own portion. How could I not make sure you had the same? That way, if my grandson turns insufferable you have your freedom."

"The horse protected her, you know. He was meant to be hers." Agnes reached to stroke the satiny red neck. "And now she has your Timothy too."

The women rode into the village of Waimea. People lined the streets to join the celebration, smiling and waving as the bride's party went by. She waved back, touching her hand to her heart each time as she reached out. Extending her love, her *aloha*, to all.

Letty should not be surprised at the crowd. Timothy was popular with both landowners and his workmen. And she was one of the Princess's own goddaughters. Diablo curvetted, his neck arched, showing off as if he were proud to bear her. The wings of her *pā'ū* overskirt swirled behind. Her stomach took another lurch. Her flames smoldered in contentment.

Ahead was the green church, tall steepled. In front, a line of men. Timothy flanked on one side by her father, Lot, and Liam. And on the other, Bull and Tom Kalama. Timothy swept off his hat, running his hand through the unruly curls. This time it was her heart that lurched. She would recognize that gesture anywhere. Her Timothy. Her *kahu*. Her love.

Now bound together, always, forever, in flame.

AFTERWORD

Akalani

AFTERGLOW

In telling this story, I was privileged to rely on many elements of Hawaiian history for inspiration. Just as the colors are deeper, the smells sharper, and the sun brighter in Hawaii, the stories of the people carry richness beyond imagining.

Because this is a work of fiction—and of fantasy—I have taken great liberties. I have changed names. I have moved dates. I have sped travel times. All of the characters are entirely fictitious, although inspired by real people in some cases. The intentional magic of *mana'o pono* is entirely my own creation. The prophecy of the Gates is my invention as well.

It was never my purpose to give a historically accurate version of life and politics in Hawaii before statehood. Those stories are for others to tell. That being said, I always like to know some of what really happened; I thought you might too. Here are a few highlights:

The Lang family is loosely based on the Lane brothers, famous Hawaiian freedom fighters. Of Hawaiian and Irish descent, they were ardent supporters of Queen Lili'uokalani throughout the overthrow of the monarchy and were imprisoned at one point during the conflict. The Lane brothers were known to be extremely tall, and one of them was named Lot.

A young woman like Letty might definitely have studied science. Many young Hawaiian women of means were sent to elite mainland boarding schools. The Redwood School is modeled after Castilleja in Palo Alto.

Letty might also have sought to be a veterinarian. By 1909, the best records I can find show no more than three women who were trained veterinarians in the entire Western Hemisphere. There were at most two in the UK. The excuse for keeping women out of the profession was that they were not big enough to handle large animals. Letty would confound that notion. There was a veterinary school in San Francisco at the time.

The inspiration for our fictional princess, Elizabeth Victoria Kahōkūlani Claiborne, was historical. Much has been written about the woman who was the last crown princess of Hawaii, Victoria Ka'iulani Cleghorn. Born in 1875, she was next in line for the crown when Hawaii was finally annexed to the United States in 1898. The kingdom of Hawaii was no more.

Beautiful, cultured, and strong-willed, Princess Ka'iulani had spent her entire life preparing to sit on a throne that no longer existed. A passionate advocate for her people, she found she no longer had a path to serve them.

The historical Ka'iulani died in 1899 at the age of twenty-three, less than a year after the annexation. She had fallen from her horse in a storm and become ill. Her doctors called it "inflammatory rheumatism," but most people of the time agreed that she died of a broken heart.

But what if she had not died? What if instead she had found the will to live? What if she knew that her people needed her as never before, and that she must go on? Our fictional

Kahōkūlani explores that possibility. There is more to her story to be told in future books. Much more.

There was a real "oil queen" of Los Angeles, a piano teacher who began buying oil fields in the early 1890s and went on to become one of the largest oil producers in her day. Her name was Emma McCutcheon Summers. At one time she controlled more than 50 percent of the producing wells in Los Angeles. Unlike our Mrs. Simmons, she did not have the foresight to sell at the peak in 1903, but she held on to later recover and profit from the need for oil with the onset of World War I.

Chen Zhou, the police detective, is also inspired by a real person, Chang Apana. In the early 1900s, Apana was a well-known lawman in Honolulu and became the inspiration for the Charlie Chan movies. Apana grew up in the Waipio Valley on the Big Island. He originally worked as a *paniolo* and learned to carry a bullwhip instead of a gun. His first police job was rescuing abused animals and children. From that, I can only assume he was a very compassionate fellow.

It would have been entirely possible for Kahōkūlani and Artemus Chang to attend Stanford, as that university was one of the first to allow students of color to study law.

The "red barn" on the Stanford campus was a center of equestrian activity during the formative years of the university. It was originally the site of Leland Stanford's racing stable. Stanford University formed its polo team around the turn of the century, so someone like Letty might have exercised ponies there.

Ladies' riding societies that promoted the cultural practice of *pā'ū* riding began to form in the early 1900s. Ladies' civic societies were also common. Some of those started in the early 1900s survive today. It is not clear if these societies had suffragist leanings, but I would like to think they did.

Automobiles and other motorized vehicles started to take the place of horse-drawn conveyances in Honolulu by 1905. In other parts of the United States, many livery owners became car dealers. It seemed natural for the Lang family to do the same.

Oldsmobiles were very desirable cars; in fact, there was a famous model called the Limited. Although the historical Limited was not sold until 1910, the song "My Merry Oldsmobile" was a huge hit in its day. It is very likely that the sheet music made it to Hawaii, as Hawaiians have always been great lovers of music of all kinds. The Lang ʻohana would be no exception.

The interisland steamers were an essential means of transport connecting the islands of Hawaii. Because the channels between most of the islands are essentially open ocean with treacherous currents, the captains had to be very skilled. And yes, animals were winched over the side to swim in to shore. They were loaded the same way.

The ranches in Hawaii were some of the most successful cattle-producing operations in the world. The biggest of all, the Parker Ranch on the Big Island, remains in operation today, with more than half a million acres. The MacHenry Ranch is loosely based on it. The trustee of Parker Ranch, Alfred Wellington Carter, was also the inspiration for the character A. J. Chartwell.

There is so much more I could share with you but let me stop here. For now at any rate. *Mahalo* for your interest in the world of the Hawaiian Ladies' Riding Society. I hope you are intrigued enough by all the magical possibilities of Hawaii that you will choose to ride along with the ladies in our next adventures.

Aloha!
Katherine Kayne

Hawaiian Language Glossary

Before annexation to the United States, Hawaii was one of the most literate countries in the world. This was a particularly stunning achievement given that before 1820, there was no written Hawaiian language. In their eagerness to convert the "heathens" to Christianity, the missionaries assembled a method of reading and writing Hawaiian that is the basis for how it is recorded today. However, it was the Hawaiian people themselves who seized upon all the opportunities that written language provided.

Hawaiian is a language rich in vowels but sparse in consonants. Words are pronounced phonetically. The rhythm of the words matters too. Some words contain a reverse apostrophe, the *'okina*. This means there is a very slight pause in the word, called a glottal stop. Words may also contain a *kahakō*, a macron that lengthens and adds stress to the marked vowel.

'āina: land
ali'i: chief
aloha: greeting, salutation, love
'auana: drifting
haku lei: crown of flowers

hapa: of mixed blood, a mixture of things

hau: a kind of tree

haupia: a pudding made of arrowroot and coconut cream

Hawai'i nei: beloved Hawaii

hilahila: shame

holokū: a type of loose dress, often of patterned material

honi: kiss; inhaling one another's essence.

ho'oponopono: ritual of reconciliation, literally to make right

'ilima: a delicate flower related to the hibiscus

imu: underground cooking oven

kāhili: feathered standard

kahu: honored attendant, guardian

kahuna: magician, priest, expert; the plural is *kāhuna*

kaikuahine: sister

kānaka: persons, Hawaiians; sometimes used derisively by non-Hawaiians; the singular is *kanaka*

kāne: men; the singular is *kane*

keiki: child

koa: a kind of wood, brave

ku'ialua: a martial art

kuleana: estate, homestead, responsibility, duty

kumu: teacher

kupuna: elder

lau: wrapped foods, usually in banana leaves

lauhala: a leaf used in weaving

lehua: the flower of the *ohia* tree, or the tree itself

lomilomi: massage

lū'au: feast

mahalo: thank you

mākāhā: gate, particularly the sluice gate to a pond or irrigation canal

malolo: flying fish

mana'o: thought

mana'o pono: righteous thinking

mele: song

Menehune: a legendary race of small people

na'au: gut, temper, heart

Nā wāhine holo lio: Ladies, let us ride.

Ni'ihau: one of the islands in the Hawaiian chain, also a
	reference to rare shells from that island

'ohana: family

paniolo: cowboy

pā'ū: a type of skirt worn by female horseback riders

pau: done, finished

pīkake: peacock flower, a type of jasmine

pilikia: troubles

pono: goodness, righteousness

pule 'anā'anā: black magic spell

pūliki: hug, embrace

pu'u: a volcanic cone, either recent or ancient

tūtū kāne: grandfather

wāhine: women; the singular is *wahine*

wāhine ali'i nui: women who lead people

wikiwiki: fast

A note about place names in this book. When mentioning each of the islands of Hawaii as a specific location, no diacritical marks have been used. In the early 1900s this was the common practice and can be seen on the territorial maps of the time. Now, with the welcome renaissance of the Hawaiian language, the names are more often presented with their correct punctuation. Today when you visit, you will likely see them listed with the proper marks: Hawai'i, Maui, O'ahu, Kaua'i, Lāna'i, Moloka'i, Ni'ihau, and Kaho'olawe.

ACKNOWLEDGMENTS

I have always told stories. As a girl, my stories were filled with horses and poetry and magic and happily-ever-after. With heroines both fierce and fearless who always *always* found true love. As happens to so many of us, age and the necessities of life stilled that voice.

Now in the third chapter of my life, I have found my childhood voice again. The horses and the magic are back. So are the happily-ever-afters. And the fierce and fearless heroines? Yes! Only better! Because now they are daughters of Hawaii, with all the richness that entails.

I could not have found my voice again without help. I count myself blessed to have the sort of friends and family who give me love *and* hold my feet to the fire. If I were to call them all out here, it would take pages. You know who you are. This would not have happened without you.

A few people I must mention, though.

In Hawaii, Barbara Nobriga has been my guide since the early stages of this project; she has been a resource, a *kumu*, and a friend. The islands are fortunate to have someone so committed to the survival of the *pā'ū* riding tradition. Barbara graciously assembled a group of cultural readers whose deep love for Hawaii informed their comments and bettered my work. Thank you all: Faye Daniels, Cynnie Salley, Anna Akaka, Moana Roy Kuma, Karen Anderson, Lisa Twigg Smith, Sally Inkster, Lolly Davis, and one very brave man, Jerry Benson.

On the mainland, another group of readers proved invaluable: Sonya Campion, Nancy Mee, Jordan Brown, and Marianne Sao. Not to mention my inimitable assistant, Corene Caley. Thank you all as well.

My guiding star is author Susan Mallery. Her wit, wisdom, and encouragement kept me going through dark moments. When that failed, she could be counted on for the necessary swift kick precisely delivered. Thank you, Susan, for believing in me. That is friendship.

And finally, the one person who has patiently been there since long before I saw my first *pāʻū* princess: my own love, my *kahu*, my husband, Michael. This man is the reason I know that happily-ever-after really can come true. Thank you, my darling, for every precious bit of our life together.

Mahalo,
Katherine Kayne

Hawaiian Ladies Riding Society

If you would like to keep up with all the happenings in the world of the Hawaiian Ladies' Riding Society, please sign up for Katherine Kayne's email list at www.katherinekayne.com. You can expect news, prizes, recipes, and all things Hawaii. And sneak previews of the next books in the series! *Bound in Roses* will release in fall of 2020.

Aloha!
Katherine Kayne
www.katherinekayne.com

ABOUT THE AUTHOR

Katherine Kayne now writes the romances she only dreamed of reading as a girl. With horses and magic and happily ever after . . . and heroes strong enough to follow their heroine's lead. Counting herself fortunate to live in Hawaii a part of each year, Katherine created the world of the Hawaiian Ladies' Riding Society to tell the stories of the fearless horsewomen of the islands' ranches. Because who doesn't love a suffragist on horseback? With a bullwhip? Wearing flowers? If you come along for the ride, be prepared for almost anything to happen. Katherine can promise you fiery kisses, charming cowboys, women who ride like the rainbow to save the day, and that rarest of beasts—handsome men who like to dance.

Made in the USA
Middletown, DE
23 November 2019